LOVE'S DARK SECRETS

"I'm afraid I don't know what you're talking about, Mr. Sinclair."

"Oh, it's quite simple," he explained, taking a step forward. "Either you're a thief or a whore."

"I already explained about the money." Her bravado was beginning to crumble.

"Then you're a whore."

Ashlee's head shot upward. She caught herself before she had said the wrong thing and forced a laugh. "I'd rather think of myself as a courtesan." Even though he stood several feet away from her, Ashlee could feel the heat of him.

"Really?" he smiled in the silvery glow of the cabin. Slowly and purposefully he reached toward her and tucked two bills into the low-cut neckline of her dress. "Then prove it to me."

Before she could think of a reply, his arm was around her and he pulled her to him, his mouth crushing hers. He had trapped her hands between them, and the feel of his rock-hard muscles against her palms awakened in her an explosive passion she didn't know existed. This was wrong, she knew that. But at this moment, she wanted to learn all the dark secrets of love. . . .

RIVER RAPTURE

KAY McMAHON

ZEBRA BOOKS
KENSINGTON PUBLISHING CORP.

ZEBRA BOOKS

are published by

Kensington Publishing Corp.
475 Park Avenue South
New York, NY 10016

First printing: December 1986

Printed in the United States of America

For Joan Hess,
A true friend.

Chapter One

The smell of salt air carried on gentle breezes wafted across the long wooden dock while overhead scores of sea gulls screeched their hungered cry against the backdrop of a bright, clear sky. Fishermen, their boats full of lobster, shrimp, crab, and oyster, skillfully maneuvered their crafts toward the pier after a morning's successful run, navigating their vessels between the huge paddle wheel steamers crowding the jetty. Hundreds of people lined the wharf, many of them passengers waiting to board the *Mississippi Queen*, a gambling steamer that would take them upriver toward Baton Rouge, Vicksburg, and finally St. Louis before heading back to the port of New Orleans once more. Since the end of the Civil War more than a year ago, this once beautiful, peaceful seaport had become a haven for the carpetbaggers from the north, and resentment ran high even though it was their money that kept the town alive and prospering.

From within the crowd of people gently pushing their way toward the lowered gangplank of the *Mississippi Queen*, Rhys Sinclair eyed the steamer with more than casual admiration. He had won the ship in a card game a little more than a month ago when its previous owner fell victim to Rhys's expertise at the game of poker. But because he was still considered a Yankee in a city of hostile southerners, even though he had resigned his commission as captain in the Union Army at the close of the war, he elected to keep his ownership a secret, knowing few of them would believe he truly sympathized with their animosities toward the north. To them, he would appear to be just another fortune hunter preying on the hardships of the southern people. Thus, he paid the captain of the *Mississippi Queen* a little extra each month to manage the staff and see to her upkeep. Spotting the man as he stood at the helm observing the passengers board the ship, Rhys's tanned brow wrinkled in a frown. Of course, paying Edward Longley any additional amount wouldn't guarantee him that the *Mississippi Queen* would escape the bandits that had been working the river for the past year.

"Don't tell me I'm about to lose all my money again," a voice behind him proclaimed with a hint of laughter.

Turning slightly to look at the one who had addressed him so good-naturedly, Rhys smiled warmly once he recognized a fellow cardplayer. "Good afternoon, Phillip," he said, courteously stepping aside to allow the other passengers to board ahead of him and give Phillip Sanders a chance to catch up. "Who knows . . . maybe I'll have a turn of bad luck this trip."

"Rhys Sinclair," Phillip admonished, taking the black silk top hat from his head to run his fingers through his thinning gray hair, "even on your worst day I seldom beat you."

"But you always come back for more," Rhys laughed.

Sanders's lined face grew serious. "But that's the sport of it, friend, to continue wagering until I do. What enjoyment would I get out of it otherwise?"

"Oh, I don't know," Rhys grinned. "I merely thought spending one's winnings was always enjoyable."

Phillip's white brows came together. "And you, dear

boy, have not grown up with more money in your pocket than you knew what to do with. I have." Distracted, his gaze moved past his companion as he added, "Besides, losing is a way of spending it, don't you think?" His expression changed to one of satisfaction.

Knowing Phillip Sanders had spotted a beautiful woman, Rhys smiled and turned to look in the same direction, chaffing, "It certainly is a blessing that you never got married, Phillip. Your wife would have never understood your wandering eye for the ladies."

"And probably the very reason you haven't either," he countered with a chuckle. "I've seen the way your eyes darken whenever a femme fatale comes near you." He stroked the perfectly sculptured white goatee on his chin, approving of what he saw. "And this one adds a hint of mystery. My, doesn't black become her?"

Rhys had espied the woman dressed in the garb of a widow the moment he turned his head away from Phillip. A black veil hid her face, but the cut of the gown could not disguise the shapely figure. One sandy brow raised, appreciatively. "Yes," he murmured, "but it also marks her as unapproachable, my good man."

"Why?" Phillip's voice raised a pitch. "Simply because she mourns the loss of her husband? Good lord, man, she's ideal."

"And you, sir, are a scoundrel to play on the weaknesses of a lady," Rhys laughed, though his attention never wavered from the gentle sway of hips as the woman ascended the gangplank. His eyes lifted suddenly when he realized the widow had stopped and turned slightly. Ebony lace obscured the color of her hair and the direction of her gaze, but Rhys had the distinct impression she was looking at him.

"See there," Phillip exploded, nudging Rhys's arm. "If that isn't an open invitation, I don't know what is."

A faint smile sparkled in Rhys's brown eyes and he

9

wanted to agree. But whether the lady was inviting him or not didn't matter to Rhys. To woo a woman in mourning clothes went against his principles. "Maybe," he replied softly instead, then forced himself to turn his attention to the man at his side. "But right now, I suggest you and I board the ship before we're left behind. I spent a little more than I intended this past week and need to refill my wallet."

"Ho-oh," Sanders roared. "And you think to have mine?" He plopped his hat back on his head and started up the gangplank ahead of Rhys. "Well, we'll just see about that, Rhys Sinclair. When the *Mississippi Queen* docks in Baton Rouge, *you'll* be the one who's poorer."

Chuckling, Rhys watched the man a moment before his gaze drifted up to where the widow had stood, and he was mildly disappointed to find that she had gone. He shrugged his wide shoulders, wishing his father hadn't insisted his sons always remain gentlemen, and followed Sanders to the main deck of the steamer.

"I could use a drink," Phillip admitted. "How about you?"

"Not right now," Rhys declined, spotting Captain Longley's tall thin shape coming down the narrow flight of stairs that led to the second deck and the pilothouse. "I'd like to talk with the captain first, but I'll meet you later."

"Well, you know where you can find me," Sanders relented. "And please, Rhys, don't take too long. I do look forward to leaving you penniless."

"I'll be there before you can order seconds," Rhys promised with a grin, watching the man's well-dressed, plump physique being caught up in the flow of the passengers moving inside out of the sun. The smile faded, and he turned to face Captain Longley. "Good afternoon, Edward."

"Mr. Sinclair," the captain nodded.

"Has everything been arranged?"

"Yes, sir. Just like you ordered. Do you really think the *Mississippi Queen* will be next?"

Rhys reached up and combed his fingers through his light brown hair streaked golden by the sun, unaware of his strikingly good looks. He had always envied those men with dark features, thinking that facet of their character had an influence on what other men thought of them, giving them a forceful, rugged appearance, while in truth Rhys was the one everyone—especially the ladies—noticed first. And, of course, the faint scar that ran from the corner of his left eye to his cheekbone didn't help either as far as he was concerned. It only meant that someone else had gotten the better of him at one time.

"Logically thinking, it would stand to reason, Edward," he pointed out, mentally taking note of the last passengers to board. "We're about due." He glanced over at the man. "And if these outlaws are as smart as they seem, they'll have taken the time to find out who booked passage on this steamer. I don't need to tell you that the five men who will be sitting around that poker table are probably the wealthiest in all of New Orleans."

"Yes, sir, I know. That's why I've posted Parkins outside the cabin. He's been ordered not to let anyone or any*thing* inside without your permission."

"Good," Rhys replied, then frowned. "Now all we have to do is pray they haven't decided on a new method." Smiling lopsidedly, he turned and strolled away.

"Just set it on the bunk," the darkly cloaked woman instructed, a gloved hand-searching through her purse for a coin to give the young red-haired boy who had carried in her bag.

"Are ya goin' to St. Louis, ma'am?" he asked, hoisting

11

the heavy satchel onto the mattress. "Or are ya gettin' off before then?"

"Before then," she replied, smiling secretively behind the gossamer veil as she reached out to hand the youngster his tip.

Eyeing the amount, the boy's chin sagged at her generosity. "Golly, ma'am. Ain't nobody ever given me this much."

"Well, I believe in paying for a job well done," she said, putting her arm around his narrow shoulders to guide him toward the door. "Now, I want you to spend that on whatever makes you happy." She glanced down at his bare feet. "Maybe for a pair of shoes?"

"Yes'm," he blushed, coming sharply to attention when he heard the bell clanging out its warning for all visitors to go ashore. "And if ya ever come back to New Orleans, I'll be real glad to show ya around."

"Thank you," she smiled. "And if I do, I'll be sure to look for you." She lingered at the doorway a moment, watching him hurry away, noticed the interested stares she received from the people passing in the corridor, and quickly stepped back into her cabin and closed the door. "Ashlee Redington, you'd better be careful," she muttered irritably to herself. "Mistakes like that could get you caught."

With a sigh, she pulled the veil from her head and shook out the long flowing mane of silky black hair, ready to get to work. Timing was crucial, and wasting even a moment in idle chatter or drawing attention to herself like she did by giving the boy a sizeable tip could be her ruination. John wouldn't be pleased if he knew. Crossing to the bed, she tossed aside the veil and unhooked the latch on the bag, spotting the blond wig lying on top and suddenly remembering the man who had flattered her with his eyes. A demure smile lifted the corners of her mouth, and without realizing it she straightened and looked at her reflection in the mirror hanging over the three-drawer chest on one wall. Her father said she had a pretty shape, but Ashlee always thought she was too thin. Apparently the stranger agreed with her father because it wasn't disapproval she had seen in his dark brown eyes. Noticing how the color in her cheeks had heightened with the thought, Ashlee's smooth brow wrinkled angrily.

"He's probably just a damn northerner, anyway," she snapped venomously, knowing her father would be appalled to hear her swear. She yanked the wig and other articles from the bag in a huff. Ashlee didn't have time for the social graces of a young woman her age, so there was no sense in daydreaming about it. And right now she had to concentrate on finishing her job and meeting John upriver at their preplanned destination. Crossing back to the door, she twisted the key in the lock and began to unfasten the buttons up the front of her dress, thinking how this disguise was the one she hated wearing most.

"I don't know what good that guard outside the door is going to do," Benjamin Jones rebuffed, taking his place at the table. "Those thieves are slicker'n axle grease when it comes to slipping that drug in our whiskey. I oughta know. It's happened twice to me already. It's gettin' so a man can't enjoy a little game of cards anymore."

"Then why are you here?" Phillip Sanders baited with a grin.

"For the same reason you and everybody else is," Jones snarled, his green eyes flashing. "I happen to like playin' and there ain't nobody who's gonna stop me." His deeply lined face brightened with his smile. "'Sides, I figure if I'm lucky, I'll be around when these men are caught and I can get back some of my money."

"There's not much of a chance for that, Ben,"

13

William Lott cut in. "I imagine they spend it as quickly as they can. The only money you'd get back is what they took right then."

"Yeah, well, at least I'd have the pleasure of seeing them arrested," Jones proclaimed, settling down in his chair, the multiple layers of his chin resting against his chest. "And if it's near Baton Rouge, I'll make sure *you're* the judge they face in court."

"Cover your ears, Judge," Phillip laughed. "Ben's about to pay somebody off again."

"I've never paid anybody off," Jones exploded irately. "I've given them a loan, but they always paid me back. There's a difference, you know."

Sanders and the judge exchanged amused grins.

"Of course the fact that these people couldn't get loans from anyone else has nothing to do with it," Phillip challenged humorously, receiving a murderous glare in return.

"Someday, Phillip Sanders, you're going to need a loan and I'll remember what you said," Ben rebuked testily.

Never being one to pass up a chance to needle the pompous merchant from Baton Rouge, Phillip replied, "As long as I sit across a poker table from you, Benjamin, I'll never have to borrow money—from anyone."

"As I recall," Ben corrected, his bald head gleaming with perspiration, "the last time the three of us sat down at a poker table with Rhys, none of us went home with so much as a dollar in our pockets."

"And I had a difficult time explaining that to my wife," the judge proclaimed with raised brows, pushing himself up from the table. "May I get you two a drink while we wait for Rhys and Thomas?"

"You mean you still haven't told her how you spend your time traveling back from New Orleans?" Ben moaned. "Why, if my wife tried to lead me around by the

14

nose the way yours does, William, I'd blacken her eye for her." Doubling up his fist, he slammed it against his opened palm. "Just like that."

William Lott had been a judge for more than twenty years. He had probably heard every insult anyone could throw at him, and since the majority of them came from the criminals he sentenced to prison or worse, he had managed to ignore the comments because the kind of men who said them had very little education—if any. Except for the fact that Benjamin Jones had always shrewdly stayed above the fine line of right and wrong, William considered the man to be of the same caliber. This time, however, he couldn't let the remark pass as he had done on previous occasions. Having filled three glasses with whiskey from the bottle on the buffet, he returned to the table, set each one down in front of the two men, then looked Jones squarely in the eye.

"There's a great difference between our situations, Ben. For one, my wife is a lady. And a gentleman would never hit a lady. That's something you wouldn't know about." He raised one eyebrow, waiting for the man to comment, but when it appeared the insinuation hadn't registered in Ben's thick skull, William added, "If Agnus had any intelligence at all, she would have walked out on you years ago."

"Ahh, that old witch knows she wouldn't have it so good with anybody else." He shifted his meaty frame to look at Phillip. "Who'd take an ugly hen like her, huh?" he roared, then downed his whiskey in one gulp and held the glass out toward William. "Get me another while you're up, will ya, friend?"

William rolled his eyes. "Friend," he muttered, taking the glass to do as Ben asked.

The group fell quiet as the roar of the huge engine set into motion marked their departure from New Orleans. Giant pistons rhythmically pulsed in perfect synchronization, jerking the steamer backward as the paddle wheel chugged the water and pulled the floating palace from the dock. A moment later the vessel slowed then jerked again and started on its journey upriver. Most of the passengers didn't notice, but for Rhys it was always a time of excitement. He secretively moved away from the crowd in the saloon, out onto the promenade deck, and toward the aft of the ship to watch the monstrous paddle wheel churn up the murky waters of the river.

The *Mississippi Queen* was a far cry from the magnificent sailing ships he had always dreamed of owning, and it certainly didn't meet his father's expectations for the kind of life he wanted his son to have. But Rhys had always been restless—his mother had been aware of that—and although his father would be disappointed to hear the young man had not only purchased land in Louisiana but owned a gambling steamer as well, Rhys was sure Carroll Sinclair would understand. A faint smile softened his rugged features while thinking that if he talked long and hard enough, maybe someday he could persuade his father into leaving the lumber mill in Maine for a few months and together with Rhys's mother spend the time visiting with their wayward son. Of course he'd argue, stating that even though he had three other grown sons to run the mill, he and Virginia shouldn't abandon their daughters. Leaning forward, he braced his hands against the railing, chuckling softly and envisioning the Sinclair brood.

Rhys was the oldest of eight children, but even so, the youngest, Billy, was twenty-one, making his four sisters well over the age of needing parental supervision. Katie and Kathy, twins, as well as Sara were all married. Jennifer, the youngest of the girls, had been widowed during the war and returned home to live at their mother's insistence. The other set of twins in the family, Robert and Ryan, were only two years younger than Rhys, and

16

they along with their wives and children lived less than a mile away. The neighbors of the Sinclair family often teased its members about starting their own city, for it seemed every time one of the sons or daughters got married they would build a house close to Carroll and Virginia and continue to help cut lumber from the multi-acred estate or work the mill for the eldest of the clan. The family was close-knit, and their greatest attribute was the overabundance of love they shared. Yet, with everything they had to offer a young man, Rhys wasn't satisfied. He had a burning ache to see some of the world before he settled down. Turning, he perched a hip on the railing, wrists crossed over one knee, and absently watched the swirling foam that lapped angrily against the side of the steamer, fondly remembering Melody.

Rhys and she had grown up together, and there had been a time shortly before the outbreak of the war when he seriously considered asking her to marry him. Thinking about it now, he wasn't sure if he would have done it out of love or because his family and everyone for miles around expected it of him. He had cared a great deal for the petite, pretty blonde, but not enough to bring him home after he resigned his commission in the army a year ago. And it wasn't long after that that he had gotten a letter from his mother saying Melody had finally married someone else. He was happy for her. Melody deserved a good man to care for her—not an adventurer like himself. Sucking in a deep breath of salt air, he raised his chin and studied the swarm of sea gulls overhead, knowing that the announcement had broken all ties he had with home.

"Rhys?"

Thomas Bryan's deep voice brought Rhys out of his reverie with a start. Embarrassed at having been caught daydreaming, he reached up and tugged at his earlobe, smiling.

17

"Thinking of home again, Rhys?" Thomas observed. He chuckled when the man shrugged one shoulder. "When are you going to break down and pay that family of yours a visit? From what you've told me about them, I don't think they'll bind and gag you in order to keep you home with them." He tilted his head to one side. "Or are you afraid you'll find out how much you'd like to stay?"

Coming to his feet, Rhys idly readjusted his charcoal-gray coat, hooked the top button on his black vest, then yanked on the cuffs of his shirt. "Something like that, I suppose," he replied.

"Or," Thomas continued, enjoying how easily he could make his friend uncomfortable, "are you worried about facing Melody?"

Surprised by the comment, Rhys's head shot up to look the man squarely in the eye. "How long have we known each other now, Thomas? More than a year? I thought you knew I didn't love Melody."

"That's what you claim," Thomas chaffed. "But every time I find you like this, your mind is a thousand miles away. I think you're trying to decide if you should go home and marry that young lady."

Rhys's dark brown eyes sparkled. "That would be a little difficult. She's already married . . . about two months ago."

"Oh?" The humor faded from Thomas's narrow face.

Chuckling, Rhys reached out and draped his arm around the other's shoulders. "Now don't let it upset you, my good man," Rhys teased, walking them back down the promenade deck toward the entrance to the saloon. "Another will be along any minute to catch my eye and give you the opportunity to play big brother again."

"Big broth—Is that what you think I'm doing?" Thomas exploded, stopping in the middle of the narrow walkway.

18

But before Rhys had a chance to answer, a young boy came rushing out of the saloon, made an abrupt turn, and collided headon with him, nearly knocking them both to the floor. In an attempt to save the youngster from falling on his backside, Rhys caught the scruffy-looking child by the shirt collar and yanked him up. But his kindness was misread by the youth who, in turn, promptly landed the heel of his shoe on Rhys's shin, loudly demanding his release.

"Why you little beggar," Rhys growled through clenched teeth, letting go, for the assault left his leg smarting a bit. His tan brow frowned even more once he saw the shabby way the boy was clothed. "Does your mother permit you to dress like that or is there a chance you're a stowaway?"

Round, fearful blue eyes stared back at him through a sea of dirt smudges. Before Rhys could voice the question again or latch onto the child's arm and, for appearance's sake, haul him to the captain for just punishment, the blond-haired boy whirled around and quickly vanished into the crowd milling about the deck.

"Are you all right?" Thomas asked worriedly when Rhys limped nearer the railing where he could lean against it and rub his injured extremity.

"I'd feel a lot better if I could catch that brat by the seat of the pants," Rhys scowled, still searching the throng of people for the boy's whereabouts. "I think he broke my leg." He frowned all the more when he heard Thomas laugh. "You think it's funny?"

"No," Thomas grinned. "I just find it amusing that a man your size can be brought to his knees by a mere child."

Dark brown eyes glared up at him through lowered brows. "I'm not on my knees," he said wryly.

"Close enough," Thomas laughed again and reached out to help Rhys to his feet. "Come on. Let's go play some

19

cards. A drink or two and a pocketful of money should ease your pain."

"Only if it's your money," Rhys replied and hobbled toward the saloon.

Ashlee didn't stop running until she had scrambled down the steps to the main deck and found a place to hide among the huge bales of cotton in the cargo area. Her heart was pounding so loudly in her ears that she was sure she wouldn't hear the man chasing her until he grabbed her by the arm. She was sorely tempted to jump overboard and forget about the reason she had donned boy's clothing. But after a quick, courageous glance at the stairway to learn he hadn't followed her, she leaned back against the massive bundle of cotton and slithered to the floor. There had always been risks involved in the plan, but none of them had ever seemed to unnerve her as much as today. The smudges on her brow wrinkled with her frown. And all because of one man. Who was he, anyway? And why was she getting this awful feeling about him? Stealing one more peek back at the staircase to make certain he hadn't suddenly materialized, she settled more comfortably out of sight between the collection of bales and took her father's gold pocket watch from inside her shirt.

The *Mississippi Queen* was scheduled to dock in Baton Rouge sometime early tomorrow morning, the first and only town of substantial size along the river—a place where there were sure to be people who could recognize the daughter of Arthur Redington, a businessman in New Orleans. Of course she didn't look much like a girl right now with the rolled-up pants, suspenders, tattered plaid shirt, and blond wig. But that was all a part of Ashlee's success for the past year. The rest relied on timing. She had to drug her victims, steal their money, and get off the boat before the theft was discovered. The tricky part came in having to accomplish all that before the steamer sailed past the rendezvous point. If she missed John and the rowboat . . . Ashlee cringed. She didn't even like thinking about the consequences.

Half of the fun Ashlee had in taking the northerners' money was the way she could boldly mingle with the arrogant sots—at times even strike up a conversation with them—then turn around and make complete fools of them. But that man just now—the one who showed too much interest in the widow and the one who so rudely put his hands on her—he ruined all that. Her upper lip curled unflatteringly. Actually, it was her own fault. She had let her temper get the better of her . . . as usual. Now she'd have to wait until it got dark before she could dare venture topside again. That way it would be easier to elude the handsome stranger by stepping into the shadows whenever she spotted him. She'd truly hurt him when she landed that blow to his shin. She knew that by his enraged bellow and the pain she saw registered in his deep brown eyes. And he didn't strike her as the type to simply forget about it. He'd want revenge.

An unexpected yawn caught her off guard, and Ashlee decided that maybe now would be a good time to take a nap. She'd worked the blackjack table last night until well past midnight, gotten up before dawn to pack her things and see John off, made her excuses to her father for planning to be away all day, and avoided Dominique the rest of the morning. There were times when merely thinking up good reasons to be away from the casino proved more difficult than the actual execution of the theft. But all in all, Ashlee thrived on the excitement. It was her own private kind of poker, a game her father forbid her to play. She was the dealer and her victims were the other players. And she won every hand by bluffing her way through. The satisfied smile that had brightened her pale blue eyes faded slowly. Her father would be proud to know how well she had mastered the game . . . if only she could tell him. But there were a lot of things lately on which Ashlee and her father didn't see eye to eye. Politics was one, marriage to a total stranger was another, and of course allowing Dominique to manage the casino had always brought about their most bitter of arguments.

Bright reflections of the late afternoon sun sparkling in the murky water caught Ashlee's attention, and as the steamer chugged upriver she turned her head to watch the glittering contrasts of golds and browns through a space in the bales of cotton. Its effect was hypnotizing and within minutes Ashlee had fallen asleep.

Her slumber wasn't a peaceful one. The tension that accompanied her rather strange profession and the fear of being apprehended put a constant strain on her, enough that her dreams frequently ended in nightmares. They always began the same: She would be working the blackjack table in the casino, dressed in her customary black silk gown, a ploy to entice the customers to bet a little more than they had intended simply to enable them a few more moments in her company. When no one could win a single round from her, she would invite them to try poker. A crowd would form around the table where she played, and when the ante had been raised to an amount that would make the Louisiana Purchase seem small, she would lay down her royal flush and scoop in the winnings. Her father would appear then to congratulate her, and that was where she would usually wake up, feeling refreshed and ready to challenge the world. However, on occasion, the dream wouldn't end there. Her next vision would have her standing in the stateroom of a luxurious gambling steamer about to stuff her victim's money into a bag when a knock sounds at the cabin door and the sheriff marches in. She's hauled off to prison, and from her cell's window she watches the construction of a new scaffold being completed, knowing

22

that at sunrise she would be hanged. The shrill laughter of a woman makes Ashlee perspire, and just before she bolts upright in her bed, visions of the smiling Dominique come to mind. But today's dream was different. It wasn't the sheriff at the door but rather the stranger who had complicated things by noticing the widow and then by getting in the way of the blond-haired boy. Ashlee came awake with a jolt.

It took her several seconds to figure out exactly where she was. Once she did, she fell back against the bale of cotton with a nervous sigh, her body gleaming with perspiration. Her scalp itched beneath the wig. She had a tickling sensation between her breasts that she couldn't scratch since she had bound her chest with a long piece of cloth to further her disguise, and short of taking it off there was nothing she could do to stop the agony. But her torment was quickly forgotten when the sounds of merry laughter floated down from the upper deck, and Ashlee suddenly realized she had slept the afternoon away. Scrambling to her feet, she rushed toward the bow of the ship and the lantern hanging near the steps, awkwardly pulling the watch from her shirt as she went. Ten-thirty!

Ashlee silently cursed the stupidity that had allowed her to fall asleep when she should have been concentrating on her reason for being on board in the first place. Providing the steamer hadn't had engine trouble or come upon too many obstacles in the river to slow its progress, the place where John would be waiting for her was less than an hour away. She had to get to work, and fast, or this trip would be a waste of time. Glancing up the steps leading to the promenade deck while she readjusted the wig, Ashlee prayed her dream would never come true— and that she had seen the last of that man. Inhaling deeply, she closed her eyes, letting out her breath in a rush and longing for this to be the last time she had to steal. But she knew it wouldn't be. Things weren't going well for her father. With a determined lift of her chin, she climbed the stairs.

Although the *Mississippi Queen* was well known as a gambling steamer, it also carried the reputation of being one of the most elegant steamboats sailing between St. Louis and New Orleans. It was this type of vessel that Ashlee and John usually selected since it meant there would always be a crowd. The more people there were, the easier it would be for Ashlee to lose herself among them should something go wrong. Nothing had so far, but as she reached the last step and moved onto the promenade deck a strange chill embraced her, and she stopped abruptly to glance all around her. It was almost as if something inside of her was trying to warn of impending doom, and had it not been for the promise of a rewarding bagful of money, she would have gone back to her cabin, gathered up her things, and returned to the cargo deck to wait for John. But once she heard the sharp, clipped, almost nasal-sounding accent of the couple who passed by in front of her, she remembered why she had been forced into stealing and why she had chosen northerners as her victims. Hatred overriding her fears, she set her gaze on the entrance into the saloon, beyond which she would find the stateroom and the men who played poker for very high stakes.

Earlier, while dressed as the widow, Ashlee had skillfully struck up a conversation with the steward who had pointed the way to her cabin, on the pretense that she thought she had recognized one of the other passengers, a wealthy businessman from New Orleans whose name she couldn't remember. The young man, eager to please, had dutifully recited the titles and occupations of each well-to-do gentleman, but to no avail since none seemed to register. Feigning surprise at the number of affluent men on board, Ashlee then asked if they were all going to an important meeting or something terribly secret, and

24

again the young steward willingly supplied the information Ashlee needed. But once the blond-haired youth with dirt smudges on his face had passed through the saloon and into the passageway leading to his destination, his steps slowed and a look of dismay darkened his blue eyes. There outside the cabin's door stood a man, his arms folded over his chest, his back against the wall. From all indications, he appeared to be quite satisfied to remain right where he was, barring anyone entrance to the stateroom.

Ashlee was about to chance drawing him into conversation in order to learn if he intended to spend the night there, when another steward passed her in the narrow corridor, carrying a chair. Hoping they wouldn't notice her, she turned her back to them and listened to their exchange of words.

"You gotta stay here all night?" the younger of the two asked.

"Yeah," came the reply. "The captain said I wasn't to let anybody in without his permission. He's not taking any chances. Figures the *Queen* is next. And you know what else?"

"What?"

"He told me that no matter who offers to buy these gentlemen a drink, I'm not to let them. If they need another bottle, it's to come from the captain's own private stock."

Ashlee nearly moaned aloud at the news. The success of her scheme had always been the seclusion of the game—that once the players were drugged, no one on board would know what went on behind closed doors. It had been her practice to send a fresh bottle of whiskey to the group by one of the stewards—a bottle she had laced with laudanum—then wait long enough to be sure everyone had drunk from it, and quietly enter the cabin. Now, not only wouldn't she be allowed inside, but the guard standing watch would refuse to take her gift to the men. She heaved a disgusted sigh. She'd have to think of something else. Glancing back at the two to find them still engaged in conversation, she turned and headed back to her cabin.

"What did I tell you? Didn't I say it's impossible to beat you, Rhys Sinclair?" Phillip groaned, throwing in his cards along with all of the others at the table. "Why don't you get married and settle down somewhere before you have us all penniless?"

Laying aside his cheroot in an ashtray, Rhys leaned in and pulled the heaping mound of coins toward him, smiling. "Trade all this for a woman?" he joked. "Phillip, you know better."

"Humph," he snorted, pushing himself up from his chair. "Yes, I know. You're the type who enjoys having his cake and eating it too, as they say." Snatching his glass from the table, he crossed to the buffet to pour himself another drink. "If you got married, you'd have to give up a lot of things, the most important being your *variety* of women."

"And why would he have to do that?" Ben piped in with a hearty laugh. "It hasn't stopped me."

"Because there are some of us," William corrected with an indignant curl of his lip, "who take our wedding vows seriously. And knowing Rhys the way I do, I think I'm safe in saying he'll be counted as one. Am I right, Rhys?"

"I can answer that," Phillip cut in, grinning broadly. "It's because he'll be faithful to his wife that he hasn't gotten married yet. He's having too much fun to be tied down."

"And I disagree," Thomas offered, reaching over to squeeze Rhys's shoulder. "He simply hasn't gotten married because he hasn't found the right woman . . . yet. She'll come along, and when she does, she'll be the luckiest woman in the entire north and south combined."

"And wealthiest," Ben grumbled, not the least bit impressed by the others' summary of Rhys's finer points. "I've lost practically everything I came with." Pushing his meaty frame away from the table, he added, "If nobody minds, I'm going to stretch my legs while I go back to my cabin and get the rest of my money. By God, I'm not leaving this boat until I've won some of it back."

"Well, don't be too long, Ben," Phillip told him. "I've got a feeling *I'm* going to be the next winner."

"Not if I can help it," Ben growled, yanking the door open wide and leaving it that way as he marched into the corridor, down the passageway, and out of sight.

"I don't know why you feel you must invite that man to play poker with us, Rhys," William confessed, gathering up the cards. "He's so . . . so crude."

A devilish twinkle appeared in Rhys's eye as he leaned back in his chair and took a puff on his cheroot. "Because I like taking his money."

"Well, isn't there someone else's money you'd like to take besides his?" William exclaimed, slapping down the unshuffled deck. "I know a lot of wealthy men who'd enjoy testing their talents against yours. Some of them are pretty good, too. It would be more of a challenge for you and a pleasure for me if I didn't have to put up with that man's barbarism." He glared at the empty doorway a moment, then turned back to Rhys. "In fact, I know a man who's a damn good cardplayer. Maybe you've heard of him—Arthur Redington? He owns Belle Chasse in New Orleans."

Holding up his glass to receive the whiskey Phillip offered to pour, Rhys shook his head. "No, I haven't. But I have heard about his hotel and casino. I've been intending to visit there, but I never seem to find the time. I thought someone told me the place wasn't doing

27

so well."

William shrugged. "For a while there, during the war, it was having a rough go of it. But things have picked up for Arthur in the past year. I'm glad. He's a fine man. And he's thinking seriously about entering politics. New Orleans needs a good Republican to help bring her back on her feet. The whole state needs him, for that matter. Did you know—"

The terrified scream of a woman followed by excited shouts and the rush of footsteps coming from the saloon seemed to explode inside the cabin, and all four men instantly bolted to their feet. Rhys was the first to reach the door and step into the passageway, only to see Parkins's broad back as the guard raced down the corridor.

"Sam! What is it?" he shouted after him.

"A fire, sir, on the main deck," he called back without breaking stride.

Although the *Mississippi Queen* wasn't the sailing ship he had dreamed of owning, it was probably the closest Rhys would ever come, and thoughts of her going up in flames was something he couldn't bear. Dashing off after Parkins, Rhys slowed his pace only long enough to grasp the wooden bucketful of water that was kept beside the bar in the saloon for just such a purpose, then shoved his way through the crowd that had gathered on the promenade deck to watch. Clearing his first step leading to the cargo area, Rhys could then see the bright orange reflections of the fire against the faces of the men who tried to control it. A mixture of fear and anger coursed through his veins as the vision of his steamer—a roaring inferno—flashed briefly in his head. But once he had descended the flight of stairs and joined the others, the dread of losing his ship eased considerably when he saw that the fire was contained to a single bale of cotton.

"Don't waste time dousing it with water!" he shouted

28

to the men. "Dump it overboard!"

At his command, boat hooks were taken from their holders and thrust into the canvas binding while Parkins drenched his head and brawny shoulders with water. As the others pulled, he leaned his weight against the bale and pushed, and after what seemed an eternity to everyone, it slipped over the side of the boat and fell into the dark waters, hissing and steaming as it quickly bobbed beneath the surface. A moment later it emerged, a black, smothering omen of what could have been a disaster.

"Are you all right?" Rhys frowned, wrapping the blanket someone had given him around Parkins. "You could have been seriously hurt."

"Oh, I'm fine, Mr. Sinclair," Sam assured him with a smile. "Just a little wet."

"Well, why don't you change into dry clothes and get yourself something to eat. I don't think our minds will be on the game for a while."

"That's all right, Mr. Sinclair. I'm not really hungry." He jerked his head toward the bale of cotton floating down the river. "Too much excitement, I guess."

Rhys nodded. "Yes. More than I care to have in one evening." He frowned suddenly, looking all around them. "Does anyone have any idea how it started?"

A deckhand standing near them heard Rhys's question and quickly came forward. "The captain sent the crew to their quarters for the night, sir, except for me and two others. We work the engine room. I'm the one who spotted the fire, but none of us can figure out what started it unless one of the guests decided to take his pipe down here and was careless with the ashes." He pointed to the floor. "Charred the deck some, but a little sanding and some linseed oil will have it good as new."

"I'll bet you were planning on a quiet card game this trip," another voice cut in, and Rhys turned around to find Captain Longley walking toward him.

Rhys smiled. "Actually, I enjoy excitement. I just prefer it to be connected with poker."

"Well, I can't guarantee that something else won't break your concentration, Mr. Sinclair, but I'll sure try to see that it doesn't happen again," the captain chuckled. "And as for you, young man," he continued, turning to Parkins, "that was a very courageous and stupid thing you did. You could have been hurt."

"Yes, sir," Sam agreed, lowering his eyes. "Sometimes I do things without thinking."

"Well, as captain of this vessel, I personally want to thank you for risking your own safety for that of the passengers and to tell you that there will be a little extra in your pay at the end of the month. But," he quickly added when Parkins opened his mouth to reply, "should something like this ever happen again, God forbid, I don't want you playing heroics. We could have used a bucket brigade."

"Yes, sir," Parkins grinned.

"Now go change into dry clothes," Longley instructed. "I'll walk back with Mr. Sinclair and wait there until you return."

The young man nodded then hurried off. Once he had disappeared from sight, Edward Longley turned to face Rhys. "One of the best crewmen I have. He'll be the captain of his own ship someday. Will I ever be able to say that about you?" he grinned.

Rhys shrugged and started for the stairs. "I wouldn't make a very good captain, I'm afraid. I don't know that much about ships. I'm the sort who'd prefer owning it but not commanding it."

"Then why the interest in them?" Longley frowned, puzzled.

"I've always been curious about the places they sail to."

"But you don't have to own a ship to go there," Edward argued as they stepped onto the promenade deck and went into the saloon.

"True," Rhys agreed, gently elbowing his way through the crowd. "But if I did, *I'd* be the one to decide which direction, and be able to change my mind if I wanted."

"Well," Edward chuckled, pausing outside the stateroom, "maybe someday you will." He leaned to the left to peer in at the group seated around the table. "How's your luck holding out so far?"

Rhys's brown eyes twinkled mischievously. "As far as they're concerned . . . too well. A few more nights like this one, and I'll be able to buy that ship and a couple of others." Cupping one elbow in his hand, he tapped his chin with a fingertip as if giving something great consideration. "I think I'll name one of them the *Sir Benjamin*." He straightened and raised his brows, mockingly. "It's the least I can do, seeing as how the man's money will buy it."

Edward broke into laughter as he watched Rhys do an about-face and enter the stateroom, unaware of the pale blue eyes observing their every move from the end of the passageway.

"Well, gentlemen," Rhys said, closing the door behind him, "now that we've had our fun, shall we get on with business?"

"Fun?" Ben exploded. "You call nearly getting killed fun?"

"We weren't in any real danger, Ben," Phillip scoffed, pouring everyone a drink. "It was only one bale of cotton. It wasn't like the whole lower deck was burning. Besides, Rhys was there. He wouldn't have allowed anything to happen that would end this game. He isn't ready to quit yet. Are you, Rhys?"

"It depends," he replied without a trace of humor in his voice as he took the glass Phillip held out to him.

"On what?"

"Do you still have money left?"

"Ho-oh," Phillip roared. "See there. I knew he wasn't ready to call it quits. And yes, my dear man, I have money left, and I'm going to use it to up the ante and wipe you out."

"Then sit, friend, and let's see if you can," Rhys grinned, reaching for the deck of cards lying near him.

Twenty minutes later only Rhys and Phillip remained in the game, each stone-faced and watching the other across the table. Rhys had raised the bet, and although Phillip was confident his hand would win, he wanted to see Rhys's cards. Thus, he threw in the needed coins and called his companion's hand, shouting with glee when Rhys laid down a pair of aces to his three of a kind.

"I knew my luck would change," Phillip laughed, drawing in the pot.

"Luck?" Rhys asked before downing the remainder of his drink. "Or might there be a chance I felt sorry for you?"

Phillip's mouth sagged open at his friend's carefree bantering, and he stopped sorting out the various coins he had won. "You never felt sorry for a fellow poker player in your life, so just keep your comments to yourself and pour us all another drink. Sorry, indeed," he muttered, glancing over at William. "Have you ever known . . . him . . . William? Don't you feel well?"

Judge William Lott had a reputation in Baton Rouge as one of the best dressed businessmen in the city. Even on the hottest of days he always looked neat and fresh. But at this moment his appearance didn't seem to matter to him, for he had removed his coat and tie and was unfastening the top button of his shirt.

"Is it warm in here?" he asked. "I feel so . . . so sleepy."

"I . . . I was thinking the same thing," Thomas said,

awkwardly pushing himself up from the table. "Maybe I should open the window."

"Would you like a glass of water?" Rhys frowned, pulling his handkerchief from the breast pocket of his coat and handing it to the judge when William's halfhearted search for his own failed.

"Yes," he nodded. "Maybe that would help."

"Ben, get William some water, will you?" Rhys asked, rising. "I think he should lie down for a while." But when Ben didn't reply or get up from the table to do as asked, Rhys sent him an angry glare only to find that Ben was sound asleep, his arms folded over his massive chest and his multilayered chin resting comfortably in the rows of fat around his thick neck. It took Rhys only an instant to figure out what was happening, and when he heard Thomas fall to the floor unconscious, he knew the culprit behind the thefts had somehow gotten into the stateroom.

"Damn," he growled, feeling the effects of the drug himself when his vision of Phillip and William blurred suddenly. He shook his head and grabbed for the edge of the table to steady himself, knowing that he probably only had a few minutes to reach the door and warn Parkins. But when he staggered forward, intending to cross in back of Phillip who had somehow managed to get William to his feet, both men teetered precariously and promptly fell to the floor right in Rhys's path, joining their friends in the same blissful sleep. Stepping over them was an impossible maneuver in Rhys's condition, but to reverse direction and go around the table was something he knew he couldn't do. His head was spinning and it grew increasingly more difficult for him to keep his eyes open and focused on the door that seemed to move farther away from him. Yet, he knew he must try.

Stepping back, he straightened and set his sights on the closed entryway into the cabin, vowing that no matter

33

how long it took him he would find the one responsible and beat him within an inch of his life. The oath spurred him on, but the drug dulled his wits and he didn't see the chair in his way until it was too late. The edge of the seat caught him in the knees. He lost his balance and reached out to grab the table but missed. The last thing he saw before his eyelids drifted shut was the floor coming up to meet him, and unconsciousness blocked out the pain he would have felt otherwise.

It had been Ashlee's plan to create a diversion that would draw everyone's attention, including the men playing poker. She had come up with two choices: someone falling overboard or starting a fire. Since the former would mean the victim could identify her as the assailant and therefore force her into hiding—something she couldn't do—she had decided on the alternative. Knowing it couldn't be much of a fire since she didn't want the entire ship to go up in flames, she had gone to the cargo deck and selected the bale of cotton nearest the edge of the ship, hoping someone had the intelligence to simply push it overboard before any real damage was done. Soaking only the top section of it with kerosene from the lantern she had smuggled out of her cabin, she had waited until the fire had a healthy start then raced up the stairs, screaming. Since everything else seemed to be going poorly for her, Ashlee could hardly believe her good fortune when the guard standing outside the stateroom was one of the first to respond, leaving his post to help fight the fire that had all the passengers in an uproar.

She had hidden herself among the crowd and counted the men coming out of the cabin, her bright blue eyes widening in dismay to discover one of them was the same man who had haunted her dreams. She had taken a step backward, about to run, when he dashed on by her without so much as a glance her way. It had taken her several moments to calm her racing pulse and force her feet to move, but once she had, Ashlee wasted no time in entering the cabin. She had stopped dead center in the room, her eyes locked on the huge amount of money scattered about the table top, struggling with the urge to scoop it up in her arms right then and run off. But she knew that would be a fatal mistake. The robbery would be discovered right away, and she still had more than half an hour before the steamer sailed to the spot where John waited. She had to stick to her plan. Turning, she went to the buffet.

After removing the cork from the whiskey bottle, she pulled out the pouch she had hidden inside her shirt and added all but a pinch of laudanum to the amber liquid, a devilish grin twisting her mouth. But just as she placed her thumb over the spout of the bottle and was about to give the mixture a good shake, she heard someone walking toward the cabin. In blind panic, certain it was the man who had constantly plagued her thoughts since boarding the steamer, the bottle slipped from her trembling hands and thudded against the buffet, teetering dangerously. The impending catastrophe snapped her back to her senses and she quickly latched onto the bottle to steady it as she scanned the room for a place to hide. The door stood open, and once she noticed the shadowy darkness standing behind it would offer, she dashed across the room and quietly slipped out of sight just as the man entered. Several moments ticked painfully by while she listened to him move about, and her reward for being patient came with the tinkling of glass as the man poured himself a drink. Taking the chance, Ashlee peeked out at him. She saw that his back was to her and that he wasn't who she thought he would be, but instead a rather obese man, and seized the opportunity to noiselessly slip out of the room to safety.

Ashlee had then returned to mingle with the crowd and

wait for the gamblers to resume their game. But her work hadn't stopped there. Once the door to the stateroom had been closed and Parkins once again took up his vigil outside, Ashlee had to execute her plan to get rid of the guard. Having stolen a mug of ale from one of the passengers while his back was turned away from the table, she had added enough laudanum to make the muscular Parkins sleep for hours. Then, in her boyish disguise, she had brazenly walked right up to him and shoved the glass in his hand. In response to his puzzled look, she had told him that she had seen how courageous he had been in helping put out the fire—while in truth she had only heard others talking about it—and said that he deserved a good mug of ale for having risked his life. He had argued with her, saying that he really shouldn't be drinking while he was supposed to be standing guard and that he hadn't done any more than anyone else would have done. Ashlee quickly assured him that there wasn't a soul on board who would agree with him or see anything wrong with accepting such a minor token of gratitude.

"Besides," she had said, lowering the pitch of her voice, "who's gonna know? Ain't nobody gonna see ya, and one mug of beer ain't enough ta get ya drunk." She had grinned up at him, shoved her hands deeply in her pockets, and leaned back against the wall opposite him. "I'll bet you could drink ten times that much and never even feel it."

Parkins had smiled back at her, and Ashlee knew then that she had found this huge, brawny man's weak spot. But then, it was every man's weak point. They all loved to brag. Especially northerners.

They had spent the last ten minutes discussing the fist fights, arm wrestling matches, and other contests requiring exceptional strength in which Sam Parkins had participated and won. And Ashlee, dressed as a young boy, pretended to be thoroughly impressed. Yet as the minutes continued to tick away and Parkins showed no signs of being affected by the laudanum in his drink, Ashlee started to worry. Perhaps her innocent claim that one drink wouldn't bother him had been closer to the truth than she suspected—even with the extra amount of a sleeping potion she had added to it. Frowning, she absently glanced down the hallway as if looking for an answer in the empty corridor.

"Where ya from, boy?" Parkins asked, stifling a yawn.

"New Orleans," Ashlee replied thoughtlessly, stiffening the instant she realized what she had said. "I mean my ma lives in New Orleans. I just came here ta visit. I live with my pa in Illinois. That's where I'm headed now . . . back home."

Spotting the vacant chair next to him, Sam stretched his shoulders and slid down on the seat. "Your folks split up?" he asked, setting his empty glass on the floor.

"Yeah," Ashlee nodded, her bright blue eyes anxiously trained on the man settling comfortably in his chair.

"Mine, too," Parkins confessed, leaning his head back against the wall and closing his eyes. "My ma wanted the excitement of a big city and pa wouldn't give up the farm." He smiled lazily. "I agreed with ma, so I stuck with her. Sure glad . . . I . . . did. I . . . wouldn't . . . be . . ." Suddenly his head bobbed forward, and a moment later he began to snore.

Pulling out her watch, she checked the time. She would have to hurry if she was to collect the gamblers' money, return to her cabin, gather up her things, and get below deck before John arrived. Glancing down the passageway one last time to be sure no one would see her, she crossed to the stateroom door, twisted the knob, and peeked inside. What she saw was as she expected it to be. One gambler was asleep in his chair, another lying on the floor near the window, two beside the table, and the fifth partly hidden from view on the other side. She had heard them fall, but Sam had been too busy reciting the boring details of his life style to give much notice to anything else. That had been some time ago, and since she had no way of knowing how much of the laudanum each man had ingested, she couldn't be sure how long it would be before one of them started to come around. Her heart thundered in her ears. This was always the part of her scheme that made her the most nervous. Everything she had done up until this point hadn't involved getting close to her victims. Now she would have to search their pockets and then step over them to move on to the next. It nearly scared the wits out of her but was also the part she enjoyed most, for in an odd way she was doing to them what they had done to her father.

Once Ashlee had stepped into the cabin, she closed the door behind her and went directly to the table where she hurriedly scooped up the money lying there and stuffed it into the cloth bag she had carried inside her shirt. When that was completed she moved toward the man sitting in the chair, quickly changing her mind about rifling through his pockets when she saw that his meaty arms were folded over his chest. Not only did she think it would be impossible to lift his elbow out of the way, but the thoughts of touching the perspiring behemoth curled her upper lip. She moved on to the man sprawled out near the window.

She had searched the pockets of every man in the cabin except for the one lying face down in the center of the room. From his position on the floor, Ashlee guessed he had been trying to get to the door before the drug took affect, and she lifted one finely arched brow in silent thanks that he hadn't succeeded.

Kneeling, she reached out to take his arm and roll him over, and froze when she realized who he was. Instinct warned her to be satisfied with the money she had already collected, get up on her feet, and leave the cabin as quickly as possible. But there was something about the man that piqued her curiosity and she settled back on her haunches to study him a moment. He wore the usual garb of a wealthy man, yet she couldn't help noticing that the gray pin-striped trousers hugged his muscular thighs in a most complimentary way. His hips were narrow and Ashlee felt herself blush when her gaze absently followed the contour of his well-formed buttocks. She blinked and forced herself to concentrate on the black linen coat he wore, which failed to hide the sinewy shape of his upper arms and shoulders. She smiled timidly, wondering what it would be like to be held by those powerful arms, for it was an encounter she had yet to experience with any man. Shrugging it off since she knew it was something that would never happen, she came back up on her knees, grasped his arm, and pulled him onto his back, ready to empty his pockets and be on her way. Her delicate chin sagged. She had seen how handsome he was from a distance, but being so close to him now took her breath away. Light brown hair with golden streaks enhanced his bronze complexion. Although his eyes were closed, it wasn't difficult to imagine how their shade would darken if he were provoked or their hypnotizing affect should his gaze be centered on her. She sucked in a deep breath. And he certainly had reason to be angry with her. Mentally scolding herself for taking so long to finish her task, she focused her attention on the wallet she found inside his coat, removing the wad of bills and stuffing them into the bag. But when she started to rise, she spotted the diamond stickpin in the lapel of his jacket, and a devious smile kinked one corner of her mouth. It was her practice to only take the northerners' money, but for some reason Ashlee found that she couldn't resist having a memento

39

of how she had duped them all—even when they had expected her. Snatching the piece of jewelry from his coat, she tossed it in her bag and stood.

"Maybe we'll meet again," she whispered to the unconscious man lying at her feet. "And if we do, I'll best you again, Yankee." With a triumphant smile, she turned and quietly left the cabin.

Chapter Two

Ashlee woke up with a start, a thin veil of perspiration dampening her brow and matting the dark hair around her oval face, and she sat straight up in bed. She had been dreaming again—the same dream she had had every night for the past week, ever since her little escapade on the *Mississippi Queen*. It wasn't her usual nightmare. Dominique wasn't in it. But that stranger was. She wiped her brow with the back of her trembling hand then swept the long, heavy strands of raven-black hair off her neck and shoulders, staring at the closed bedroom windows. The warm nights of spring with their cool breezes were late this year, but Ashlee knew that even if she had gone against her father's wishes and slept with the window cracked open a ways, the crisp air would have had no effect on her.

Glancing at the clock hanging on the wall opposite her, Ashlee fell back on the bed with a moan. It wouldn't do any good for her to try to go back to sleep. Dominique would be sending the maid with Ashlee's breakfast soon. Then, as a matter of course, the maid would recite her mistress's instructions to Ashlee on how the young woman's day would be spent. Growling, Ashlee rolled to her stomach and covered her head with a pillow. Why

41

couldn't her stepmother accept the fact that she was a grown woman with a mind of her own? Stepmother! God, how she hated even thinking the word, let alone admitting that her father had married such a creature. Couldn't he see what the little bitch was after?

"Bitch, bitch, bitch!" Ashlee proclaimed loudly as she tossed aside the pillow and slid out of bed, feeling only slightly appeased that she could call the woman names. It would have suited her better if she could have said them to her face! Yanking her robe from the foot of the bed, she jammed her arms into the sleeves and went to the dresser to stare at her reflection in the mirror.

Maybe if I were an ugly old crone with a wart on the end of my nose, Perrin wouldn't want to marry me, she thought rebelliously, spying the potbellied stove over her shoulder. Struck with a mischievous idea, Ashlee spun around, crossed the room, and hurriedly took the griddle from its resting place, rubbing a fingertip against its underside. Satisfied with the amount of soot she had collected, she absently laid the iron plate back down as she delivered the black substance to the tip of her nose, giggling impishly. Twirling about once more, she paused midway across the room where she promptly bent over and shook out the thick mass of dark hair, sending it in wild disarray about her shoulders once she stood again.

"Hello, Perrin, my sweet," she cackled, shoulders hunched as she strolled back toward the mirror. "Won't I make a be—e—e—autiful bride?" Letting her mouth fall open, she crossed her eyes and curled her upper lip at the image gaping back at her, fighting the laughter that threatened to destroy the grotesque face she had created. Finally, having lost all control, she gave way to the need until her sides ached and tears ran down her cheeks. But her amusement quickly ebbed and turned to despair when the thought raced through her head that nothing she could do or say would stop the marriage her stepmother had arranged. A frown shadowed her pale blue eyes as she thought about Perrin Fabron and how horrible her life would probably be married to him.

"How could you agree to such a thing, Papa?" she uttered in a painful moan. "You've never even met the man!"

Forlorn, she returned to her bed and threw herself across it, wadding up the pillow to rest her chin upon as she stared out through the window at the rooftops of New Orleans. Perhaps she was a bit spoiled and even headstrong as Dominique constantly told Ashlee's father, but did that warrant marrying her off? Did they think a gold band around her finger would be enough to tame her wild nature? A chilling thought flashed in her brain and Ashlee quickly buried her head beneath the pillow. Maybe he was of the sort that beat his women! Dear lord, what would she do then? Dominique would never allow her to come home. After all, Perrin was Dominique's cousin.

Rolling onto her back, the pillow hugged against her chest, she stared up at the ivory lace canopy above her, longing to have things the way they were a few years ago. It had been only Ashlee and her father, and John. No French seductress ordering her about and getting in the way. Why did her father marry that woman, anyway?

"Because she bewitched him, that's why," she grumbled disdainfully. A sadness shone in her eyes and she sighed. "And Papa was lonely," she admitted reluctantly. Turning her head, she stared over at the portrait hanging on the wall.

The first real fight Ashlee and Dominique had had came the day the woman tried to take the painting of Ashlee's mother from its hook in Ashlee's room, proclaiming loudly that it was time the young woman stopped living in the past. Ashlee remembered the scene as if it happened only yesterday. Arthur Redington was away at the time, but even if he hadn't been and he had agreed with his new wife about the removal of the portrait, it wouldn't have prevented Ashlee from grabbing the woman's arm and spinning her around.

"I don't care if you are married to my father," she had hissed, blue eyes shooting sparks of rage. "If you ever touch that painting or have someone else remove it, it'll be the sorriest day of your life!"

Dominique had retreated a step or two, surprised by Ashlee's outburst, for until that moment the youngest Redington seldom voiced an opinion or thought on anything. But the shapely Frenchwoman's awe quickly turned to anger. No one—not even Arthur—talked to her in that tone, and she wasn't going to tolerate it.

"All right," she had replied, turning for the door, "keep the damn thing hanging right there where you can see it. And every time you look at it, think how much your mother must have hated you. What other reason could there have been for her to desert a three-year-old girl?"

"She didn't desert me!" Ashlee had screamed, tears burning hotly in her eyes.

"Oh?" Dominique had challenged, one finely arched brow raised. "Then tell me why she hasn't come back for you in seventeen years? Or written a letter? If she cared at all for you, she would have tried to send word to you. She hates you, Ashlee, and the sooner you realize that and get on with your life, the better off you'll be. That's what your father's done."

Even now as Ashlee lay alone in her room staring up at the portrait she could hear that deafening slam of the door after Dominique had marched out, and the tears came again. Dominique was right. Veronica Redington had deserted her husband and young daughter, but Ashlee would never admit it to anyone.

"Oh, Mama," she whispered with a sob, "why did you

leave us? We loved you. Papa still loves you. He only married Dominique because he was lonely. He waited fifteen years and he would have waited his entire lifetime if *she* hadn't worked her evil on him and made him think divorcing you was for the best." Pushing herself up from the bed, she crossed the room and stood before the painting of a woman whose likeness Ashlee mirrored. "If you came home now, he'd take you back, Mama. I just know he would."

Ashlee jumped at the light rapping that sounded at her door and interrupted her thoughts, certain her step-mother had heard every word. "Who is it?" she asked, stalling for time as she hurriedly brushed at the tears streaming down her face.

"It's me, Ashlee," John's deep voice replied, and Ashlee breathed a sigh of relief. "Are you dressed? We need to talk before the others are up and moving around."

To anyone who didn't know him, John Hardin's gruff tone and almost evil-looking appearance could frighten a nonbeliever into never missing church services on Sunday. Well over six feet tall, he carried his huge, barrel-chested physique on thickly muscled legs with the lumbering gait of a grizzly. The size and strength of his hands were capable of crushing a man's skull if so provoked, though no one had ever been brave enough— or stupid enough—to find out. It took a lot to anger him, but if anyone ever did, the only sure way of escaping with their life was to run as fast and as far as they could. John Hardin wasn't the type who forgave easily.

His most distinct characteristic was his shiny bald head. He had begun losing his hair in his early twenties, and since he had never considered himself to be handsome anyway, he shaved his scalp clean and kept it that way for the past fifteen years. Ashlee had told him many times that all he needed was a gold ring in one earlobe and he'd look like a swarthy pirate ready to take on the entire United States Navy. And only Ashlee could speak to him that way. He loved her for the daughter he never had, and everyone knew that John Hardin would lay down his life before ever letting any harm come to the beautiful raven-haired woman with the bewitching eyes.

Ashlee responded to the urgency in John's voice without a thought to her appearance except to haphazardly smooth down the tangled strands of hair falling over her shoulders. Clutching the lacy lapels of her robe in one tiny fist, she went to the door and opened it wide, motioning her friend into the room. "Is something wrong?" she whispered, glancing back outside to make sure no one saw them. Dominique had spies everywhere, ones who were too frightened of the woman to keep a secret. If someone saw John go into Ashlee's room at such an early hour, even though they were close friends, it might raise Dominique's curiosity. And that was something they couldn't afford.

"No, nothing's wrong," he answered, crossing to the decorative barred window in the room as if to look outside. Ashlee's bedchamber was located in the back of the hotel on the main level, overlooking a spacious rolling lawn lined with trees and shrubs in the center of which stood a magnificent gazebo for use by the patrons of Belle Chasse. As Ashlee grew from a young, troublesome little girl into a beautiful, headstrong woman, John and her father recognized the need to protect her. The heavy metal bars were added to the windows in her room to prevent an overzealous and unwanted suitor from entering through them. But many times Ashlee wondered if they weren't put there to keep her in, since as a child she had oftentimes sneaked out that way after being sentenced to her room for punishment. And it was always John's custom whenever he came to visit her there to check the grate for any tampering. Having done so, he turned to face her, ready to explain his reason for wanting to talk with her while the others slept, pausing once he noticed her red-rimmed eyes.

"Thinking about your mother again?" he asked tenderly.

Ashlee's anxious expression quickly vanished, and she dropped her gaze. "Among other things," she admitted quietly.

"Like what?" John pressed, for he knew forcing her to talk it out would soon have her back in high spirits. The world could be crumbling around her head, yet Ashlee Redington always managed to find something amusing on which to focus her attention. It was one of her best qualities and the one John enjoyed the most.

Ashlee shrugged one delicate shoulder. "Where would you like for me to begin? It seems my life is full of depressing thoughts." Remembering her earlier performance, she reached up, caught both hands full of her long, thick hair, and gave it a shake. Then, holding a limp wrist in front of her as if the limb were immobile, she asked, "Would Perrin want to marry me if I looked like this?"

John's green eyes sparkled with laughter but he somehow managed not to make a sound. "Probably," he answered. "But maybe you should try a little more dirt on your face. It might change his mind."

Ashlee's cheeks flamed instantly. She had forgotten all about the soot she had smeared on the tip of her nose. Turning away, she vigorously wiped the spot clean with the palm of her hand. "So," she said, pretending as if nothing out of the ordinary had happened, "what brings you here this early?" Crossing to the dresser, she picked up her brush and began to pull the tangles from her thick, dark mane.

"Ashlee," John sang, "what happened to that optimism of yours? It's going to be some time yet before Mr. Fabron arrives."

"Optimism?" she echoed, looking at him in the reflection of the mirror. "You mean like the possibility his ship will sink on the way from France? Or that he'll trip and fall of the gangplank and drown? How about his falling in love with one of the dealers in the casino and—" Suddenly, Ashlee's chin quivered as she fought not to laugh. "Male or female." She bit her lower lip, but joyful tears glistened in her eyes. "How will I ever face everyone if I have to tell them that my fiancé chose George over me?" She blinked coquettishly and turned around to look at him. "George is rather cute, though, don't you agree?"

Ashlee stared at her friend without so much as a smile, but the mischief shining in her eyes was more than John could handle. Unable to hold it back any longer, he burst into heartfelt guffaws. "Now that's the Ashlee I know," he chuckled, wiping the tears from the corners of his eyes.

Grinning openly, Ashlee watched him a moment until a devilish thought crossed her mind. "Of course," she added, feigning a serious air, "if all else fails, I still have one option."

"And what's that?" John laughed.

"You and I can get married before Perrin can do anything about it."

John's mouth fell open. "You can't be serious?" he exclaimed, his suntanned face paling noticeably.

"And why not? We love each other."

"It's—it's not that kind of love, Ashlee," he stammered, failing to realize that Ashlee had turned her back to him so that he wouldn't see the smile that flashed across her face. "We love each other as friends. It could never be any more than that. Besides, your father would have me shot! God, Ashlee, I'm nearly as old as Arthur.

No father in his right mind would—" Suddenly, John knew her game, and he let out a long, surrendering sigh. "I wonder if I'll ever learn," he muttered, sinking down in the rocker next to Ashlee's bed and nightstand.

"I hope not," Ashlee giggled, coming to wrap her arm around one of the tall bedposts. "It would ruin all my fun."

"Hmmm" was John's only reply.

"So, tell me what was so important that you had to see me at this hour if it wasn't to propose?"

John gave Ashlee one of his most berating looks as he folded his arms over his wide chest, staring silently at her for several minutes. "If it wasn't to help your father, I wouldn't even mention it," he finally said. "But I owe the man a great deal, and since we haven't come up with any better way, I'm forced to continue with our little scheme."

"You've heard something," Ashlee proclaimed excitedly, sitting down on the mattress, her hands clasped tightly in her lap as she waited to hear him out.

"Yes, I have. In a couple of days there'll be a steamer docking here called the *Spirit of Dubuque*. It's a small boat, used only for gambling, and it won't be here for long before it makes its way back home—a small river town somewhere in Iowa." His sandy-colored brows came together in a frown. "I didn't think the people in Iowa did anything but farm," he commented with a shake of his bald head. "Anyway, rumor has it that there's to be a high stakes poker game taking place there, and from the sounds of it, we should come out of it with twice the money we got last time." John leaned forward with his elbows braced on his knees. "It'll be risky, Ashlee. More so than ever before because of the small amount of passengers. And I'll agree to help on one condition."

"What's that?" she asked cautiously.

"That if anything should go wrong—if you suspect

49

anything isn't as it should be, even if you just have a gut feeling about it—you'll abandon the plan and get off the ship. Agree?"

"What could go wrong?" she smiled, wondering if he could see right through her. She hadn't told John about the guard that had been posted on the *Mississippi Queen* or the fire she had started to distract everyone. And she most certainly wouldn't tell him about the man that had her nerves on edge. She had had a gut feeling on their last caper, but everything turned out all right. As far as she was concerned it went along with the job.

"I mean it, Ashlee," he warned. "The only reason I'm not the one who boards these steamers is because I know you can't handle a rowboat in that swift of a current. And the biggest factor in managing to pull this off is simply because you're not there to be questioned or searched once the theft is discovered. We've been damn lucky for the past year, but just like everything else, good things don't last."

"And the only way I'll quit is to get caught, John," Ashlee stated, all trace of humor gone from her eyes. "Even if you refuse to help me, I'll keep on with it . . . alone, if I must. Papa doesn't deserve to lose everything after he's worked so hard."

"I'm not disagreeing, child," John assured her. "But I know your father would rather give up Belle Chasse than have you in prison. He loves you too much, and if he had any idea of what we're doing, he'd"—a faint smile crossed his lips as John fell back in the chair—"he'd probably put me on the first ship back to England and lock you up in your room for the rest of your life."

"I don't think he'd do that," Ashlee smiled softly. "Oh, he might lock me in my room, but I truly doubt he'd ever send you back home. He loves you like a brother."

"Then I guess we better see to it that he never finds out," John chuckled.

"Agreed. And I better talk with Priscilla today. How long do we have before the steamer docks?"

"It's expected this afternoon sometime, but it won't weigh anchor until Sunday."

"Hmmm," Ashlee frowned. "Day after tomorrow. Doesn't give me much time, but at least I won't have to come up with some excuse for Papa. He and Dominique are going to some political dinner Sunday evening, and you know how those affairs can last all night. I'll just ask Elaine to fill in for me at the blackjack table." The gleam appeared in her pale blue eyes again. "I can feel a migraine coming on."

"And something tells me you'll be fine Monday morning," John laughed, pushing his broad frame up from the chair. "Now, I better get out of here before someone spots me and I find myself trying to explain to your father." He headed for the door, ready to make a quiet and unseen exit, when he absently glanced at the dresser on his way by and spotted an unfamiliar piece of men's jewelry lying there. "Ashlee," he said, stopping to pick up the diamond stickpin, "where did this come from?"

Ashlee could feel the blood rush to her cheeks. John had told her time and time again never to steal anything from the gamblers except their money. She hurriedly left the bed and went to the window to open it, an excuse to keep her back to him while her mind raced for some lie to tell him. "Oh—ah—I broke a rule at the table last night. Some poor fool lost all his money and I let him bet the stickpin." She forced a laugh. "As you can see, he lost that, too."

"Oh?" John questioned, and Ashlee could hear the doubt in his voice. "Then why didn't you turn it in with the rest of the house winnings?"

Ashlee shrugged and rearranged the lace curtains. "I—ah—I forgot."

"No you didn't. You took this from one of the men on the steamer. Ashlee, turn around and look me in the eye and tell me I'm wrong."

It never ceased to amaze her how easily she could lie to her father and he would believe every word she said, yet John seemed to know she was stretching the truth before a single word left her mouth. To confront him now with anything but fact would be foolish and a bit ludicrous, for the expression on her face alone would confirm his suspicions. Ashamed of the stupidity that had tempted her to take the jewelry, Ashlee bowed her head and idly toyed with satin ribbon on her robe.

"Oh, for God's sake, Ashlee," he moaned, coming to stand next to her, "don't you ever listen?" He held the stickpin in front of her nose for her to see. "It's mistakes like this that will get us both hanged! Stealing this is the same as signing your name to a confession. It puts you on that steamer the night of the robbery, and I doubt the man who owns this would excuse you for taking it with a simple pat on the head. Get rid of it, young woman, before it becomes the key that will lock your prison cell." Grabbing her wrist, he dropped the item in the opened palm of her hand, turned, and marched from the room.

Ashlee flinched at the loud bang that echoed all around her when John slammed the door shut behind him. He was right and she knew it, but admitting it didn't make her feel any better. Nor did his advice to dispose of the evidence have any affect on her desire to keep the souvenir. The strange part of the whole thing was her reason. It wasn't the value of the stickpin she treasured, but to whom it belonged. Some would call it a young girl's fantasy—John would label it madness—but this stranger was the first real man in her life to make her feel like a woman. And he hadn't even said a word to the lady in black. There had been plenty of customers in the casino that had begged her to marry them, but they were either already married, too old, too ugly, too fat, or too drunk for Ashlee to even consider their proposals.

Lifting the pin between her thumb and first finger, she raised it to the sunlight coming in through the window, hypnotized by the rainbow of color the tiny gem produced. Was it truly too much to ask to have a man court her, play for her affections, win her love, and whisper his own? Apparently her father thought so or he never would have arranged a marriage between his daughter and a man he had never seen. Ashlee's lip curled at the thoughts of Perrin Fabron, and she turned away from the window so abruptly that it sent her long, flowing mane swirling out around her shoulders. She'd keep the pin and if Perrin ever asked her where she had gotten it, she would tell him that her lover gave it to her to remember him by.

Returning to the dresser, she opened the top drawer, took out the ornately decorated jewelry box, and lifted the lid. No one would ever find the pin among the many necklaces and earrings she had. And even if they did, she'd tell them it belonged to her grandfather on her mother's side. Pleased with her decision, Ashlee closed the box and returned it to its place, leaning a hip against the drawer to slide it shut. Besides, she'd never see its owner again, so what possible danger could there be in keeping it? Silently applauding her brilliance in the matter, she turned for the armoire, hearing the clock strike half past six. She would have to hurry if she were to talk with Priscilla before her father came looking for her . . . or worse yet, Dominique.

The hired conveyance rolled to a stop in front of the hotel. A moment passed before its only passenger stepped down, bag in hand, to stare in quiet admiration of the place he had heard so much about. Belle Chasse was

53

indeed a magnificent spectacle. It had earned its favorable reputation not only because of the skilled staff that managed it and the immaculate, spacious rooms the hotel offered, but for the exquisite design of the structure as well. The three-story brick building resembled one of London's Roman Catholic cathedrals, with its arched windows of multicolored panes on the first floor, rose windows on the second, louver windows on the third, and high towering spires adorning the red tile roof line. Of those who had stayed in the hotel, many of them wondered if Arthur Redington hadn't designed the place with the idea of giving an outward appearance of respectability for anyone who required it while inside, those same patrons gambling away their life's earnings at the blackjack tables in the casino. Yet, whatever reason may have brought them, scores of customers passed through its doors at all hours of the day and night.

Setting down his satchel, Rhys reached inside his coat pocket, withdrew his wallet, and handed the required fare to the driver of the rig, thanking him for a smooth ride from the docks. He lingered a moment longer, watching the buggy pull away, then turned, picked up his bag, and started up the wide stone staircase that led to the tall double front doors with their stained glass panels and shiny brass hinges and knob. He was about to lift the latch and walk inside when the door was suddenly flung open, nearly hitting his shoulder before he agilely stepped out of the way.

"Good lord—" the young red-faced doorman exclaimed once he realized what had almost happened. "Excuse me. I didn't mean—"

"That's quite all right," Rhys cut in. "It's a little early for guests, and I'm sure you didn't see me."

"No, sir, I didn't," the man replied. "But it's never too early around here. My shift started ten minutes ago, and I"—he looked sheepishly down at his feet—"overslept," he admitted, glancing back inside, his brows drawn together. "I have an excuse, but nothing is good enough for Mrs. Redington, I'm afraid." The doorman straightened suddenly when he realized how he had rattled on to a perfect stranger, and he reached to take Rhys's bag. "If you'll allow me, sir, I'll carry that in for you. Will you be staying long?" he asked, following Rhys into the lobby.

"About a week," Rhys smiled, amused by the young man's uninhibited nature. "What's your name?"

"Harold, sir, Harold Brown."

"And I'm Rhys Sinclair," he nodded, turning to offer his hand once they had reached the front desk.

Harold was quick to accept it. "An honor, sir," he said with a bright smile. "And I hope your stay here is pleasant." He set down Rhys's bag and glanced back at the front door. "Well, I better get to my station. The other guests should start arriving soon. It was a pleasure talking to you, Mr. Sinclair." Leaning in, he hit the desk bell with his opened palm then turned and strode away.

Rhys absently watched the young man's tall, lanky figure until the clicking of Harold's shoes against the marble floor sparked his attention, and for the first time since stepping inside the arched entryway, he studied the elegant interior of the place. Opposite the front entrance on the far side of the lobby was a huge staircase that rose to the second floor and a row of French doors that Rhys assumed opened up to a balcony. At the top of the stairs the way divided and circled around overhead, revealing the large amount of rooms for rent by their dark mahogany doors with raised brass number plates. On the other side of the lobby Rhys noticed a wide archway through which he could see numerous tables and chairs. Each was elaborately set with fine china, silver, crystal glasses, and a candelabrum filled with delicate ivory tapers. To the right of him he espied another set of French doors and could only surmise they opened up to

55

the casino. Judge Lott had been correct in telling Rhys that Belle Chasse was, indeed, the most prestigious enterprise in all of New Orleans.

A door closed behind him, and Rhys turned back to the desk to greet the clerk coming from a back room. "Good morning," he smiled.

"Good morning, sir," the clerk replied. "How may I help you?"

"I'd like a room . . . for a week, if you have one available."

The clerk, dressed in a crimson jacket and dark trousers similar to Harold Brown's uniform, opened the large leather-bound book lying on top of the desk. He studied it a moment, turned to pluck a key from one of the pigeonholes in the cabinet behind him, then laid it on the desk before his guest. "Room 3A, sir. I'm sure you'll find it suitable. It overlooks the gardens in back and catches the late afternoon breeze." He turned the register around. "If you'd be kind enough to sign here—" He pointed to the line below the last entry.

"Is the restaurant open?" Rhys asked as he took the quill from its well and penned his name in the book. "I just got off a steamer and haven't eaten yet this morning."

"Yes, sir, it is," the clerk replied as Rhys returned the quill to its place and slid the register toward him. "But if you'd care to freshen up first, Mr."—he glanced at the book—"Sinclair, I'd be happy to show you to your room."

"I think I can find it," Rhys smiled, picking up his key then his bag and turning for the stairs.

"Well, if there's anything I can do for you, Mr. Sinclair, just let me know. My name is Michael," the clerk called after him.

"Thank you, Michael," Rhys threw back over his shoulder as he mounted the stairs. He had nearly reached the top when he heard a door open and close from somewhere below him, followed by the distinct sound of delicate heels against the marble floor as someone walked into the lobby.

"Good morning, Miss Redington," he heard Michael say, and Rhys stopped once he reached the landing to glance back down out of curiosity.

"Good morning, Michael," came the light, airy reply, but all Rhys was allowed to see of the woman was the swish of pink taffeta skirts before she disappeared into the dining room. Shrugging off his misfortune with the thought that he might catch a glimpse of her later, he turned and walked to his room, pausing to unlock the door before stepping inside.

Although the room was spotlessly clean, the first thing Rhys noticed was the slightly frayed rug at his feet, and he remembered William Lott telling him that Belle Chasse was having a hard time of it during the war. Yet, William had gone on to say that its owner was doing better now. Swinging the door shut behind him, he crossed to the bed and tossed his bag down. Maybe the hotel wasn't doing as well as William thought.

Turning, Rhys threw his room key on the dresser, then slid off his coat and laid it on the bed. He'd shave first before going down for breakfast, and while he ate he would go over his plans again. He had to be sure of everything if he was to succeed in catching the bandits who had stolen from him a week ago. Moving to the nightstand, he lifted the pitcher from the washbowl and poured water into it.

For the past seven days, Rhys had gathered all the information he could get about the thefts that had occurred on various steamers along the Mississippi River during the last year. Comparing it to the events in which he had unwillingly participated, he had uncovered some very interesting facts. All the victims had been drugged after drinking from the same bottle, a bottle that had been brought to them by an anonymous well-wisher. In the case where some of the gamblers were drinking beer, others whiskey, a round of drinks had been brought to the stateroom—all laced with laudanum. In Rhys's instance, the culprit had created a diversion that would lure everyone out of the cabin since they weren't accepting any presents, giving the person enough time to add the drug to the bottle already used by the victims. Once Rhys's initial rage had waned and he had set his mind on catching the thieves, he had had to admit that it had been a very good scheme, one that had caught even him off guard.

Even though Parkins had told him that a young boy had given him the mug of beer that put him under, Rhys decided the child had nothing to do with it and that someone else must have given the mug to the boy. And that someone else had been a woman—the widow Rhys had noticed boarding the ship that day. When Rhys had finally regained consciousness, he had gone to Captain Longley and ordered a thorough search of every cabin and piece of luggage before the steamer docked in the next port. But the investigation failed to turn up any money or Rhys's diamond stickpin. It did, however, produce one empty cabin—the one that had been used by a woman who had booked passage on the steamer under the name of Mrs. Jesse Smith.

It was this bit of knowledge that prompted Rhys to check the passenger lists of all the steamboats that had been hit by the thieves. Thus, another similarity. Just like the *Mississippi Queen* they, too, docked with one less passenger on board. However, their descriptions ranged from a little old lady with white hair, to a preacher with a beard and dressed in a black suit, a young English lad, and a Confederate soldier, leading Rhys to believe that there was a gang working the gambling steamers. Another interesting tidbit Rhys had discovered was that all the victims were northerners who had settled in the south, and he had come to the conclusion that the band might be a group of rebels still fighting the war. It might prove quite a feat to capture them all, but after studying the evidence he had, he was sure his trap would snare at least one—and if he were lucky, it would be a woman, one who wouldn't be too difficult to break.

"Mrs. Jesse Smith, indeed," Rhys chuckled as he toweled his face dry. He, himself, knew three married men by that name, so finding such a woman would be impossible. Of course, he doubted that was the mysterious widow's name in the first place. If these people were crafty enough to pull off something of this size for over a year without getting caught, they certainly wouldn't be stupid enough to use their real identity.

Slipping on his black coat, Rhys adjusted the collar, then the cuffs of his shirt beneath it. He reached for the large envelope he had carried in his satchel and checked the time on his pocket watch. Thomas was expected to arrive at the hotel around eight, and from there they would discuss what was to happen next. Rhys had wanted to do this alone, but the more he had thought about it, the more he realized he needed someone's help, and Thomas Bryan was the only man Rhys could trust to do as he asked. With the envelope held in one hand, he picked up his room key and started for the door.

"Miz Ashlee, where you goin' dis time o' de mornin'?" the black woman frowned when she glanced up from her work and spied Ashlee trying to sneak out the back door of the kitchen. "You ain't goin' to de theater, is you?"

"Shhh!" Ashlee warned, spinning around to face the cook with a finger pressed to her lips. "Someone might hear you."

"And ah reckon dey oughta. Yo' papa doan want you anywheres near dat place and you knows it," she scowled.

"And what Papa doesn't know won't hurt him," Ashlee rallied. "And besides, Eunice, it's important that I talk to Priscilla."

"Impo'tant nuff fo' you to go again' yo' papa's wishes?" Eunice snapped, pounding her fist into the ball of bread dough she was making. "Ah is sorely tempted to tell yo' stepmama."

"Oh, God, Eunice, don't do that," Ashlee moaned, rushing toward the table and the woman who stood beside it. "I'd be locked in my room until I'm ninety-three."

"Den tell me whad's so all fired impo'tant," Eunice demanded, leaning her weight on her fists pressed against the table top.

Ashlee's slender shoulders drooped. "I can't, Eunice. I've told you that before. If I tell you anything, it will only make matters worse."

"And why's dat?"

"Because—" Ashlee's smooth brow wrinkled as she fought for the right words. "Because if you knew why, you'd understand and not stop me from talking to her. Then you'd be a part of it, and it's better that you're not. That way Papa would only be angry with me if he ever found out."

"And you think he ain't gonna be once he finds out ah knew, but didn't tell?" Shaking her head, she lifted the bread dough and dropped it into a greased pan, adding, "Miz Dominique would love to know somethin' like dat. Dat woman is lookin' fo' any excuse she can find to set yo' papa again' you."

Hearing the concern in the black woman's voice, Ashlee's nervous excitement ebbed, and she rounded the table to take Eunice's hand. "Would it make any difference if I told you that even if Papa or Dominique found out, I would still try to talk with Priscilla? I know this won't make any sense to you, Eunice, but I'm doing it for Papa, for his hotel, for the things that are important to him. Having him angry with me is a very small price for the rewards my disobedience brings. There will come a time, I'm sure, when I'll be forced to tell him why. And he'll be very upset. But until that moment, I'll keep on with what I'm doing. All I ask of you is that you turn your back until I'm ready to discuss it with him. Will you do that much?"

The deep frown that had furrowed the other's brow faded with Ashlee's confession. "Only 'cause ah know how you love yo' papa. If'n you feel dat strong about it, it gotta be fo' a good reason. Now hurry up and skedaddle 'fore ah change my mind." Picking up the bread pan, Eunice turned away and went to the stove, humming to herself as if no one else was around. Ashlee quickly left the kitchen through the back entrance.

Priscilla Krayer was a middle-aged actress who worked in the theater next door to Belle Chasse. Ashlee and she had become friends more than eight years ago when the older woman took a room in Arthur Redington's hotel while doing a play. Ashlee's father had violently objected to the budding relationship between his daughter and the theatrical tart, as he called her, and banned the woman from his hotel. Since her father refused to explain, the young Ashlee hadn't understood why until Priscilla took the twelve-year-old child to one side and as gently as possible told her about Arthur's hatred for people of the stage.

Veronica Darnell, Ashlee's mother, was seventeen when she and the acting troupe appeared at the Claiborne Theater next to Arthur Redington's hotel and casino. Her stunning beauty had caught Arthur's eye the first moment he saw her, and he had fallen hopelessly in love

61

with her. After one short week of taking her to dinner, carriage rides to the country, and visiting the many boutiques in New Orleans to buy Veronica anything she wanted, Arthur proposed marriage. Veronica had been terribly flattered to think that an older, wealthy man would ask her to be his wife, but marriage wasn't what Veronica wanted. She had dreamed of being a renowned Shakespearean actress, and to succeed she had to be free. Yet, she found that she adored Arthur and didn't want to hurt him. Thinking to let him down easily, she had allowed him to make love to her, and while nestled in his arms she told him the truth.

He hadn't been discouraged by her rejection and continued to court her, hoping that in time she would change her mind. Two months later, Veronica accepted his offer after she learned that she carried his child. She had been very happy for the first year and deeply loved their daughter, but the haunting dream of appearing on a stage in London soon wedged its way between them. A few weeks after Ashlee's third birthday, Veronica ran away.

That was all Priscilla could tell Ashlee about her mother, claiming to have met Veronica only once a long time ago. But Priscilla constantly reassured Ashlee that her mother truly loved her and that someday, if she could, Veronica would come back and tell her so.

"We're a strange breed of people, Ashlee," Priscilla had said. "There's something about the sound of applause that gets into our blood and won't let go. We can control it for a while, but sooner or later it takes over again, and nothing else matters in our life. It doesn't mean we're incapable of love, just that sometimes we forget what's truly important."

There had been a few times while Ashlee's father was busy entertaining guests that Ashlee would sneak off to the theater and watch Priscilla perform. She had to admit that she didn't know much about acting, but Ashlee always thought Priscilla outshone all the others on the stage. It never ceased to amaze her how young and healthy Priscilla appeared to be while dramatizing her part, when backstage the woman would have to drink a shot of whiskey to dull the pain in her knees and shoulders. It had been her reason for settling in New Orleans when traveling the country with her troupe became too difficult for her. The doctors she had seen told Priscilla that she had arthritis, and that before she reached her fortieth birthday she could be confined to a wheelchair. Maybe that was what Ashlee loved so about her, for Priscilla would always laugh it off even though her suffering shone clearly in her eyes. She loved life and the excitement of it, and that had been why Ashlee had gone to her for her help more than a year ago.

"Priscilla?" Ashlee called out once she had entered through the back door of the theater. "Are you here?"

"Yes, darlin', I'm in the prop room. What brings you here so early?" came the distant reply.

"I need your help again," Ashlee answered, starting toward her friend through the dimly lit backstage area.

"So soon? Aren't you pushing it a bit?"

Ashlee grimaced when her shin kicked the leg of a table that seemed to jump in her way. "It's been a week."

A shadow crossed the yellow light coming from the prop room, and a moment later Priscilla appeared in the doorway, several costumes draped over her arm. "That long?" she mocked, her brightly painted red lips stretched into a smile.

The bump to her shin still aching a little, Ashlee stopped and leaned against the back of a sofa to rub the bruised area. "Well, you made it sound like it was yesterday," she mumbled.

Priscilla's smile vanished. "Are you all right?"

"Yes," Ashlee replied, although her tone hinted

63

otherwise. "I just kicked something in the dark." She straightened and started toward Priscilla again. "I don't know how you manage not to have both legs black and blue all the time."

"Talent, my dear," the older woman laughed, reaching out to lay her arm across Ashlee's shoulders and guide them both into the prop room. "So what will it be this time?"

"Well, after the trouble I ran into last trip, I better come up with a disguise that will get me into the stateroom," Ashlee said, crossing to the rack of clothes opposite them. "I was thinking of dressing like a"—she paused when she realized what the woman's reaction would be—"a prostitute."

"Oh, that would get you into the stateroom, all right, and into some man's bed as well." Priscilla shook her blond head. "It's not worth the risk. We'll find something else."

"Like what?" Ashlee objected, turning around. "A nun? Or how about an old maid schoolmarm? I don't think either one of them would go unnoticed in the midst of a poker game."

"You know how to play poker, don't you?"

"Yes."

"Then why not disguise yourself as a wealthy businessman who wants to join the game?" Priscilla suggested.

"I'd love it, but there's two things wrong with the idea," Ashlee replied, turning back to sort through the clothes again. "First of all, I'd have to have a lot of money to gamble with, and you know who keeps it under lock and key. Dominique wouldn't loan me a penny. But secondly, and most importantly, it's a closed game. John said the players have already been selected. Besides, it's easier for me to move around as a woman rather than having to remember how to walk and sit and talk. It frees me up to concentrate on my job. Ah, this one should do," she smiled, pulling out a bright crimson satin gown with a black sash and lace trim. "Now all I need is a feather, a blond wig, and lots of makeup."

"Ashlee—"

"Nothing will happen, Priscilla. I'll stay in my cabin until the game starts, then go to the stateroom, pretending I'd like to watch. I won't get near any men who'd be interested in"—her face flooded with color at the thought—"you know," she finished sheepishly. "And the ones I will see will be too interested in winning to pay me any attention. Now, I'll need this the day after tomorrow. Can I count on you to help with the makeup?"

Priscilla's blue eyes darkened with her disapproving frown. "Yes, I'll help. But I want you to know that I'm not in favor of this."

"Thank you," Ashlee grinned, hurrying over to place a kiss on the woman's darkly rouged cheek. "I'll be back sometime Sunday after Papa and Dominique leave for their dinner engagement."

"You make it sound far away," Priscilla laughed as she took the dress from Ashlee.

"It is, sort of. They're going to Laplace to meet some other people from Baton Rouge. Couldn't have timed it better." She gently squeezed the other's hand, then headed for the door, calling back over her shoulder, "See you later."

"Yes, Ashlee, I'll see you later," Priscilla whispered sadly once she knew the girl couldn't hear her. "And I pray everything goes as planned." Glancing down at the red gown hanging over her arm, she wondered if there would ever be a time when she could shed her costume, take off the makeup, and just be herself. She was tired of pretending.

*　　*　　*

"All right, Rhys, I'm here," Thomas sighed impatiently as he plopped down in a chair across the table from him. "So tell me what's so all-fired urgent that I had to drop everything and sail here to meet you."

Rhys motioned for the waiter. "Would you care for some breakfast while we talk, or just coffee?"

"Yes, yes," Thomas frowned. "I'll have whatever you ordered." He sat back in the chair, watching the servant fill his coffee cup then Rhys's before moving on. Once the man was far enough away, Thomas leaned in, his arms resting on the edge of the table. "All right. Why all the mystery?"

A vague smile enhanced Rhys's good looks as he lifted the cup to his lips and took a swallow. "How would you like to get back some of the money you lost?"

"Ha!" Thomas exploded. "Playing cards with you? Why? Are you planning to let me win?"

"I don't mean playing poker."

Thomas's green eyes narrowed, and when he spoke it came in hardly more than a whisper. "Are you planning to rob somebody?" He glanced around them as if checking to make sure no one would hear. "Then it better be in Canada, my friend, because I'm trying to get elected to the Senate, and I don't think the good people of Mississippi would want their senator to steal out of their own pocket." He made a silly but rather sarcastic grin and picked up his coffee.

"No, Thomas," Rhys laughed, "that isn't what I had in mind, but if everything goes as I expect, you'll further your career as a politician."

Thomas raised an eyebrow. "Go on."

Pushing aside his plate and silverware, Rhys leaned forward with his elbows braced on the table. "I've got a plan—one that I've already started into action—but I need your help. I've asked Judge Lott, Phillip Sanders, and Ben Jones to join us in another poker game. But this time it will be different. I intend to catch the men—and women—responsible for ruining our last get-together."

"Women?" Thomas repeated, surprised.

"I've been doing some research for the past week— studying the facts related to all the other robberies—and came up with some very interesting points. After the thefts are discovered and the steamers docked in the next port, each one was short a passenger. Some were men, some women, and on occasion a boy, which leads me to believe there's a gang working the river. Every victim was drugged, just like we were, and they are always northerners who have settled in the south. Give you any ideas?"

"Somebody who carries a little hatred, I'd say."

"Uh-huh," Rhys nodded. "It's always a private game in a private stateroom, enabling the thieves to come and go without being noticed and allowing them time enough to get off the steamer. And the interesting thing is the robberies always take place somewhere between New Orleans and Baton Rouge."

"Meaning?"

"Meaning that the thieves board here—in New Orleans. Now either they live around here or it happens to be their meeting place."

"So what's your plan?"

"I've been spreading it around that this high stakes poker game will be on the *Spirit of Dubuque*, which weighs anchor Sunday evening. What I want you to do is hit the casino for the next two nights, pretend you've had a little too much to drink, and tell everyone you can about the game Sunday night. These bandits must have spies and I can't think of a better place to find them than in a gambling house. Will you do it?"

"I'd love it," Thomas smiled. "But what happens once we're on board?"

"Nothing out of the ordinary. We all meet in the

stateroom to play poker. The whole trick of this plan is to act natural. I even want you and the others to drink the whiskey that's brought to us by some generous admirer of the game."

"But you won't," Thomas added.

"Right," Rhys grinned. "I'll pretend to be just in case our thief is watching, and when the rest of you start feeling the effects, I will, too. Or so it will appear."

"And when our uninvited guest joins us . . ." Thomas chuckled.

"I'll be waiting for him."

Thomas fell back in his chair. "I like it, Rhys. And I think it will work. Do the others know?"

"No. And I don't want them to. They might give it away. That's why I need your help in making sure they all have something to drink."

"Consider it done," Thomas nodded as the waiter returned to their table carrying a tray with their breakfast order. While he set the food down in front of them, Thomas asked, "So what are your plans for tonight?"

"It's been a long time since I've seen a play," Rhys admitted, unfolding his napkin and laying it across his lap. "There's a theater next door. I thought I'd spend the evening there and then tomorrow I'd try my luck in the casino." He glanced up at his friend with a smile, only to discover that Thomas's attention was somewhere else. "Thomas?" he frowned.

"Oh, I heard you," Thomas replied. "I was just enjoying the scenery. What a beautiful young lady."

Turning in his chair in an effort to see the woman and decide for himself, Rhys's suntanned brow wrinkled when the only person he saw was an elderly gentleman sitting some distance away. "Either I'm blind or you've been drinking this morning," Rhys chuckled, holding out his cup to receive the coffee the waiter offered to pour.

"You missed her. I spotted her just before she went into the lobby. Who is she?" Thomas asked the waiter.

"Miss Redington, sir. Her father owns the hotel."

"*Miss* Redington," Thomas repeated. "Did you hear that, Rhys, old friend? The lady isn't married. Maybe you should—"

"Eat breakfast," Rhys warned playfully, picking up his fork.

"Right," Thomas conceded reluctantly. "Just trying to help."

"Well, don't," Rhys laughed. "I have more important things to think about." But even as he said the words his curiosity about the elusive lady in pink taffeta doubled, and he decided that after he and Thomas had eaten he would plot out a discreet way of meeting her.

Chapter Three

Rhys's efforts to meet the daughter of the owner of Belle Chasse failed miserably, for it seemed he was always one step behind Miss Redington wherever she went. When he learned that she was in the dining room having lunch, he decided to have a cup of coffee. But once he had taken a table that gave him a clear view of everyone there, the waiter who served him explained the current shortage of help as due to the staff meeting Miss Redington had called in the kitchen. He had waited until they all filed out again, quickly realizing Miss Redington wasn't one of them, for he doubted she would wear the customary color of the restaurant staff—the waiters in white shirts and black trousers, the waitresses in plain white blouses and aprons, and black skirts—especially since he recalled having seen her in pink taffeta that morning.

He had lingered a while longer, in hope that she would appear, until he was sure every customer, waiter, and waitress suspected his real reason for being there. Feeling strangely uncomfortable, as he had never purposely trailed a woman before, he paid for his one cup of coffee and left, deciding to take a walk around the streets of New Orleans and forget about trying to meet her. If it were meant to be, it would happen on its own.

The last place he had visited before starting back to the hotel was the docks. The *Spirit of Dubuque* was expected to arrive shortly after noon, and he wanted to be sure nothing had delayed it. Rhys had gone to too much trouble to have his plans ruined because the steamer hadn't docked, and he had given a mental sigh of relief when he saw it nestled there among the much larger steamboats. As he had turned to leave, however, he had spotted a carriage some distance away. Rhys wouldn't have given it much thought if not for the driver, who was pointing toward the steamers. The rig was too far away for him to clearly see the man's face, but his identity didn't interest Rhys once he noticed the bright pink gown of the passenger sitting in the back seat. A huge white bonnet with satin ribbons tied beneath the lady's chin hindered Rhys's chance of seeing her face or the color of her hair. He took a quick step forward then stopped. He couldn't very well just walk right up to her. And what if she wasn't Miss Redington? He had argued with himself just long enough for the driver to turn the mare around and head away from the docks and Rhys, and he couldn't help but laugh out loud. In all of his thirty years it had never been this difficult for him to meet someone.

That night he had dinner in the restaurant, attended the theater, then retired to his room after the performance. The following morning he had breakfast with Thomas who, during the course of their conversation, told him that Miss Redington was one of the blackjack dealers in the casino. Rhys acted as if it made no difference to him as he finished off the last piece of ham and mouthful of scrambled eggs. When Thomas asked if he had heard him, Rhys had nodded and stated that blackjack had never been one of his favorite types of gambling. But it had only been a way of getting Thomas to change the subject. If the man knew Miss Redington had

72

sparked Rhys's interest, he would more than likely do everything possible to get them together, as he had done with other ladies in the past. It wasn't that Rhys objected to his friend's help. But there had been a few occasions when he had wanted to end an affair and Thomas had unknowingly prevented it by inviting both Rhys and the lady to various dinners, balls, or other events he was giving. Because Rhys liked the man he never got angry with his interference, but this time, he decided, he would be the one to make the first move. If it turned out not to be what he wanted, he would be able to terminate it without anyone's feelings getting in the way. Thus, he told Thomas that if nothing better came up before then, he would probably try his luck at the roulette table later that evening. But as for how he would spend the day, he was planning on checking out the steamer and its passenger list.

The night before a robbery was always the same for Ashlee. Her nerves were on edge, her hands shook, and to others she seemed preoccupied. John, however, never appeared to let anything bother him. *That's because he has the easy part,* she would tell herself many times. Just once she wished she could be in charge of the rowboat. Then she'd see how calm John would be! Yet, Ashlee knew better. John Hardin wasn't afraid of anything, except maybe dying.

He had grown up on the streets of London after his mother had died and his father deserted him. He had fed and clothed himself by stealing from the local merchants. By the time he was twenty, he had mastered every sort of card game imaginable and could cheat with the best of them. He had come a long way from the street urchin sleeping in back alleys, and at one point in his young life had owned his own tavern. His only weaknesses, however, were poker, whiskey, and women, all of which brought on the hasty departure from his homeland on the first ship bound for America.

He had fashioned himself in love with a pretty brunette whose background wasn't unsimilar to his own. He had only known her a few days when she and four men came into John's tavern one evening. She said the men were her brothers and that they were looking for a friendly game of poker. Never one to pass up a chance to win some money, he sat down at the table with them. Before an hour had passed John had lost everything, including his tavern. Devastated, he had drunk himself unconscious and woke up the next morning in an alley on the other side of town, put there, he assumed, by the brothers. Because of his skill with cards, John rarely lost more than a few hundred pounds and couldn't understand what had happened. He did some checking around on the young woman and her brothers, only to find out that he had been taken in by a gang of professional swindlers from Portsmouth. Enraged, he set out to win back his property, but he had to do it quickly, before word of his misfortune spread.

When John had gone into business for himself, he had given up cheating to win, thus earning a reputation as a fine and honest businessman. Although he didn't like lying to the merchants who trusted him, he used the tavern he didn't own at the moment as security in guaranteeing repayment with each man he visited, praying that if any of them ever found out, they would understand his need. After all, it would only take him an hour or so to win back his tavern. But things hadn't worked out that way for him. The moment he stepped inside the place he realized his mistake, for the four men were expecting him. Caught off guard, he was easily overcome, knocked unconscious, and dumped near the docks, his pockets empty. For the first time in his life,

John Hardin knew real fear. The merchants would want their money, and it was his word against four others that they had stolen it from him. And once the shopkeepers learned that he had lied to them about the tavern, his life would be worthless.

The same afternoon, using the money he'd won after a quick roll of the dice with a tar he'd met at the pier, John booked passage on a ship sailing for America. He hid out until the ship weighed anchor the next morning. It made several stops along the eastern sea coast of the United States, but John elected to go all the way to New Orleans, thinking the farther away the better. The night he arrived, while looking for a place to sleep where no one would bother him, he came upon three men in an alleyway. John quickly realized that the better dressed of the trio was being held at gunpoint while the larger of the other two demanded his money. Visions of his own disastrous confrontations back in London filled his brain. Although he didn't know the man, he was compelled to help, for in an odd way he felt it was one method of seeking revenge. John's hulk and vengeful determination ended the brawl before the thieves had a chance to do anything. He simply ran up behind them, grabbed them by the scruff of their necks, and banged their heads together, knocking them both to the ground unconscious.

When John refused the money the man offered as a reward for his bravery and selflessness in helping him, the gentleman had looked him up and down, then insisted that he come to work for him. His name was Arthur Redington, and he needed someone of John's size and ability to handle the rowdy customers who sometimes patronized his casino. But John turned him down, telling Arthur that gambling, liquor, and women had nearly gotten him killed and being so close to these things would only tempt him to try again.

"Then I'll make you a deal," Arthur had told him. "I'll give you a room in my hotel in the servants' quarters, I'll feed you, and any extra money you earn, I'll keep on record. Then if you need clothes or shoes or money to buy presents at Christmas, you can come to me and I'll give you a note clearing your credit at any store you choose. That way, you'll never be wanting for anything and you'll never have any money in your hand to waste on whiskey or the gaming tables. As for the women . . ."

Arthur Redington's proposal was too good for John to let slip through his fingers, and it had taken him only a moment to say yes.

He had worked at Belle Chasse for nearly six months before two men showed up at the casino looking for him. They had been sent to the United States by the merchants in London who wanted their money, and they told John that they were instructed not to return without either the money or proof John Hardin was dead. He had reluctantly gone to Arthur and asked for all the money he had earned, to pay off a loan. But when he learned it wasn't enough, he gave notice that he would be leaving.

"Are you in some sort of trouble, John?" Arthur guessed. When John simply frowned and looked away without answering, Arthur Redington went to his desk and withdrew a bank voucher. "How much?" was all he asked.

"I'll pay it all back," John promised, his throat tight. "I swear to God."

"Pay me back?" Arthur smiled up at him as he filled in the huge amount. "I'm the one who owes you, remember?"

That had been nineteen years ago, and with each season that passed, their friendship grew until it no longer could be measured by dollars. But John never forgot what Arthur Redington had done for him. When Belle Chasse started losing money, he was more than eager to help the man's daughter find a way to save the hotel and casino, but only if Arthur never found out about it.

John had been amazed at Ashlee's capabilities in handling the danger involved in what they did. Except for the jitters the night before each job, she had never panicked during its actual execution, and he could only credit their success to that fact. However, if he had known what was going through her mind at this very moment, he would have insisted they pass this opportunity by.

Ashlee had managed to avoid her stepmother during the entire day. The morning hadn't been difficult at all, since it was Dominique's practice to sleep until noon. The rest was relatively simple. Just before the woman's expected appearance in the dining room, Ashlee had told her father that John would be driving her to Miss Gloria's, with the excuse that she wanted to select the linen for the new tablecloths in the restaurant as soon as possible and that it would probably take the rest of the afternoon. John, of course, was more than glad to act as her coachman, since he and Dominique shared a mutual dislike for one another and would invariably come to heated words sometime during the day.

Their hours away from Belle Chasse and Dominique had been pleasant. They rode through the streets of New Orleans then out into the country, where they stopped and ate the food Ashlee had packed for them. Their last stop before going back was at the docks to take a look at the steamer Ashlee would be boarding. It was then that she was filled with an eerie sense of doom that tickled the hairs on the back of her neck. John noticed her tremble, and when questioned Ashlee blamed it on the cool breezes near the docks, and he had quickly turned the rig toward the hotel. If she had told him the truth, he would have called off their little adventure, and Ashlee wouldn't have liked that. They hadn't missed one yet, and she wasn't about to cancel just because of a strange feeling she had. Call it superstition—Priscilla felt that same way about a theater performance—but Ashlee felt that if she gave in to the odd stirrings in the pit of her stomach, their luck would change . . . for the worse.

Her uneasiness had intensified that night in the casino as she listened to the customers talk about the poker game that was to take place on the *Spirit of Dubuque* Sunday night and how many of them wished they had been invited to play. As the night wore on, Ashlee's head started to pound.

She had slept late the next morning, spent the afternoon somewhat peaceably since Dominique was at the dressmaker's checking on the wardrobe she was taking with her to Laplace, then eaten dinner alone in her room. But as the time had neared for her to don her black satin dress and go to the casino to work for the evening, the food she had eaten only an hour before suddenly felt like a rock in her stomach.

"It's always like this the night before," she scowled back at the reflection in the mirror as she put the finishing touches to her beautifully thick hair. "And it will be like this the next time. It will always be like this until we don't have to do it any more."

To comfort herself, Ashlee glanced over at the aging photograph of her mother, wishing there were some way to stop it from getting darker with each year that passed. It was all she had of her mother, and it was growing increasingly difficult to distinguish Veronica's dark hair from the black background or realize that her eyes were blue like Ashlee's instead of brown as the portrait made them seem.

"Oh, Mama," she whispered sadly, "am I truly a bad person? Are we two of a kind like Dominique says? If you were here right now, would you help me the way Priscilla does, or condemn my actions?" Ashlee's pale blue eyes lightened with a spark of mischief. "I bet you'd help. I bet you'd even disguise yourself and go with me," she grinned. "Of course, John wouldn't like that too much. Then he'd have twice as much to worry about." Laying aside her hairbrush, she walked over to stand before Veronica's picture. "You'd like John. He's kind and sweet and—"

The knock on her door made Ashlee jump. "Who—who is it?" she called, rushing back to the dresser to check her appearance again.

"Just me, Ashlee," John replied. "Your father sent me. Are you all right? You're late for the casino."

"I'm fine," she called, hurrying to open the door. "Just thinking about—" She glanced past him into the foyer dividing her father's quarters from hers, making sure Dominique wasn't there. "Well, you know."

"Have you changed your mind?" John frowned worriedly.

"Of course not," Ashlee replied with a forced smile. But John's expression didn't change and she quickly went on to explain. "I'm always like this the night before, you know that. What I have to do sounds simple enough, but something unexpected could always come up, and it makes me nervous. I'll be all right once I'm on the steamer, so you can stop looking like that." When John continued to stare at her suspiciously, she laughed and stepped into the foyer, pulling the door to her room shut behind her. "And unless you want Papa to start asking questions, you and I better get to the casino," she warned playfully, slipping her arm into his and guiding them toward the front entrance of the rooms set aside as the Redingtons' living quarters.

After dinner Rhys always enjoyed a good cigar and the

crisp, clean air of early evening, when the sun painted bright golds and oranges across the sky before settling behind the horizon. It was for this reason that he left the restaurant, climbed the elegant staircase in the hotel lobby, and stepped out onto the balcony through the French doors. The courtyard below was lit by torches placed around the perimeter, illuminating some of the dark corners the dying sun failed to reach. It was peaceful there, and he would have lingered a while if his attention hadn't been drawn to the couple he heard walking along the stone pathway that circled the border of the gardens and disappeared beneath the balcony on which he stood. Ordinarily, he would have thought them nothing more than young lovers seeking a chance to be alone, until he heard the man address the woman at his side.

"You're right as always, Miss Redington," he joked, and Rhys quickly leaned out over the railing to get a look at her. But to his dismay, all he could see was the black satin of her skirts and the dark trousers of the man who walked beside her.

"Damn," he muttered, straightening back up. This whole thing was beginning to irritate him. Heaving a disgusted sigh, he turned away from the courtyard and lifted the cheroot to his mouth, clamping it between his teeth as a frown settled on his brow. *Wait a minute,* he thought. *Thomas said she worked the blackjack table every night. And to get to the casino, she has to come through the lobby.* Grinning victoriously, he snuffed out his cigar in the ashtray on one of the tables and hurried back inside.

The lobby was filled with customers coming and going from the restaurant and casino. Rhys's brown eyes darkened all the more once he realized how difficult it would be to spot her among them. But he decided to try. Pausing at the top of the stairs, he scanned the crowd below, looking for a beautiful woman in a black satin dress and smiling broadly when he saw her. But his glee quickly faded when the redhead turned in his direction to respond to something someone said to her. She was far from his description of beautiful. And for some reason he had pictured her as having dark hair. Thomas knew he always favored brunettes. Disappointed, Rhys started down the steps, thankful that he hadn't shown Thomas an outward interest in meeting Miss Redington. He came to an abrupt stop when he noticed that there were at least four other women in the lobby wearing black satin dresses.

"If I didn't know better, I'd think someone was trying to play a trick on me," he mumbled, starting down the steps again.

"Good evening, Mr. Sinclair," Michael called to him as he passed the front desk. "Are you going to try your luck at the poker tables tonight?"

"I was considering it," Rhys admitted, "until a few minutes ago." He paused to lean an elbow on the desk top, watching the redhead walk into the casino. "Now I'm not so sure my luck is any good."

"Sir?"

Glancing up, Rhys smiled at the man when he realized how confusing his statement must have sounded. "Can you keep a secret, Michael?"

"I've been known to a few times," Michael grinned.

"Good," Rhys answered, tugging on one earlobe. "Then maybe you can help me out. A friend of mine told me that Miss Redington looked exactly like a woman he saw me with in Baton Rouge last month. Now, seeing as how that lady was the most beautiful woman I've ever known, I told my friend that that possibility wasn't very likely. So we placed a little wager on it. I've been trying for two days to get a look at her, and every time I get near her, she disappears before I get the chance."

"That's understandable," Michael laughed. "Miss Redington is a hard person to track down."

"So I've noticed," Rhys replied with a sarcastic curl of his lip before turning to watch the patrons of Belle Chasse once more.

"But this time I think you'll succeed, Mr. Sinclair," Michael smiled as he folded his arms in front of him and braced them on the desk. "I just saw her go into the casino with Mr. Hardin. But," he added, lowering his voice, "I think I should warn you. Her father is very protective of her. If you get too close, you'll find yourself explaining why to her escort."

"Oh?" Rhys questioned, his curiosity aroused.

"Your friend was right on one point. Miss Redington is a very beautiful woman, so you can imagine how difficult it is to keep a customer away from her who's had too much to drink. Mr. Hardin watches her like a hawk."

"So tell me what she looks like and I'll admire from a distance," Rhys grinned.

"Oh, it won't be too hard to recognize her. There isn't a woman in there that even comes close. But I'll save you a little time trying to figure it out. She has raven-black hair and the most exquisite blue eyes you've ever seen in your life."

"Hmmm," Rhys murmured. "And what is she wearing?"

"Well, all the dealers in the casino wear black, just like those who work the hotel wear red and black, and those in the restaurant wear white and black. Mr. Redington's way of dividing up the staff and knowing whether or not he has enough help in each place. But like I said, you'll know her the minute you see her."

"All right, Michael, we'll see if you're right," Rhys nodded, pulling on the cuffs of his shirt.

"I might add, Mr. Sinclair," Michael grinned, "that I think you're going to lose your bet. Miss Redington might not look like the woman you were with, but I think I'm safe in saying she's more stunning than any you've ever seen."

"Well, if that's the case, Michael," Rhys laughed, "I won't mind losing." His dark brown eyes danced with a spark of humor before he turned and strode toward the casino.

"Good evening, gentlemen," Ashlee smiled politely as she pulled up a tall stool on which to sit behind the blackjack table. "Are you ready to try your hand?"

There were four roulette wheels, six crap, five poker, and five blackjack tables to choose from in the casino. Ashlee's table never had a vacant chair as many of the others occasionally did, and she always assumed it was because hers was near the bar. But Arthur Redington knew it had nothing to do with a man's thirst for liquor that sometimes had them standing three-deep waiting their turn, thus influencing his decision to have John stationed close by at all times should one of Ashlee's customers suddenly become too friendly. Ashlee was glad to have him there, but not because it made her feel safe. After a few hours of being forced to laugh at old jokes told hundreds of times, she'd discreetly glance over at John and roll her eyes or make some other sort of funny face at him. And he'd always laugh and wink in return. Tonight, however, was different. She doubted even John's presence could ease the knot in her stomach.

It was her custom to deal blackjack for one hour then have Elaine take over for a short while. She had dealt only two hands, paying the winner of one, the house the other, when she looked up at one of the men with a smile, catching sight of the newest arrival to the gaming room coming through the doors of the casino. Her heart lurched in her chest.

"It's him!" she breathed in hardly more than a whisper. A thousand thoughts raced through her head,

83

ranging from the possibility that he was in the casino merely by a strange coincidence to the fear that he had somehow figured out who the boy on the steamer was and had come with the sheriff to arrest her. Her hands trembled as she gathered up the cards from the table as if to begin another game, but her eyes never left his tall, muscular build as he made his way through the crowded room to the bar.

"Miss Redington, are you all right?" one of the players asked, and Ashlee jerked her attention back to look at him.

"I'm fine," she answered quickly, even though her mouth had gone dry.

"Then why are you shuffling the discarded pile?"

"What?" she frowned, glancing down at her hands to discover that was exactly what she was doing. She dropped the cards as if they burned her hands, looking over at the man near the bar whose attention at the moment was focused on ordering a drink, back at the players, and finally toward Elaine who stood a few tables away.

"Elaine," she called in a loud whisper, motioning the woman closer. "Take over for me, will you?" She touched shaky fingers to her brow. "I have this awful headache."

"Sure, honey," the big blonde smiled comfortingly. "You go lie down for a while."

"Thanks," Ashlee sighed, stealing one quick look toward the man at the bar then racing for the doorway.

She didn't slow her pace as she cut through the lobby, circling around in back of the staircase and out the door to the stone walkway in the gardens. Concentrating on the path leading to her living quarters, she didn't even notice the people she passed along the way or hear John's deep voice calling out to her. If someone had touched her arm to get her attention, she probably would have let out a bloodcurdling scream. Ashlee had never been so frightened in her whole life.

Dashing through the wide foyer, she didn't pause to look at the huge marble fountain and the cherub whose pitcher steadily poured a sparkling stream of water over the rocks at his feet as she so often did. Instead she went directly to her room, twisted the doorknob, and rushed inside, slamming the portal shut behind her. Collapsing back against the door, Ashlee closed her eyes and listened to her heart pounding in her ears, wondering how long it would be before the sheriff came bursting into her room.

"How did he find me?" she moaned. "How did he even know who the boy was?" She quickly scanned the length of her huge bedroom, as if looking for the answer, when she heard the door to the foyer open and close, and the sound of heavy boot heels against the floor outside her room. Jerking away from the door, she whirled around to stare at it, realizing the trap in which she had placed herself, for the barred windows in her room prevented any escape. Tears flooded her eyes.

"Ashlee!"

Dear God, he even knew her name!

"Ashlee, are you all right? It's me, John."

She stiffened, a frown marring her smooth brow. John? Her mind called out to him, but no sound passed her lips. She gulped, fighting for control. Of course, it was John. That man hadn't seen her leave the casino. She chewed on her lower lip. But she mustn't let John know how upset she was, and most of all, why. She took several deep breaths, letting them out slowly until her pulse had returned to normal and she was sure she could talk convincingly.

"I'm—I'm not dressed, John."

"Why?" he demanded. "What's wrong? Why did you leave in such a hurry? And especially without me? You know how your father feels about your being unescorted

85

in this place."

"I—I got sick. I—I have a terrible pounding in my head, and my stomach— I just wanted to lie down for a while, that's all. I'm sorry I didn't tell you first." Ashlee tilted her head, listening, and several long moments passed before he answered.

"All right then," he conceded. "But I want you to go to bed and forget about the casino tonight. You've been acting strangely all day. I'll make your excuses to your father, and we'll decide about tomorrow in the morning. Do you hear me?"

"Yes, John," she quickly replied. "I'll go right to bed. See you tomorrow."

"Good night, Ashlee," came the muffled response, and she hurried forward to listen to him cross the foyer and close the door behind him on his way back to the casino.

You've got to stop doing this, Ashlee! she silently scolded herself. *That man has no idea who you are, but you'll give yourself away if you continue to behave like this. It's merely a coincidence, and he'll be gone in the morning. Now go to bed and get some rest. The job tomorrow promises to be the biggest yet.*

Her little speech made her feel considerably better, and since she was so free with the advice, she decided to listen to it. With her shoulders squared, her chin raised high, she marched across the room toward the adjoining chamber used for her personal grooming, unfastening the buttons of her black satin dress as she went.

"Ashlee, now tell me the truth," Priscilla demanded as the pair walked down the wharf toward the *Spirit of Dubuque.* "What did John say about your disguise?"

"Nothing," Ashlee replied, avoiding the woman's eyes.

John didn't know about it nor would he ever find out,

since she always changed into dungarees before leaving the steamer. After her first experience, she had learned that too many skirts and petticoats made it difficult for her to climb into the rowboat. So from that time on, she had always taken along a pair of boy's pants and a faded red flannel shirt to aid in her departure. And since Priscilla had already voiced her disapproval of the outfit Ashlee had chosen, she wasn't about to tell the woman that she had kept it a secret from John. If Priscilla knew that, Ashlee was sure her friend wouldn't hesitate informing him.

"Nothing?" Priscilla repeated. "Nothing at all?"

"No, nothing." Ashlee nervously reached up to touch the side of her wig as if to fluff out a blond curl, forcing herself to stare at the gangplank of the steamer.

"Somehow I just can't believe that," Priscilla murmured with a shake of her head, her steps slowing as she gave the matter great consideration. Then suddenly a thought struck her, and she knew the answer. She stopped in the middle of the walkway. "Ashlee, how long ago did John leave?" she asked, bringing her companion to an equally abrupt halt.

"Leave?" Ashlee questioned with a weak smile as she turned back to face the woman. "I . . . er . . . I'm not sure. The usual amount of time it takes him to reach the rowboat, I suppose." She hoisted her satchel up in both arms. "Come on, Priscilla. You'll make me miss the steamer."

"He doesn't know, does he?" Priscilla insisted, one fist resting on her hip. "He didn't say anything because you never told him. And you didn't tell him because you knew he'd object, maybe even forbid you to go this time. Oh, Ashlee—"

"Now don't get yourself all heated up, Priscilla," Ashlee groaned, reaching out to take the woman's elbow and pull her along. "I can take care of myself. I have so

87

far, haven't I? I know what I'm doing."

"Do you?" Priscilla challenged, drawing her arm away.

Ashlee's shoulders fell, and she stopped and turned around. "Yes," she replied.

"And what will you do if someone mistakes you for a harlot by the way you're dressed? What will you do then? You'll be all alone on that boat, Ashlee. John won't be there to help you out."

Ashlee's blue eyes sparkled with mischief. "Then why don't you come with me? There's safety in numbers, you know."

Priscilla lowered her chin and met Ashlee's smile with a hard look. "I have trouble climbing a flight of stairs. How would I ever manage to lower myself into a rowboat?"

"You wouldn't have to. As long as there's no money found on you, no one would suspect you were in on it," Ashlee explained excitedly, liking the idea the more she thought about it. "It would be thrilling. Oh, please come with me."

Priscilla shook her head. "I've had enough thrills in my life already, thank you. And besides, I'd be the first one they'd question once the theft was discovered."

"Why?"

"Because by now someone has seen us together, and if you're missing, along with the gentlemen's money, they'd want to know my connection with you. And I have a rehearsal this afternoon that I can't miss," she added, taking Ashlee's elbow and turning her around toward the steamer.

"Next time?" Ashlee grinned.

"No," Priscilla flatly refused.

"But you'd like to, wouldn't you?" Ashlee smiled. "After all, what I'm doing isn't much different than acting on the stage, is it? I wear a costume and pretend to be someone else—just like you've been doing all your life." The clanging of the steamer's bell took Ashlee's attention away from the woman, and she missed the sad look on Priscilla's face. "Well, since I can't seem to change your mind, then I better be going." She leaned, kissed Priscilla's cheek, and rushed off before her friend could wish her good luck.

"It isn't what I'd like to do, Ashlee," she whispered, watching the bright red skirts swaying with each step the young woman took. "I'd like to tell you why I wear a costume and —"

The thought vanished instantly when Priscilla suddenly noticed the tall, well-built gentleman with light-colored hair watching Ashlee's slender shape ascend the gangplank. And when he turned his head to look at her, a chill ran down Priscilla's spine. Fearful, she dropped her gaze, a million thoughts running through her head. She didn't know who he was, but she had seen him at the theater two nights ago. Did he suspect what Ashlee was planning to do? Or was he merely enjoying the beauty of the lanky, blond-haired woman in a scarlet dress? Frowning, Priscilla wondered if she should board the steamer and tell Ashlee. Maybe she should drag the young woman off the boat and call an end to this madness. Dear God, what *should* she do? She looked up in his direction again, only to find that he had disappeared into the crowd. Standing on tiptoes, Priscilla strained to see him, but he was gone. Had he gotten in that carriage that was pulling away? She glanced at the boat whose gangplank was already being hoisted. Or on the steamer? Grabbing her skirts in both hands, Priscilla took a quick step forward and stopped. It was too late. Ashlee was on her own now.

Rhys had chosen the stateroom nearest the bar on the

Spirit of Dubuque for two reasons. Not only did it place the men in the thick of things, but that compartment had double doors, which he planned to leave open for a while, thus encouraging the thief to watch the game. The culprit would be free to size up his work lost among the crowd, but it would also give Rhys the opportunity to study anyone who seemed more interested in what was going on around him than the cards being played. Knowing that this band wasn't an ordinary group of thieves and would notice any changes, Rhys hired a man to stand guard outside the door as had been done on the *Mississippi Queen*. What he didn't want was to scare the person off by thinking something was wrong if extra precautions weren't taken as before. Now all Rhys had to do was to be sure he drank only the whiskey he had brought with him. Once he sensed the robbery was about to take place, he would put his own plan into action.

"You know, Rhys," Thomas said as he stood in the doorway of Rhys's cabin watching his friend unpack his bag, "I've been thinking about this little adventure of yours. What if these people change their methods and send two to rob us? You'd need help, especially if they're both men—men with guns."

"You can stop worrying, Thomas," Rhys grinned, setting aside his bag. "There have been fourteen robberies in the past year and a half, and their style hasn't changed. There's no reason for them to start now, since it's always worked before."

"Hmmm, I suppose," Thomas relented, leaning a shoulder against the framework. "I was just hoping I could be in on this."

"You will be," Rhys assured him. "Without your help the others might get suspicious and not allow themselves to be drugged. I can't really do it without you."

"Yeah, I know. What I meant was that I'd like to see the bastard's face when you suddenly wake up." He

90

chuckled at the vision he saw. "I'll bet his heart will stop."

"Or hers."

Thomas frowned. "You truly think a woman has the nerve to do something like this?"

"Remind me to introduce you to my sister Jennifer sometime. She was always more trouble for mother than all of us boys put together." He straightened and walked over to stand before his friend. "In fact, if she didn't live so far away, I'd be tempted to ask her where she was at the time these robberies took place." Grabbing the edge of the door, he pulled it shut behind him as Thomas and he stepped into the corridor. "Are the others here?"

"Yes. William and Phillip are waiting for us in the stateroom, and I saw Ben in the bar with some harlot." Thomas shook his head. "I don't know why his wife stays with him."

"Have you ever met his wife?" Rhys asked with a wry grin.

"No."

"Then that explains it."

"Explains what?" Thomas frowned, stopping in the middle of the passageway.

Rhys suppressed a laugh and turned back to face him. "Because if you had met her, you'd know why." Holding his arms away from his sides, he mimicked an obese shape.

"Ohhh," Thomas sang. "I get it. Two of a kind. Right?"

"Right," Rhys nodded. "In more ways than one. She's about as faithful to Ben as he is to her. And I ought to know. I got stuck with her one night, and if I hadn't found a graceful way of leaving, I'm sure she would have lured me to her room and raped me!"

Thomas burst into laughter. "You mean there's one lady in the entire world you found objectionable?" he

91

teased, wrapping his arm around Rhys's broad shoulders to start them on their way again.

"Lady, no. Woman, yes," he corrected as they walked into the crowded bar. He came to a dead stop when he spotted Ben talking with the blonde he had seen on the wharf.

"What is it, Rhys?" Thomas asked, dropping his hold as he searched the group for whomever it was that had caught the other's focus. "Do you see someone you know?"

"Not exactly." Rhys's dark eyes narrowed with his frown. "See the woman Ben's with?" He waited for Thomas's nod then continued. "I saw her on the pier as I was boarding. She was with another woman. They were too far away for me to hear what they were saying, but I got the distinct impression this one's friend didn't want her on this boat. I probably wouldn't have thought much of it if this was an ordinary cruise, but right now everyone is a suspect."

"You mean you think she could be a part of this gang we're after?"

"It's possible. Look, do me a favor, will you?" Rhys asked, keeping his voice low in case someone near them was a friend of the woman's and would tell her what they overheard. "I want you to find out if she approached Ben or it was the other way around. If it was the former, then suggest to Ben that he invite the woman to watch the game."

"All right, but what are you going to do?"

"I'm going to tell William and Phillip what the plan is so they'll let her stay. If my instincts are right, we'll soon be putting an end to the thefts." Smiling, he patted Thomas's shoulder and hurried away.

Ashlee couldn't believe her luck when she had gone to the bar, after putting her things away in her cabin, and spotted the same huge, smelly poker player from the

Mississippi Queen. It could only mean one thing. He had been invited to play. So all she had to do was flirt shamelessly, tell him how much she loved watching great big, strong men play poker, and win herself entry into the stateroom. The rest would be easy. Her delight heightened even more once the man's friend joined them, bought them a drink—one Ashlee had to force down as if she enjoyed it—then suggested that Ben's companion be their good luck charm and come with them to the stateroom. Ashlee had acted as if it was an honor and promised not to get in their way. In fact, she had added with a coy smile, she would gladly be the one to fetch their drinks from the bar so that the game wouldn't be interrupted. Glancing up at the clock, Ashlee realized she had several hours before she would have to administer the drug that would bring an end to her charade, and she eagerly followed the men across the room.

"My name is Thomas Bryan," the tallest and slimmest of the men announced. "This is Benjamin Jones. And you are?"

"Sally," Ashlee replied coquettishly, cleverly choosing the name of the character Priscilla played. "Sally White."

"Where you from, Sally?" Thomas continued as he took her elbow and guided her toward the cabin where the others were waiting.

"Oh, nowhere in particular," Ashlee smiled. "I travel around a lot . . . if you get my meaning."

Thomas raised an eyebrow. "I'm sure you do," he chuckled, stepping aside to allow Ashlee to enter the stateroom ahead of him and Ben. He had centered his gaze on the man standing near the window with his back to them and failed to notice the way his shapely companion stiffened the moment her eyes found Rhys's tall figure. "Gentlemen," Thomas proclaimed, "I'd like you to meet Miss Sally White. Sally, this is Phillip

Sanders, William Lott, and the one by the window is Rhys Sinclair."

Ashlee's knees trembled violently, but she somehow managed to appear as if she had never seen any of them before, especially the one who turned dark brown piercing eyes on her. He had chosen to shun the customary black attire of most gentlemen for the flattering shade of midnight-blue, a hue that complimented his sandy-colored hair and bronze complexion. Now Ashlee knew all too well why he had constantly haunted her dreams. He was, without doubt, the most handsome man she had ever seen.

"Sally White," he murmured, moving away from the window. "The name sounds familiar. Have we met somewhere before?"

Just once, but you weren't aware of it, she thought, forcing a smile. "I don't know, honey," she said aloud, imitating Priscilla's interpretation of a whore. "Have ya ever been to Florida? I work a lot of the saloons down there."

Rhys continued to stare at the young woman, thinking how under all that makeup there was a hint of real beauty but the yellow pile of bleached hair detracted from it. His eyes lowered to the plunging neckline of her scarlet dress. Nothing hid the firm contour of her bosom or the narrow waist, and he wondered how long it had taken her to clinch up her corset.

"No," he went on as he pulled out a chair and sat down next to Phillip. "I heard the name just recently." It bothered him that he couldn't remember where, figuring it might have something to do with the robberies, at least maybe a clue. He picked up the deck of cards and began to shuffle them. He'd think about it for a while. "Shall we get started?" he questioned the men at the table.

As usual, Rhys won nearly every hand, only this time no one really seemed to care—no one except Ben. Rhys knew it was because the others figured they would have their money returned to them just as soon as he had trapped the woman. For a while, as he watched the heavily painted girl from across the table, he wondered if he might have been wrong about her, for it appeared as if she thoroughly enjoyed Ben's affection. But then he noticed how she seemed more interested in the clock hanging on the wall and the nearly empty bottle of whiskey than in the amount of money lying in the middle of the poker table. Could it mean that the time was drawing near for her to make her move? He was sure of it when Ben grabbed her wrist, pulled her down on his lap, and asked for a good luck kiss. He could almost see the revulsion in her blue eyes, and he quickly looked away to keep from laughing out loud. This was no harlot. He'd bet his entire winnings on it. But she was a good little actress.

"I'll tell ya what, sweetie," she smiled at Ben after managing to satisfy him with a kiss on the cheek. "I'll go and get a fresh bottle of whiskey, and when I come back, I guarantee your luck will change." She slid off his lap before he could object but didn't move fast enough to escape a hearty slap to her backside. She squealed, jerked around to glare at him, caught herself, and smiled instead. "Why you ol' devil," she scolded and hurried from the cabin.

"I think you're right about her, Rhys," Thomas whispered while the other three discussed Ben's improper behavior.

"I think so, too," Rhys agreed. "And we'll find out in a few minutes. But I'm going to change the strategy a little."

"How?"

"I'm going to try and set her up."

"How do you mean?"

"Well, we've already established the fact that these robberies are the work of a gang. Right?"

Thomas nodded.

"Then why not catch as many as we can?"

"You mean you think someone else on board might be one of her partners?"

"It's a possibility," Rhys agreed. "And a smart idea should something go wrong. But it's not what I was getting at."

Thomas shifted in his chair, excited with the prospect of bringing an end to the rash of thefts along the Mississippi. "All right, so tell me what is."

"I'm going to try to entice her to my stateroom by letting her know there's a lot of money there. Then when I get her alone, I'll confront her with what I know about her and her cohorts, and that I might just let her go if she'll give me the name or names of the masterminds behind it all. Shouldn't be too hard convincing her. She doesn't strike me as the type who'd go to prison if she didn't have to."

"It might work, but how do you know she'll be the one to come and not her partner—or anyone at all?" Thomas pointed out. "She just might be satisfied with the money she gets here and not want to run the risk of stealing yours as well. Then what? You'll be in your stateroom waiting for nothing, while she cleans us out. And we'll all be unconscious and unable to stop her."

"I've already thought of that," Rhys smiled reassuringly. "Right after I excuse myself from the game on the pretense of going to my room for more money, I'm going to tell the guard outside to keep an eye on Miss White. If she looks like she's headed anywhere other than my cabin, he's to stop her, then come and get me."

Thomas didn't answer, shrugging his shoulders instead.

"Either way, we'll at least have one of the gang," Rhys grinned, reaching for the stack of cards when he spotted the pretty blonde coming back toward the stateroom, a bottle of whiskey held in her hands and a confident smile on her painted lips.

A half hour passed, and to the other's surprise, Rhys began to lose. Sally, on the other hand, eagerly refilled the gambers' glasses from the bottle she had brought back with her. And each time she poured a little into Rhys's glass, Thomas would secretly exchange his empty one for it, making it appear as if Rhys had drunk as much as the rest of the men. Thus, Thomas was the first to feel the effects of the drug, and when it became difficult for him to focus on the game, he leaned closer to his friend and whispered that it was time.

"Well, gentlemen," Rhys sighed, "you've just about wiped me out. But," he added, setting the bait and pushing himself up from the table, "I have a *lot* more where that came from. If you'll excuse me for a moment, I'll go to my cabin and get it." He masked his grin when he saw the attentive look that came over Sally's face, knowing his plan was beginning to fall into place.

"Rhys, ol' buddy, I sure ain't gonna stop ya," Ben proclaimed with a loud laugh. "Seein' as how I took most of it to begin with, I'll be more than anxious to win some more. And I have this little lady to thank for it," he howled, reaching out to grab Ashlee around the waist, haul her to his beefy lap, and press his wet mouth over hers while his free hand came up to squeeze her breast.

A sickening wave of repugnance shot through every inch of her, and at that moment Ashlee wished she had a long-bladed knife in her hand. She longed to see how far she would have to ram it into the obnoxious cretin's fat belly before it hit any vital organs. And maybe someday she'd have the honor of doing just that. But right now, she had to pretend she enjoyed his smelly breath and revolting advances, or give herself away. Yet, before she had a chance to display her greatest performance, her wrist was seized by another's strong grip and she was yanked from the first's embrace into someone else's.

"Then maybe you should share, Ben," her captor's deep voice stated, and Ashlee's body trembled anew when she looked up in the deep brown eyes smiling back at her. "You don't mind, do you, Sally?"

It took Ashlee a moment to react, to realize that this wasn't part of the dream that had plagued her since the first time she had seen this man. Calling on every ounce of skill she had developed in the art of acting, she smiled, secretively gulped down her nervousness, and said, "Of course not, honey. That's why I'm here. To change everyone's luck."

"Somehow I knew you'd say that," Rhys murmured, lowering his head.

A bolt of searing heat exploded within her when his mouth covered hers, and Ashlee thought she would faint from the pleasure of it. She had never imagined a man's kiss could be so exciting, and in that moment, she forgot why she was there. Unaware, she slipped her arms up around his neck, savoring the feel of him, his strength, the masculine scent, the hard muscles of his powerful frame as he pressed her full against him. Then it was over, and Ashlee stood weak-kneed as she watched him walk to the stateroom's door, open it, then pause, leaning heavily against it as if he had lost his sense of balance for a moment. It was all it took to shatter Ashlee's illusion that he had kissed her because he truly wanted to and not out of superstition, and her hatred for the northerners who had invaded the south and stolen her father's money rose to the occasion. She was here for one thing—to steal it back, including Rhys Sinclair's.

"Well, gentlemen," she smiled with a flutter of lashes once he had left the cabin and shut the door behind him, "why don't I pour all of you a drink while we wait for Mr. Sinclair to return." She'd deal with him once these barbarians were all sound asleep.

"Good idea, sweet thing," Ben grinned up at her. "But before you do, open a window, will you? It's gotten awfully hot in here for some reason." Rising, he moved away from the table to take off his coat and unfasten the top buttons on his shirt. "It's what I've always hated about this damn south. The weather is so humid all the time." He turned back then, intending to take his place at the poker table beside Phillip Sanders, when his vision suddenly blurred and he stumbled to his knees.

The loud thump his body made hitting the floor brought everyone's attention to him. Ashlee slyly stepped to one side as Phillip hurriedly left his chair to go to Ben. But by the time Phillip had reached him, Ben had fallen forward on his stomach, his eyes shut in blissful unconsciousness.

"William," Phillip called over his shoulder as he rolled the huge man onto his back, "help me get him on the bunk."

"Ha!" came the reply. "And what do you propose we use to hoist that ton of lard? I don't see a pulley and rope anywhere."

"Well, we have to try," Phillip snapped. "We can't leave him on the floor all night."

"And why not? I'm sure he's used to it." Laughing, he turned to look at Thomas. "Don't you agree—" William's face paled instantly once he saw that Thomas had not only not heard him, but had cleared off a space on the table in front of him on which to lay his head. He, too, was sound asleep. Rhys had told Phillip and William that he suspected the harlot Ben had latched onto might be involved with the gang of thieves working the Mississippi, and he had asked them to allow her to watch the game. But William, being the sort that never wanted to believe a woman would purposely go against the law, had agreed only to prove Rhys wrong. Now he was sure he wasn't, and as William turned to look at Phillip, his own head began to spin, and he moaned softly when he saw the man slump to the floor next to Ben.

Ashlee stood stock-still, afraid that if she moved she might draw the last man's attention to her and that he might call out a warning to the guard outside the door before the laudanum took affect. But only a few seconds passed before he made a feeble attempt to rise, lost his balance, fell against the table, then slid to the floor in the same state of sleep as the others. She glanced at the clock once more. She had twenty minutes in which to finish her job and get off the boat.

Moving toward the table and the pile of money sitting in the middle of it, she hiked up her skirt and untied the cloth bag she had fastened to the strings of her petticoats before leaving her cabin. Once it was filled, she returned the bag to its hiding place and went to the door, pausing a moment to gather her composure. She rather doubted Sinclair could have made it to his cabin, retrieved the money he had gone after, and started back down the passageway to the stateroom before the laudanum hit him, but there was no sense in taking chances when she was this close to succeeding. If she were to open the door and find him standing there, she would have to act as if she had just stepped out for a breath of fresh air, convince him to walk with her for a while, and somehow get him back to his cabin before he passed out. It would be easy enough to explain to anyone who witnessed his collapse that it was due to too much whiskey, but it would also mean someone would want to inform his poker partners that Mr. Sinclair would not be joining them again. And that meant disaster for Ashlee. She turned the knob and stepped out into the hallway, pulling the door shut behind her.

"Mr. Bryan asked me to check on Mr. Sinclair," she told the guard when he turned a questioning look her way. "He seemed a little under the weather . . . if you know what I mean. Can you tell me where his cabin is?"

"Yes, ma'am. End of the corridor on the right. Stateroom twelve," the young man willingly obliged.

"Thank you," she smiled, starting off toward her own room and thinking how easy this had been. The next time she had nervous thoughts about pulling off a job, she'd remember this one. Men were such fools—especially northerners.

It took Ashlee only a couple of minutes to hide the bagful of money in the bottom of her satchel, thus disposing of the curious lump beneath her skirts. Although she was sure nothing would happen, it was better if she tucked her booty safely away just in case something went wrong. Locking the door to her cabin behind her, she headed toward Mr. Sinclair's. She'd have to hurry if she was to help herself to the man's money, then return to her room, change into the dungarees, and go to the cargo deck in time to meet John. A soft smile played upon her lips. He would be so proud of her. The amount of money she had stolen was more than any two other jobs combined, and acquiring it had been the simplest of all.

The laughing couple she met in the corridor snapped Ashlee back to the present. There would be time to gloat later. Right now she had something important to do. Glancing up at the brass-plated numbers above each stateroom door, she paused outside the one marked twelve, waiting until the hallway was empty again before she rapped softly against the thick wooden barrier, then tilting her head to listen for a response. When none came, she tried the knob, found the door unlocked, and hesitated a moment before opening it. The yellow glow from the kerosene lamps in the passageway spilled into the darkened room, falling upon the bunk on the opposite wall and the man lying facedown upon it. Ashlee's heart thumped loudly in her chest. Even asleep as he was, this man's mere presence unnerved her, and she found it difficult just to breathe. She pulled her gaze away from him, quickly glanced down the long, vacant corridor, then pushed the door open wide. At that moment, she noticed something lying on the floor midway across the room, and her eyes grew into huge circles. Scattered over the rich oak flooring was nearly as much money as she had seen in one night at the blackjack table! Tens, twenties, even one hundred dollar bills were just waiting for her to scoop them up! A trickle of laughter escaped her as she eyed the treasure, thinking how easy this whole affair had been and how stupid northerners were. Checking the corridor again to make certain no one saw her, she turned and hurried inside.

Ashlee quickly reaped in the pile of her newfound wealth, following the trail of money out of the stream of light coming in through the doorway to the shadowy darkness away from its owner and the only means of escape. Caught up in the excitement of her easy victory with its exceptional reward, she failed to see the dark figure rise from the bunk, cross the room, and grab the edge of the door, giving it a gentle push to swing it shut. But the sound of the latch clicking into place exploded in Ashlee's head and spun her around as the cabin was plummeted into darkness. In that instant, she realized her nightmare as a chilling reality. Frozen with fear, she fought for every breath she took as she searched the shadows for the one who held her fate in his hands.

"I thought your greed might lure you here, Miss White."

His deep voice seemed to fill the room, and Ashlee felt her knees quiver. The drug obviously hadn't worked, although she couldn't understand why. Ashlee knew she'd have to think fast if she were going to get out of this one. She forced a laugh. "I know how this must look, but I honestly came here to make sure you were all right. The others were worried when you didn't return to the game."

"Oh?" His tone marked his disbelief.

"I wasn't going to steal it," she assured him, hurriedly laying the wad of currency on the chest near her. "I was just putting it away for you. When you left the stateroom, you looked as if you'd had too much to drink, and I came here to check on you. When I peeked in, you were asleep and I saw the money laying on the floor. You should be thanking me instead of accusing me. Anyone could have walked in here and—"

"The game's over, Miss White," he cut in.

Ashlee's heart pounded loudly in her ears when she heard him twist the key in the lock. She wanted desperately to ask him how he knew about her and John, but to do that would be admitting her guilt. Trying to run would cinch it. She had to keep pretending to be Sally White, a prostitute who had simply come to his room out of concern and nothing more.

"Game?" she echoed. "What game?"

He was quiet for what seemed an eternity to Ashlee. "I suppose you expect me to believe that my friends were playing cards when you left them in the stateroom, and not lying on the floor unconscious—the way you thought you'd find me. Must have been quite a shock to see that I wasn't. And just in case you're thinking to stand there and wait until the drug affects me the same way, I should tell you that it won't. I didn't drink any of the whiskey you so kindly offered everyone."

Ashlee could feel the blood drain from her face. That had been exactly what she was hoping for. Now she'd have to think of something else. And she'd have to hurry. John would be rowing out to meet the steamer very soon. She touched a hand to the plunging neckline of her dress. She still had some laudanum left in the tiny pouch she had hidden there. But short of wrestling him to the floor

103

and pouring it down his throat, she had no idea how she would get him to take it.

"I'm afraid I don't know what you're talking about, Mr. Sinclair."

"Oh, it's quite simple," he explained, taking a step forward. "Either you're a thief or a whore."

The cabin had only one window, but it was enough to allow the moonlight to filter in, and Ashlee's pulse quickened as she watched his tall, broad shape move into it. He had taken off the dark blue jacket, and she noticed how perfectly the white shirt clung to his wide shoulders and the way he had unfastened several of the top buttons, allowing the silky fabric to fall open in gentle folds over his muscular chest. Ashlee wasn't sure if the strange feeling she had in the pit of her stomach was born out of fear or the unnatural desire to run her fingertips over the sinewy ripples he displayed. She pulled her gaze away from him and took a step backward.

"I already explained about the money, Mr. Sinclair." Her bravado was beginning to crumble.

"Then you're a whore."

Ashlee's head shot upward. "I beg—" She caught herself before she had said too much and forced a laugh. "I'd rather think of myself as a courtesan, Mr. Sinclair." Even though he stood several feet away from her, Ashlee could feel the heat of his body over every inch of her.

"Really?" he smiled in the silvery glow of the cabin. "Then suppose you prove it to me."

Ashlee's flesh tingled. "What?"

Moving closer, he reached past her, picked up two bills from the chest where she had put them, then slowly and purposefully tucked them into the low-cut neckline of her dress. "You see, Miss White—or whatever your name really is—I'm willing to admit there's a chance you weren't in on this little scheme . . . that someone else drugged that bottle of whiskey. But there's only one way you'll convince me that you're not a thief, and that's by proving you are what you claim to be. Do you understand?"

Oh, I understand, you son of a bitch, Ashlee fumed in her strongest of tirades, wishing she could hurl them to his face. *Either I admit to stealing and allow you to send me to prison, or behave like a back street trollop just to save my own skin. You are detestable, Mr. Sinclair, and I pray someday I can pay you back for this humiliation, but right now, I see where I have no choice. Bedding you is a small price to pay in return for my father's happiness. I just hope I can get through this without losing my supper.* But even her thoughts that this engagement would be anything more than sickening failed to cool the heat his touch had aroused, and she unknowingly rubbed her fingertips over the spot before plucking the money from her dress as if to count it.

"The way I see it, honey," she sighed, "you ain't never been with very many prostitutes or you'd have recognized me as one right off. And I don't mind telling ya, I take offense to your insinuations that I'm here to steal rather than earn my money." She reached up and yanked the red feather from her wig. "Sure is gonna cool me off some. But as long as you're paying, I suppose I can pretend to enjoy this." She waved a slender hand toward the bunk. "Go on . . . climb in. But take your clothes off first. There ain't enough money here for me to do it for ya." She turned her back to him, praying she wouldn't faint. How had she ever managed to say such things? "Ya got something to drink? I work better after I've had a shot or two." Ashlee closed her eyes, thinking the whole bottle would be better, and suddenly hit upon an idea. She'd get him to share a drink with her. One she had laced with laudanum! Then all she'd have to do was stall him, and she'd be able to leave the steamer with her virginity intact and his money in her hands.

"To loosen you up a bit or boost your courage?" he mocked softly, opening the top drawer of the chest.

Ashlee bit back her angry retort. "If I was any looser, honey, you wouldn't be paying." She picked up the bottle she saw laying there. "Got a glass? I don't like drinking it this way."

He pointed to the top of the chest then walked away, and Ashlee gave a quiet sigh of relief. His closeness was too much to bear. Popping the cork, she poured a stout measure and raised the glass to her lips. She truly detested liquor, but at this moment she needed all the help she could get just to stand up. She swallowed the entire amount, waited for the burning sensation to subside, then stole a glance his way. He had gone to the window to open it, standing with his back to her, and Ashlee knew this might be the only chance she had to fix his drink. In a rush, she pulled the pouch from her dress, poured the laudanum into the glass, and filled the rest with whiskey.

"So, sweetie," she said, turning around, glass in hand, "ain't ya gonna shed your clothes?" She walked close enough to him to hold out the glass for him to take.

"No," he murmured, covering her delicate fingers with his much larger hand as he accepted her offering. "I thought I'd pay the extra to have you do it."

A knot formed in Ashlee's throat big enough to strangle her. Was Belle Chasse truly worth this? She sucked in a deep breath, hoping to sound indifferent. "Don't matter to me," she shrugged, surprised that her feet even moved when she took a step closer. Her hands trembled as she lifted them to unfasten a button on his shirt. "Where ya from, sweet thing?"

Ashlee had watched Priscilla play the part of Sally White on stage, and that along with the talks they had had about men and romance had guided her moves thus far. But Priscilla had always gotten too embarrassed to explain to Ashlee what came next after the couple had made it to the bed, and Ashlee had always wound up having to be content with her imaginings. She had longed to know what sweet words a man would whisper in his lover's ear, how he would hold her, touch her. She blinked suddenly. But this wasn't the way she wanted to find out. Not with this northerner, anyway! She popped the last button loose, ready to pull the shirttail free of his trousers, and froze. She had thought that if she avoided looking into his eyes, her torture wouldn't be as great. But now as the shirt fell completely open and all she could see was the wide, iron-thewed expanse of his bronze chest, she fell victim to her womanly desires. It seemed that her blood had turned to liquid fire, pulsing through her veins and daring her to touch him.

"Are you, perhaps, stalling for time, Miss White, while that ingenious little mind of yours works out some alternative to win your freedom?"

The deep timbre of his voice and the fact that he had, in part, struck upon the truth snapped Ashlee out of her daze. "No . . . I . . . I was just thinking that a man like you shouldn't have to buy a woman's affections."

His laughter seemed to bounce off each knot in her spine. "There's been a few times," he admitted, throwing back his head as he swallowed the drink she had given him. "But like I said before, I don't think that's the case now." Leaning slightly, he set the empty glass on the windowsill. "Shall we find out?"

Before a thought had entered her mind or she could open her mouth to say anything that would stop him, Rhys caught her with one hand at the base of her skull, the other around her tiny waist, and jerked her to him, his mouth swooping down to take hers. If Ashlee thought she was on fire before, it was mild compared to the raging inferno she experienced now. He had trapped her hands between them, and the feel of his rock-hard muscles against her palms awakened in her an explosive passion she didn't know existed, clouding her mind and reeking havoc with her emotions. He was everything she had learned to hate, yet that mysterious magnetism that had made her flesh tingle the very first time she saw him returned twofold, destroying her will to push him away and to call an end to her charade. It was wrong. She knew that. But at this moment, she wanted to learn all the dark secrets of love.

Ashlee's head began to spin when his mouth slanted across hers and his tongue lightly traced the curve of her lips before pushing inside, and she couldn't imagine why Priscilla hadn't told her how titillating the sensation could be. It was probably the most exciting experience she'd ever had. Then suddenly, he lifted her in his huge, powerful arms, their lips still touching as he carried her to the bunk, and Ashlee had to fight back the giggle that made its way to her throat. But her girlish pleasures quickly disappeared when he slid his arm from beneath her knees and began to unfasten the hooks up the back of her dress.

Wait! her mind screamed, and she pulled her lips from his, gasping for air. This had gone too far! Priscilla never told her that the woman had to disrobe. In fact, she wasn't sure if it was necessary for the man to do so. She had only recited the words she had heard her friend use in the play, the words Sally White had spoken. Filled with panic, Ashlee couldn't move, and when she opened her mouth to demand that he put an end to this shameful behavior, nothing would come out. The scarlet satin dress slid to the floor at her feet. *What are you doing?* she wailed, but the only sound that penetrated the stillness in the cabin was the gentle lapping of water against the bow of the steamer.

A sudden, frightening chill embraced her when he tenderly pushed her down upon the bed to remove her

108

stockings and shoes, and the snowy white camisole that he tossed carelessly aside. She couldn't see his handsome face in the shadows of the cabin, but she was sure he had taken on a demonic vision. Ashlee simply lay there, afraid that if she moved, she would be consumed by the fires of hell for the evils she had done. Yet, while she stared, she saw him slip the white shirt from his wide shoulders, letting it glide to the floor with her things, then kick off his shoes and reach for the fastening of his trousers. Ashlee frantically squeezed her eyes shut, unable to bear watching a second longer.

Go away, she silently begged. *Let me wake up from this nightmare to find myself alone in my own bed. I swear by all that I hold scared to give up stealing if . . .*

Ashlee's heart leaped in her chest when she felt his weight upon the bed, and her body turned to granite. Nothing would move even though she willed it, and for an instant she wondered if she had died. But as he pressed his body down upon her, she knew that she hadn't for the heat of him scorched every inch of her flesh. His mouth covered hers again while his hands roamed freely over the smooth curves of her hips and thighs, and her breath caught in her throat when his kisses seared a hot trail down her slender neck to the taut peak of one breast. She was powerless to stop him, for it seemed as though he had beguiled her with a mystical force that had turned her mind and body into the clay of a sculptor. His caresses lingered on, touching her everywhere, driving her mad, but when he parted her knees with his own, Ashlee's trance vanished instantly.

"Oh, please—" she whimpered, willing to admit to her deceitful ways if he would only stop. But the confession was never spoken, for in that moment his passion soared beyond control, and as he thrust his manhood deeply inside her his mouth captured hers again, smothering the scream that tore at her throat. Ashlee felt as if he had torn her apart, and she wanted nothing more at the moment than for him to be finished with her. Yet, as his moves deepened, long and sure, a strange stirring erupted in the pit of her stomach. Before she knew what had happened, Ashlee's womanly instincts guided her, and she was lifted high above the foolish imaginings of the young girl she had once been. It was as if her entire body ached to possess this man, to unite as one, to draw herself into him. Then it was over, and he lay quietly at her side, one hand tracing the delicate curve of her cheek.

"Who are you really?" he murmured. "An illusion of my daydreams or a seductress sent to melt my soul?"

Ashlee smiled in the darkness that surrounded them, but she wouldn't answer. She wanted to savor this moment, to burn it into her memory, for she was sure it would never happen again.

"I was wrong about you," he laughed softly. "I thought you were part of a gang who wanted nothing more than to steal from me. Now, I'm more confused than ever." He raised up on one elbow to look at her more closely. "And you're not a prostitute." He tilted his head to one side. "Who are you?"

But before Ashlee could open her mouth to reply, he had pushed himself up onto one hip, his brow cradled in his hand. He sat quietly for a moment, not moving or uttering a sound, and a prickling of fear tickled the flesh across her arms and shoulders. With her eyes trained on him, she blindly fumbled for the coverlet and awkwardly sat up with it tucked beneath her chin, painfully aware of her nakedness and too frightened of him to ask what was wrong.

"You conniving bitch," he growled, the cold, hard look he gave her chilling Ashlee to the bone. "It was a trick! All of it!" He swung his feet to the floor, swaying dizzily as he tried to rise from the bed. "You put something in my drink, and I was fool enough not to—

not to expect it."

Ashlee huddled in the far corner of the bed as she watched him clumsily pick up his trousers from the floor and don them. It took a lot of effort and several minutes before he had completed the task, and all the while she stared wide-eyed and terrified that he would suddenly turn on her in a wild rage and beat her senseless. She had given him enough of the drug to knock out two men his size, and although she could see that it was starting to take hold, it amazed her how he was able to fight it off as long as he had. He stood with his back to her now, but she could tell by the direction of his head that he was looking at the door, and Ashlee knew what that meant once she spotted the key protruding from the lock. Yanking the coverlet free, she came up on her knees, swirled the fabric around her, and scooted off the bed.

"Damn you," he hissed when the slender figure darted past him for the door. "Give me that key." He took a step forward, staggered sideways, and fell to one knee. In the ashen glow of the room, Ashlee could see the fury burning brightly in his deep brown eyes. "I may not know your name . . . but someday . . . someday I'll find you, little lady. And you won't see me coming."

Ashlee's whole body trembled violently when he suddenly reached out, caught the edge of the coverlet, and tried to pull himself to his feet. In a panic, she jerked the cloth from his grip and stumbled back as he collapsed to the floor in front of her. A long while passed before the pain in her chest disappeared and she could breathe easily again, but the pledge he had made still rung loudly in her ears.

Chapter Four

The fresh scent of lavendar, girlish laughter, long,
flowing silky hair, and the gentle thrust of feminine
curves played upon Rhys's sleep-filled mind. He stirred,
moaning softly, vaguely aware of the hand that shook
him.

"Rhys. Rhys!" a voice called out to him.

One eyelid fluttered open.

"Rhys, it's me, Thomas. What happened here?"

Struggling to sit up, Rhys squeezed his eyes shut,
trying to shake off the lingering effects of the drug and
clear his thoughts. Bits and pieces of what had transpired
flashed through his brain, all scrambled together. He
rubbed his eyes, trying to make some order of it. His
throat was dry, he had a horrible taste in his mouth, and
it seemed every bone in his body ached. He stretched,
wincing as he kneaded the stiff muscles in his neck and
fought off the dizziness that swirled around in his head.

"Here, drink this," Thomas ordered, depositing a glass
in Rhys's hand.

Unconsciously, he took it, but as he raised the drink to
his lips and smelled the heady aroma of whiskey, he was
ruefully reminded of the last offering he had so carelessly
accepted. With a feeble shake of his head, he passed it

back to his friend and staggered to his feet, silently grateful for Thomas's help when his knees started to buckle beneath him.

"Sit down on the bunk until you feel better," Thomas sharply instructed. "And for God's sake, tell me what went on here! Where's the girl? Was I right? Did she bring someone with her? Is that what happened to you, Rhys?" He straightened and quickly took in Rhys's lack of attire. "For the life of me, I can't imagine why they found it necessary to practically strip the clothes from you."

Bent forward with his elbows braced on his knees, Rhys cradled his brow in his hands. "Where are the others?" he asked quietly.

"William and Phillip are recovering in their cabins much the way you are, but Ben is still out." He frowned suddenly. "My God, Rhys, she didn't drug . . . you didn't drink . . ." Whirling, he tossed his hands in the air. "I don't believe it. She tricked you, too."

"I'm afraid so," Rhys sadly admitted, massaging his temples.

"But how?" Thomas howled, jerking back around to stare incredulously at his companion. "*You* were the one who suspected her in the first place. What did she do, show up with a gun in her hand and demand that you take off your clothes and drink—" He stopped suddenly, a knowing twinkle gleaming in his eye. "Why are you only half dressed, Rhys, ol' friend? It seems to me that if she wanted to make sure you wouldn't be able to follow her once you woke up, she would have thrown your clothes—all of them—out the window."

The massaging stopped, but Rhys wouldn't look at him.

"Uh-huh," Thomas grinned. "Just as I thought." He folded his arms in front of him, his head tilted to one side. "So tell me, was she worth it?" He paused a moment,

114

waiting for Rhys to say something, and when his friend simply began rubbing his temples again, Thomas asked, "Did you, by chance, happen to get her name? How about the money she took? Did you make her a trade?" Thomas jumped when Rhys suddenly sprang to his feet and rushed past him to the chest.

"Damn," Rhys bellowed, slapping the top of the sturdy piece of oak. "She took it all!"

"What? What did she take?"

"Your money, Phillip's money, Ben's, William's, *mine!*" He turned in a rage, and Thomas knew not to tease anymore. "Yes, she tricked me, but only because I let her." He stormed back to the bed, leaned over and scooped up his clothes from the floor, then sat down to put on his stockings and shoes. "But it won't happen again. And I'm not going to stop until I find out who she is. Then, by God, she's going to wish she never laid eyes on me."

"But how, Rhys?" Thomas frowned, watching him jerk on his shirt and hurriedly fasten the buttons. "Where will you start?"

Jamming his shirttail down into his trousers, Rhys headed for the door. "In her cabin."

"But she's not there. We already checked."

He paused in the framework of the doorway. "I didn't imagine she would be. But I'm not getting off this steamer until I've searched every inch of it. There's got to be something on it that will give us a clue. Then I'm going back to New Orleans and find the woman I saw her talking to before she came on board this ship. Somebody knows who she is, and I won't stop until I find them. You interested in helping?"

"Of course," Thomas quickly replied. "She's got some of my money too."

"Then start by finding out if any of the passengers talked to her or heard her talking to someone else. She's probably the shrewdest woman I've ever run across, but even the best can make mistakes. How long before we dock?"

Thomas shrugged. "Half hour, maybe an hour, I'm not sure."

"In either case, we better hurry. I want some answers before I catch the next steamer back to New Orleans."

"Well, don't leave without me," Thomas told him. "I'm going along. I want to see the look on her face when you catch up to her."

The examination of Sally White's cabin turned up nothing, just as Rhys honestly expected it would. The passenger list he acquired from the captain, however, told him that she had booked passage only as far as the first stop along the way to Baton Rouge, which was no surprise to Rhys. The little thief never truly intended to go even that far, and by now was probably headed back to meet with her conspirators. But since Rhys didn't want to leave a single stone unturned, he requested that the entire boat be searched just in case he had been wrong about her method of departure. That, too, failed. But his determination to win only intensified after Thomas reported back that none of the passengers other than the poker players had spoken to the woman, and that the guard outside the stateroom was the last to see her. Somehow, she had vanished into thin air without a trace or a single clue. Still, Rhys wouldn't accept that. He, more than anyone else, knew that she was no illusion, no unearthly being who could simply disappear at will. He returned to his cabin to think about it for a while and to wait for the steamer to dock.

"Rhys," Thomas said, following his friend into the compartment, "I know you're angry, more so than I am. And I know it's none of my business, but I really wish you'd tell me how she managed to catch you so off guard. We've known each other for a long time, and I can't remember a single incident when someone got the better of you. I swear I won't tell anyone if you'd like to confide in me."

Smiling, Rhys strolled to the chest and picked up the red feather lying there, fondly recalling the shapely figure of the mysterious temptress bathed in the silvery glow of moonlight. He was quiet for a long while, then lifted his gaze to look out at the early markings of sunrise through the window.

"I would think the answer would be obvious to you, Thomas," he spoke softly, idly running his fingers across his shirt front as if the warmth of her pressed against him still lingered. "It's my biggest weakness." He laughed once he glanced over at the man and saw his frown. "I always allow a beautiful face to cloud my judgment. And in this case, I made two mistakes. I underestimated Sally White—or whatever her name is. She wasn't a harlot. I was sure of that. So I thought I would back her into a corner and force a confession from her in exchange for her . . . favors." He laughed softly and went to the window, where he casually leaned against the framework, listening to the steady rhythm of the steam engine. A moment passed before he spoke again. "It was the worst thing I could have done."

"Why?" Thomas asked, his tone comforting and sympathetic. "I would have been too angry to think of it, but now that you mention it, it would seem like a suitable answer."

"For the average woman," he shrugged, "it probably would have worked. But this little lady isn't average. As for me—" He smiled over at his friend. "I'm the one who's average."

"What do you mean?"

"The moment she touched me, I forgot everything. She beguiled me, Thomas. Just like a schoolboy. I stood right here"—he pointed to the floor at his feet—"and watched her pour us a drink, never once suspecting that she had drugged it. She handed it to me, and I drank it— as simple as that."

Thomas raised a brow. "Then you didn't—" He let the question go unfinished.

"Oh, yes. I made love to her if that's what you're asking." His eyes darkened as he recalled the pleasure of that blissful moment they shared. He ran the scarlet plume over the tips of his fingers. "I have to find her, Thomas. I have to stop her before someone else does."

"And what will you do with her if you're able to succeed where no one else has for the past year?"

Rhys chuckled. "Take her under wing? Reform her? Make a lady out of her? Maybe I'll just turn her over to the authorities and let her rot in prison." He stared out at the swirling dark waters of the Mississippi again.

"Will you listen to a word of advice from a friend?" Thomas asked, stepping closer. He waited for Rhys to look at him. "You say she beguiled you then, but I think she still has. She probably doesn't feel the same way about you, Rhys, and that could be dangerous. She could lead you down a rosy path and hand you over to her partners before you knew what happened. Be careful. That's all I'm saying."

A lazy smile stretched across Rhys's mouth. "Don't worry, Thomas. I will be. She fooled me once, but now that I know what I'm up against, I won't let it happen again. I'll be on the defensive. And you can tell the others that I'll get their money back for them. I can't say when exactly, only that I will."

"I'm sure of that," Thomas laughed, slapping Rhys's broad shoulder. "So, where do we begin?"

"Back in New Orleans. In fact, I think we should start with the casino."

"Why?"

Rhys absently tapped the feather against his opened

palm. "Well, we already know that there are men involved in this thing, and they're obviously the sort that like the excitement of a gamble. Stealing is always a gamble. Now, if you enjoyed that kind of game and had some extra money to spend, what would you do with it?"

"Go to a casino," Thomas grinned.

"It's a start," Rhys nodded. "We might get lucky. And while we're there, I can keep an eye open for the woman I saw Miss White talking with on the pier. Right now, she's our only lead."

"But aren't you afraid of scaring them off should one of them recognize you?"

"The only one who's ever seen me is Miss White." His dark eyes took on a faraway look. "And I'll know her the minute I see her," he replied in hardly more than a whisper. If only he knew her real name . . . He blinked, straightened, and draped his arm over Thomas's shoulders. "Well, Thomas my good man, we better pack our things and wait for the steamer to dock."

"All right," Thomas agreed. "I'll meet you on the promenade deck in ten minutes."

Rhys walked his friend to the door. He lingered at the threshold until Thomas had disappeared down the corridor, then turned back to look for his bag. The pale yellows of sunrise had strengthened and flooded the cabin with a bright glow, drawing his attention to the unmade bunk on the far wall. Visions of the beautiful coquette filled his head and brought a smile to his lips. Before he realized it, he had crossed the room and stood beside the bed.

"There isn't a place in this world for you to hide that I won't find you," he whispered, idly lifting the coverlet in one hand. "And I won't stop looking until I do."

Tossing down the spread, he started to turn away when he noticed a dark stain on the sheets. Rhys froze, his lips parting in a breathless groan. Blood! He knew she wasn't

119

a whore, but he had never suspected this! God, what had he done? He staggered away from the bed. Why had she allowed it? She hadn't fought him. In fact, she even seemed to enjoy it. A thousand different thoughts raced through his head at one time. If she were a virgin, how could she have known what to do? How could she have possibly figured out what pleased a man without ever having laid with one? Frowning, he ran his fingers through his hair. It was all so confusing. She dressed as a harlot, played the part of a . . .

"That's it!" he exploded with a snap of his fingers. "Playacting! That's where I heard the name. Sally White was a harlot in the play I saw back in New Orleans a few nights ago." Was it possible that the actress on stage and the one who had so cleverly outfoxed him were one in the same? A calculating smile kinked one corner of his mouth as he studied the red feather that he spun back and forth between his thumb and finger. "There's always one way to find out," he whispered.

"You're not serious," Thomas exclaimed as he and Rhys stood on the promenade deck waiting for the other passengers to disembark. "Could it honestly be that simple?"

Rhys struck a match and lit the cheroot he had clamped between his teeth. "We'll know tonight, just as soon as I pay Sally White a visit."

"God, how could she be so stupid? You'd think an actress with so many costumes to choose from would at least pick something other than the character she plays."

"Not if she thought she could get away with it," he grinned, glancing down at the gangplank and the steady flow of people moving across it. "Lucky for us she did." He straightened suddenly when he spotted a familiar shape among the crowd and urgently tapped Thomas's

120

arm. "See that boy just stepping onto the pier?"

Thomas quickly surveyed the group. "The one in the red shirt?"

"Yes. He looks like the little hellion who kicked me in the shins. You remember, don't you?"

"Yeah, I remember. But I didn't get a very good look at him then, and I sure as hell can't see him clearly from up here. And even if he is the same one, what difference does it make?"

"Possibly none, possibly a lot," Rhys frowned, steadily watching the youth edge his way through the people on the wharf in an obvious hurry.

"What do you mean?"

"Well, don't you think it's a little odd that this boy was a passenger on the *Mississippi Queen* and the *Spirit of Dubuque* on the same nights a robbery took place?"

"If he's the same boy, yes. But you can't be sure."

Rhys's gaze drifted to the satchel the child carried. "There's one way to find out."

"How?" Thomas argued.

Rhys flipped his cheroot out into the river, then turned a broad grin on his companion. "By looking in his bag. I'm willing to bet we'll find our money in it. Would you care to come along?"

Thomas glanced from Rhys to the boy and back again, his frown fading into a devious grin. "If you're that sure," he said, "I wouldn't miss it." Extending his hand for Rhys to lead the way, the two men hurried down the steps to the cargo deck, politely but quickly shoving their way through the throng of people still going ashore. "Can you see him?" Thomas asked as they stepped out onto the wooden pier.

"Over there," he pointed, once he spotted the child again, and suddenly broke into a run. "Hurry, Thomas! He's getting in a buggy."

The boy had just enough of a head start that by the

time Rhys and Thomas had cleared the end of the long wharf the rig, with the youngster sitting in the back seat, had jerked forward, wheeled around in the opposite direction, and thundered past them before either man could call out to the driver.

"Damn!" Rhys shouted, angrily swiping at the thin cloud of dust enveloping him. "I'd stake everything I own that that little heathen is involved in this in some way." In a rage, he whirled and slapped the open palm of his hand against the tall supporting post of the wharf. "I don't know whose throat I'd like to wrap my fingers around first, that imp or Sally White." His hands placed low on his hips, he lifted his chin in the air and heaved a disgusted sigh. "Of course, I have to find one of them first."

"That might not be as hard as you think, friend." Thomas grinned once Rhys had turned a questioning frown on him. "I'm not positive, but I think I recognized the driver."

"The driv—" Rhys glanced at the rapidly disappearing rig, then back at Thomas. "From where?"

"Now don't go and fetch the sheriff right away. I said I'm not sure. If he hadn't had on that hat, though, I would be. He reminds me of one of the men who works at Belle Chasse—in the casino. I noticed him the first night I was there. He's bald. I mean there isn't a single strand of hair on his head—kind of like he shaves what little he might have."

"You mean the one who's built like an ox?"

"Yes," Thomas replied enthusiastically. "Did you notice him, too?"

"Uh-huh," Rhys murmured, his gaze drifting back to the road the carriage had taken. "And isn't it strange? He and the boy are headed in the direction of New Orleans." A wide grin stretched his lips. "You're right, Thomas. Finding the boy might not be too difficult after all."

Catching his friend's shoulders in one arm, Rhys turned Thomas toward the steamer where they would retrieve the luggage they had left behind, knowing that within the next hour they would be on their way back to New Orleans.

John didn't slow the rig until they had traveled a good distance away from the dock, and even then Ashlee thought it was too soon. Crouched in the corner of the seat, she clutched the bag and its contents tightly against her chest, fearing that at any moment Rhys Sinclair would appear from out of nowhere and rip it from her fingers. Her body shook uncontrollably as she envisioned the rage burning in his eyes and the huge hand that stretched out to entrap her shirtfront and draw her to him. In her mind, there was little doubt that he'd kill her if he ever had the chance. And if John hadn't been waiting for her at the pier, she'd probably be dead right now.

When Rhys had finally fallen victim to the drug she had given him and collapsed to the floor at her feet, it had taken Ashlee several minutes to react. Until that moment, none of the men she had stolen from were anything more than nameless faces. He was something special—someone whose dark eyes, ruggedly handsome features, and masculine physique would forever frequent her dreams and spill over into her waking hours. She would never be able to get him out of her mind. Nor would she ever forget the terror she experienced after she had collected his money, gone to her cabin to change, then warily traveled through the empty corridors of the steamer to its cargo deck, only to discover that the ship had already passed the rendezvous point. She had stared at the swirling waters of the Mississippi for a long while before abandoning the idea of trying to swim to shore, certain its powerful current would drag her beneath its surface long before she reached the muddy banks. The only alternative left her had been hiding somewhere on board until the steamer docked. Then, if God were on her side, she would be able to sneak off the boat and disappear among the crowd at the pier. For an indefinite amount of time, she huddled between the tall stacks of wood near the boiler room, waiting, praying. She never slept, and by morning she hardly resembled the beautiful, carefree Ashlee Redington.

She had stood in the shadows while the gangplank was lowered, but the moment the way was opened up, she gripped the bag in both hands and raced for the dock. No one seemed to pay her any heed as she darted in and out of the mass of bodies all moving in the same direction. Yet for some unexplainable reason, she was compelled to stop midway, turn, and glance back up at the ship. Early morning sunlight penetrated the leafy overhang of trees on shore, spotlighting the one man she hoped never to see again as he stood by the railing on the promenade deck. He hadn't seen her, and she probably would have lingered for several moments if someone hadn't bumped into her and snapped her out of her daydream. Head down, she dashed off again, not knowing where she would go, only that it had to be far away.

The flow of people moved out of the way of the carriage stopped at the end of the pier, and Ashlee was about to go around it as well when a strong hand seized her arm, yanking her toward it. Horrified that somehow Rhys Sinclair had managed to catch up to her, she stiffened, ready to fight. As she thought about it now, she couldn't remember if she had actually hit John with her fist or merely thought about it. If she had, she was sure he would forgive her. But could she say that again after she told him why she hadn't been there to meet the rowboat? Or why those two men raced to catch the buggy before it pulled away? And how would she tell him? Exactly what would she say? The carriage lurched and rolled to a stop in a clearing at the side of the road, and Ashlee closed her eyes. She hated it when she made John angry.

"Ashlee, I'm so sorry," his deep voice apologized, and she bolted upright in the seat. He had twisted around to look at her, and from the pathetic expression on his face, she was sure he knew every detail of what had happened. How could he have possibly found out? And why was he asking her forgiveness when he should be hollering his head off at her?

"If I had only known someone had stolen the rowboat before I got there, I never would have let you on the steamer. God, you must have been scared to death not to find me waiting for you."

She slumped back in the seat. "Someone stole the rowboat?" she weakly repeated. "You—I—I thought—" She closed her eyes again and bit her lip to keep from smiling, letting her head fall back against the soft leather cushion.

John's frown deepened. "You didn't think I deserted you, did you? Is that what you're trying to say? Oh, Ashlee, I thought you knew how much you mean to me. I would never do such a thing! I'd die before I'd let anything happen to you."

"No, no," she quickly amended, sitting up to pat his arm reassuringly. "I—er—I thought it was my fault. I thought I had mistimed it and that you were going to lecture me." She smiled coyly, lowered her chin, and glanced up at him through thick dark lashes. "I never have liked being told I was wrong."

"Hmmm," John agreed, the sparkle returning to his green eyes but disappearing into a frown again when he remembered the reason for their hasty departure from the dock. "Why were those men chasing you? Did you have some trouble?"

Ashlee hoped the heat that rose in her cheeks hadn't darkened them enough for John to notice, and that her tone wouldn't betray her. "They—ah—they were two of the gamblers. I'm not sure, but I would guess that after the robbery was discovered everyone on board was searched. I was hiding down by the boiler room all night, and I suppose once they saw me this morning they realized I was one they missed." She laughed nervously. "It's a good thing you saw me when you did. I hate to think where I'd be right now if you hadn't."

"Behind bars waiting for me to figure a way to break you out," John sighed, turning back to grab the reins. "We were lucky this time, Ashlee, but if I don't get you home before your father returns, we'll have a hell of a time trying to explain where we've been." Calling out a sharp command as he laid the leather straps to the mare's rump, John guided the rig back onto the road and headed them toward home, unaware of the faraway look in Ashlee's eyes.

They traveled the distance to New Orleans in silence, never stopping along the way except to rest the mare and have something to eat. By early afternoon they had reached the outskirts of the city, and John reluctantly allowed Ashlee to get out of the carriage. Because their routine always brought them back in the middle of the night, it was easy for Ashlee to secretively sneak into the theater where Priscilla waited to help her change back into her own clothes, then return to her room as if she had only gone for a stroll. But the bright sunlight created a problem, and she certainly couldn't be seen with John. Someone would be sure to ask questions about the boy they had spotted riding with him. Thus, they had decided that the only safe way to cover their tracks would be for Ashlee to return to the theater on foot and alone.

Oddly enough, Ashlee found that she actually enjoyed the walk. It gave her some time by herself, and the fresh air was invigorating. She didn't notice if anyone she passed along the way paid any attention to her, for she was too busy caught up in her own thoughts to worry about the looks she might receive. Now that the initial danger was over and she would be able to shed her disguise in a few minutes, she discovered, much to her surprise, that she wasn't truly in any hurry to do so. Taking off the wig, red shirt, and dungarees meant putting an end to her escapade as well as closing out a chapter in her life. She had left Belle Chasse as a young, innocent girl, and she was returning as a woman who had experienced her first encounter with passion.

A delicious chill tickled her spine in spite of the warm sunshine falling all around her. She hugged her arms to her, pleasantly recalling the feel of another's strong arms embracing her, the fiery kisses, the masculine scent, and that wild, explosive magic that had sent her blood coursing through her veins in a glorious siege of ecstasy. Rhys Sinclair. Mrs. Rhys Sinclair. Ashlee Sinclair. An impish smile teased the corners of her mouth. It had a nice ring to it. Her steps lightened to almost a skip as she turned the corner and headed toward the theater near the end of the street.

I wonder what it would be like married to someone like him, she thought with a sigh. Her upper lip curled suddenly. *It would have to be better than Perrin Fabron!* Her fanciful daydreams shattered, Ashlee lowered her chin and set an angry, displeased glare on the tall, dark building several hundred feet farther on. It didn't matter anyway. Rhys Sinclair was a northerner, and she hated northerners!

Ashlee followed the sidewalk that circled around in back of the theater to the rear entrance, covertly watching for any of the employees of Belle Chasse that might spot her. She doubted any of them would recognize her dressed as she was, but she didn't want to take any

127

chances. Pulling open the huge wooden door, she hurriedly slipped inside into the darkness backstage, pausing a moment to let her eyes adjust to the dim light before heading in the direction of Priscilla's dressing room.

Priscilla, she thought with a silent groan. Fate had been kind to her by allowing someone to steal the rowboat. John had blamed himself for not being there to meet her, and because of it, he'd been too overwrought to suspect Ashlee's fear stemmed from another cause. But Priscilla was a different case entirely. There was very little Ashlee could hide from the woman. Being late would only make it worse. Taking a deep breath, she straightened, squared her shoulders, and quietly opened the door to Priscilla's room.

The female members of the troupe usually shared a place to change into their costumes and apply their makeup before a performance. But Priscilla had been given a room of her own since she never traveled with the group, and although it was similar to the other much larger dressing room, the difference was that she had turned it into a small apartment. Instead of paying rent as she would have done at a boardinghouse, Priscilla had worked it out with the theater owner that, in exchange for allowing her to live there, she would act as manager in charge of its maintenance as well as keep an eye on it at night when the others had gone to their hotel rooms. She was thought of by many of the young actresses as "the mother of the theater," and when there wasn't a part in the play for Priscilla, she would act as their coach. Priscilla loved the arrangement, since it gave her the chance to work with the play in some way or another and because it meant she was rarely alone. It kept her too busy to think about her own problems. Yet, when Ashlee didn't return during the night as expected, she had closed herself off in her room, telling everyone that she preferred not to be disturbed for a while.

With the coming of daylight, Priscilla began to pace the floor until the inflammation in her joints forced her to sit down and rest. Knowing that it wouldn't do her any good to worry, she had picked up her script and tried going over her lines, even though she knew them by heart. When that failed to help get her mind off Ashlee, she had taken out her sewing basket and needles and altered the costume one of the young actresses had complained was too big. But when the distant church bells struck the hour of twelve noon, she broke one of her own rules about never trying to contact John and sent one of the stage hands to the casino with a message. Her fear increased when he returned to tell her that no one there knew where to find John Hardin.

She continued pacing until the pain in her elbows and knees drove her to pull up a rocker and sit by the window where she could look out at the street. When someone opened the door to her room, she didn't even bother to look up but waved them off with a flip of her hand. She was on the verge of tears and didn't want anyone to question why.

Ashlee stared at the woman for a long while, sensing that something more than a friend's concern bothered Priscilla. Yet Ashlee honestly had no true idea what it might be. And knowing Priscilla as well as she did, there was no use in asking her. Priscilla wouldn't talk unless she wanted to. She stepped further into the room and quietly closed the door.

"Priscilla, I'm sorry if I worried you. Will you forgive me?" she spoke softly. "Can we still be friends?"

The slightly plump, crippled shape in the rocker straightened at the sound of Ashlee's voice, but Priscilla refused to look at her. Ashlee noticed how the woman reached up to dab at her eyes. "We'll always be friends, Ashlee," she finally answered, turning a smile her way.

"And I'll always worry about you." She motioned for Ashlee to come closer. "So tell me what happened."

Ashlee sat down on the end of the bed and kicked off her shoes. "Someone stole the rowboat," she said, pulling off the short-cropped blond wig and shaking out her long black hair, "so I had no way to get off the steamer until it docked this morning."

"Dear Lord," Priscilla frowned. "What did you do until then?"

"Well, I didn't know about it, of course, until after I had followed through with the plan, so it was too late to change any of it." She began unfastening the buttons on her shirt. "I did the only thing I could do. I hid in the wood pile near the boiler room until the gangplank was lowered, then ran like hell—er—heck." She glanced up sheepishly, knowing Priscilla wouldn't like her choice of words. "Sorry," she mumbled and stood to pull the shirt loose from her dungarees.

"Mmmm," Priscilla answered in her usual disapproving tone as she left the rocker to go to the wardrobe where she had hung Ashlee's dress. "So how did you get back here so quickly? It's too far to have walked."

"Well, luckily for me, John must have realized I wouldn't try to swim to shore. He was already waiting for me when the steamer docked." She unhooked the fastening of her pants and slid them off.

"Luckily?" Priscilla repeated, gathering Ashlee's petticoats, shoes, and stockings, as well as the bright blue dress, in her arms. "Why does that word sound like trouble? I mean more than just the obvious." She turned to confront the young woman with a raised eyebrow. "Something else went wrong, didn't it?"

Ashlee could feel the perspiration start to pop out of every pore. She'd have to tell her something. Otherwise, Priscilla wouldn't let it rest. She gave a surrendering sigh as if she was about to reveal everything. "Yes. Well, sort of. I mean it could have been disastrous. One of the men from the stateroom spotted me leaving the boat, and he must have realized I wasn't one of the regular passengers because he started to chase me." She moved closer to Priscilla and took the garments she held. "But I had too much of a head start." She smiled and then quickly turned away, silently praying it would be enough to satisfy Priscilla.

"Who was he?"

Ashlee gulped down her nervousness and crossed to the bed to sit and put on her stockings. "Actually there were two of them. I'm not sure of their names." She purposely didn't look at her friend as she spread out the petticoats and stepped into them.

"But one of them was a tall, good-looking man with light brown hair. Am I right?"

Before she could catch herself, Ashlee glanced up in surprise. "How—"

"How did I know?" Priscilla asked, coming to help fasten the hook at Ashlee's waist. "I saw him at the pier yesterday. He seemed to have a special interest in the blond harlot boarding the steamer. Who is he, Ashlee? And why has he made you so edgy?"

"Just a man," she replied, reaching for the dress she had laid on the end of the bed.

"And one who poses a problem," Priscilla snapped.

Big blue eyes looked worriedly at her. "Not really," Ashlee said.

"Oh, but he does," Priscilla went on. "When I saw him, he was looking right at me, which means he saw me with you, the prostitute who stole his money. And as a result, I can almost guarantee you he'll be paying me a visit very soon. I'm a good actress, Ashlee, but only when I know my part. You're not leaving here until you've told me everything that happened last night—and I mean everything—every little detail, young woman, because if

131

he says something that I'm not expecting, he'll know he's on the right trail by the expression on my face. Do you understand?"

Ashlee couldn't bring herself to look at Priscilla any longer. Dropping her gaze, she sank down on the bed, the blue dress clutched in her hands. "Yes, ma'am," she mumbled.

"Then start at the beginning," the older woman instructed.

Ashlee toyed with the lace collar on the gown for several moments before she answered, knowing of no way out except to tell the truth. Priscilla Krayer's friendship meant too much to her to put the woman in any kind of danger. "His name is Rhys Sinclair. I don't know where he's from or anything about him other than that. By the time I realized I was in trouble, it was too late to do anything about it."

"What do you mean?" Priscilla asked, sliding the rocker closer to the bed and sitting down.

"Rhys Sinclair—in fact all of the men in that stateroom—are the same ones from the *Mississippi Queen.*"

"What?" Priscilla breathed.

"Too much of a coincidence, right?"

"That's an understatement. So what did you do?"

"Well, I decided to just watch them play for a while, as if that was the only reason I was there. But what I was really doing was testing them. I mean I was listening to what they said and how they said it. I figured if they knew why I was there, one of them would give it away. But they never did, so I decided I was safe in following through with the plan." She vented a long, surrendering sigh. "I couldn't have been more wrong," she admitted, shaking her head.

"Why? What did they do?"

"I don't honestly think they were all in on it, but Mr.

Sinclair was for sure. I still haven't figured out how he managed it, but he never drank any of the whiskey I had drugged, even though he acted like it."

"A trap," Priscilla moaned, falling back in the rocker.

"Yes. But the mistake he made was thinking that he was dealing with a woman who didn't have any brains. He excused himself from the game to go to his cabin for some more money. He'd been losing pretty heavily, but now that it's over, I think he was actually hoping to lure me there."

"Did it work?"

Ashlee looked at her hands. "Yes. But only because I wanted to make sure the drug had taken affect so that he wouldn't come stumbling out of his cabin and tip someone off to what was going on."

"So how did you get away?"

Ashlee glanced up with a devilish smile. "I put some laudanum in the drink I gave him."

"What?" Priscilla laughed. "How did you ever manage to do that if he was sure of who you were?"

Ashlee shrugged. "That was my advantage. He wasn't positive. He wanted to force a confession from me, but I wouldn't budge. I just kept pretending to be Sally White." Rising, Ashlee lifted the dress over her head and slid it down over her slender figure, adding, "Men can be so stupid at times."

"Oh, really?" Priscilla mocked, waiting for Ashlee to look at her again. "And you think it was smart to use the name of the character I portray every other night in the theater right next door to where you live?"

Stunned, Ashlee retreated a step. "I—I didn't see any harm in it."

"Of course not. You think men are stupid. Well, I hate to be the one to tell you this, Ashlee, but most of them only pretend to be while they're around women. It's their way of flirting. If Mr. Sinclair guessed the true reason you were in that stateroom, then it won't take him very long to connect you, me, and Sally White." Wincing from the discomfort in her knees, she slowly pushed herself up from the rocker and went to the window to stare outside. "About the same length of time it will take him to appear at my door," she mumbled with a frown. "You're lucky he didn't get a good look at John."

"John?" Ashlee repeated nervously, knowing that if Rhys Sinclair hadn't, he must have been blind.

Priscilla jerked her head around to look at the young woman. "Are you trying to tell me that he did?" She groaned, certain of the answer when Ashlee didn't reply. "Does John know all of this?"

Ashlee shook her head and concentrated on fastening the buttons up the front of her dress. "I didn't want him to be upset over nothing."

"Nothing?" Priscilla exploded. "Ashlee, you're in about as much hot water as a stewing chicken. Now I suggest you tell John everything you've told me so that he'll have the right answer when he's confronted by Mr. Sinclair. And you can bet your father's casino that it's going to happen." She pointed a thumb toward the dressing table. "Now, run a brush through your hair, then go and find John. And until I send word, you're not to come here again."

Tears gathered in Ashlee's eyes. "Priscilla, please don't be angry with me. You're the only real friend I have."

A confused frown settled on the other's brow until she realized that Ashlee had misunderstood. She came to stand next to her, wrapping one arm around Ashlee's narrow waist. "It's for your own safety, darlin', not because I'm angry with you. Sinclair is looking for a woman, one he saw with me, and every woman I'm seen with from now on is going to be suspect. If we act as though we don't even know each other, he'll give up after

134

a while. At least he won't be looking in your direction. Don't you agree?"

Feeling much better, Ashlee smiled with a nod of her head. "I don't know what I'd do without you, Priscilla. You've been like a mother to me these past years." She moved away to retrieve the hairbrush and stroke the long, silky strands of raven-black hair. "I'll never understand why Papa dislikes you."

"He has his reasons, I'm sure," Priscilla whispered, turning away. "Now hurry up. It's important that you find John as soon as possible."

Laying aside the brush, Ashlee headed for the door. "I hope this is over soon. I don't like the idea of not talking to you for a while."

"Nor do I," Priscilla smiled. She ushered Ashlee out with a wave of her hand. "Get going!"

"Yes, ma'am," Ashlee laughed, hurriedly making her exit.

For the next hour, Ashlee sat in her room trying to decide exactly how she would explain her reasons for lying to John. What made it worse was the fact that he had blamed himself for the danger she had been in when he failed to meet the steamer as planned, while the truth of the matter was that even if he had, Ashlee wouldn't have been there anyway. The only thing in her favor was that her father and Dominique hadn't returned from their trip to Laplace, therefore sparing her the most difficult of explanations. But all in all, she was still in a lot of trouble, and if Priscilla was right, it had only just started.

The outer door to the foyer of the Redingtons' living quarters clicked open, followed by the sounds of dainty heels walking across the marble floor. Ashlee sighed disgustedly, knowing that her stepmother had returned. She had always longed to find a way of making herself invisible whenever Dominique was around, but since

Ashlee knew that was an impossibility, she forced herself up from the rocker where she had sat staring out the window and crossed to the door of her bedroom. She might as well be the one to make the first move, since it always aggravated Dominique to have to come and find her.

"Good afternoon, Dominique," Ashlee said from her doorway. "How was your trip?"

Coal-black eyes trimmed in equally dark lashes glanced over at her. "Boring as usual," came the caustic reply, "but I would imagine you enjoyed it."

There was only one reason why Ashlee never said the things she wanted to say to the woman, and that was because of her father. Although Ashlee couldn't understand why, Arthur Redington deeply loved the petite, shapely Frenchwoman, and she could only guess that it had something to do with the woman's ability to make him feel young again. Didn't he realize that marrying someone fifteen years his junior had nothing to do with how he felt about himself? She had to admit, however, that they made a strikingly good-looking couple and that despite Dominique's nasty nature she was a beautiful woman.

"Where's Papa?" she asked instead, allowing her stepmother's remark to pass without comment.

Dominique paused in the middle of the foyer as she pulled the black shawl from her slim frame and motioned for the two young boys carrying her bags to take them into her bedchambers. "All your father thinks about, my dear, is politics. You should know that." Neatly folding the shawl, she draped it over one arm and testily brushed a piece of lint from it. "As we were coming through the lobby he stopped to talk to a man he'd been told was running for the Senate in Mississippi." She raised her chin and sighed irritably. "Which can only mean we'll have company for dinner tonight." She set a cold, hard glare on her stepdaughter. "So do try to wear something that won't embarrass your father." She raised one finely arched brow at Ashlee and, without waiting for a reply, turned away and disappeared into her chambers.

Ashlee glared at the empty doorway, her upper lip curling in an unflattering snarl. "Yes, Dominique," she mocked. "Would it please you if I wore something black as you obviously think is becoming?" She shook her head. "No, no. That isn't necessary. You're the only one who must worry about your appearance. Bright colors would show the wrinkles around your eyes!" Reaching behind her, she grabbed the doorknob and yanked the portal shut with a bang. Dominique was the only one who found fault with anything Ashlee did. Her father loved her, and a simple thing such as the selection of a dress never bothered him one way or another; someday, she'd prove it to her stepmother. But for now, Ashlee wanted to welcome her father home. Lifting her chin in a defiant show of bravado, she crossed the foyer and stepped out into the courtyard, certain she would find him in the lobby engaged in conversation over an issue that was extremely important to him—the political rebuilding of Louisiana.

Her mood lightened as she walked toward the back entrance into the hotel. No matter how violent the argument between her and her stepmother might be, the warm smile and twinkle in her father's eyes always soothed Ashlee's hurt. She hurried her steps, anticipating the comfort and reassurance she would experience wrapped in his strong arms.

It was never difficult for Ashlee to spot her father among a crowd of men. She saw him the moment she entered the lobby and moved away from the staircase toward the front desk. Arthur Redington was a handsome man with thick ebony hair and blue eyes much like his daughter's. The distinction that set him apart from others his age was the silver gray patches at his temples and the youthful physique he had maintained for the past forty-five years. Many times Ashlee pictured him as the senator he wanted so badly to be, standing before Congress fighting for the rights of the people of his state. She had even entertained the thought that someday he might be president. What made him special to her, other than the fact that he was her father, was the respect they had for each other. Although they didn't always agree, Arthur would never shut her off. It mattered dearly to him to hear what the young woman had to say. Their discussions could become rather heated at times, but they never argued in a fit of temper, and there were only rare occasions when Arthur would use his authority to bring an end to their debate. She doubted he realized it, but allowing her to voice her opinion where politics was concerned—something Dominique was never permitted to do—always confirmed the fact that he valued her ideas many times over those of his closest friends. She loved him more than anyone else in the whole world and if, for some unexplainable reason, God only allowed her to watch him from a distance as she was doing now, she would be content with that. A bright, confident smile spread across her face when he glanced up and spotted her. Of course, Papa would never let that happen.

"Ashlee," he called, motioning her near. "Come and say hello to your father and help me welcome our new guests."

Anxious to be held in his warm embrace, Ashlee quickly made her way through the group of people standing between them, her attention focused only on the man who held out his arms to her. "I'm glad you're home, Papa," she whispered, hugging him tightly to her. His deep laughter rumbled in his chest and sounded good to her.

"I've only been gone for a day, child," he chuckled,

holding her at arm's length, "not the entire month. But I always enjoy being missed no matter how long or short the time." He enveloped her slender shape in one arm and turned her to greet the men who had quietly observed the reunion, failing to notice how her face paled instantly. "My dear, I'd like to introduce Thomas Bryan and his friend, Rhys Sinclair. Gentlemen, my daughter, Ashlee."

Ashlee found it nearly impossible to draw a breath. Her feet wouldn't move, and she doubted she'd fall if she fainted, for it seemed her entire body had turned to stone. Everything around her became a blur except for the handsome face turned her way with its dark brown eyes, the wide cheek bones, full mouth that was slightly parted in a soft smile, the square jaw, and thick, beautifully light-colored hair that caught the sunlight streaming into the lobby from the balcony above them. The charcoal-gray coat he wore lay perfectly over his wide shoulders, complementing the white silk shirt beneath it, opened to the breastbone, hinting at the powerful muscles they concealed, a strength Ashlee was well aware of. Had he come to confront her? To have it out? To tell her father that the daughter of whom he thought so much was nothing more than a common backwater thief? Would he handle this discreetly? Or was the sheriff waiting outside in the street to haul her off to jail? And how had he figured out who she was so quickly? Priscilla would have died before telling him. John? No, of course not. John would never abandon her. Then . . . Ashlee couldn't explain why, but all of a sudden she sensed that he *didn't* know, that the lady standing before him was simply the daughter of a man he had just met. Was it because of the puzzled look in his eyes or the way he tilted his head to one side, as if searching his memory for another time when they had stood face to face, that made her draw such a conclusion?

She swallowed the lump in her throat and snapped to attention when she realized her father had called her name.

"Are you all right?" he frowned.

"Yes, Papa." She smiled bravely and extended her hand. On the chance that she was right and neither man recognized her, she would act as if she had never laid eyes on either one of them. Besides, they had no way of proving anything. "I'm pleased to meet you, Mr. Bryan." She would have preferred pretending the man's friend wasn't even there, but rather than risk her father's curiosity, she turned to shake the other's hand. "Mr. Sinclair."

The moment his long brown fingers encased her much trimmer ones, Ashlee felt a disturbing electrical charge shoot through her entire body that sent her pulse racing. She withdrew her hand almost abruptly and sucked in a deep breath to calm her nerves. She stepped back and slid her arm around her father's waist, hoping to give the impression that she was totally at ease. She could feel that Rhys's gaze hadn't left her, and she settled her own on Thomas Bryan, the lesser of two threats, confused why one would bother her more than the other when there was a chance either man could recognize her at any second.

"Ashlee, Mr. Bryan is hoping to get elected to the Senate as a representative from Mississippi."

Oh? she thought sarcastically. *And what does his friend want to be? President?* Unwittingly, her gaze shifted to Rhys. The smile he gave her was nothing more than pleasant, but it was enough to rattle her confidence. She quickly looked back at Thomas.

"And that's the reason I've invited both Mr. Bryan and Mr. Sinclair to dine with us this evening. I'd like to discuss our views on what will help the south."

If her father said more, Ashlee didn't hear him. She

was too busy trying to come up with an excuse that would allow her to eat in her room. The last thing she wanted was to sit at the same table as Rhys Sinclair!

"I think that would be wonderful, Papa," she smiled sweetly up at him, smoothing the lapel of his coat, "but I'm going to have to beg my leave. It's my turn to work the blackjack table, so I'll just have dinner in my room." She stood on tiptoes and placed a kiss on his cheek before he could reply. She turned to their guests. "It was nice meeting you Mr. Bryan and Mr. Sinclair." Forcing herself not to race off, she nodded politely and walked away.

Arthur watched his daughter until she had disappeared into the casino, a frown on his face. "That's strange," he murmured with a shake of his head. "That little lady has never passed up a chance to talk politics." He shrugged and looked at the men again. "Well, if you'll excuse me now, I have some paperwork to attend to. I'll see you both in the dining room . . . around seven?"

"We'll be there," Thomas smiled, waiting until Arthur had gone before turning to his friend. "Am I wrong, or did Miss Redington seem to take an instant dislike to you?"

A soft smile lifted the corners of Rhys's mouth as he pulled a cheroot from the inside pocket of his coat. "Thomas, old friend, I know you find it hard to believe, but it does happen on occasion." He struck a match and lit the end of the cigar.

"But you never said a word to her," he pointed out. "And you heard her father. He was surprised that she chose not to join us for dinner."

Taking a puff on the cheroot, Rhys squinted when the smoke drifted into his eyes, and he shrugged in response to Thomas's observation. "Who can explain the workings of a female mind?" he grinned.

Thomas's mouth crimped sarcastically. "No one," he

remarked. With a tired sigh, he glanced down at his attire, haphazardly swiped at the dust on his coat, and said, "I don't know why I let you talk me into hiring a rig back to New Orleans instead of waiting for a steamer." He frowned irritably. "Damn dirty way to travel. I'm going to my room to clean up. You coming?"

"You go on ahead," Rhys answered. "I'm going to finish this cigar out in the gardens."

"All right," Thomas said. "Then how about meeting me in the dining room in a half hour. I haven't had anything to eat all day."

"Agree," Rhys smiled, walking his friend toward the stairs. But long after Thomas had climbed the wide staircase and disappeared into the crowd, Rhys lingered there, one arm resting on the thick wooden banister and his eyes trained on the entrance into the casino. He had never met Ashlee Redington before today, but for some strange reason he felt as if he had.

Chapter Five

"So," Thomas sighed, putting his empty coffee cup back in its saucer, "whom do we talk to first, our little actress or Mr. Goliath?"

Smiling, Rhys dabbed at the corner of his mouth with his napkin, knowing what Thomas's choice would be if he asked him. "Well, I don't think either one will be going anywhere," he said, laying the piece of linen cloth next to his plate. "It would arouse suspicion. But if I'm right about the boy, chances are our money went with him. He's the one we should find."

"Then we have to talk to this Hardin character," Thomas concluded with a frown.

"What good would it do, Thomas?" Rhys challenged. "We don't have any proof to confront him with, only that you *thought* you recognized him and that I think the boy we saw was the same one from the *Mississippi Queen*." He leaned forward with his elbows braced against the edge of the table. "We'll have to have some good, hard evidence before we can accuse him of anything."

"Then what do we do?"

"Watch him for a while. If he is who we think he is, sooner or later he'll contact the boy." He gave a short laugh. "That is if the boy is a part of this."

"You're beginning to make it sound hopeless, Rhys," Thomas complained, reaching for the coffee pot to refill his cup.

"Not hopeless," Rhys grinned. "But it will take some time. These people have been successful for over a year. We can't expect to solve this very quickly. In fact, I even doubt that I'll find Miss White at the theater."

Thomas's coffee cup clanked against its saucer. "Why?"

"Well, if you were in her place, wouldn't you go into hiding for a while?" Chuckling, he fell back in the chair and shook his head, mumbling, "If she hadn't kept her wits about her, I would have nailed her right then."

"Then does that mean you're not even going to try the theater?"

"No. As soon as you finish your coffee, that's where we'll head. If I word it right, I'll find out Miss White's real name and go from there. And if we're lucky, someone will tell us where she lives."

Thomas picked up the napkin from his lap and tossed it on the table. "Then what are we waiting for? I'd like to see this through to the end, but I've got to get back home fairly soon before they think I've changed my mind about running for the Senate." Taking his wallet from an inside coat pocket, he laid several bills on the table. "I'll even pay for that outrageous amount of food you ate if you'll get up right now."

Never one to pass up a free meal, especially if it came from Thomas Bryan, Rhys quickly stood up, grinning broadly. "Whatever you want, Senator."

The good-natured remark instantly brought Thomas to his feet with a silly smirk on his face. Taking his friend's elbow, he leaned closer and whispered as they walked toward the door, "And the first thing I'll do in office is see that all you northerners are sent back where you came from."

"I'm not really a northerner anymore," Rhys playfully objected. "I own a plantation near Vicksburg."

Thomas grunted. "But you were born in Maine and fought with the Yankees. In my book, that makes you a Yankee."

Rhys waited until they had left the hotel lobby, descended the front steps, and moved down the sidewalk toward the theater before he replied, "And what would all your southern friends think if they knew you associated with a Yankee?"

"Associating and liking are two very different things, Rhys Sinclair," he quipped, trying to keep a straight face. "There are a lot of things we southerners have been forced to endure because of the war, and tolerating cocky Yankees is one."

"Cocky?" Rhys laughed loudly. "Maybe this cocky Yankee ought to send you back home and just keep your share of the money once I've gotten it all back."

"At the rate you're going, I'll be cold in my grave before then. And by the way," he added before Rhys could say a word in defense, "if you come up with anymore ideas on trapping these culprits, you can count me out. I've lost enough of my hard-earned money already on account of you."

Rhys stopped in the middle of the walkway, his jaw sagging. "I'll admit my plan didn't exactly work the way I intended it to, but—"

"That's putting it mildly," Thomas chaffed.

"But," Rhys went on, "you knew the consequences. And as for it being your hard-earned money . . . well, both of us know that you haven't worked a day since you sold the shipping lines and went into politics."

"It's still hard-earned," Thomas argued, his green eyes sparkling.

"At the poker tables," Rhys finished. Grinning, he started down the sidewalk leading to the back of the theater, listening to his friend's hurried steps as Thomas rushed to catch up to him.

"Wait just a minute—" Thomas protested.

But their conversation came to a quick end as the two moved into the shade of the brick building and espied someone coming out through the back entrance. From the bucket of paint and stage scenery the person awkwardly carried, Rhys could only assume the young man worked in the theater. He watched in silence until the man set down the bucket, propped the rather large piece of board against the sawhorses already there in the middle of the yard, and started to roll up his sleeves, then he motioned Thomas to follow him.

"It's a great afternoon to be painting outdoors," he smiled.

The young man's head snapped up to look at the intruders as he hadn't heard their approach. "Yes—yes, it is." His tone of voice wasn't the friendliest, and his reluctance to chat was evident by the curious look he gave them as his gaze shifted from Rhys to Thomas and back. "Something I can do for you gentlemen?"

"Yes, as a matter of fact, there is," Rhys nodded, stepping closer as he held out a hand toward Thomas. "Mr. Washington and I own a theater in Boston. We're opening a new play next fall, but right now we're in a bit of a problem."

"Problem?" the man asked, his interest stirred.

"Yes. We've cast all the parts but one, and until two nights ago we figured we never would. We saw the production of *Murder in the Dark* and were quite impressed with the actress who portrayed Sally White. We're prepared to pay her handsomely—"

"Forget it," the man cut in, turning to lift the board across the sawhorses. "Miss Krayer doesn't travel."

Rhys shot Thomas a quick smile, then said, "Well, perhaps we could change her mind."

146

"I doubt it," the other laughed, picking up his brush. "But if you care to try, you'll find her inside." He jerked a thumb toward the door. "Through there and around the back of the stage. Last time I saw her, she was working on one of the backdrops with a stagehand."

"Thank you," Rhys replied, then lowered his voice so only Thomas could hear. "Come on, George. Let's go and talk to Miss Krayer."

"George?" Thomas repeated in a loud whisper as he fell into step with his friend's long stride. "George Washington?" He sucked in a deep breath and let it out in a groan. "Sometimes, Rhys, I find your sense of humor leaves something to be desired."

A bright smile flashed against Rhys's bronze complexion. "I thought it fitting seeing as how you'd like to revolutionize the south." He paused, grasped the doorknob, and pulled the portal wide as he swept out his hand. "After you, Mr. President."

Rather than banter further, for Thomas was eager to find Miss White and have his money returned, he simply gave Rhys a mocking smile and led the way into the theater.

Both were surprised by what they found, for neither of them had ever been backstage before, and each silently marveled at all the props needed to present a play. It appeared as if an entire household of furnishings were scattered about the place. Chairs, paintings, a sofa, lamps, a rug rolled up and tied with twine lined one wall, while overhead hung several curtains of various size and lengths. A wooden walkway circled high above the stage floor, and the men assumed it was the only way one of the hands could get at the enormous amount of ropes and pulleys should any of them need repair. Although there were no windows in this part of the building, the stage was well lighted by numerous kerosene lamps. It was easy for Rhys and Thomas to spot the couple on the opposite side of the stage as they concentrated on the huge piece of scenery being hoisted above their heads by a third person on the catwalk.

"That's not Sally White," Thomas frowned when Priscilla moved to get a better view of their work. "I've never seen her before."

"I have," Rhys told him, a vague smile parting his lips.

"Where?"

"At the pier where I first saw our Miss White. She's the one who didn't want Sally to board the steamer. This lady might not be the one we're after, but I'll bet she knows where we can find her."

"Well, if that's true, she isn't going to willingly tell you."

"Oh, I'm sure of that."

"Then what do you plan to do?"

"Just let her know that we're on to them. If we can put a little fear in Miss Krayer, she just might try to contact Sally."

"And then again, she might not," Thomas pointed out.

"It's worth a try," Rhys smiled.

Thomas shrugged indifferently. "At least we'll know for certain by her reaction once you tell her why we're here."

"Don't count on that, my friend. This woman is a professional actress. She knows how to disguise her real feelings." His smile returned when he saw Thomas's discouraged frown. "Stop worrying. Sooner or later one of them will make a mistake, and we'll be there when they do. It's simply a matter of time."

"That's what they said about the war and it lasted four years," Thomas muttered. "And since I haven't had the practice on stage, please introduce me by my proper name." He turned then to watch Priscilla, praying his friend would be wrong about her and that she would help bring this matter to an end.

148

Priscilla had noticed Mr. Sinclair and his friend the moment they entered, and she had busied herself with the backdrop in order to allow time to gather her wits. She knew he would come, but she hadn't honestly expected him this soon. Now all she could do was pray that she had the right answers and that her performance was the greatest she'd ever given.

"I think that should do it, Miss Krayer," the young man at her side observed.

"Yes," she agreed. "Let's just hope it works properly tonight. It's rather difficult creating the illusion of night with the wrong piece of scenery hanging behind you. Thanks, Jimmy."

"Anytime, Miss Krayer," he replied with a smile, then straightened when he noticed that they had visitors. He turned to confront them. "Can I help you?"

"No," Rhys declined politely, "but Miss Krayer can. I'm sure she was expecting us."

Confused Jimmy looked at Priscilla to discover the same expression on her face as well.

"I was?" she asked, unconsciously sweeping a stray tendril of blond hair from her brow. The glimpse she had gotten of this man on the wharf had been brief and at a distance. She had considered him to be handsome, but now that he stood before her where she could get a good look at him, handsome wasn't the right description. He was more than that . . . if that was possible. Strange that Ashlee never mentioned the fact. "Then I must apologize sir," she went on. "If we had an appointment—"

"No, Miss Krayer," Rhys interrupted, " we didn't."

"Then I'm afraid I don't understand your meaning. Have we met before?"

"Once," Rhys smiled, extending his hand in the direction of the back entryway. "Maybe we should talk in private. Outside, perhaps?"

"All right," she conceded and turned to her companion. "Jimmy, go ahead with that other backdrop. You know what I want done with it." She waited for his nod, then added, "I'll be back in a few minutes to help."

"Yes, Miss Krayer," Jimmy replied. He glanced at both Thomas and Rhys, as if hesitant to leave her in their company, then walked away.

"You have me at a disadvantage, sir," Priscilla said as they crossed the stage and went outside into the bright sunlight, away from the young man still absorbed in his job of repainting the piece of scenery. "You seem to know my name, but I don't know yours." She smiled at Thomas. "Or your friend's."

Rhys led them to the weathered settee, which was haloed by sweetly perfumed lilac bushes clustered all around it, and motioned for her to sit down while he and Thomas stood on either side. "My name is Rhys Sinclair and this is Thomas Bryan. But I'm sure you already knew that."

Priscilla settled back in the piece of wicker furniture and studied him a moment. "Oh?" she questioned, feigning her bewilderment. "Then again I must apologize. It seems I have forgotten. Where is it you seem to think we've met?"

"On the pier yesterday afternoon," he said, supplying the information.

"The pier? Yesterday afternoon?" She sighed with a shake of her head. "I'm sorry, Mr. Sinclair, but you must have mistaken me for someone else. I wasn't at the pier yesterday. I spent the whole of the day in my room—going over my lines. I'm an actress."

A soft smile spread wide across his face. "Yes, I know. And a very good one."

Although Priscilla presented him with a look of perplexity that outwardly meant she sensed an ambiguous tone to his words, she braced herself for the warning she was sure he was about to give. Her gaze dropped to the polished leather shoe he lifted to the edge of the settee, drifting upward to his knee and the arm laid across it, then to the dark brown smiling eyes staring at her as he leaned his weight forward and clasped his wrist with the other hand.

"Rather than spend the rest of the day bantering words, Miss Krayer, I'll come right to the point. I'm looking for the woman I saw you arguing with at the pier yesterday, the one who boarded the same steamer my friend and I were on, the one who said she was Sally White, the one who robbed us, the one who was a virgin until she came to my cabin." He paused a moment, waiting for her reaction. But when she simply continued to look at him with an unwavering expression, he smiled lopsidedly, glancing up at Thomas and back again before continuing. "Now I'm reasonably certain that there isn't a thing I can do to force you to tell me where I can find her, so I'll merely ask you to give her a message. Tell her I'm here to collect." Standing erect once more, he nodded at her then turned and strode away with his friend.

Priscilla remained seated on the white wicker bench long after the two men had gone. Her gaze centered on the exquisitely designed building next door to the theater as she wondered how Ashlee could have been so stupid and how long the girl had before Rhys Sinclair figured out who she was.

"You did what?"

Ashlee cringed and squeezed her eyes shut, waiting for the blow she was sure would strike her at any moment. John had every right to be angry, and she deserved a beating.

"And Rhys Sinclair of all people! Damn it, Ashlee, I told you that if something didn't seem right, you weren't to go through with it." Throwing his hands in the air, John growled and turned away, stomping off a few steps before he stopped and spun back around. "Did you, at least, have the decency to inform Miss Krayer so that she can be on the lookout for him?"

Unable to bring herself to look at him, Ashlee continued to wring her hands. "Yes," came her feeble response, her gaze quickly surveying the courtyard in which they stood for any who might have heard John's outburst.

"You've never heard of him, have you?" John went on, stepping closer and lowering his voice.

Ashlee glanced up sheepishly. "You mean Mr. Sinclair?"

"Are we talking about anybody else?" he snarled. "Yes, Mr. Sinclair."

Ashlee studied her hands again. "No."

"Well, I have. Would you care to know how I obtained the knowledge?" He didn't wait for her answer. "I was on my way to see you just now because of something one of the customers told me. Although the gentleman couldn't verify it, rumor is that Mr. Sinclair owns the *Mississippi Queen*. You remember the *Mississippi Queen*, don't you? Well, it seems Mr. Sinclair won it in a poker game a few months back, and it's probably the reason why he seldom travels on any other steamboat. Now, because of all the recent robberies involving steamers and poker players, Mr. Sinclair figured the culprits would sooner or later target his. So he posted a guard outside the stateroom door to keep any strangers from getting in. And the customer I mentioned? Well, I questioned him on how he knew this, and he said it was fact because he just happened to be a passenger that night." Settling back on his heels, John fixed an irksome glare on his young companion and folded his arms over his massive chest. "Was there a guard, Ashlee?"

"Yes," she mumbled. What good would it do to lie?

"And the fire, did you start it so you could distract Mr. Sinclair and the others long enough to put the drug in their whiskey?"

Raven-black curls bounced up and down with the nod of her head.

"Ordinarily I would say that that was a bit of ingenuity, Ashlee, but all you managed to do was infuriate Mr. Sinclair enough that he set out to trap you. The gentleman from the casino told me that he overheard Mr. Sinclair vowing to get even, that if it was money that lured you, he'd put enough within reach to make you careless. The gentleman didn't know how or when, only that it would be soon. Well, soon was last night, and you walked into it with both eyes open. Are you that stupid, Ashlee, that you didn't suspect a thing when you saw him?"

Ashlee knew she had been wrong in going through with their plan. But at the time, it had seemed like a challenge instead of a threat. Here was this arrogant northerner who thought he could catch her on the first try—and probably more so because she was a woman. She'd wanted to prove him wrong and hopefully, at the same time, make a fool of him. And it had worked! On both counts! And besides that, she was tired of being yelled at.

"I don't know why you're so upset, John. He tried, but he failed. And I got us more money than—"

"Oh, really," he cut in, his tan face darkening as he fought to control his rage. "Well, let me ask you something, Miss Smarty Pants. Just because you beat him at his own game, do you honestly think he's given up? Do you think a man like that—one who went to all that trouble—will simply throw in his cards and say, 'I quit. She beat me.' No, Ashlee, he won't. And you can bet all that money you got us that before very long he'll be paying us a visit." Misreading the look she gave him for that of concern, he added, "That's right, Ashlee. I expect him to show up at Belle Chasse any day."

"He's already here," she mumbled, fidgeting with a thumbnail.

John's jaw slackened. "What?" he breathed. "What did you say?"

Suddenly, Ashlee had had enough. She had taken more than her share of berating from both John and Priscilla for what she had done, and she couldn't honestly see what all the uproar was about. There was no way Rhys Sinclair could ever prove she was the one who had stolen from him unless one of them told him, and they'd never do that. Sucking in a deep breath, she let it out in a rush and set her gaze on the man frowning back at her.

"I said he's already here. In fact, Father asked Mr. Sinclair and his friend to join us for dinner tonight." She looked away, venting a short laugh. "I think it will be rather fun sitting across the table from him expressing my sympathy over his misfortune."

"As much fun as you had letting me go on thinking I was to blame for the danger you were in by not being able to meet the steamer?"

The color in Ashlee's cheeks paled. "No, John. That's not true. I didn't do it for the fun of it. I simply wanted to spare you the worry of knowing how close I came to being caught."

"And you think the danger is any less now?" He roughly took her arm and gave her a shake. "Wake up, Ashlee. You're not playing with a schoolboy. Rhys Sinclair is a grown man, and a damn dangerous one!"

His hand suddenly fell away as if he regretted losing his temper. But when she glanced up at him to silently reassure him that he had the right, a cold chill ran through her as she saw that his eyes were no longer on her but cast in the direction of the balcony behind her. Without thinking, she turned to see who it was that brought such a reaction from him, instinctively knowing that it could be none other than Rhys Sinclair. At that moment, her heart seemed to thunder in her ears.

He sat casually with one hip on the banister, wrists crossed over his thigh, his head turned their way as he leaned back against the post to quietly observe them. Ashlee knew the distance was too great for him to have heard anything they said to each other, but there was something about the way he stared at them that turned her blood to ice.

"Before you look away, Ashlee," John warned, "nod at him. He mustn't think his presence has bothered us. Do you understand?"

Ashlee gulped down the knot in her throat. "Yes," she whispered. "But do I have to smile? I don't think I can manage it right now."

"No. Just nod."

She had oftentimes pictured herself on a stage in London before an audience of hundreds, imagining she was the greatest actress that ever lived. Ashlee drew on those fanciful daydreams for the ounce of courage it took to simply bob her head, as if it were an indifferent gesture of acknowledgment toward the newcomer, then she looked away, fighting just to breathe.

"From this point on, child, we're not going to discuss what happened. It's over and done with, and too risky. We can't take the chance of being overheard anymore. Do you agree?"

"Yes, John," Ashlee replied, closing her eyes in an effort to calm her rapidly beating pulse.

"And we're going to act as though nothing is wrong. If there's any change in our behavior toward each other, someone is sure to comment on it, and with the kind of luck we're having lately, Sinclair will hear it. And stay away from Miss Krayer for a while."

"She and I already decided that."

"Good. Then see that you do." His expression softened as he stared at her, realizing how terrified she must be. "If we keep our heads about this, Ashlee, we'll be all right. Just be careful whenever you're around him, and watch what you say."

"I'll try," she offered, smiling halfheartedly at him. When he turned to leave, she caught his arm. "I'm sorry, John, for not telling you about—about the—"

He covered her hand with his. "Apology accepted," he answered tenderly. "And one more thing." He smiled devilishly at her questioning look. "At dinner tonight wear that emerald-green dress of yours—the one Dominique thinks is too revealing."

"Why?" Ashlee frowned, surprised that John of all people would suggest it, much less approve.

He reached out and tapped the end of her nose with his fingertip. "What better way to keep Mr. Sinclair occupied with other thoughts?"

She fought not to laugh, but couldn't. "John, you're awful. But I'll do it."

"That's my girl," he beamed, leaning in to place a kiss on her brow before turning around and walking away.

She watched his steady gait until he had crossed the courtyard and disappeared through the entryway into the hotel lobby, feeling greatly relieved to have the truth out. Rhys Sinclair's presence was something she was sure she couldn't deal with alone. She needed John, and she needed him on her side. Thinking of the other again, she lifted her eyes toward the balcony and stiffled a gasp. Rhys had vanished without either her or John noticing, and she didn't like it. He could come and go as quietly as the wind, and it unnerved her. Deciding it would be best for her not to get caught alone with the man, she made an abrupt turn for her room and nearly collided head-on with him. She stumbled backward, her mouth dropping open in breathless surprise.

156

"Forgive me, Miss Redington," Rhys smiled softly. "I didn't mean to startle you."

Ashlee wanted to tell him how rude he was for sneaking up behind her like that. But since the courtyard was designed for the use of its customers, giving him the liberty of walking wherever he pleased, and because she doubted the words would come out if she opened her mouth—not to mention the fact that John had warned her to be careful of what she said around him—she merely bit on the inside of her lip instead of commenting. With a noncommittal shrug of one delicate shoulder, she moved to step around him.

"I don't mean to pry, Miss Redington," he went on, and Ashlee paused to look questioningly at him, "but it seemed as if your companion might have been threatening you."

"John?" The name was issued forth in a burst of laughter. "Hardly that, Mr. Sinclair. Mr. Hardin is a very close family friend, and more like a second father to me. He treats me as any kin might do." She laughed again and looked away thoughtfully. "In truth, John knows more about me than—" Ashlee could feel the color drain from her face. Damn! Didn't John warn her to be careful? She forced a smile to her lips and looked up at him again, positive he knew exactly what she meant and that he would tell her so at any moment. But from the expression on his face, Ashlee quickly realized that he hadn't even heard her. He was frowning as if something confused him or he was possibly trying to recall something from his past.

"Is anything wrong, Mr. Sinclair?" she dared to ask.

A bright smile instantly warmed his face, and Ashlee suddenly wondered if the man had any imperfections—other than being a northerner, of course.

"We've never met before, have we, Miss Redington?" Ashlee's heart thumped in her chest. "No," she hurriedly replied. "Why do you ask?"

The frown returned as he gazed off to his left toward the beautifully flowering magnolia trees at the end of the courtyard. "I didn't honestly think I could forget if we had, but there's something about you—" His gaze found hers again. "Maybe it's your eyes." He shook his head. "I'm not sure."

"Not sure of what?" she blurted out, then mentally cursed herself for her recklessness. Why couldn't she just let it drop instead of tempting fate?

The puzzled frown disappeared and the warm smile showed once more. "I rather doubt there's another as beautiful as you, Miss Redington, but I can't seem to shake the feeling that I've seen you somewhere before." He shrugged his wide shoulders. "Perhaps only one who bears a resemblance."

Ashlee felt as if a great pressure had lifted from across her chest, and she was able to breathe easily for the first time since this man's arrival. The fool had no idea that she was the one who had stolen from him . . . and not once, but twice! It almost made it worth all the tension he had put her through for the past few hours. Feeling a little smug, she relaxed, deciding to enjoy his ignorance.

"Why, thank you, Mr. Sinclair," she smiled demurely. "It's been a long time since anyone paid me such a nice compliment."

Rhys's laughter was warm and sincere. "Now I find that hard to believe."

"Well, actually I get a lot of them working in the casino," she admitted with a shrug. "But they're not quite the same. Most of them precede various forms of proposals to wed, none of which can be taken seriously." Remembering one such episode, she laughed. "And after I turn them down, the compliments are usually retracted for something not quite as flattering."

"Well, I assure you, Miss Redington," Rhys grinned.

"I'm very sober and meant every word—without any conditions. Unless, of course, you consider my asking you to change your mind about dinner this evening as one."

Ashlee knew she should turn him down. She should stay as far away from him as possible and not encourage his visit at Belle Chasse to last any longer than necessary. But the deep, rich timbre of his voice and his exquisite features, as well as the fact that she had him completely fooled, dared her to play him along a bit more.

"I suppose I could," she replied with a sweet, yet incongruous smile, thinking to do exactly as John suggested and wear the emerald dress cut low over her bosom. She'd take this arrogant northerner for a ride he'd never forget. "But I won't be able to stay for very long. I have to fill in for Elaine at the blackjack table tonight." She glanced back toward the building. "And right now I really should make sure the new tablecloths arrived while I was gone." A full moment or two elapsed before Ashlee realized what she had said, and rather than look at him and confirm the fact that he had understood, she turned and started toward the restaurant, calling back over her shoulder, "I'll see you at dinner, Mr. Sinclair."

Ashlee wasn't sure if he answered her or not . . . nor did she care. She was too busy trying to think of a sound alibi that would logically put her somewhere other than the hotel *and* the steamer. Visiting Priscilla was always a good excuse for not being where she was supposed to be, but not this time. Until Rhys Sinclair left New Orleans, Ashlee had to pretend that she didn't even know the woman.

"How do I manage to get myself into these messes?" she mumbled irritably as she yanked open the door to the lobby and went inside. "It's quite simple, Ashlee," she continued, ignoring the quizzical stares of the people she

159

passed. "You don't think any further ahead than the end of your nose." Venting a throaty growl, she stormed across the marble floor of the lobby and hurried into the dining hall.

It wasn't until later that evening, while Ashlee sat soaking in a tub full of lavendar-scented bubbles, her thick black hair piled high on top of her head, that another disturbing revelation came painfully to mind. Had the young woman Rhys Sinclair lured to his cabin and then to his bed meant so little to him that once he stood face to face with her the intimate moments they had shared failed to spark his memory? Did he look upon bedding a woman with the same degree of importance as selecting a clean shirt to wear? Tears gathered in Ashlee's eyes, and she sank low in the tub until the bubbles tickled her chin. He should have known her the minute he saw her! Or had he found her so lacking that she wasn't worth remembering? Sitting up abruptly, she reached for the sponge near her feet, splashing water out onto the floor.

"Well, you're no prize either, Mr. Sinclair," she fumed, vigorously scrubbing her knee. "And the day you walk out of Belle Chasse will be the day you walk out of my life, and I shan't think of you again."

But even as she made the pledge, Ashlee knew it wasn't so. How could she ever possibly forget the man who stole her virginity? The one who awakened a strange passion in her that she never dreamed herself capable of feeling? Her expression softened as she recalled that moonlit night and the way the silvery beams caressed his tall, muscular frame. Even now, her fingers tingled as they had when she touched him, and her lips burned with the memory of his kiss. Maybe their romantic interlude meant nothing more to him than a pleasant way to pass the evening, but for Ashlee it was something she would always cherish.

"But *he'll* never know that!" she spat in a burst of

160

renewed fury, pushing herself up from the tub. "God forbid he should ever come to know who I really am, but if he should, *I'll* be the one to act surprised!"

Yanking the towel from its peg, Ashlee hurriedly wiped herself dry, then slid into her chemise and sat down on the chair to pull up her stockings and fasten them with lacy garters just above her knee. Next came the flowing yards of white petticoats and finally the emerald satin dress with its tight bodice and plunging neckline. After struggling with the buttons up the back of the gown, Ashlee looked down at her chest, wishing she had chosen to wear her corset and add a little more fullness to her bosom. She heaved a disgusted sigh. What difference would it make? Not being well-endowed to begin with, all the corsets in the world wouldn't help, so if she'd put one on, she'd simply wind up spending the evening trying to hide her discomfort. Maybe a dab or two of perfume would make up for it. Lifting her skirts with both hands, she hurriedly left the small bath chamber and went into her bedroom to examine the selections sitting on the dresser. But once she caught sight of her reflection in the mirror, her shoulders drooped in dismay. About the only thing that would help would be a gunnysack over her head. She hated her dark hair and pale blue eyes, even though they looked much the same as her father's. She had always thought that blondes were much more striking in appearance . . . like Priscilla.

Priscilla, she thought, reaching up to pull the pins from her hair. Life had been hard on the woman, but she never allowed it to get her down. Even on her worst day, Priscilla Krayer looked exquisite. If there was anyone Ashlee wanted to be like, it was she. Or, perhaps, Veronica Darnell. Even her mother's name was exciting. Ashlee's upper lip twisted in an unflattering snarl as she brushed the long dark curls into a shiny brilliance. Anything was better than Ashlee Redington! Her name was boring, her looks were boring, *she* was boring! Grabbing the thick mass of hair, she twirled it into a knot and secured it on the top of her head, irritated that no matter what she tried, she could never catch the few single strands of hair that defiantly insisted on falling down the back of her neck. Resigned to the fact that there wasn't anything she could do to change her appearance, she picked up the lace handkerchief from on top of the dresser, tucked it into the sleeve of her dress, and left her room.

"I consider myself to be a very lucky man," Arthur sighed as the three men sat waiting for his wife and daughter to join them for dinner. "I have the love of a beautiful woman, a good business, a charming daughter, and the potential of becoming a senator." The last immodest attribute was followed by his good-natured laugh. "At least that's what Ashlee keeps telling me." The smile disappeared. "Of course, it takes a lot of money to campaign for office. I just wish I had enough."

"Don't you have any backers, Arthur?" Thomas questioned, lifting his coffee cup to his lips.

"A couple," Arthur replied, "but they're having trouble just like I am."

"Trouble? What kind of trouble?"

"Well, being a Republican who's trying to get Louisiana accepted back into the Union has left me wide open for criticism and harassment. We spend a lot of time just watching our backs. The war isn't over for a lot of southerners." He vented a long, weary sigh. "And then there's the casino."

"The casino?" Rhys asked.

"Yes. It's losing money."

"I find that hard to believe, Arthur," Thomas objected. "I've spent a couple of nights in there myself—

lost some money like most of the men at my table. And the place is always full of customers."

"I know," Arthur agreed. "I can't figure it out myself. The odds are always with the house, but for some reason my casino barely breaks even."

"Every night?" Rhys asked, curious.

Arthur nodded. "There's even a few nights a week when we lose."

His interest aroused, Rhys leaned forward with his elbows braced against the edge of the table. "Who does your books?"

"My wife, Dominique," Arthur easily admitted. His attention fell away from the men for a moment as he traced a fingertip around the rim of his cup. "I really feel sorry for her."

"Why's that?" Thomas asked.

"Because I can see how much it bothers her to have to tell me that the casino is costing us." He glanced up with a smile. "I would have sold it long ago if it hadn't been for her. She keeps telling me to hang on, that once the United States is finally at peace again the place will start to show a little profit. But I don't really think it will and I've lost the desire to fight for it. My interest is in politics now. I'm just holding onto it for Dominique's sake."

"Have you considered the possibility that you've got a thief in your employment?" Rhys proposed.

"A thief!" Arthur exclaimed. "Heavens, no. Every single person who works for me has been with me for more than ten years. Our losses only started happening at the outbreak of the war. I'm sure it's got nothing to do with them."

"But it's something to think about, Arthur," Rhys pointed out. "You just said the odds are with the house. It doesn't make sense otherwise."

"You should listen to him, Arthur," Thomas broke in. "Rhys earns his living at the poker tables. I'd say he's an authority on the subject."

Arthur sucked in a quick breath to object but changed his mind. "Yes, I know. It's just something I don't care to admit."

"Who would?" Rhys replied sympathetically. Leaning back in his chair, he took a cheroot from his pocket and struck a match. "It might be in your best interest, Arthur," he added, lighting the cigar, "to hire someone to do a little investigating for you rather than lose the place."

"You mean spy?"

Rhys shrugged. "A little harsh, but I guess you could call it that."

"Oh, I don't know . . ."

"I think it's a good idea, Arthur," Thomas agreed enthusiastically. "It can be done very discreetly. And once you know who's been helping themselves to your money, you can decide how to handle the situation. If you want it that way, no one would ever have to know except you, the investigator, and the one behind it." He leaned in, looked all around them to make sure no one would hear, then glanced briefly at Rhys and back to Arthur. "In fact, I know just the man for you."

"Thomas," Rhys warned. He knew that look in the man's eye.

"And why not?" Thomas argued. "You're going to be sticking around here for a while anyway." He turned his attention back to Arthur. "I've never known a sharper mind for detail than this man right here, Arthur. I'd give Rhys a week and he'd have the matter settled for you. And what better cover? Rhys is a gambler. No one would suspect his real reason for being in the casino."

"I'll tell you why," Rhys cut in. "I'm here on business. I can't be doing two jobs at one time."

"And how do you know the two aren't connected?"

"Why should they be?"

Thomas opened his mouth to recite the reasons, but when none came to mind, he shrugged instead. "All right, so the chances are pretty slim. But I still don't see why you can't help Arthur out a little since you'll be staying at Belle Chasse anyway." He raised both eyebrows at him. "Well? Got an answer for that one?"

Rhys couldn't refrain his laughter. "No. But I have a question."

"What?"

"You only met Arthur this afternoon. Why are you so insistent on helping?"

"Yes, Thomas," Arthur agreed. "Why?"

Thomas raised his nose in the air. "Well, I've always considered myself a good judge of character." He cast Rhys a mocking look. "Of course, in your case I could have been wrong. But after talking politics with you, Arthur, I've learned you and I think a lot alike. I want to see that opinion put to good use in the Senate. If your business problems affect your bid for office, then I want to do something about it. I don't see where that's too hard to understand." He shifted his gaze back to Rhys. "Even for a Yankee."

The corners of Rhys's mouth twitched, fighting back a grin. "So now you're going to attack my intelligence in order to get me to agree."

"Did it work?" Thomas smiled.

Rhys's immediate reaction was to say no. But as he thought about Thomas's offhand remark about the two situations being somehow connected, Rhys's inventive mind calculated all the facts he had gathered over the past few weeks with those he had learned just this morning. And the bottom line added up to John Hardin. If Thomas was correct in identifying Hardin as the man they saw helping the young boy escape, then it meant Hardin was a thief—or at least a part of the gang. And if he stole from one place, what would prevent him from

165

stealing from another? He took a long puff on his cheroot and watched the smoke drift upward for a moment. And, of course, he never passed up a chance to further his business ventures.

"On one condition," he said, looking at Arthur. "And the decision is yours."

"Let's hear it," Arthur replied amiably.

"Most people who know me think my only source of income is from the gaming tables. It isn't," he confessed, flicking the ash from his cigar into a glass dish on the table. "I own property and a steamboat. I'd like to expand my business interests, but not enough that it would interfere with my . . . social life, shall we say. In other words, I prefer that no one knows about my holdings except those involved. I'm not out to earn a reputation as a wealthy businessman, just enough money to allow me to live comfortably—to do absolutely nothing if that's what I want. You stated earlier that you had considered selling Belle Chasse." He waited for Arthur's somewhat hesitant nod. "In exchange for my help, I want to buy in—only fifty percent, mind you. I'm not interested in taking over. In fact, nothing about your place will change outwardly. And you can take the money I pay you and use it on your political campaign. I may be a Yankee," he smiled, "but I'm one who wants to see the south get back on its feet. With men like you and Thomas, it can be done."

Arthur stared at him for several moments, digesting the offer. It sounded good, almost too good to be true. "Is there a catch?" he finally asked.

"Only one," Rhys admitted. "No one, including and especially your wife, is to know about our deal."

Arthur's dark brows came together instantly. "My wife?"

Rhys leaned forward against the table. "Now don't misunderstand my reason, Arthur. I'm not accusing

166

anyone. But if someone is stealing from you, nothing about your operation must change. Otherwise it will scare them off. And there's always a chance your wife might let it slip."

"But she keeps the books. If you're a partner, you've the right to examine them. If she doesn't know about our deal, she'll never allow you near them."

"Well," Rhys grinned, "unless she carries them around all the time, I'll find plenty of opportunities to look them over—with your help, of course."

"I can see one flaw in your plan, Rhys," Thomas said, continuing when his friend gave him a quizzical look. "How will you explain your sudden interest in Belle Chasse without raising suspicion?"

"I could give you a job as one of my dealers," Arthur suggested. "Everyone knows I've been thinking about hiring one to help out. We might not turn a profit, but we've had more customers than we can handle. Even Dominique talked about it, and it would give you the freedom to be places our customers aren't allowed."

"Great idea," Thomas exclaimed. "So—are you two agreed?"

Catching sight of Ashlee coming into the dining room, Rhys rested his elbow on the table and casually raised his fist in front of his mouth to mask the words he said to Arthur. "Perhaps you should think about it and give me an answer later. We're about to be joined by your daughter."

"There's nothing more to think about," Arthur whispered. "We'll settle on a price, and I'll have my lawyer draw up the papers tomorrow." Smiling, he pushed himself up from the table. "And we can shake hands on it then."

The man's quick answer surprised Rhys, but it also told him how strongly Arthur Redington wanted to be a senator. Even though he claimed to have lost interest in his business, he truly hadn't, and when his gaze shifted to the beautiful young woman walking toward them, Rhys was sure of the reason. No one had to tell him how much the man loved his daughter. Rhys could see it in the older gentleman's eyes. Looking at Thomas, Rhys smiled and stood up to greet the newest arrival to their group, that strange feeling that he had seen her somewhere before turning his smile into a curious frown.

Ashlee had lectured herself all the way from her room, through the lobby, and into the restaurant on how Rhys Sinclair's presence wouldn't—*mustn't*—bother her. Yet the moment she saw him garbed in dark brown, with a ruffled ivory-colored shirt and gold brocade vest, and saw how well the clothes fit his muscular build, her heart began to pound all over again. After seeing him dressed in the dark blue outfit the night before, she couldn't imagine any other color would suit him better. But this . . . this ordinary shade of brown richly enhanced his bronze complexion and added golden highlights to his hair. And when he smiled at her, displaying a flash of strong white teeth, Ashlee thought she would faint. Unknowingly, she pulled the kerchief from her sleeve and lightly dabbed at her neck.

"We were beginning to think you changed your mind again," Arthur smiled, pulling out a chair for her. "Did you see your stepmother anywhere?"

A frown flitted across Ashlee's brow as she stared at the place her father had selected for her to sit. Although she was glad he hadn't chosen a place next to Rhys, being opposite him where the Yankee could ogle her all through dinner wasn't much better. She blinked, glanced up at her father, and shook her head. "No, Papa, I didn't change my mind, and I don't know where Dominique is. I haven't seen her since this morning."

"Well, I'm sure she'll be along any minute," he replied, helping her with her chair. "You look very pretty, Ashlee. I've always liked that dress on you."

"Thank you, Papa," she mumbled, suddenly wishing she had disregarded John's suggestion and worn her blue one with the high neckline. She could almost feel Rhys's eyes devouring every inch of bare flesh.

"May I pour you some coffee, Miss Redington?" the man at her left asked.

Somewhat startled, she glanced up at Thomas and laughed nervously. "Y—yes, please." She concentrated on watching him lift the pot and fill her cup, wondering if there were some way she could avoid looking at the man directly across from her. But she had no sooner questioned her ability when Rhys moved to tap the ash from his cheroot into the dish in front of him, drawing her attention to his long brown fingers, well-manicured nails, and the diamond ring he wore. Surprised by the size of the gems—a total of three set in a wide gold band—and by the fact that he wore it on the little finger of his left hand, Ashlee forgot about her decision to ignore him and curiously studied the piece of jewelry and its ascent as Rhys lifted the cheroot to his mouth once more.

"It belonged to my grandmother," he said, having noticed her interest. "I plan to give it to my wife."

"If he ever decides to settle down," Thomas added with a chuckle. "Lord knows what woman would have him."

Ashlee smiled at the man's playful remark, although she disagreed. There were probably plenty of women who would eagerly accept his proposal of marriage. "The ring is very beautiful, Mr. Sinclair," she added, picking up her coffee.

"Please call me Rhys," he smiled, showing a hint of those white teeth, and Ashlee could feel the heat rising in her cheeks. She nodded over the rim of her cup.

"My grandmother thought it was beautiful, too. That's why she gave it to me just before she died. She wanted my wife to have it," he sadly reminisced. "And I guess she chose me to give it to because I'm so much like my grandfather." Laying aside his cheroot in the dish, he pulled the ring from his finger and absently studied the sparkling stones. "He and I were both in love with the sea."

"I've never seen a ring quite like that one, Rhys," Arthur observed. "Where did your grandfather get it?"

"He was the captain of his own merchant ship before he married my grandmother and spent most of his time sailing between North and South America. They hit some rough weather down there one time and had to dock for repairs somewhere in Brazil. To hear my grandmother tell it, she'd say he bought the ring. But I rather doubt it. Grandpa was an adventurer, to say the least." He tossed the ring in the air, caught it, then shoved it back on his finger. "I think he worked the diamond mines down there for a while. It's the only logical explanation for the sudden wealth he brought back with him."

"Maybe he stole it," Ashlee scoffed and took a sip of her coffee.

"Ashlee!" her father rebuked, frowning angrily. "Mind your manners. Mr. Sinclair is a guest."

"That's all right, Arthur," Rhys laughed, settling a warm look on the youngest Redington. "Knowing my grandfather, it's possible."

The conversation ended there when Rhys's gaze suddenly left her at Arthur's announcement that his wife had finally arrived. Ashlee felt a stab of jealousy at the appreciative expression she saw come over Rhys's handsome face. Dominique might be well into her thirties and a married woman, but she never failed to draw any man's attention to her beauty and shapely figure. Nor did the woman ever pretend she didn't notice.

"Darling, I'd like to introduce you to our guests," Ashlee heard her father say. Rather than look up and acknowledge her stepmother's presence, Ashlee elected to drink her coffee. "This is Thomas Bryan, a fellow candidate for the Senate, and his friend and our new casino dealer, Rhys Sinclair."

It was Ashlee's misfortune to have only half swallowed the sip of coffee she had taken. Although she managed not to choke on it when she heard her father's shocking news, she did, however, jiggle the cup she held when she tried to gulp down the hot liquid, spilling the dark brew over the rim and onto her lap. Her muffled groan bore evidence to the scalding heat that penetrated her skirts and burned her leg, and she came instantly to her feet, the china cup clanked hurriedly back into its saucer.

"Oh Ashlee, really," Dominique barked crossly. It wasn't so much Ashlee's clumsiness that disturbed Dominique as it was the fact that her stepdaughter had drawn everyone's attention away from her. After a brief examination of the damage done to Ashlee's dress, she curtly ordered, "Go to your room and change. But don't expect us to wait dinner on you."

For once in Ashlee's life, she was thankful the woman had dismissed her from the table. Under ordinary circumstances, she would have been embarrassed; but not this time. All she wanted to do was get as far away as she possibly could and not waste a minute doing it. Without bothering to look at any of the men watching her, especially Rhys Sinclair, she whirled and raced off.

"I'll be very glad when Perrin arrives, Arthur," Dominique sighed irritably as she purposely sat down next to the handsome man with sandy blond hair. "Maybe he can straighten her around."

"Dominique, it was an accident," Arthur argued.

"Just like it's an accident every time she goes behind your back and spends the afternoon with that Krayer woman?" She unfolded her napkin and spread it across her lap. "She may have you fooled, Arthur, but I know where she goes at least once every day. And if you're not careful, she'll wind up with the same notions her mother had about being an actress."

Rhys wasn't sure exactly when it all fell into place, only that he had Dominique to thank for it. And now that he knew, it explained a lot of things, the most puzzling being why he thought he knew Ashlee Redington before today. Settling back in his chair with his arms folded over his chest, a vague smile sparkling in his eyes, Rhys mentally plotted out a sure way to trap the beautiful little thief that had plagued his thoughts of late.

Chapter Six

As usual, the casino was crowded when Rhys entered through the wide double doors and edged his way toward the long black lacquered bar with its brass foot rail. Thick leather trimmed the edge of the white marbled top, and behind it was a huge mirror that ran the entire length of the bar. Three monstrous chandeliers hung from the richly painted cathedral ceiling overhead and illuminated every inch of the place. But as Rhys ordered a drink, he knew that even in a dimly lit cafe he'd have no trouble spotting the illusive woman in his dreams, for now that vision had a name—Ashlee Redington.

Cupping his glass in one hand, he leaned against the thick padding at his elbow and centered his attention on a far table crowded with players, in the middle of which stood Ashlee. She had changed from the dark green dress she had worn into the dining room to the customary black attire of the dealers. Its style, intended to be subtle, failed to hide the feminine curves he knew so well. She had not returned to dinner and although Thomas thought it was because she was embarrassed, Rhys suspected it had nothing to do with how she felt about spilling coffee on herself. If he was right about her—and he was reasonably sure he was—she had stayed away because of him. He smiled as he watched her and took a sip of his drink. It must have been horrifying for her to learn that the man who could identify her as a thief would be staying around for a while—and worse, yet, to be living *and* working right alongside of her!

Through the course of dinner, Rhys got the distinct impression that Dominique and Ashlee were constantly at each other's throats and that while Arthur presented a front of being his own man, it was truly his wife who ruled the lives of the Redington clan. Rhys sensed the man's love for both his women, but because of the one minor flaw in Arthur's character, he allowed Dominique free rein in the handling of his daughter. That became evident when Dominique told Rhys that Ashlee would be marrying Perrin Fabron, Dominique's cousin, just as soon as the young man arrived from Paris. It was rather obvious the marriage had been prearranged when Rhys saw the frown on Arthur's face at the mention of Fabron and heard the man's comment on how he hoped he was doing the right thing by his daughter. He went on to explain to Rhys and Thomas that Ashlee had grown up without a woman's influence, that other than himself and his close friend, John Hardin, Ashlee never received the guidance a young woman should have, and that growing up in the midst of gamblers wasn't a proper education. He blamed Ashlee's reluctance to accept Dominique's authority on that fact and justified his willingness to allow her to marry a total stranger by stating that a change in her life style, such as living in France, would be the best solution. He hadn't, however, admitted that part of it until after Dominique had excused herself from the table in order to change before going to work in the casino. Rhys had no way of knowing if Arthur felt the same toward him, but he was comfortable with the man, sensing a good friendship would develop between them given half a chance. Thus,

174

he took the opportunity to gently pry into Arthur's personal life by asking about Priscilla Krayer and what kind of persuasion the woman might have had over Ashlee. The man's reaction hadn't been at all what Rhys expected.

There was an unmistakable look of hatred in Arthur's expression and the muscle in his cheek flexed repeatedly as he sat there, apparently trying to control his rage at the mention of the woman's name. A long while passed before his blue eyes softened and he visibly relaxed. He poured a fresh cup of coffee and added a scant teaspoon of sugar as he related his story about Ashlee's mother and why he strongly objected to his daughter's friendship with anyone connected to the theater. Yet, as he calmly retold the painful happenings of his past, he confessed that some good had come out of Priscilla and Ashlee's relationship. Miss Krayer had taught Ashlee to read and write. It might have been from the scripts of a play but, just the same, Ashlee could read. And before Arthur married Dominique, Ashlee had managed the business's books. A smile had broken the serious line of Arthur's mouth when he reluctantly admitted he suspected Ashlee of taking the ledgers to Priscilla for help. Maybe Ashlee was rebellious, but Arthur had to admit it was the one thing about her he loved most. No one would run her life for her unless she wanted it that way. Then he laughed. It would be interesting to see how she would get out of marrying Perrin Fabron. His last statement before leaving his new friends had been that although he had a lot to thank Priscilla Krayer for, he would never be able to forgive people like her for what they had done to him and his family. They had broken his heart and forced his daughter to grow up not knowing her mother.

Rhys had remained quiet as he watched Arthur walk away. The man had tried to convince them that the day Veronica Darnell had walked out on him had been the day he closed her out of his life. He had tried, but Rhys hadn't believed him. Arthur still cared for his first wife even though he was married to another.

Thomas had excused himself then, telling Rhys that all the excitement and travel of the past two days had him exhausted and he wanted nothing else but to collapse in a soft feather bed. Evidently Thomas hadn't drawn the same conclusions about Ashlee Redington as Rhys had, and since Rhys wasn't absolutely sure at this point— although he would have bet his plantation and steamboat on it—he decided to get the proof he needed before telling Thomas. Thomas was a fairly good poker player, but whenever he held an exceptional hand, he'd tug on his earlobe and give it away. Rhys often considered telling Thomas about it, since in a way he felt like he was cheating the man. Once he presented Thomas with the facts in this little venture he would tell him, explaining that the reason he hadn't done so right off was because he couldn't take the chance of Thomas's spoiling everything by pulling on his ear. He was sure Thomas wouldn't be able to mask his glee at uncovering Sally White's true identity the first time he looked into Ashlee's beautiful blue eyes. The truth of the matter was that Rhys wasn't sure he could either. She was a foxy little creature and he'd thoroughly enjoy catching her in his lair.

Content now to simply watch her from across the room, he lifted his glass to his lips and blinked when the diamond in his ring, reflecting a flash of pastel colors, caught his eye. Remembering Ashlee's comment on his grandfather's acquired wealth, he laughed softly at the irony of it. Todd Sinclair might have tricked someone out of his money, but he never would have stolen it. Ashlee, on the other hand, had and she had quite flippantly accused someone she didn't even know of the very crime she had committed. Staring at the wide gold band with its gleaming stones, he suddenly remembered another piece of jewelry his grandmother had given him. It had been the stickpin Ashlee had taken from his lapel as he lay unconscious, a victim of her scheme. That pin meant nearly as much to him as his grandmother's ring, for it had been the lady's gift to her husband on the fiftieth anniversary of their wedding day. Of all her grandchildren, she had wanted her oldest to have it. Unlike Rhys's three brothers, he had the blond hair and dark brown eyes of Todd Sinclair and, more importantly, his carefree, adventurous nature. Part of Rhys's anger that morning after the robbery on the *Mississippi Queen* had been the thought that he would never see that pin again. Now it was a different story. Ashlee had it, or at least she knew where it was and he was going to get it back if he had to wring her pretty little neck to do it. A devilish gleam twinkled in his eyes. He'd prefer a friendlier form of incentive, one she knew all too well because of him. His gaze shifted back to her as she dealt the cards she held and laughed at something one of the players had said. Suddenly an idea came to mind when he remembered a method his grandfather used to trap a thief. There was no reason why it wouldn't work with Ashlee. He'd visit a jeweler in the morning and hopefully within a few days he'd put his plan into action.

Lifting his drink once more to finish off the whiskey, Rhys's gaze drifted out over the rim of the glass and fell upon the one man who held the key to this mystery— John Hardin. This burly character knew why Ashlee would steal from her own father and what she did with the money. Yet Rhys's first deduction was more logical: a good friend gone bad. But if he were right, could it mean Ashlee hated her father or just wanted some way to get rid of her stepmother? Rhys had seen through Dominique the moment he met her. She was a fortune hunter and maybe Ashlee knew it too. Could the solution then be that Arthur's best friend, along with his daughter, had come up with a way of exposing Dominique for what she truly was? Were they stealing every dollar they could lay their hands on, putting it in a bank account under a phony name, and just biding their time until Arthur was forced to sell for little or nothing, praying then Dominique would leave him? Would they, by chance, be the new buyers of Belle Chasse, done by a proxy? An inventive plan, if that was the case, but one that was doomed from the moment they made the mistake of stealing from Rhys Sinclair.

He smiled as he set his empty glass on the bar and ordered a second drink, imagining how surprised the alluringly naive young woman would be once she learned who her father's new partner was, and more so that he had figured out what she did when she was away from home for an evening. Tossing down a coin to pay for his drink, he picked up his glass and started toward the blackjack table surrounded by a great number of men, the majority of whom Rhys doubted wanted to play as much as flirt with the dealer.

One of the things that made Belle Chasse a class above all the other casinos in the area was that Arthur had as many women dealers as men, and none of them were allowed to share a drink or an amorous moment with any of the customers during hours or on their own time. If they did and he heard about it, he fired them. Arthur wasn't running a brothel and didn't want his girls acting like it. That aspect of the gambling house added a little second interest to its customers to see if they would be the one to make the girls break the rule. It never worked, but the men never quit trying. And of all the women dealers Arthur employed, his daughter was considered the grand prize—and the least likely ever to be won. She was friendly enough to the customers, but only at the tables. When her job was finished for the night, she wouldn't waste a moment securing her privacy behind

178

the locked door of her room. And wherever Ashlee Redington went, John Hardin wasn't far behind. Rhys had already been cautioned about the man's protectiveness toward the young woman the first day he arrived at the hotel. Under different conditions, he might have paid attention to the warning. But Ashlee and he had shared something everyone else had to be content only thinking about, and Rhys felt he had the right to say and do anything he wanted . . . not to mention that she owed him! Given the time, Rhys was sure Ashlee would slip and say something that would give her away. For now, he'd work on John.

The man had stationed himself about fifteen feet away from Ashlee's table and near the bar. He sat comfortably on a tall stool where he could keep an eye on his young ward and any rowdy customers who might have to be unceremoniously escorted from the place before tempers flared and a fight broke out. His huge muscles strained the seams of his black coat as if in some obscure way he warned that he was no man to be taken lightly. The grim expression on his face added to the menacing air his bulky physique displayed, and although he couldn't be deemed ugly even with the shaved head, he wasn't the type with whom most ladies would choose to flirt nor any man tempt into conversation. Rhys Sinclair, however, wasn't just any man. Setting his glass on the bar next to John Hardin, he leaned back against the leather padding and took a cheroot from his inside pocket.

"Miss Redington seems to be quite popular," he said, lighting the cigar. He tossed the match in the ashtray next to his glass.

John's green eyes moved to look at Rhys then returned to watch the game, the only acknowledgment he made indicating that he had heard Rhys's comment.

"But then it's understandable," Rhys went on, not the least bit discouraged. "She's very beautiful and can play a game quite convincingly. It's a novel way to win—by using a distraction. Most men would be fooled by it."

"A distraction, Mr. Sinclair?" John's deep voice asked after a while. His eyes remained on the young woman, who hadn't noticed that John had been drawn into conversation by another. "None of the dealers at Belle Chasse cheat, sir."

"I'm sure they don't," Rhys replied smoothly, taking a puff on his cheroot. "Forgive me if I made it sound as though I thought they would."

John sensed he shouldn't respond. He knew Sinclair was testing him, hoping to trick him into saying something that would give the man an edge, a slight glimmer of a clue. But then again, John wasn't positive Rhys Sinclair had the vaguest inkling of what he and Ashlee were up to. He decided not to press his luck.

"I think I should warn you, Mr. Sinclair," he answered instead, folding his arms across his wide chest, "that just because you'll be working here now won't give you any special privileges with other members of the staff." He briefly turned dark green eyes on his companion. "Especially Arthur Redington's daughter."

Rhys smiled secretively at the man's shrewd ability to change the subject. "And you, sir, misunderstand," he calmly replied as the man's threat had little effect. Rhys was never one to openly challenge another in a show of strength. Actually, he'd had enough of fighting during the war and would prefer other means of solving a disagreement. But, so pressed, he'd never back down either. He covertly studied the man's size from the corner of his eye, certain that if it ever came to blows he would no doubt have a few bruises to show for it. "The only privilege I seek is to learn Miss Redington's secret."

John could feel the perspiration begin to fill every pore, but his expression didn't change. He turned his head toward Rhys and asked unobtrusively, "Secret, Mr.

180

Sinclair? What secret is that?"

Rhys studied the cheroot he rolled between his fingers. "How she manages to play the game so well."

Just a hint of a smile appeared in John's eyes. "Practice, Mr. Sinclair, practice." He watched the game again. "And having a good teacher."

John Hardin's words to anyone else would have seemed the mere stating of fact. To Rhys, they held an ambiguous tone. "You, perhaps?"

"Perhaps," came the simple, noncommittal reply.

Rhys took a long puff on the cheroot, silent for a time as he too watched the beautiful raven-haired temptress deftly deal out the next round of cards. "And what would it take for someone like me to learn such a skill?"

"Mr. Sinclair, your reputation at cards precedes you. 'Tis why I suppose Mr. Redington hired you and rumor of it spread so quickly," John chuckled. "You are the one who should teach."

Realizing that John Hardin would probably excuse himself from his company rather than chance exposing his lovely friend by a slip of the tongue, Rhys decided to try elsewhere for the proof he needed. Turning around, he snuffed out his cheroot in the ashtray, swallowed his drink, and looked over at John. "It's exactly what I plan to do, Mr. Hardin," he smiled crookedly then walked away, missing the worried frown that came over the other's face.

An hour later after Rhys had returned to his room, removed his coat and shoes, and stretched out on the bed, cradling his head in his folded arms, he lay staring up at the dark shadows on the ceiling above him. A vague smile parted his lips as he thought of Ashlee and how panicky she must be, wanting to run away from him yet knowing she couldn't. The last piece of evidence he needed in confirming his idea that he was on the right track had come from talking with Michael, the desk clerk, Elaine,

181

and two of the waitresses from the restaurant. None of them could remember seeing John or Ashlee any time during Sunday afternoon or evening, and it was well past noon today before either of them made an appearance.

Elaine had given him an interesting bit of information when she said that she had had to close up the casino that night because Ashlee never showed. Whenever Dominique was gone overnight, it was Ashlee's job to see the money locked in the safe; because Ashlee wasn't there, Elaine had had to do it. When Rhys asked if that was uncommon, Elaine said yes, that it had never happened before, and the only reason Mr. Redington didn't hear about it was because Ashlee had made her promise not to tell, giving Elaine some feeble excuse about having been sick and gone to bed early.

Michael had told him that John and Ashlee often spent their afternoons off together going for carriage rides or a picnic when the weather allowed, and usually because of Dominique. Few people at Belle Chasse liked the demanding Frenchwoman, including Ashlee and John, but they were the only ones that seemed able to escape her. Therefore, Michael didn't find anything wrong with their disappearance, except that the pair seldom left the hotel if they didn't have to. And that aspect of it puzzled Michael. Mr. and Mrs. Redington had traveled to Laplace early Sunday morning and everyone knew they wouldn't return until the next day. There had been no need for Ashlee and John to leave, but they had.

Oh, there was a need, Rhys grinned in the ashen streams of light coming through the window of his room. *But neither one of them expected their little adventure to turn out the way it did. Especially Ashlee.* His brown eyes darkened lustfully as he thought of the shapely blonde who came to his cabin the night before, and he wondered what the little vixen would have done if he hadn't been so careless and drank the whiskey she had drugged. Could it be they

182

would have made love until the morning intruded and drove them apart? He groaned suddenly, recalling the blood stains he had found. Ashlee had been a virgin until then, a fact that caught him completely off guard and totally confused him. If he had been drinking, he would have blamed his intoxicated state for not having known the minute he touched her. But he wasn't drunk and he hadn't met any resistance on her part. Obviously, she thought he'd be unconscious before it went too far, and that's what confused him. Why hadn't she found a way to stall him off long enough to save her . . . virginity? God, he hated even thinking the word. There was only one virgin he had planned to bed, and she was to have been his new bride.

He was suddenly struck by a sharp barb of jealousy and his mouth tightened in a hard line. Dominique had said Ashlee was engaged. He had known his share of women and had even considered marrying Melody. But he had never experienced the same kind of feeling for them that he felt right now for Ashlee. Nor could he honestly say what it was. All he knew for certain was that he didn't want her marrying Perrin Fabron. Angered by the thought, he sprang off the bed and yanked down the covers. Well, a lot could happen before then, so he wouldn't worry about it. Stripping off his clothes, he slid into bed and pounded out his frustrations on the pillow before irritably finding a comfortable spot in which to lie. He closed his eyes, intent on going to sleep as quickly as possible. A moment later, he rolled onto one side and stared at the platinum beams of light falling softly into the room, a troubled frown marring his handsome brow.

The ticking of the clock on the dresser began to grate on his nerves. Thinking a damning look its way would silence the noise and allow him to fall asleep, he cast his attention upon it, groaning out loud once he saw what time it was and realizing he had been lying in bed wide

183

awake for more than an hour. Heaving an exasperated sigh, he threw the covers off his naked frame and reached for his clothes. By now the casino would be closed so he couldn't go there and have a drink. Maybe a walk in the crisp night air would help tire him out. He jerked on his clothes, leaving his coat behind, and irritably left his room.

The lobby was empty as he descended the stairs, except for the night clerk who sat reading the newspaper and didn't bother looking up at him as he stepped onto the marble floor. Although the way was well lighted, the solitude of the usually busy place had an almost eerie feeling to it, and he paused a moment to consider what made it so. As he did, he heard a door open and close from somewhere close by, followed by the light sound of dainty high heels against the floor. A moment later, Ashlee appeared before him on her way from her father's office. Rhys smiled brightly at the startled gasp his unexpected presence had caused once she looked up and saw him.

"I didn't mean to frighten you, Miss Redington," he apologized. "But then I didn't expect to find you here, either. Are you on your way to your room?"

Ashlee had just spent a rather trying ten minutes with her father, attempting to explain why Belle Chasse didn't need another dealer, least of all a Yankee, only to be told that whatever decisions were to be made about the casino were up to him and that she should mind her own business. Nor had Dominique been any help. She had agreed with her husband, and Ashlee knew it was only because the woman found Rhys attractive and having him under her employ meant she could flirt any time she wanted. Totally frustrated and knowing any further argument might only raise a few suspicious questions, she had given up trying to persuade her father—for the time anyway—and left the office to go to her room and sulk. Finding the one who was the cause of her dilemma standing there in the lobby didn't help her mood any, either, and rather than give him an answer she turned abruptly and started for the door leading into the courtyard.

"You really shouldn't walk alone, Miss Redington," he advised, hurrying to catch up and hold the door open for her. "It's late and you never know who might be lurking out there in the shadows just waiting for a chance to get a beautiful woman alone."

Ashlee paused, then cast him a sidelong glance. "Too late," she jeered, bringing an amused chuckle from her companion.

"My intentions are honorable, Miss Redington, I assure you," he smiled, following her outside.

"Depends on one's definition of honorable." She hurried her step when he moved in beside her, but his long strides were not easy to outdo. Short of running, she realized she wouldn't be able to get away from him. Venting an irritable sigh, she stopped in the middle of the stone path. "What do you want, Mr. Sinclair?"

"Want?" he repeated. "I don't want anything except maybe to make peace between us, since I'll be working here from now on."

"We don't have to be friends for you to work here," she crisply told him. "And if I can figure out how, I'll see your job is short-lived."

The soft light from the torches danced across her face, enhancing the anger shining in her pale blue eyes, and Rhys thought he had never seen a more beautiful woman in his entire life. It was baffling to him why he hadn't recognized her right off. He had never seen eyes of that particular color before, and it should have been enough to jolt his memory and discover the connection. He mentally shrugged it off. It didn't matter now anyway. He knew who she was, and with a little effort he'd trick her into admitting it.

"I'm sorry you feel that way," he said, gently taking her arm and starting them off again at a slower pace.

The warmth of his casual touch sent a searing heat charging through her, and Ashlee's head began to spin. She had never met anyone like him, and she couldn't understand why she didn't find the mere sight of him repulsive. After all, he was a northerner, and she hated northerners. She sucked in a breath and let it out slowly, quietly.

"I didn't have an opportunity to ask if you were all right after you spilled your coffee earlier. I trust no harm came of it."

Ashlee could only manage to shake her head in response.

"Good," he smiled down at her. They traveled a few more steps in silence, then, "Have you ever seen the play being presented next door at the theater? If you haven't, you should. Miss Krayer is an excellent actress. She really should consider teaching drama." He stopped suddenly and faced her. "Or does she already?"

Ashlee's cheeks burned. "I—I don't really know. I mean, I hardly know the woman, so I couldn't say," she explained in a rush of nervousness.

Rhys hid his smile. "Hmmm," he frowned. "I would have thought the two of you would be friends."

Ashlee could feel herself tremble apprehensively. "Why would you think that?"

"Oh, I don't know," he leisurely replied, gently reaching up to brush a stray tendril of hair from her brow. "Your stepmother doesn't appear to be the type a young woman can relate to and I figured you'd need a friend to talk to from time to time. Miss Krayer seems the obvious choice—being single and living right next door."

He let his fingertips lightly trace the delicate bone structure of her temple, cheek, and jaw. Though he

186

planned to only tease her, to trap her into saying something that would force her to admit to the truth, he found the temptation to kiss her slightly parted lips more than he could resist. Without a thought to her reaction, he lowered his head.

Ashlee's mind reeled. She knew she should stop him. But for some unexplainable reason, she couldn't. After all, it wasn't like they were strangers. As his handsome face descended slowly toward hers, her pulse raced in an explosion of wild titillation as she anticipated the rapturous sensation of his lips pressed against her own. Certain she would faint, she closed her eyes, raised her chin, and waited breathlessly.

Rhys felt his blood warm the instant he touched her, and he desperately longed to sweep her up in his arms and carry her to his bed. They had met under some very peculiar circumstances, but he had known then that she would play an important part in his life. Kissing her now only reaffirmed it. Slanting his mouth across hers, he brought his arms up around her and pulled her into his embrace, feeling her delicate body molded willingly against his own. His breathing as well as his pulse quickened. He kissed her tenderly, passionately, running the tip of his tongue over her lips then pushing inside. Every nerve in his body came alive. Had there been no danger of intruders, he would have stripped away their clothes and made love to her there in the courtyard on a bed of grass and beneath a blanket of stars.

Ashlee couldn't stop the sensuous excitement that coursed through her with his fiery kiss, nor did she want to. It was a heady intoxication that no other man had ever aroused in her, and she wanted it to go on forever. The thin cloth of his shirt failed to mask the hard muscles of his chest and she slowly ran her hands up over the sinewy ripples beneath it, reveling in the wild sensation she experienced and sensing the power he possessed but held in rein. She answered his kiss with equal passion, thinking that if they had met under different conditions and if he wasn't a Yankee, maybe . . . Suddenly, painfully, Ashlee realized what she was doing. Giving him an ounce of encouragement would be disastrous! He'd never go away if he thought she liked him! God, what was wrong with her? Hadn't John warned her not to come near this man? That he was very dangerous? She jerked away from him, gasping for air as she glared up at him. And the damn northerner didn't even know who she was—didn't even remember—probably didn't care! Ohhh, how she loathed him! Without warning, she brought back her hand and slapped his face with enough force behind it to rock him back a step.

"How dare you!" she seethed, turning on her heel and stomping off.

Rhys grinned recklessly as he rubbed his cheek and watched Ashlee hurry away. He should have expected as much from her and wasn't really surprised by it. He had taken advantage of the situation, but he honestly didn't regret it. Feeling her soft curves against him was well worth the slap to his face.

"Think you can get some sleep now, ol' boy?" he chuckled and turned for the lobby.

"I hope you understand why I must return to Jackson, Rhys," Thomas said as the two men finished their breakfast the next morning. "I'd like to stay and help with this, but the telegram said they needed me right away."

"Mmmm," Rhys nodded, chewing on the last bite of bacon then washing it down with a sip of hot coffee. "Of course I do. You've more important things to do and I'm not sure how long this will take me to unravel. It's perfectly all right."

188

"Will you promise to keep me posted on everything?"

"Most assuredly," Rhys guaranteed him.

Thomas was quiet a moment, a thoughtful frown darkening his eyes. "Rhys, what I said yesterday, about not wanting to help financially? I didn't mean it. I hope you know that. If you need some money to—"

Rhys quickly raised a hand. "Say no more. I knew you were only playing and I don't think I'll have to go to that extreme again. Besides, I want you to use every penny you have on your campaign. Mississippi needs you as its senator."

Thomas chuckled mockingly. "I hope its people feel the same way."

"They will after they hear your arguments." After wiping his mouth with his napkin, he tossed the cloth on the table. "So when do you leave?"

Thomas finished off his last bit of coffee and pulled out his pocket watch. "In one hour—that is, of course, if the train is on time." With a sigh, he pushed back from the table and stood. "And right now I better get my bag packed and settle my account with Michael. Will you see me off at the station?"

"Someone should," Rhys joked. "We can't have our new senator getting lost on the way there."

"Very funny," Thomas moaned. He started to say more when his gaze suddenly shifted past Rhys toward the entryway into the restaurant, and he smiled appreciatively instead. "My only regret in leaving," he sighed with a silly look on his face.

Confused by his friend's admission, Rhys frowned and twisted in his chair to see what it was he meant, smiling in accord once he saw Ashlee and her father walking toward them. She wore a soft pink cotton dress trimmed with white lace around the sleeves and the hem of its full skirts. Although the collar flared up around her slim neck and stood in gentle ruffles beneath her chin, the yoke of

189

the gown was made of a sheer, gauzy fabric that only slightly hid the smooth, silky flesh beneath it. Rhys found it difficult to lift his gaze and study the exquisite face haloed in a thick mass of dark, shiny curls. As the couple neared his table, he came to his feet and extended his hand to the eldest Redington.

"Good morning, Rhys, Thomas," Arthur said, shaking both men's hands. "I hope we're not interrupting your breakfast."

"Unfortunately, I was just on my way to my room," Thomas sadly admitted. "I received a telegram asking me to return home on business. The train leaves in an hour."

"I'm sorry to hear that," Arthur frowned. "I was hoping to talk at length with you about your ideas on how to help the south. Is there a chance you might return?"

"Well, I'll make a point of it, but I can't say exactly when right now," Thomas replied. "I only live in Jackson, you know. Maybe I could talk you and your lovely wife and daughter into visiting. The ladies could spend the day at a dress shop while you and I meet with some of my political friends."

Arthur smiled agreeably. "You name the time and we'll be there."

"Good," Thomas grinned.

"And if you'll wait a moment while I talk to Rhys, I'll walk you to your room," Arthur added. "We still have a little time left to discuss a few issues."

Thomas nodded his consent and centered his attention on the bills he pulled from his wallet to pay for his meal, while Arthur turned to the other, his hand gently touching Ashlee's elbow. "I've instructed my daughter to show you around Belle Chasse, Rhys, and introduce you to its personnel. If you'd like, you can keep the room you have or move your things to the staff's quarters in back of the casino. It's a little more private there and most of the employees prefer it. But it's up to you."

"The staff's quarters will be fine," Rhys smiled, thinking it would be the best place to hear rumors or a conversation that might give him an idea on why Arthur's friend and daughter were stealing from him.

"All right. Then after Ashlee's introduced you around, she can show you to your new room," Arthur said. "I've some business to take care of after I talk with Thomas, so if you could come to my office around—oh—ten o'clock, we can discuss the details of your employment and I'll answer any questions you have. Will that be suitable?"

"That would be fine," Rhys agreed. "I have a little business of my own to finish up as well."

"Then I'll leave you in my daughter's care," Arthur nodded, leaning to gently kiss Ashlee's temple. "Show him anything he wishes to see, Ashlee."

"Yes, Papa," she replied quietly, having yet to look at Rhys. And once she had, she could feel her cheeks flame instantly. The expression on his face and the place where his gaze rested blatantly hinted at seeing things her father hadn't had in mind when he said to show Rhys anything he wanted to see. She desperately longed to cross her arms over her bosom and distract his attention away from her rather revealing neckline, but more so to repeat last night's performance and slap his face. When her father had shown up at her bedroom door just after breakfast and announced that he wanted to make Rhys Sinclair feel welcome at Belle Chasse starting with her, she had tried to argue her way out of having to be the man's escort for the next hour or so. It would be very difficult to pretend last night never happened. But her father wouldn't hear of it. Dominique had had to go to the bank on business a short time earlier, and since Arthur wasn't sure how long his wife would be gone, the responsibility fell on Ashlee. John wanted Ashlee to avoid Rhys Sinclair, and her father kept pushing them together. He'd certainly change his mind if he knew what had happened between them and what reason brought him to Belle Chasse. She heaved a mental sigh of exasperation and turned to bid Thomas Bryan farewell. God, how she yearned to do the same for his friend!

"Well, shall we start with the kitchen?" Although it was stated as a question, Ashlee gave him no time to reply. She simply turned around and walked away. If he chose to follow her or not didn't matter one way or another to her. Actually, she'd prefer he didn't or better yet that he fell in the Mississippi and drowned. Shoving open the wide, swinging door, she went into the kitchen, sensing more than seeing his tall, muscular frame right behind her.

The kitchen was about one third the size of the dining hall, with two sets of swinging doors, one for entering, the other for exiting. Eunice had come up with the idea after several crashes occurred that resulted in spilled trays, wasted food, double work, and angry customers too impatient to understand why they must wait twice as long as usual. Two long trestle tables were situated in the center of the room where the cook's assistants peeled potatoes, diced carrots and onions, filleted fish, or prepared bread dough and pastries that would bake in one of the three huge stoves lining the back wall. Overhead hung an enormous variety of pots, pans, and other utensils needed in maintaining the efficiency of a kitchen this large. At one end of the room was a smaller stove used only for heating huge pans of water that were poured into larger pans set on a separate table from the other two. Three people manned this area, washing, drying, and stacking dishes. In all, twelve people worked in the kitchen, all under the management of one, the black woman called Eunice. It was one of the hardest and hottest jobs at Belle Chasse and why the kitchen staff frequently took a break, as they were doing now, out back in the courtyard where they could cool off a moment before the noon hour rush began. However, Eunice seldom did, although both Ashlee and her father repeatedly told her that she should. Therefore, Ashlee wasn't surprised to find the woman at her usual spot, supervising the huge kettles bubbling rhythmically on the stove.

"Good morning, Eunice," she said once the black cook looked up and saw her.

"Mo'ning, Miz Ashlee," Eunice smiled back at her. The warm greeting was short-lived when she spied the gentleman standing next to her mistress.

"Eunice, this is Rhys Sinclair. He'll be working at Belle Chasse for a while. He's Papa's new blackjack dealer, and he'll be staying in the staff's quarters, which means an extra meal has to be sent over." Ashlee intended to make it a brief stop before moving on. If she rushed through this, she wouldn't have to tolerate his presence for very long. But her impassive expression changed to a curious frown once she heard Eunice laugh.

"So's, you is de one whad's got all de girls a'gigglin'," she grinned, her chubby cheeks gleaming with perspiration as she wiped the back of her hand across her brow. "Ah reckon ah kin understand why now's ah sees you fo' myself." Her sparkling brown eyes looked back at Ashlee. "Makes me kinda jealous ah ain't a young thin' like you, Miz Ashlee. Been a long spell since we had us a handsome one like Mistah Sinclair."

Appalled by Eunice's boldness, Ashlee sucked in a breath to remind the servant of her place and that no comment was needed for this one. Handsome or not, he was a northerner and one who came to pick the bones of the failing merchants in the south. He made her giggle, but only because she had duped the pompous Yankee. She found little else about him to make her smile. Eunice should be told that if Mr. Sinclair and others like him had their way, she and everyone at Belle Chasse would be out in the street with no money in their pockets to buy the meagerest sampling of a meal. She opened her mouth to recite every word, quieting when Rhys's deep voice laughed at the black woman's comment.

"And I can't remember when I've received such a fine compliment," he grinned, presenting Eunice with a slight bow. "Nor am I deserving."

Ashlee's eyes narrowed, thinking how she couldn't agree more.

"And please call me Rhys," he went on. "I've never been one who likes formality." To Ashlee's amazement, he crossed the room and paused in front of the huge stove. Lifting the lid on one of the pots, he waited for the cloud of steam to dissipate then sniffed the air. "Smells wonderfully delicious. Lunch?"

"Yassuh," Eunice beamed. "My specialty. French veal stew. Secret is ta let it simmer all mornin'."

Dipping a spoon into the broth, he sampled the hot liquid and moaned approvingly. "Excellent, Eunice. But so far everything that comes out of your kitchen is. My compliments, madam."

Eunice laughed almost as giddily as a young girl experiencing her first encounter with a man. "Thank you, suh. And anytime you want, you can sample anythin' ah is a-fixin'."

Ashlee rolled her eyes, groaning silently. "If you two are finished," she jeered, "I have a lot to show, *Mr.* Sinclair." Her cheeks burned hotly when dark, twinkling eyes glanced back at her. He certainly had a one-track mind! She knew what that look meant. "Shall we go?" she asked, her delicate mouth twisted derisively.

"Whatever you wish," he grinned, waiting until she had turned her back on him before he stole the opportunity to wink at the woman by his side. "She dislikes having to play hostess to me," he whispered confidentially, then smiled brightly and followed Ashlee from the kitchen.

Eunice remained unmoving long after the couple had left her, a puzzled frown wrinkling her dark brow. She had to agree with the gentleman. Miss Ashlee wasn't too pleased about the situation, but Eunice couldn't imagine why. Shrugging her thick shoulders in dismissal, she began whistling a cheery tune and set about stirring the batter for a chocolate three-layer cake.

"Since all the girls are giggling already," Ashlee said, more crisply than she intended, "I'll forego introducing you to them. They obviously know who you are and it won't take long for a man like you to learn their names . . . one at a time." She walked a brisk two steps ahead of him, unaware that he was thoroughly enjoying the sight of her trim waist and swaying hips, the curve of her spine, her long, slender neck, and the thick black hair that hung in soft ringlets down the back of her head.

"A man like me?" he asked, masking his amusement at her cool aloofness to him. "And what kind of a man am I?"

She stopped abruptly and spun around. "A Yankee . . . a northerner . . . a—a—carpetbagger!" she snapped, her blue eyes flashing icy sparks.

A lazy smile spread across his face. "I can't deny the first two, Ashlee, but I hardly see myself as a carpetbagger. I haven't settled in the south for financial gain."

"Then why don't you go home?" she sneered. "And my name is Miss Redington to you."

One tawny brow lifted. "I can understand your resentment of those who have come for that purpose, Miss Redington, and I expect it from most. Your father, however, doesn't lump us all together as you so obviously have. While you're busy condemning all northerners, he's busy using our help to rebuild Louisiana. It would be to the south's as well as your advantage if you did the

195

same instead of letting your prejudices and narrow-mindedness affect your judgment of people before you get to know them."

"Narrow-minded—" She uttered the word in mounting rage. "I'll have you know, Mr. Sinclair, that until the war things were going along very smoothly here. Everyone was happy with the way things were. Then some brilliant congressman decided to mess it up. We didn't want war, but you Yankees asked for it."

"How old are you, Miss Redington?"

The question caught Ashlee so off guard that it took her a full minute to respond. "Twenty. But what has that to do with anything?"

"It means you were old enough to understand the events of the war and that you probably know it was General Beauregard, a Confederate officer, who fired on Fort Sumter. The north had no alternative but to take arms. And just to set you straight, Miss Redington, *no one* wanted war. But it's over now and all of us should do our best to join together and reunite the states as one nation—the way our forefathers intended it to be." He hadn't meant to lecture, but her attitude baffled him. Her father didn't see things the way she did. How could two members of the same family disagree on such an important issue?

Ashlee's temper soared. How dare he insinuate that she didn't want peace . . . or unity! Of course she did. *She* was the one who pushed her father into politics! Her nostrils flaring, she took a deep breath and stood with arms akimbo. "Just to set *you* straight, Mr. Sinclair," she grated out, keeping her voice low when she noticed the curious stares of some of the customers, "that's exactly what I want. It's you vultures I'd like to see sent back where you came from."

"Vultures?" he echoed in surprise.

"Yes, vultures," she hissed. "That's what people like

you really are. You're preying on innocent victims of war, stealing all they have left, and laughing while you do it. Well, we'll just see who has the last laugh."

The heat of anger in his dark brown eyes disappeared, and although the smile didn't reach his lips, she could see it sparkling in the hypnotizing look he gave her. "*I'm* not the one who's been stealing," he said calmly, quietly.

The muscles across Ashlee's chest tightened instantly and a flood of panic nearly forced her to flee. Was this his subtle way of telling her that he knew who she was? Unable to look at him a moment longer lest he know the truth for certain in her eyes, she cast her gaze away from him. It was best to change the subject, and quickly, before she gave way to her emotions. "I think you will agree, Mr. Sinclair," she said somewhat shakily, "that you and I do not see eye to eye, and if we chanced discuss the issue at length a hundred years, it would do naught to change our differences. Therefore, I suggest we discontinue any mention of the matter and try to get along, since *father* has thought you worthy of his employ. I shall do as he instructed and show you around Belle Chasse. But once you're settled and your questions answered, we shall have no further reason to speak to one another. Is that acceptable, Mr. Sinclair?"

He was quiet a moment before he spoke. "If that's what you wish," he answered softly, and Ashlee could feel his eyes rake over her. "But I think we'll be hard pressed to keep it that way since we'll be working . . . eating . . . sleeping under the same roof."

There was a hint of intimacy in his tone that made Ashlee's pulse quicken. The rogue! She'd have to make doubly certain her door was locked every night! And she'd be very careful about being alone in the courtyard again. Forcing herself to pretend that his words, his very closeness, didn't affect her, she sucked air into her lungs and gave him her most contemptuous look. "I seldom eat in the dining hall, and the courtyard divides our quarters. The only time we shall see each other will be in the casino, and I'll make every effort to have your table as far away from mine as possible."

His smile wrinkled the small scar near his eye. "Then perhaps there'll be no problem after all, Miss Redington."

Ashlee hadn't expected him to give in so easily and a momentary pang of disappointment kinked the smooth line of her brow. She blinked it away, feeling suddenly uncomfortable over her outburst, and spoke more quietly. "If you're to meet with my father at ten, then we'd best hurry, Mr. Sinclair. There is much of Belle Chasse to show you."

He nodded politely and extended a hand for her to lead the way, his eyes lowering to continue his appraisal of her trim form once she walked ahead of him.

They spent the next hour touring the restaurant, hotel, and casino, making introductions and going over the rules each employee was expected to follow. The uniform of the dealers, he was told, was black, with a white shirt for the men. If he preferred, Belle Chasse would furnish his clothes for less than regular cost by using the hotel seamstresses. Everyone greeted the handsome newcomer with equal warmth, a few with obvious reservation once they learned he was a northerner. It annoyed Ashlee that more of them didn't feel the same as she about the man. But then, they hadn't experienced what she had, only to be forgotten as if the interlude had never occurred.

The last place they visited was the deserted casino that didn't open for business until noon. It was there Ashlee informed him that none of the dealers were allowed to drink while working, no matter how much the customer insisted on paying for it. If there was any trouble, Rhys was to motion for John Hardin, Jason Palmer, or Hank

Newell, the casino's safeguard against any ruckuses that might disturb the other customers, before trying to handle it on his own. His job was to deal, nothing more. He was to work one hour, have a fifteen-minute break, then work another hour, and so on. His shift would be from eight o'clock in the evening to two o'clock in the morning, with Sundays off. Any tips the patron gave him were his to keep. Every hour on the hour house winnings were collected from the dealers by John Hardin and taken to the office where Dominique handled it from there.

Rhys had quietly listened to everything she had to say, thoroughly enjoying the smooth, velvet quality of her voice, the ravishing profile she presented him whenever she turned away to point something out or speak to one of the employees, and the way the soft shade of her pink dress added a rosy hue to her flawless skin—he listened until her last comment. If his assumption about John Hardin were correct, then the man must have taken a detour en route to the office more than once while entrusted with the casino's profits. And catching him would be simple enough. Rhys would follow him. Pulling a cheroot from his pocket, he smiled to himself, thinking how right Thomas had been about solving this mystery in a week's time. He struck a match and exhaled the smoke from his cigar, a vague frown drawing his sandy brows together. *Simple?* he thought. *Yes, too simple.* Something wasn't quite right, but he'd check it out anyway. Lifting the cheroot to his lips again, his gaze absently drifted back to Ashlee, who stood glaring at him.

"I detest those things," she said, watching the opaque cloud curl upward.

Rhys chuckled lightly. "The cigar or the one who smokes it?"

Her dainty nose was elevated a notch. "Both," she replied. "Either one makes me sick. Together, they're insufferable."

Unaffected by her insult, he held the cheroot out to study it more closely. "Yes, I guess they are offensive to some women. I know my mother could never tolerate their odor whenever she was carrying a child." His brown sparkling eyes shifted to look at her as if to suggest her possible state of motherhood as the cause.

Ashlee stifled a gasp at his bold implication, but her outrage quickly vanished at the sudden revelation that because of him there was a chance of that being true. She could feel her brow dampen with perspiration. Not wanting to even think about the possibility, much less discuss anything related to it, she turned away from him.

"Do you have any questions about the casino?" The words came weak and unsteady.

There could be more than one reason why Ashlee reacted to his statement the way she had. Rhys elected to think it was because he was right about Ashlee Redington being Sally White, and until he reminded her of what had happened in his cabin, she hadn't given much thought to the consequences of spending an evening in his arms. His blood warmed with the notion of their doing it again, though he couldn't see much chance of it.

"Only one," he answered. "Which table will be mine?"

"That one," she said, pointing a slender finger.

He cocked one brow. "I thought they played poker over there," he replied, jutting a thumb over his shoulder in the opposite direction indicated by his lovely companion.

"They do," she told him. "But you're dealing blackjack . . . over there." She stressed the location with another point of her finger.

"Mmm," he sighed, as if confused. "Then Arthur must have changed his mind."

"About what?" she asked with a suspicious frown. She had a dreadful feeling she already knew his answer, and

200

before he opened his mouth to reply, she stiffened her spine and faced him with tiny fists resting on her hips. "No, don't tell me. Papa hired you on to deal poker." When he stood mutely still with the cheroot clamped between his teeth, she demanded loudly, "Well?"

Rhys hid his smile and took the cigar from his mouth. "You told me not to tell you," he teased, and gave serious consideration to retreating a step when he saw the rage flare up in her beautiful blue eyes.

"Well, we'll just see about that," she fumed and spun around, heading for the exit. "The tour is over, Mr. Sinclair," she called back to him without breaking stride. "And if you have any questions, ask somebody else!"

Rhys watched her go, admiring the slim waist he was sure he could easily encircle with his hands, the agitated swish of pink skirts, and the bouncing black curls that he longed to feel between his fingers.

"I think Mr. Redington is about to wish he had stayed in Laplace," a voice behind him said, and Rhys turned to see a young man walking toward him.

"I got the feeling someone was in for it, but I wasn't sure who," Rhys half laughed. "Have any idea why my being a poker dealer upsets her?"

A bright smile flashed across the other's freckled face as he reached up and ran his fingers through his flaming red hair. He wasn't much older than Ashlee and even though he was nearly a head shorter than Rhys, his width made up for what he lacked in stature. Rhys suddenly wondered what this man and John Hardin ate for breakfast. If he weren't one of the men hired to keep peace in the casino, he should have been. A meaty fist to the jaw or a beefy arm locked around an opponent's neck would certainly change a rowdy customer's mind in a hurry.

"You must be Rhys Sinclair," he said, holding out his hand in a warm greeting. "I'm Hank Newell. Sorry I

201

wasn't around when Miss Redington introduced you to the rest of the staff. I—ah—went to see my girl."

"I guessed that's who you were," Rhys admitted, amazed by the gentleness of the man's handshake.

"I've known Ashlee since she was a little girl. My father used to work for Mr. Redington until a couple of years ago when he was killed in the war. It's always been her dream to be a dealer at a poker table. She has quite a fascination with the game." Plucking an overturned chair from its resting place on top of the table, he settled it easily on the floor and straddled it. "The truth is she wants to play not deal. I always tease her about it being a man's game and she'd lose every penny she had, but that only seemed to make her more intent on getting in a game. She's been after her father for years to let her deal, and the only way he could postpone it a while longer was to tell her that the next time the job came open, she'd have it. He doesn't want her doing it."

"Oh," Rhys laughed. "No wonder she's angry."

"Yeah, you certainly haven't won her friendship," Hank chuckled. "She'll pout about it for a while, but give her time. She'll get over it. She's a great little lady, that one." He smiled and crossed his thick arms along the chair's back rail. "And she certainly loves her father. Too bad he had to marry Dominique."

"I get the impression no one likes Mrs. Redington."

Hank shrugged. "Mr. Redington does," he replied, his green eyes alight with humor. "Oh, she's not too bad, really. Not to the staff. It's just that we don't like the way she treats Ashlee."

"Yes, I got a taste of it last night," Rhys admitted with a lift of sandy brows as he glanced toward the doorway where Ashlee had gone.

"Have you heard it was Dominique's idea Ashlee marry this Perrin Fabron character?" he went on in a rush. "Ashlee wasn't meant to marry some Frenchman

202

she hasn't even met!"

His interest aroused, Rhys leaned an elbow against the edge of the bar and clasped his wrist. "Does that mean she already has someone else in mind?"

Hank shook his head. "Not that I know of. We all gave up trying a long time ago. But there's got to be someone special just waiting to find her."

"We?" Rhys queried with a faint smile that made Hank laugh, embarrassed.

"Yeah, we. There's a lot of young men in New Orleans that want to marry her. I've been in love with Ashlee since she and I were no taller than this table," he confessed, slapping an opened palm against the mentioned item. "And about the same time I realized it would never happen. We're too different. So I'm content to act as her . . . *big* brother." He laughed as he rubbed his wide belly with both hands.

"Maybe that's why she hasn't found that special someone," Rhys observed playfully. "Between you and Mr. Hardin, you scare off any potential hopefuls."

"Only the wrong ones," Hank grinned. "That's what will make him special. He won't scare."

"She and Mr. Hardin are close, aren't they?"

"Very."

"Perhaps he's the one."

"Not a chance," Hank strongly objected. "John's too old for her."

"Age shouldn't matter."

"Well, it does with John. Besides, he's a friend of Mr. Redington, and he's known Ashlee since she was a little girl. He looks at her like the daughter he was cheated out of."

"Cheated?" Rhys responded, most curious.

"Yeah, John never got married. I doubt he ever will. And why should he now? He's got Ashlee."

Rhys lifted the cheroot he still held and studied its

long, slender shape, wondering just how far this man would be willing to talk about Ashlee and her huge friend. Hank might unknowingly give him the answers he needed. But he had to be careful how he worded his inquiry. Hank had already admitted he loved Ashlee, and if he didn't threaten to blacken Rhys's eye for asking too many personal questions, he most certainly would change the subject or walk away.

"You make it sound like Mr. Hardin would do just about anything for her."

"Rob, cheat, or steal," Hank laughed. "Like most of us here at Belle Chasse would do if she asked." He cocked his head to one side, studying his companion. "Given time, so will you."

Rhys met the man's amused look with a smile. "Perhaps. But right now with the way she feels about me, I don't think she'd trust me. She already thinks I steal . . . from her."

"Yeah, she's a little bitter toward northerners. I am too, I guess. But you seem different, and I try to judge the man, not the place where he lives."

This was the opening he had hoped for. "Then maybe you'll tell me if you agree with Miss Redington."

"About what?"

"I've heard Belle Chasse is losing money. Miss Redington blames—to quote her—people like me, meaning northerners. But after she explained the security in the casino, I can't see how anyone could manage to steal a dime from the place."

Hank sighed thoughtfully. "Yeah, I know Mr. Redington is having trouble. Started at the outbreak of the war. For a while there, just before he married Dominique, things were getting better. Now, all of a sudden, they ain't. Nobody can figure it out, and unless you look over the books to balance out the cost of running the place versus what's taken in, you'll never know for certain." Cautiously, Hank glanced toward the door then over his shoulder to make sure no one had come in while his attention was on Rhys. "Some of us think maybe—and I do mean maybe 'cause we don't have no way of knowing—somebody who works for Mr. Redington might be helping himself to something that isn't his."

"Really?" Rhys tried to sound surprised. "Any guesses on who?"

"Naw," Hank replied with a shake of his red head. "Besides Mrs. Redington, John's the only one who can get his hands on the money, and he'd cut off his arm and both legs before he'd ever steal from his friend. Nobody knows the whole story about John but rumor has it that Mr. Redington saved his life once, a long time ago." Pushing himself to his feet, he added, "But somebody, somewhere, must have his hand in the till. Don't figure otherwise. Well, I gotta go. Nice talkin' to ya, Rhys, and welcome to Belle Chasse. I think you'll like it here."

"Thank you," Rhys replied, exchanging a warm handshake with the man before he leaned back against the bar to watch Hank walk away.

So Rhys wasn't the only one who suspected a thief among the employees. Yet, his thoughts on who the culprit was differed from Hank's, even though Hank admitted John was the only one who had the opportunity. And then, of course, the motive was a little shaky after Hank's rendition of the friendship between Hardin and Arthur Redington. Lifting the cigar to his lips, Rhys noticed that it hadn't stayed lit and turned to place it in a nearby ashtray. But on the other hand, Hank openly said anyone would do anything for Ashlee—including John— and Rhys had to agree with that. He was helping her steal from unsuspecting gamblers. Why wouldn't he help with this if Ashlee's reason was good enough? Well, he sighed, there was only one person who could answer that. He doubted she would just come out and admit everything, and thanks to Hank Newell, Rhys knew how to trick a confession from her. But he needed Thomas's help before the man boarded the train back to Jackson, and a moment with Arthur to insure he would agree to bring Dominique to visit Thomas in three days.

Chapter Seven

"I hope the pin meets with your satisfaction, Mr. Sinclair," Marcus Wetherly said nervously, his gray-green eyes looking much too large for his head through the thick-lensed spectacles he wore.

Rhys held the piece of jewelry up toward the light to examine it more closely. "Perfect," he said after a moment.

"Well, I must tell you, sir," Wetherly went on as he wiped his brow with his handkerchief, "that I've never been asked to make such a fine piece as that and not"— he glanced at the other customers in the jewelry shoppe and lowered his voice—"not use a real stone. Are you sure this 'friend' of yours won't know?"

"By the time it's realized, the pin will have served its purpose," Rhys guaranteed him, slipping the stickpin back in its box then tucking it away in his coat pocket. He withdrew his wallet. "Did you have to spend more than the price you quoted me earlier?"

"No, sir," Wetherly answered, frowning, "but to be quite honest, Mr. Sinclair, I feel guilty charging anything."

"Nonsense," Rhys replied, handing the sum over to the man. "You were hired to do a job and should be paid.

And I've given you a little extra to insure that no one knows about our transaction. It would ruin everything if my friend learned about it too soon."

"Not from me," the little man quickly assured him and wiped his brow again.

"Good," Rhys smiled. "And perhaps we can do business again—on a more serious level." Nodding a farewell, Rhys turned and left the store.

A devious grin kinked one corner of his mouth as he walked back toward Belle Chasse. Hank Newell had unwittingly given Rhys an idea on how to place Ashlee in a situation where she would—with a single look or gesture—give herself away. And it would happen tonight. Having learned that it was Ashlee's responsibility to put the casino's winnings in the safe on the nights Dominique was away, Rhys knew Ashlee would be unable to accept Thomas's invitation for the Redingtons to visit him in Jackson for the weekend. Alone with Arthur, Rhys had told the man why he wanted him and his wife to go to Jackson, other than the obvious opportunity for Arthur to meet some of Thomas's political friends—the Redingtons' absence from Belle Chasse would give Rhys the chance to look over the casino's records. Until Rhys forced a confession from Ashlee, he couldn't be sure if Arthur knew about his daughter's somewhat shady pastime. And if he didn't—as Rhys suspected—it would have to be Ashlee who told her father. Thus, the true reason why Rhys wanted Arthur and his wife to leave Belle Chasse went unsaid. Arthur would never understand nor permit Ashlee to play poker, and that's exactly what she would be doing tonight if things went as planned.

He had spent the last three days observing—Ashlee, John, and the normal routine of the casino. If John were responsible for the problems at Belle Chasse, Rhys couldn't figure out how he managed it. Once an hour, just as Ashlee had said, John would go to each table, collect the money and put it into a bag, then take the bag to the office. Dominique always met him at the door, then locked herself in once John handed the winnings over to her. And there was always a guard standing outside in case some distraught player had lost his life's earnings at the roulette wheel and decided to get it back any way he could.

As for Ashlee, her habits during the day were easy to follow. After breakfast in the dining hall with her father—Dominique never appeared that early—she went to the kitchen for a staff meeting and then to her father's office to work on ordering supplies and posting invoices that needed to be paid. She either ate lunch with her father or alone in her room. The afternoon was spent with Michael going over any hotel problems, supervising the laundry, and deciding which of the rooms needed redecorating the most and how inexpensively it could be done. She ate dinner in her room, and Rhys guessed it was because Dominique always joined her husband in the restaurant at that time and Ashlee preferred being somewhere else rather than endure her stepmother's company if she didn't have to. Then around seven o'clock she came to the casino, went directly to her table, and seldom looked Rhys's way.

As he neared the hotel's front steps, Rhys assumed one of the reasons she ignored him was because of the argument she'd had with her father about who should be the new poker dealer. Obviously it hadn't gone in her favor, and looking at him would only add to her anger and humiliation. He grinned as he opened the huge front door and went into the lobby, remembering their accidental meeting yesterday afternoon.

He'd heard the *Mississippi Queen* had docked about an hour earlier and wanted to talk with Captain Longley. He had left Belle Chasse through the courtyard out back, intending to walk the alley to the pier. When he stepped through the iron gate, he found Ashlee arguing with the driver of a wagon filled with supplies for the restaurant. She hadn't known he was there at first since her back was to him, and a pleased smile flashed across his face at the splendid sight she presented. Her thick black hair was pulled back from her face and tied in a knot at the nape of her long, slender neck. The pale blue gown she wore hugged her narrow waist then fell in yards of flowing skirts, hiding the shapely limbs he remembered with a great deal of pleasure. Each time she shook her fist at the driver or motioned toward the building in back of her, the hem of her gown swayed just enough for Rhys to see a trim ankle covered in ivory stockings and the tiny shoe she stomped against the earth when the driver still refused to do as she demanded.

From their rather heated discussion, Rhys concluded that at the moment she was shorthanded and didn't have anyone available who could carry in the supplies for her. The driver told her he was sympathetic, but since it wasn't his job to unload the wagon and because there was no one around to help, he was left with no alternative but to come back later when she was ready for him. But before he took up the reins to snap them over the horse's rump and send them on their way, Rhys stepped into view.

"Might I be of service, Miss Redington?" He smiled at the startled look on her face when she spun around to see who it was, and Rhys couldn't mistake the expression in her eyes that changed the instant she recognized him. She wanted to decline his help and for a full moment stood there in silent frustration, glancing from him to the wagon and back again. He decided to spare her the humiliation saying yes would cause and slid off his coat before she could make up her mind. But he also decided not to make it too easy on her.

"Would you be so kind?" he asked, handing her his coat as he passed by, and Ashlee could do naught but take it when the garment was all but thrust upon her.

Boxes, crates, and barrels were lifted to the ground with ease, and Ashlee watched in reluctant appreciation, mute respect, and awe at how effortlessly the task was accomplished. The seams of the white linen shirt he wore strained as his muscles flexed with the heavy load he moved, and Ashlee remembered all too well the feel of them beneath her fingers. Her pulse raced and the anger she wanted to keep alive within her vanished. The day Rhys Sinclair appeared at Belle Chasse, Ashlee had feared he knew the truth about her and had come to expose her, to demand the return of his money or go to prison . . . or both! But as the days passed, she soon began to think he had no idea that she and Sally White were the same person, and when he avoided her, even though it was at her request, a dull ache twisted at her insides. She couldn't understand why. She truly didn't want him to learn about the riverboat escapades, but at the same time her womanly pride had been woefully injured. Though she had never deemed herself the fairest of all the women in Louisiana or even New Orleans, she thought herself at least comely enough to be remembered after a tumble in bed. Her gaze drifted to the dark coat draped over her arm, wondering what it took to have a woman linger in this man's thoughts.

"How soon before you'll have someone to help carry these inside?"

Ashlee's head jerked upward when she heard his deep voice, realizing he had finished his job. Feeling the color rise in her cheeks, she quickly handed back his coat and absently brushed a stray tendril of hair from her temple as she moved past him to sign the receipt the driver held out for her.

"John should be back in a few minutes," she replied

once the delivery man had climbed in his wagon and cracked the reins, sending the rig rattling off down the alleyway.

"I thought he never left your side, Miss Redington," Rhys grinned, slipping on his coat.

His comment, though seemingly lighthearted, wasn't received well. "He usually doesn't," she scoffed. "But I told him I didn't think I'd need his protection today. I mean, who'd ever suppose you'd find a snake in the middle of New Orleans?" She smiled sarcastically, her blue eyes flashing dangerously, then walked past him toward the tree stump where she'd laid the paper with its list of supplies. Plucking it from beneath the small rock that prevented it from being blown away in the gentle afternoon breeze, she crossed to the crated goods and began checking off each item against her list, pretending as if there were no one around.

Rhys watched her a moment as he tugged at his shirt cuffs and readjusted his collar, then brushed away the dirt smudge on the knee of his trousers before leaning back comfortably against one of the barrels he had unloaded.

"You know, Miss Redington, it would be a lot more pleasant around here if we tried to get along," he announced, his gaze drawn to the demure neckline of her dress and the rounded figure it failed to completely disguise.

"No, Mr. Sinclair," she replied tartly, "it would be more pleasant if *you* weren't around here." She continued her inventory and wouldn't look at him, missing the bright smile that added golden depths to his dark brown eyes.

"Are you still angry because your father chose me to deal poker?"

Icy blue eyes lifted instantly to glare at him. "And don't I have the right to be angry? I'm a better poker dealer than any ten men—including you—all thrown together! But he thinks that's impossible because I'm a woman. Well, he's wrong."

"Then you've dealt poker before," he said, knowing full well she hadn't, and grinned openly when she quickly looked back at her paper.

"Not exactly," she mumbled.

Rhys feigned his bewilderment. "Then how do you know—"

"I just do," she snapped, shoving him off the barrel as she continued her count.

He studied the angry set of her tiny chin and knew that it wouldn't be long before he had her right where he wanted her. He sighed as if agreeing with her father. "Well, in that case, I can understand your father's reluctance. It wouldn't be very good publicity for the casino if word got around that one of his poker dealers didn't even know how to play the game. I think you should stick to blackjack."

"Oh you do, do you?" she rallied, her voice rising in pitch. "You think that just because I've not played the game I don't know how? Well, I do, Mr. Sinclair. I've watched enough of it to know. In fact," she sneered, crumbling the paper in her fist as she rested both on her hip and pointed her pencil at him, "I can probably beat *you* at any game you chose."

"Oh, most—most assuredly," he replied, allowing just enough of a smile and doubtful tone to slip into his words.

Ashlee straightened with an indignant lift of her nose. "You think not?" she challenged. "Then suppose we find out. I'm sure you're well aware that my father and Dominique will be going to Jackson tomorrow for the weekend. So let's you and I have ourselves a little poker game to see who's the better player."

"Miss Redington," he began with a shake of his head as

213

if he found the idea absurd, "there's no need—"

"What's the matter? Afraid you can't handle the embarrassment when I win?"

The muscle in his cheek flexed as he suppressed a grin. "Actually, I was thinking just the opposite. Are you sure you can handle it when you lose?"

A wry smile wrinkled her cheek. "I won't have to," she boasted, "because I won't lose playing against you."

"Then I guess you leave me no choice," he sighed. "And since you've challenged me, by right I am allowed to pick the dealer, time, and place."

Her confidence faltered a bit, wondering what he had in mind.

"Relax, Miss Redington," he laughed softly when he recognized the worried look in her eyes. "It shall be most proper. Since neither of us wish to have the outcome of the game known to everyone should we lose, and because your father would not approve if he learned of it, I simply meant that we should keep our little rendezvous a secret. I think we can trust Hank Newell to be the dealer, and since you'll already be in the office after the casino closes Friday night, he and I will meet you there. That way should someone come to the office for any reason, it will appear as if the three of us are discussing business. Agreed?"

Ashlee would have preferred that John sit in on the game for her own peace of mind. He knew just what to say to put her at ease. Not that she needed him as a good luck piece to beat Rhys Sinclair in poker, but rather to give her that little bit of encouragement that no matter what happened, John would be there to protect her. However, the longer she thought about it, the better it sounded not to have John know about the game. He had always agreed with her father about not allowing her to play, and if asked to be the dealer, John would probably prevent the contest from taking place.

214

"All right," she had finally consented, though her tone lacked the assuredness it had before. She had turned away from him then to resume her inventorying of supplies and missed the gleam in her companion's dark eyes. If she had seen the look, she would have sensed trouble lay ahead for her.

"Good morning, Michael," Rhys beamed as he crossed the lobby toward the front desk, thinking how grand the day had begun and how equally grand its end promised to be. In a little more than twelve hours he would be sitting across the table from the most beautiful woman he had ever known, just waiting for the chance to fulfill his plan. And then . . . He frowned suddenly, once he noticed that Michael seemed more interested in what was going on in Arthur Redington's office rather than answering Rhys's greeting. "Is something wrong?" Rhys whispered with a grin as it was quite obvious the man was eavesdropping.

Nodding his head, Michael motioned for Rhys to come around in back of the desk to where he stood some ten feet away from the office doorway. "Ashlee and Mrs. Redington are in there," he answered, keeping his voice low and his eyes centered on the opened entrance. "They've been arguing for the last five minutes." He frowned back at Rhys when he saw that the man hadn't moved.

"And don't you think you should allow them to argue in private?" Rhys asked, leaning an elbow on the desk.

"If I did that, how would I learn anything?" Michael rallied in defense. A slow smile parted his lips. "Besides, it breaks up the boredom." Moving away from the office, he cast one last look toward the door then came to stand before Rhys. "Care to know what it was about?"

"Not really," Rhys smiled, amused.

"Not even if I give you a hint and say it concerns Perrin Fabron?" he tested with a silly smirk as he leaned forward against the desk top and eyed Rhys closely.

215

All sign of humor vanished from Rhys's face. He looked away. "Why should the gentleman interest me, Michael?"

"Oh, come now," the other chuckled. "Are you trying to get me to believe that you're not like every other man at Belle Chasse? Even me? And I'm married."

"You're talking in riddles, Michael," Rhys said.

"Well, then let me explain," Michael teased, his green eyes aglow with mischief. "There isn't a one of us who thinks Ashlee should marry this . . . this Fabron character—except Mrs. Redington, of course. Even Mr. Redington has voiced his doubts about it when he's had too much to drink. And from the argument the two women are having right now, something will have to be done very soon or all the opinions in the world won't help."

A frown creased Rhys's suntanned brow. "What do you mean?"

Michael crossed his arms in front of him, bracing his upper torso against his elbows on the desk, and spoke in a whisper. "Mrs. Redington told Ashlee that she's received a telegram from her cousin. Mr. Fabron is expected to arrive in New Orleans sometime Sunday, and she wants Ashlee to be sure and meet the train since Mrs. Redington won't be home from Jackson in time. It means, my thickheaded friend, that Ashlee will become a bride very soon unless something is done to prevent it."

Rhys's stomach knotted. He looked out in the direction of the long, elegant staircase without really seeing it. "And what do you suggest? That someone here at Belle Chasse ask for her hand before she can marry her betrothed? And who would that be, Michael?" His mood lightened and he glanced back at his companion. "You? Short of murdering Fabron, I see no way for Miss Redington to escape her father and stepmother's wishes." He leaned heavily on his elbow and clasped his wrist with his other hand. "And after having known Miss Redington for even a small amount of time, I've learned that if she doesn't wish to do something, she'll find a way out of it."

Michael grinned broadly. "Not if Mrs. Redington wishes it to be," he argued.

"Then perhaps someone should kidnap Miss Ashlee," Rhys whimsically proposed and laughed aloud when he saw the gleam in his companion's eyes. What man in his right mind would want to be saddled with such a devious female as Ashlee Redington? His brown eyes softened with the thought. Of course, it would be a rather pleasurable task to try and break her willful spirit.

The sounds of hurried, dainty footsteps against the marble floor brought Rhys's gaze to their source, and the sight of Ashlee made him catch his breath. She had stomped from her father's office in a rage with her stepmother close behind her. Compared to Dominique's beautifully delicate shape, Ashlee's was still by far more ravishing. She stood a good six inches taller than her companion, and although Dominique could hardly be deemed plump, it appeared she could stand to lose a pound or two when likened to her stepdaughter. Ashlee's dark hair had a much shinier gloss to it than Dominique's, and the fire in her pale blue eyes merely added a healthy glow to her fair skin. There was no denying that Dominique was a beauty—one that would catch any man's eye—but in the company of Ashlee Redington, the Frenchwoman would have to be content with second place.

"You'll do as you're told, young woman," Dominique snapped, "or you'll pay the consequences."

Ashlee stopped abruptly and spun around, her chin lowered and her shapely brows drawn together in an angry frown. "I've been paying them," she snarled, unaware of those who watched, "from the first day Papa met you!"

With that she stormed past the desk, rounded the end of it, and nearly collided with Rhys just as he was discreetly making an exit rather than inadvertently be a witness to a family squabble. Stepping out of her way, he nodded politely at her, noticing the tears in her eyes, and watched her hurry off. Oddly enough, he was tempted to chase after her, catch her in his arms, and soothe away her pain. A half smile touched his mouth and he sighed, knowing that would be the last thing Ashlee would appreciate, for he doubted she ranked him much higher than her stepmother. He turned then to go to his room, but paused with questioning brows when Dominique called out to him.

"Madam?" he asked, turning to her.

"Might we speak a moment in the office?" she queried with a smile that Rhys thought was a bit too friendly for a married woman.

He nodded consent and moved to follow her, but once she had looked away from him, Rhys glanced over at Michael for some clue to the woman's purpose. But Michael offered none when all he did was shake his head and give a short shrug of one shoulder.

Arthur Redington's office had the same tasteful elegance as the rest of Belle Chasse, but in a masculine flavor. The walls and ceiling were of a rich oak paneling with massive book shelves to the left and a white marble fireplace opposite them. Shutters muted the bright sunlight trying to seep in through the slits between the minutely carved louvers, and in the center of the room was a huge mahogany desk. Before it sat two leather wing chairs on a mauve-colored Oriental rug. Overhead hung a simple, yet refined chandelier capable of spreading light throughout the entire room. Rhys paused just inside the door, watching Dominique round the desk and sit in the chair behind it. Most females would be out of place in such a setting, yet Dominique seemed perfectly at home.

"Please close the door and take a seat," she instructed, a tiny hand raised in the direction of one of the wing chairs.

Rhys did so.

"I don't know why Arthur has taken such a liking to you so quickly, Mr. Sinclair," she began. "He's usually very selective in his choice of friends. Maybe it's because you're a northerner and he thinks your acquaintance will in some way benefit him politically. I really have no way of knowing since I won't ask him. But I must admit he's usually never wrong about the men he entrusts with his friendship, and it's for that reason I've asked to speak with you. If Arthur has confidence in you, then so shall I." Rising, she went to the buffet and the silver service sitting on top. "Would you care for a cup of coffee, Mr. Sinclair?" she asked, the pot held in one hand as she smiled back at him. "And may I call you Rhys?"

Not being unfamiliar with the various forms of flirtation directed his way by the fairer sex, Rhys recognized a dangerous situation with this woman if he didn't handle it properly. What he couldn't figure out was her interest in him when her own husband was a prominent businessman, gave her everything she could possibly want, and was far from homely. Rhys could see no reason for her to stray excepting, of course, the possibility that she merely enjoyed the risks involved in having an affair.

"Yes, coffee would be fine," he nodded, "and I'd be honored to have you call me Rhys."

Handing him a full cup, Dominique sat down in the chair next to him, her own cup and saucer perched daintily on one knee. "It doesn't take a genius to know that my stepdaughter is a very unruly young woman. You witnessed a sampling of it just now. She can't be trusted to do as she's told when her father and I are away, and asking Mr. Hardin to see that she behaves is wasted breath." Twisting slightly, she placed her untouched coffee on the small table positioned between the two chairs, then folded her fingers together and rested them on her crossed knees. "I'd like to ask a favor of you, Rhys," she smiled provocatively.

Had it been Ashlee's face he studied, Rhys would have been delighted with the unexpected attention. However, he sensed there was more to Dominique's enthusiasm than just needing his help. He smiled into his cup as he took a drink of coffee, then placed it on the table next to hers.

"Ask away," he replied, leaning comfortably on the arm of his chair.

"Ashlee's fiancé—my cousin, Perrin Fabron—will be arriving in New Orleans on Sunday. As you know, Arthur and I will probably still be in Jackson, so I'll be unable to meet his train. It's his first trip to America, so I'm sure he'll be quite lost if no one is waiting for him at the station when he arrives. I'd like you to see to it that Ashlee doesn't forget."

Fighting not to smile, Rhys reached up and traced the scar on his cheek with a fingertip. "Miss Redington and I aren't exactly on good terms, ma'am. I'm afraid that if I reminded her of anything, she'd do her best to forget it." He laughed openly. "But not until after she told me to mind my own business."

Dominique quietly watched him a moment, her gaze boldly taking in the length of him.

"Yes, I'm aware of how she feels toward you," she finally answered, a vague, suggestive smile deepening the faint lines around her mouth. "Though I fear she must be blind to find anything objectionable about you." She lifted one dark brow at him, then laughed when he merely smiled back at her. "And that's the reason I think you, above all others, will be able to control her. She has John

Hardin wrapped around her little finger. You, however, will not bend to a woman's fancy, I suspect. Am I correct?"

Rhys wisely chose not to answer, for it would have been a lie to say yes. There had been a woman who had done just that—tempted him, teased him, tricked him, then drove him to find her—and she was the very one that Dominique thought couldn't affect him.

"I won't pretend that I haven't heard the rumors, Mrs. Redington," he said, carefully avoiding her question. "The marriage was arranged, and Miss Redington doesn't appear to approve. If she doesn't wish to meet the train, no amount of reminding on my part would force her to go. How do you propose I accomplish it?"

"She will if her father tells her to go. You see, Rhys," Dominique went on to say, "Ashlee will listen to and obey only her father. But her father has spoiled her, and if Ashlee argues long enough with him, he gives in to her."

Rhys laughed with a shake of his head. "Excuse me, but I don't understand then. If Arthur told her to meet the train, she would do it, yet you're asking me to make sure she will."

"Well, the real problem is getting Arthur not to back down once he's told her. All it would take would be one excuse from her, and he'd relent. But if he knew you were acting as escort, Ashlee could beg and plead all she liked, and he wouldn't change his mind. Now do you understand?"

Rhys smiled lazily. "Yes. But it seems like an awful lot of trouble to go to. May I be so bold as to ask why you bother?"

Dominique settled back in her chair. "Ashlee is twenty years old, Rhys. She should have been married years ago. I think it's obvious why she hasn't—why, in fact, she doesn't even have any serious gentlemen callers. She's too wild and stubborn." Dominique looked away from him with a hateful twist to her mouth. "A trait of her mother's, I'm told."

"Some men like that in their women," Rhys pointed out.

Dominique's head jerked back around to glare at him. "Possibly. But I haven't the time nor patience to wait for him to come along. Ashlee's behavior puts a strain on my marriage. There have already been several occasions when she's come between Arthur and me, and I'll not tolerate another."

Dominique's voice had raised in anger, her face flushed with color, and Rhys could almost see the sparks in the woman's dark brown eyes. He wanted to believe the woman's temper had flared because she was frustrated over her failure to control Ashlee, that she honestly cared about her stepdaughter and wanted nothing but the best for her. Yet, there seemed to be more to it, and he decided that he had no desire to be a part of Dominique's plan. Rising, he stood casually before her.

"I'm sorry, Mrs. Redington," he said as politely as he could manage, "but I'd prefer not being in the middle of a family disagreement. As I said before, your stepdaughter and I are not on the friendliest terms, and my help in this matter would only make it worse. Since I have to work with her, I'd—"

"Mr. Sinclair," Dominique cut in, her voice cold and threatening, "I think you're missing the point. I'm not really asking you to do it, I'm telling you. You may work with Ashlee, but you work for me, and if you wish to keep it that way, you'll say no more." Rising, she crossed around in back of the desk and sat down in the chair. Without glancing up at him again, she opened the ledger laying in front of her and studied the first page as she said, "The train will arrive at two o'clock, Mr. Sinclair.

222

Now, good day to you."

It was quite apparent to Rhys that Dominique Redington was used to having her own way no matter what she had to do to accomplish it. But what amused him was that he was probably worth four times as much as her husband ever hoped to be and could buy Belle Chasse without having to do much more than writing a bank draft. Threatening him with anything was useless. Rhys Sinclair couldn't be intimidated. For now, however, he was forced to play along.

"I can't believe he actually listened to her!" Ashlee fumed, whirling away from the dressing mirror as she hooked up the last of the buttons on the front of her gown. "If they wanted to make sure I met the train, John would have seen to it." Lifting the hem of her skirts, she thrust her tiny feet into her shoes. "Now I must endure that Yankee's company. I'm sorely tempted to tell Papa about Mr. Sinclair and have him thrown out of Belle Chasse on his ear!" Her anger ebbed a mite as she thought of the game she and Rhys would be playing in a few hours. "But not until I've proved my point and taken the scoundrel's money."

Turning back to the mirror, she checked her appearance once more, frowning critically at what she saw. The black satin dress only made her hair look that much darker, her eyes that much bluer, her skin more pale than she liked, and those blasted tendrils of hair still refused to do anything but fall down the back of her neck. With a throaty growl, she stormed the door, slamming it loudly behind her as she stepped into the foyer. How could her life have changed so drastically over the past three years? Before that, her father had never heard of Dominique Fabron, Belle Chasse was beginning to show a little profit and promised to prosper as it had before the war, she wasn't engaged to a man she had never seen, and she had never heard the name Rhys Sinclair! Now she had it all heaped upon her with little hope any of it would change. If she didn't love her father so much and if she had a place to go, she'd run away from this madness.

Marching down the walkway encircling the courtyard, her wide skirts swaying with each agitated step she took, Ashlee was suddenly overcome with apprehension and her pace slowed. Word of Rhys Sinclair's ability with cards had been the topic of conversation from the moment he started working at Belle Chasse. Few doubted they knew of anyone who could beat him at poker, and some even ventured to say that his skill more than likely included any game of chance. What made it worse was that Rhys never mentioned any of the bouts he'd won or lost even when asked, and his reputation had grown out of pure speculation alone. Ashlee had learned long ago that one must never listen to gossip when it came to playing cards. Worry over the opponent's proficiency could make one careless and thus lose the game. But she had seen him play and knew that the rumors about him weren't far from the truth. Coming to a complete halt once she reached the door leading into the lobby, Ashlee took a deep breath and sighed heavily. Her recklessness had gotten her into trouble again. Pulling herself up, she opened the door and stepped inside, vowing that this time it wouldn't go against her.

"Good evening, Miss Redington," Michael smiled brightly when he saw her walking toward him.

"Good evening, Michael," she replied, watching the crowd of people making their way into the casino. "Looks like we'll be busy tonight."

Nodding, he leaned forward against the desk. "Usually are on Saturday night. Did your father and Mrs. Redington get on the train all right?"

"Yes," she answered. "They're probably in Jackson by

224

now." She studied the mass of richly garbed customers, mostly men, who entered through the double archway, silently wishing her father would leave Dominique in Mississippi and return home alone.

"I heard your fiancé will be arriving tomorrow," Michael confessed and smiled sympathetically when Ashlee looked back at him.

"Don't remind me, Michael," she replied with a sarcastic curl of her upper lip. "I'd like to spend my last free day thinking of more pleasurable things." A bright twinkle gleamed in her blue eyes. "For instance, the possibility that he got on the wrong train and is headed toward Maine right now." A smile lifted the corners of her mouth, and she leaned forward to add, "And that after he gets off, he's abducted by pirates and forced to serve on their ship . . . never to be seen again."

"We're all hoping for that, Miss Ashlee," Michael laughed.

"Yes, well, the chances of that happening are about as good as Papa letting me be a poker dealer or seeing New Orleans knee-deep in snow." Sighing, she looked away again. "But I'm not married yet. There's still time for something to happen that will prevent it."

Michael quietly appraised the young woman's beautiful profile for a moment, a sadness reflected in his eyes. When he spoke, his voice was soft and gentle. "Miss Ashlee," he began hesitantly, "you know that if you wanted any one of us at Belle Chasse to help you we would without any question."

"Michael," she laughed, a bit nervously, "what are you saying?"

He shrugged and turned sideways from the desk, staring off toward the casino's entryway. "That there's only two people in the world who think you should marry Mr. Fabron . . . and the rest of us strongly object, some more than others. Say the word, and he'd be"—Michael

225

fell quiet a moment before he turned his head to look at her again—"disposed of."

Ashlee could feel the blood drain from her face. She understood what he meant and was horrified. "Michael," she breathed. "My God, you aren't suggesting—" Feeling a little faint, she touched shaky fingers to her brow. "Of course, you are." She sucked in a deep breath and glanced around them to make sure no one else had heard. "Michael, swear to me that you would never do such a thing. I'll find some other way to solve my problem without using violence. Do you swear?"

A lopsided smile came over his face. "Yes, Miss Ashlee, I swear. But I want you to know that if you should change your mind or think of some other way we can help, we'll be more than eager to oblige."

Ashlee forced a smile. "I'll keep it in mind," she said and turned toward the casino.

She paused once she stood in the archway, that same old question coming to mind as she watched the throng of wealthy customers crowd around every table, eager to spend every dime they had. How could Belle Chasse possibly be failing? This night alone should put it in the black, not to mention the money she and John added to its income. If she didn't know better, she'd swear Dominique was stealing it. The deep line between her brows disappeared. If that was true, what was the woman doing with all that money? What would she need it for? She had everything she could possibly want. Ashlee's father saw to that. With a disgusted sigh, she moved into the room, heading toward her blackjack table and thinking that after her little poker game with Rhys, she'd be able to help the casino turn a bigger profit.

"Hello Elaine," she smiled once the last card was dealt. "Ready for a break?"

"I sure am, Miss Ashlee," the pretty blonde groaned. "It's been like this all afternoon and doesn't promise to let up."

"I'm glad to hear it, Elaine. Belle Chasse could use a good night." Waiting for her companion to gather up the cards, Ashlee glanced around at the new faces milling about the place, drinks in one hand and chips in the other. "I wonder what the special occasion is. I can't recall ever having seen some of these people before."

Scooping in the house winnings, Elaine laughed. "Don't know for sure, but I think Mr. Sinclair has something to do with it."

Ashlee's head snapped around. "Mr. Sinclair? What are you talking about?"

Handing Ashlee an unopened pack of fresh cards, she got off the stool and swept out her hand. "Take a look. Notice anything different?"

Failing to see much of a change except in the amount of customers, Ashlee frowned. "Like what?"

"There's more ladies here tonight than ever before," Elaine explained. "I think the women wanted to get a look at our new poker dealer, and the only inconspicuous way to do it was to come here with their husbands." She pointed toward the opposite end of the room. "Notice where most of them are standing?"

Having it brought to her attention, Ashlee had to agree that that was what it appeared had happened. The ladies indeed were clustered near Rhys's table, and none of them seemed interested in playing the roulette wheel or blackjack, the customary games for a lady. Miffed that they could find anything interesting about him in the first place, and secondly that they could be so brazen about satisfying their curiosity, Ashlee unknowingly raised her nose in the air.

"He's a Yankee. Don't they know that?" she muttered more to herself than to Elaine as she took her place on the stool and stripped the cards from their box.

"I think all they care about is that he's a man," Elaine

sighed, her attention still cast in Rhys's direction. "And probably the handsomest I've ever seen. I wonder if Mr. Redington's rule about not socializing with customers applies to fellow employees," she murmured.

"It most certainly does," Ashlee snapped, giving her companion a most disapproving scowl. The surprised look on the other's face made Ashlee realize how jealous her statement had sounded, and she quickly returned her attention to the game before her and the men who watched in silent curiosity. Why should she care with whom Rhys Sinclair chose to be? He was nothing to her. Her hands trembled as she shuffled the cards.

"I'll be back in one hour, Miss Ashlee," Elaine said, feeling the sting of her reprimand.

Ashlee couldn't bring herself to look at Elaine and only nodded, forcing a smile to her lips as she glanced up at the players surrounding her table. "Shall we begin, gentlemen?" she asked, silently wishing she had never left her room. The smile faded. What she really wished was that Rhys had never come to Belle Chasse.

The evening passed in a blur for Ashlee. To the chagrin of the customers at her table, Ashlee's mind wasn't on the game from the first moment Rhys elected to smoke his cheroot in clear view of her. He hadn't looked in her direction the entire time, a fact Ashlee found irritating, since it appeared nearly every woman in the casino at some point or another had drawn him into conversation and his attention away from her. Finally, when she couldn't stand it a moment longer, she motioned for Elaine to take her place and left the casino for the office. At least there she would find the solitude she needed in order to calm her rising ire. She couldn't have her thoughts straying off when they needed to be on the contest in which she and Rhys were about to engage.

An hour later found her alone in the office with the pot of coffee she had brought from the kitchen. She had dismissed John about fifteen minutes before, telling him that he needn't wait for her since she planned to do some last minute ordering for hotel supplies. Everything was set. The casino was closed, the customers gone, and John was out of the way. So where were Hank and Mr. Sinclair? Ashlee poured herself a second cup of coffee. If the two men didn't show up fairly soon, she was going to bed, and Rhys Sinclair could have the entire night to spend with the ladies. A frown flitted across her brow as she went to the window and opened the shutters. Was it possible that he had forgotten about their challenge? Tears gathered in her eyes as she stared out into the starlit night. Just as·he had seemed to have forgotten about the night he had held her in his arms and made love to her?

Ashlee jumped and spun around when she heard someone's hand on the doorknob. Blinking away her tears, she squared her shoulders. Whoever it was wouldn't find her crying . . . especially if it was that damn northerner!

"Sorry we're late, Miss Ashlee," Hank apologized with a delighted grin as he waited for Rhys to step inside before closing the door behind them. "We—ah—had a little trouble getting some of the customers to leave."

Ashlee didn't miss the amused look Hank gave his companion. "I can't imagine why," she jeered before settling her gaze on the taller of the two. "Maybe you should join the circus, Mr. Sinclair. You'd obviously be the main attraction."

The two men exchanged surprised looks at Ashlee's curt remark.

"I assume Mr. Sinclair has explained everything to you, Hank," Ashlee continued, picking up a cloth bag from on top of the desk.

"Yes'm," he nodded. "If anybody asks, we were discussing business."

She nodded at him then moved her attention to Rhys, a vague smile on her lips. "I hope you've brought a lot of money with you, Mr. Sinclair," she baited.

The smile he gave her was noncommittal, while in his thoughts he agreed. He would lose the money in his wallet, but he'd win something of much greater value before the night was finished.

"I couldn't have a regular table brought in here without someone getting suspicious," she told them, rounding the desk toward the gateleg drop leaf table her father would draw into the center of the room whenever he and several other politicians needed a large work space for the many papers they studied. "But I think this will be suitable."

The two men easily lifted the bulky piece of furniture away from the wall, propped up the leaves, and positioned the leather wing chairs and Arthur's desk chair around it. Each took their place, Ashlee sitting directly across from Rhys, and Hank to her left. For one brief second, Ashlee wondered if she were doing the right thing. She never had any money of her own, and in order to play against Rhys, she had had to help herself to some of the casino's winnings for the night. She frowned as she withdrew the amount from the cloth bag, silently telling herself that it was only a loan. Once she got up from the table, she would put it all back, plus the equal sum she had won from her opponent.

"Shall we begin?" Hank asked, and both players nodded.

The ante was decided upon, and the game was to be seven card stud. While Hank shuffled the deck, Rhys counted out the needed dollars and tossed them to the center of the table. Settling back in his chair, he watched the man's deft handling of the deck before he dealt out one card, face down, to Rhys, one to Ashlee, a second to Rhys, and a second to Ashlee. Rhys's third card, a ten, was placed face up, and Ashlee received a seven. After looking at his first two cards, an eight and nine—the beginning of a possible straight—he placed his bet and looked over at Ashlee. She called his bet, added the amount, and both waited while Hank turned up their fourth card. Rhys received a six, strengthening his chances for a numerical run of five, while Ashlee also received a six. Now was usually when Rhys doubled his bet, but since he wanted Ashlee to win the first game, he checked and allowed her to bet. He matched the sum and waited for the next card. By the time all seven were dealt, four up and three down, Rhys had the straight he was sure would win, especially after looking at Ashlee's cards lying face up on the table—a seven, six, queen, and jack. His gambler's blood urged him to triple the stakes, but he was afraid Ashlee would drop out if he did. Thus he bet only a moderate price, which Ashlee quickly met and raised.

"I'll call," he said with little emotion in his voice.

Turning up her last three cards, Ashlee produced another seven and jack with an odd three, or two pair—a hand that couldn't beat Rhys's straight.

"You win," he smiled, tossing in his cards unseen by the other two at the table.

A delighted, confident grin teased the corners of Ashlee's lovely mouth as she scooped in her winnings, and Rhys decided now was the time to test her. Pulling a cheroot from his inside coat pocket, he waited until she looked up and asked, "May I?"

Nothing, not even the awful odor of a cigar, was going to spoil Ashlee's mood. She nodded her approval with a sweet smile and watched him strike a match while Hank shuffled the deck a second time. She had seen enough men play poker to know that many of them oftentimes tried to display a cool nature by casually drinking their whiskey or smoking a cigar like Rhys was doing, and she was sure he was experiencing the same worry about losing as so many other men had done. A mischievous glow brightened her pale blue eyes. And he should worry. She was going to beat him!

They played for the next hour and a half. The pot shifted hands several times, but whenever Ashlee won, she picked up more than Rhys's pot offered. Her winnings began to grow. By three o'clock in the morning, Rhys's pile of money had dwindled to only a few bills, and Ashlee was sure this would be the last game before he admitted defeat and she had proved her point.

After the first six cards were dealt both players, Ashlee held only a pair of twos in her hand, with a four, ace, eight, and nine lying on the table in front of her, all in different suits. Rhys's face up cards were a mixture of everything—a jack, six, seven, and deuce—and nothing that did him any good. However, she had no way of knowing what he held in his hand, and since just about any combination beat a pair of deuces, she was tempted to drop out. Her gaze shifted to the two one-hundred-dollar bills lying at his elbow, knowing that all she had to do was wager more than what he had and the game would be over. Dealt her last card, a king, Ashlee grinned to herself, picked up three one-hundred-dollar bills, and tossed them on the pile in the middle of the table.

Rhys fanned out the three cards he held—two jacks and a deuce—then glanced down at those spread out in front of him. It had been a long while since he'd been given a full house and he truly hated wasting the three jacks and pair of twos, but he hadn't come to the table to play poker. He had come to trap Ashlee, and right now he had her right where he wanted her.

"It appears I'm out of cash, Miss Redington," he sighed, setting down his cards.

Ashlee's smile broadened. "Yes, so it does," she agreed, reveling in her victory. "And it's such a shame. I was just beginning to enjoy this."

Rhys raised a tawny brow. "Then perhaps, if you'll consent, we can continue a while longer."

Ashlee's eyes sparkled as she crossed her arms and leaned forward against the table. "To what, Mr. Sinclair? You have no more money."

"No," he replied, "I don't. But I do have something of great sentimental value. It belonged to my grandfather and is worth more than I need to call your bet." He reached into his pocket then held out his clenched fist toward her, slowly uncurling his fingers to reveal the stickpin he had purchased from Marcus Wetherly.

Ashlee stiffened the instant she saw the piece of jewelry, the light from the chandelier overhead gleaming brightly off the stone and into her eyes as though the hand of Satan reached out for her. Could it be the same—the one she had stolen from him? Had he sneaked into her room while she was gone and found it? Was he playing with her? Did this mean he knew her secret? Or could he, by some ill fate, possibly have another similar one? She swallowed hard and lifted her eyes to him, hoping to see the answer in them. But the expression on his handsome face told her nothing, and on the chance that all of this was mere coincidence, she forced herself to smile as if the pin held no specific meaning to her. The cards shook in her hands as she laid them down in front of her in unspoken approval for the game to continue, and she prayed against all odds that she would win the hand. She must regain possession of the pin, for if he had figured out who she was and thought to use the piece of jewelry as evidence, she could then deny it all. Only John knew she had it, and with Hank as a witness to her having won it fairly in a poker game, Rhys had no way of proving anything. Unwillingly, her eyes shifted back to the pin lying on the pile of money. If he had taken it from her room, why use it to call her bet? Didn't he realize that without it the authorities wouldn't believe a word he said? Was he a bigger fool than she first thought him to be? It was all so confusing. If he knew who she was, why didn't he just confront her? Frowning, she glanced back up at him in time to see him toss down his cards.

"Well, I guess you've earned the right of calling yourself a better poker player than I," he said softly, a half smile crimping his mouth. "You win, Miss Redington."

Her victory should have brought her great satisfaction. As it was, Ashlee could only numbly gather in her winnings, including the diamond stickpin, then rise from the table.

"I'd appreciate it if everything was put back where it was before you go," she said to no one in particular as she turned toward her father's desk, the wad of bills in one hand, the pin in the other. "I'll lock up when I leave."

"Yes'm," Hank replied, frowning over at his companion. Something bothered Miss Ashlee, but he couldn't figure out what it was. She had played very good poker and won honestly. Yet she was acting as if she had bet her father's casino and lost. With a shrug, he scooped up the cards, stuffed them back in their container, and stood.

Once Arthur Redington had gotten the funding he needed to build Belle Chasse, he had designed his own office and specified that he wanted a safe built into one wall, in front of which he could hang a painting to hide it. No one other than Arthur, Dominique, Ashlee, John, and Elaine knew of its existence. Accordingly, Ashlee waited until she was alone before she took down the painting and opened the safe, placed the ledgers inside next to the casino's profits, then added the money she had won from Rhys. She stared at the thick pile of bills for a moment, tempted to take a handful, pack a bag, then flee New Orleans before Rhys went to her father and told him that his daughter was a thief. Thinking of the night she had first met Rhys, she slowly turned back to the desk and picked up the stickpin she had left lying there, twirling it between her thumb and finger. The smooth line of her brow wrinkled as she studied the glittering stone more closely. It seemed to be the same one, yet there was something different about it. She couldn't quite place what it was at first, and finally decided that the gem wasn't as large as she remembered it to be. She straightened suddenly. Was this a poor attempt at a replica? Clutching the pin in her hand, she spun back around, quickly shut the safe and locked it, then returned the painting to its place. There was one way to find out. Turning out the kerosene lamp, she followed the stream of moonlight coming in through the window to the door and quickly left her father's office.

Except for the desk clerk who sat propped in his chair against the wall sound asleep, Ashlee saw no one else in the lobby or along the narrow walkway surrounding the courtyard as she headed for the back entrance of the hotel. Hurrying through the foyer that divided the two separate living quarters belonging to the Redingtons, Ashlee rushed into her room, closed and locked the door behind her, then rushed to find a match with which to light the lamp sitting on her dresser. A yellow flickering glow quickly filled the space, and Ashlee wasted no time in pulling open a top drawer and withdrawing the box where she kept her jewelry. Lifting the lid, she searched through the contents until she had found the piece she looked for, her lovely face crimped in a worried frown as she held up the diamond stickpin she had stolen from Rhys Sinclair.

"I wasn't absolutely sure about you until now," the deep voice behind her admitted, and Ashlee spun around to find Rhys sitting in the rocker across the room from her.

It seemed her heart had lodged itself in her throat and

her chest had turned to rock. She could neither swallow nor voice a word in defense, much less draw a single breath. Her knees trembled and rather than collapse to the floor, she fell back against the dresser for support, her entire body tight with fear. Her first instinct was to run—as far and as fast as she could. Knowing there was no way out through the barred windows of her room, she glanced at the door, remembered that she had locked it, then mentally calculated how much time she would have to correct the problem before he was on her. Certain it was useless to try, she considered throwing something at him, in the hope her aim would be good enough to knock him out, and frantically surveyed the items nearest her. She chewed on her lower lip, eyes glistening with unshed tears, panic rising high, and bolted when she heard the rocker squeak as he lifted his weight from it.

"If you're thinking to run from me again, you might as well forget about it, Ashlee," he said softly, closing the distance between them. "Now that I know who you are there isn't a spot in the world where I won't find you." His dark eyes lowered to her black satin dress. "Whether you're clothed as a widow, a whore, or a young boy won't matter. I'll be able to pick you out of a crowd." A half smile twisted his mouth, his eyes looking at hers again. "After all, I know you better than anyone."

Ashlee jerked to her left when he stepped close enough to touch her. "I—I don't know what you're talking about," she lied, wondering how she had managed to keep her teeth from rattling.

"Don't you?" he chuckled, following her moves. "Then maybe I should refresh your memory."

With lightning speed, he reached out, caught her arm just above the elbow, and crushed her to him, his mouth coming down hard against hers. The long black curls fell loose of their pins and cascaded down her back in a brilliant torrent of flowing silk. The suddenness of his attack took her breath away, and the searing hotness of his kiss did little to restore her courage. She hung limp and motionless in his arms, certain that if he let go of her, she would tumble to the floor like the dying petals of a rose. But when his tongue lightly touched her lips then forced them apart and pushed inside, it jolted life back into her numb limbs. Long nails came up to claw his cheek, and Rhys instantly released her with a cry of pain, his hand flying to the bright red wounds in his flesh and his eyes flashing golden sparks of absolute fury. Ashlee stumbled back.

"You have a lot of nerve, Rhys Sinclair," she choked out, her chest heaving as she fought to cool the fire his embrace aroused.

"*I* have nerve?" he grated out through clenched teeth. "Young lady, you have more audacity in your little finger than all the people in the entire state of Louisiana thrown together."

"Oh really?" she countered, her temper flaring. "You're the Yankee who's come to New Orleans to prey on those less fortunate than you. I'm simply trying to make things even."

"By stealing?" he raged.

"That's what you're doing!"

Rhys's eyes narrowed and he picked up his grandfather's stickpin from the dresser where she had dropped it. Pointing it at her, he said, "I'll ignore that comment and excuse it as one made out of stupidity, Ashlee, just as I'll keep your little secret from your father. But only if you return the money you and your huge friend took from me. I'm sympathetic toward the south and their problems, but I don't appreciate waking up with my head pounding like a kettledrum because of your misguided loyalty."

"Misguided loyalty!" she exploded.

"Yes, misguided," he returned just as loudly. "The

237

south is the one who withdrew from the Union like a rebellious child who didn't like what his father told him to do. But we're the forgiving type and we'll try any way we can to mend our broken relationship."

"By coming here and taking what isn't yours?" she screamed.

Rhys's nostrils flared. He lowered his chin and glared back at her. "Name one. Name one thing I've taken that wasn't mine to have."

Visions of that night spent in his arms flashed in her mind. Tears welled in her eyes, and when she spoke, it came in hardly more than a whisper. "How soon you forget."

The welts on his cheek suddenly didn't sting as much as being accused of rape. "Wait just a minute, Ashlee," he warned, the anger fading. "I met no resistance on your part. God, if you'd given me one sign, one hint who you really were, I wouldn't have— Ashlee, you were dressed like a prostitute. You talked like one. You accepted my payment!"

"And what did you expect me to do?" she shouted. "Admit I was a thief so you could have me arrested?"

"I wouldn't have done that," he argued with a heavy sigh.

"You expect me to believe that?" She choked back a sob. "The whole thing was an elaborate hoax to catch me. If you went to that much trouble, I didn't expect you to just let me go because I asked you to. You wanted revenge . . . just as you do now!"

"At first I did, yes," he admitted. "You'd made a fool of me. And not once, but twice."

Ashlee's chin quivered, even though she had raised it bravely in the air. "And now you don't," she mocked.

Rhys stared at the exquisite face framed in thick ebony hair, feeling the pain and humiliation reflected in her beautiful blue eyes. "No. Not any more. I didn't know then what I do now," he said softly.

"And what's that?" she sneered, blinking and sending a single tear streaming down her smooth cheek.

"That you're not really a criminal. You're stealing to help out your father." He smiled tenderly when she whirled away from him and went to stand before the window. Noiselessly, he followed, pausing behind her for a moment to smell the sweet fragrance of her hair and touch a silky curl. "I'd like to help."

She spun around to glare at him. "Would you?" she jeered. "Then why don't you pack your bag and go back where you came from?" She started to brush past him, but he caught her arm and pulled her back. "Let go of me!"

"I don't think that's what you really want me to do," he murmured with a half smile.

"Oh?" she scoffed, trying to yank free of him. "And what is?"

His brown eyes softened. "This," he whispered, his other hand coming up to trap the back of her head as he lowered his mouth to hers.

Outraged, Ashlee stomped the heel of her shoe against his toe and pushed against his wide, hard chest with all her might, instantly winning her freedom. "You conceited jackanapes!" she growled. "Hasn't it ever occurred to you that there's one woman among us all that's not interested in you?"

A devilish grin curled his lips. "Many times," he confessed. "But you're not one of them."

"Ha!" she howled and moved to step past him, but Rhys quickly blocked the way. "I'm on the top of the list!"

Rhys tilted his head to one side. "You may think so, but I don't. Otherwise, you would have taken your chances that night in my cabin and told me who you really were. You wouldn't have let it go that far if you honestly didn't want me to touch you."

"I was praying the drug would take hold!" she rallied.

He shrugged one shoulder. "Maybe. But there's no chance of that happening now." He shot out a hand, seized her arm, and crushed her to him. "Shall we find out who's right?"

Before she could answer him, Rhys captured her lips with his in a fierce, demanding kiss that shook her very soul and ignited a fire deep within her. Her mind screamed hatred for the Yankee while her body responded eagerly, and after a brief struggle, she looped her arms around his neck and kissed him hard and long and passionately. The warmth of his hard, muscular body pressed against hers seared every inch of her, setting her aflame with uncontrollable desire, and she moaned aloud, her head falling back, when his kisses moved to trail a sultry path down her neck.

Ashlee's world reeled when she felt his hands move to the buttons up the front of her dress to unfasten them one at a time—slowly, deliberately. The black satin cloth slid off her shoulders and a moment later the dress and her petticoats glided to the floor in a pool at her feet. Kicking off her shoes, she stepped out of the yards of crinoline and satin, drawing him with her toward the bed. Their lips met again, their breathing quick and labored as Ashlee pulled his coat from across his hard, muscular arms and tossed the garment on the floor with her own. Next came the buttons on his lacy shirt while Rhys held her delicate face in his huge hands and kissed the corner of her mouth, the tip of her nose, each eyelid, her cheek, and finally claimed her parted, trembling lips once more. Tugged free of his trousers, the shirt found its place on the floor beside the other discarded clothes, while Rhys's quick fingers unlaced the strings of her camisole to free the creamy white breasts aching for his touch. The light from the kerosene lamp bathed the couple in a golden glow and Ashlee's flesh tingled as his eyes roamed freely over the treasure he had uncovered. Oddly enough, she felt no shame or embarrassment.

His hand came up to brush away a dark strand of hair from her temple, then lift the luscious curls off her shoulder, while his fingers lightly traced the silkened outline of her throat and slowly descended to the firm mound of flesh. Gently, tenderly, he cupped her breast, his thumb languidly stroking its peak while his brown eyes darkened with lust and stared longingly into hers. Without a word, he lowered his head, his lips parted and leisurely tasting the sweetness of her mouth before brushing against her cheek, her slender throat, and on to greater rewards as his hot kisses trailed a molten path to her breast. Ashlee groaned in delicious ecstasy when his moist, warm mouth covered the taut nipple and his tongue played lightly with it, sending an explosive fire through her veins. Certain she would faint from the blissful rapture of his caress, she closed her eyes to stop the spinning axis of her mind and gently laid her shaking hands against the sinewy ripples across his shoulders. When he straightened to capture her lips once more, she glided her open palms down the iron-thewed length of his chest, across his thickly muscled ribs, and up the wide expanse of his back to draw him to her. Their fevered flesh touched, their lips met and clung desperately, passionately to each other. His mouth moving hungrily over hers, Rhys bent slightly, swept her up in his arms, and gently laid her on the feather bed where he quickly pulled the camisole from her trembling body. He left her only long enough to shed the rest of his clothes. Ashlee's eyes darkened with burning desire as she openly appraised his sleek, golden body, her own tingling with anticipation before he lowered himself upon her, welcomed eagerly into her opened arms.

Their bodies touched full length as his hand followed

241

the smooth outline of her waist, hip, and thigh. Then in a rush he rose above her, parting her knees with his own and kissing her savagely as his manhood pressed hotly into her. Delirious with passion, he moved deep and hard, and Ashlee met each thrust in mounding glory, lifted high beyond their earthly world on wings of wild rhapsody. Carried to the height of ecstasy, they triumphed in the joining of their souls until, spent and exhausted, they floated through endless time nestled in each other's arms as though no other universe existed.

Chapter Eight

Shrugging into his coat, Rhys paused in the foyer's entryway before stepping out into the courtyard and closing the door behind him making certain no one would see him coming from the Redingtons' quarters at such an inappropriate hour. Rumors were sure to fly if someone spotted him, and Ashlee's reputation would take the brunt of their gossip since everyone at Belle Chasse knew that she was alone for the evening . . . or at least expected to be. And if word spread that she had had a visitor for the night and the visitor had been the casino's new poker dealer, Rhys was sure John Hardin wouldn't waste any time finding him and demanding an explanation—if he'd even allow him one before he doubled up a huge fist and slammed it against his jaw. A vague smile parted his lips. John's temper would certainly cool once he learned the real reason that had brought Rhys here in the first place.

Following the stone pathway leading to the back entryway into the hotel lobby, Rhys glanced up at the starlit sky, sucking in a deep breath of cool night air and thinking how much the velvety blackness reminded him of Ashlee's hair. They had lain in each other's arms for a long while, neither of them speaking, and Rhys hoped it was because she was thinking the same thoughts as he. No other woman had touched his heart the way she had. And now that she was aware that he knew who she was, maybe things would be different between them. He frowned suddenly, setting his steps in the direction of the lobby door. Different? How? In less than twelve hours she would be going to the train depot to meet her fiancé, and according to Dominique, it wouldn't be long after that before Ashlee was married and shipped off to Paris. The lines in his brow deepened even more as he pulled open the door and went inside.

Rounding the end of the long staircase, Rhys paused to survey the lobby. He neither heard nor saw anyone else other than the desk clerk who still slept soundly in his chair. Moving as quietly as possible across the marble floor, Rhys hurried past the sleeping man whose snoring, he swore, could drown out cannon fire. He unlocked the door to Arthur's office with the key he had given him, and went inside. While everyone at Belle Chasse was asleep, he would go over the casino's records.

Fumbling through his vest pocket for a match, he scraped a thumbnail over its tip, setting it aflame and guiding his way to the desk where he lit the lamp then tossed the match in an ashtray. Once the room was flooded with light, he circled in back of the desk and took down the oil painting, assuming Ashlee had put the ledgers in the safe along with the money she had won from him. A soft smile spread over his face as he took a second key from his pocket and opened the tumblers, recalling the frightened look that had come over Ashlee when she spun around to find him in her room. He had only planned to confront her about the thefts that had taken place on the steamers, not wind up in bed with her. Lifting the books from inside the safe, he turned with them and sat down at the desk.

A half hour passed before Rhys leaned back in the

chair and took a cheroot from his pocket. According to the records, Belle Chasse was indeed losing money, but it wasn't that revelation that knotted his brows. Expenses paid out to keep the place running matched against the combined income of the hotel, restaurant, and casino proved unequal in many entries, too much in others and rarely enough to turn a profit. He struck a match and took a long drag on his cheroot, idly watching the smoke curl above him. What raised his curiosity was that on the few occasions when the casino's winnings were more than the expenses for the day, the entry was always made in the same handwriting. And since that handwriting matched the last notation made with today's date, it meant that it occurred only on the night's Ashlee took care of the books. If he was right about her and John Hardin, then it didn't make sense. Why wouldn't she take the opportunity to alter the records and keep the extra money? Clamping the cheroot between his teeth, he leaned forward, closed the ledgers, and stood. Well, he'd just have to ask her.

The magnificent grandfather clock standing stately tall in the lobby struck the hour of four as Rhys quietly locked the office door and crossed toward the back entrance, glancing briefly at the sleeping desk clerk. He'd have plenty of time to talk to Ashlee before the hotel came alive with activity. He smiled crookedly. Actually, he wasn't worried about anyone other than John at the moment. Until he confronted Ashlee and gave himself some leverage by forcing the truth from her, the huge giant posed a greater danger to his health. In fact, Rhys wasn't sure it would make any difference to the man if John ever learned what went on between him and Ashlee this night. He left the hotel in a hurry, followed the stone walkway to the Redingtons' quarters, and went inside to the foyer, wondering if Ashlee would still be asleep as he had left her. Turning the knob, he quietly pushed open

245

the door to her chambers and stepped into her room.

A soft ashen light streamed in through the window, across the floor, and onto the bed, and Rhys grinned to himself once he realized Ashlee wasn't even aware that he had left her for a time. He was tempted to strip off his clothes and climb back in beside her, but he knew that if he did that, he'd probably forget about talking and more than likely wake her up before he had a chance to do anything. He quietly closed the door, turned the key in the lock, and went to the nightstand to relight the lamp he had extinguished before leaving her room.

A bright yellow blaze penetrated Ashlee's dreams and she stirred, a sweet smile lifting the corners of her mouth. The sheets felt cool against her naked flesh and Ashlee stretched, reveling in the delicious sensation they aroused. But just as quickly the regalement vanished when visions of Rhys exploded in her mind, and she sat straight up in bed, the covers clutched beneath her chin. The excitement of her shameful behavior turned to guilt the instant she saw him standing near the window staring out into the night, and thoughts of what she had done brought a flush to her cheeks. Unable to move or speak a word, she simply stared at him, wondering what demands he would make . . . and how often. Her eyes widened fearfully when he turned to look at her, and Ashlee contemplated making a dash for the door whether she was dressed or not. But once his warm gaze fell upon her, she felt a rush of titillating exhilaration course through every inch of her body. He was the most handsome man she had ever known. The golden glow of lamplight seemed to intensify that fact as it caressed the strong line of his jaw, sandy-colored hair, wide set brown eyes trimmed with thick lashes, perfect nose, and even the mysterious scar on his cheek. She was hypnotized by the mere sight of him, and although she wanted to hate him, she couldn't. She jumped when he moved away from the window, going to the armoire and taking out her robe.

"We have to talk," he said quietly, handing the garment to her.

Apprehensively, Ashlee reached out to take it, her slender hand trembling a bit. She waited until he had gone back to the window to look outside again before quickly donning the robe. Yanking it tightly around her, she tied the sash and slid off the bed, thinking it would be best for her if she were as far away from that haven as possible. He was like an intoxicating drink to her. One sip and she would do anything he wished. She backed away and went to stand next to the dresser.

"How long have you and Mr. Hardin been stealing?" he asked, his gaze affixed to something outside in the darkness.

Ashlee swallowed hard. "A little over a year," she answered weakly.

"Why?" He turned then to look at her, his dark eyes shadowed by his frown.

A shiver ran down her spine. She gulped and fidgeted with the satin sash around her waist, trying desperately to pull her attention away from his lean, hard frame. Why couldn't he have been a skinny, bespectacled old man? And why had her courage left her? She forced herself to meet his eyes. "To help Papa."

Rhys stared at her a moment, thinking she had never looked more beautiful, and fought the temptation to go to her and take her in his arms. He glanced away. "Suppose you tell me how you think running the risk of being caught would help your father," he said, pulling the rocker away from the wall and sitting down. Resting his elbows on its arms, he interlaced his fingers, his thumbs tapping together in quiet impatience.

Ashlee chewed on her lower lip. A knot formed in her throat and she had to blink back the tears that threatened to spill down her cheeks. She took a deep breath and let it

247

out slowly before she answered. "I never planned on getting caught."

"A thief never does," he mocked.

Ashlee's spine stiffened. "Don't make it sound like John and I are backwater riffraff, Mr. Sinclair," she snapped, some of her spirit returning. "Our cause was a noble one."

A vague smile parted his lips, and he rested his chin on one fist while he considered her remark. "Somehow I never associated nobleness with stealing."

"Of course you wouldn't," she snarled, feeling her old self again. "I doubt you've done a noble thing in your life, seeing as how you're a Yankee."

The smile sparkled in his eyes. "Then suppose you explain the similarity. But put it in simple words so this Yankee can understand it."

"Unlike you, I'm sure, my family has had to work for every dime they ever had. Belle Chasse was just beginning to bring in enough money for us to live comfortably when the war broke out. I think even you can figure out what happened to it then."

He nodded, and Ashlee turned her back on him to pick up her brush and pull the tangles from her hair. The angry strokes ceased when she caught his reflection in the mirror, and the brush landed with a thud on the dresser. She spun back around.

"John and I couldn't bear the thought of Papa losing Belle Chasse, so we decided to help. Since the only people who seemed to have any money were the northerners feeding off the rest of us, John and I came up with a way to get some of our money back." A sardonic smile twisted her mouth. "I don't think I have to give a detailed account of how we managed it, since you were twice a victim."

He shook his head. "I'm just curious as to what happened to my money."

"It's quite simple," she replied, shrugging her delicate shoulders as she crossed to the bed and sat down near the foot of it. "We'd channel it back into the casino through my blackjack table."

"You mean you never kept any for yourselves?"

"Of course not!" Ashlee exploded.

"Then why is Belle Chasse still losing money?"

"If I knew that, I'd put a stop to it," she hissed, her blue eyes flashing. He made no reply, and at his continued silence, Ashlee suddenly realized what he was implying. "You don't believe me. In fact, you think I'm responsible for the losses at the casino, don't you?" She jumped to her feet, tiny fists perched on her narrow hips. "How dare you!" she raged. "Name one reason why I'd like to see my father's business fail if you can, you . . . you . . . Yankee!"

"Oh, I believe you," he assured her. "I'm just not sure about your . . . partner."

"John?" she shrieked.

Rhys stared at her for a moment, then casually reached in his pocket for a cheroot. "If you can manage to cool that temper of yours for a minute and allow me the chance to present all the facts, I'm sure you'll see the possibility and the opportunity. You, however, will have to supply the reason."

Ashlee's pale eyes narrowed. "If I had a gun, I'd shoot you for even thinking such a thing. And I'm not going to stand here and let you insult my friend. John loves my father like a brother. He owes Papa his life. He isn't about to steal from him. Now I suggest you take that blasted cigar and leave this room immediately before I start screaming and bring the bloody place down around your ears."

Settling back in the rocker, Rhys studied the cigar he held. "I'm afraid it isn't that simple. You and Mr. Hardin stole a lot of money from me and several of my friends,

249

and those men have entrusted me to get it back for them. I'm not leaving Belle Chasse until I've recovered every penny of it."

"Well, that will be a little difficult, Mr. Sinclair," she sneered. "I already told you what happened to it. So why don't you just pack your things and go back up north where you belong?" Apprehension tickled the hairs on the back of her neck as she watched Rhys calmly return the cheroot to his pocket, then easily push himself up to his feet. She took a step backward when he started to advance.

"I can't do that right now, Ashlee," he murmured, just a hint of a smile on his lips. "Not until after I've talked with your father. Besides"—he slowly, deliberately trailed her as she moved around the end of the bed and backed into the wall behind her—"I don't think you really want me to go."

Ashlee felt as if she hadn't a stitch of clothing on when Rhys's gaze leisurely traveled the length of her. Unknowingly, she grasped the lapels of her robe tightly around her neck, her eyes wide, and she jumped when he raised a hand to lean it against the wall near her head.

"But if you'll tell me the truth about your big friend and help me recover at least a part of the money, I might leave a little sooner than I planned."

Ashlee held her breath as Rhys gently curled a lock of her hair around his finger. Her entire body tingled.

"That is, of course, if you really want me to go."

His breath fell warmly against her cheek as he leaned closer, and Ashlee couldn't pull her eyes from those inviting lips that continued to descend upon her. Suddenly, something he had said earlier registered in her brain, and she stiffened.

"Talk to my father about what?" she demanded, ducking beneath his arm and racing to the other side of the room where she was safe from his mystifying power

250

over her.

Rhys could have stopped her if he had wanted. But he rather enjoyed playing with her. And she hadn't told him everything he wanted to know. Chuckling to himself, he straightened and turned around to face her.

"Why, about what you and Mr. Hardin are doing," he said most matter-of-factly.

Ashlee's tiny chin dropped. "You wouldn't," she gasped. "Oh, Rhys, say you won't tell him. He'd never understand. And he'd never forgive us. He does have his pride, you know, and if he learned his daughter and best friend were stealing to keep him from losing his business, he'd think that we thought he was a failure. Rhys, if you have any compassion at all for the man, you won't injure him so."

Slipping off his coat, he tossed it on the end of the bed, then came to the side and sat down on the mattress, kicking off his shoes as if he planned to stay a while. He forced himself not to look at her as he fluffed up the pillows, propped them against the headboard, then settled himself back comfortably on them. With his hands behind his head for support, he stared up at the ceiling above him and said, "Then suppose you convince me that I shouldn't tell him everything I know about you and John Hardin."

"How?"

"By telling me the truth . . . about everything."

Frowning, Ashlee took a step forward. "But I already have."

"Then suppose you tell me again," he said, turning his head to look at her. "Start at the beginning and explain every move the two of you made each time you pulled off one of your jobs." He studied the ceiling overhead again. "Maybe then I'll believe you."

If preventing her father from learning the truth weren't so important to Ashlee, she would have been

251

tempted to tell this arrogant Yankee to remove himself from her bed and her life. After all, he had no proof of anything now that she had a witness who saw her win that stickpin in a poker game. The lines in her brow deepened as she glared over at him. It would be only his word against hers where her father was concerned, yet Ashlee was sure that wouldn't stop Rhys Sinclair. And she didn't intend for John and her to give up their little venture with the riverboats. As long as Belle Chasse needed money, she would do everything possible to supply it. And that meant that if she weren't careful, Rhys would catch her and John in the act and have all the proof he needed. Feeling the crispness in the air, she hugged her robe more tightly to her and moved to sit down in the rocker where she could curl her feet beneath her for warmth. A calculating smile brightened her eyes. She'd tell him everything, pretend that she was truly sorry and that it wouldn't happen again, plead with him not to tell her father. Once she was sure he believed her, she and John would plan another robbery.

"John would choose the steamer," she began, "from conversations he'd overhear at the casino . . . about the ones that were planning a big game. He'd take me to the dock to board the steamer, then take the carriage upriver to where he'd hidden a rowboat along the shoreline and wait. I'd embark in disguise and go to my cabin, where I'd change into another disguise. Each job was different as to how I'd slip the laudanum into the gamblers' drinks, but the result was the same. After they had all fallen asleep, I'd sneak in, steal their money, then return to my cabin for the rest of my things. A short while before the boat reached our meeting point, I'd go to the cargo deck and wait for John to row in alongside. I'd toss in my bag, then climb down after it. We'd row back to shore, tie up the boat, and return to New Orleans in the carriage. From there, John and I would split up."

"Who kept the money?" Rhys asked.

"I did. Until I went to work the next night. Then I'd turn it in to Dominique with the winnings from my blackjack table. Since it's all thrown into one pile, she never got suspicious because she had no way of knowing my table supplied more than the others."

"And she always takes care of the books?"

"Except on the nights she and Papa are gone. Then I do."

"When is a bank deposit made?"

"The following morning. Dominique takes care of it. That's also when she pays the bills."

Rhys was quiet for a moment, deep in thought, and Ashlee frowned, wondering where all these questions might be leading.

"Before Dominique took over, was the routine always the same . . . as it's done now?" he finally asked.

Ashlee thought a moment then nodded. "Yes. Why do you want to know?"

"So other than Mr. Hardin, no one else has access to the money."

Ashlee stiffened irately. "If you're implying—"

"What about the dealers?" he went on, swinging his long legs over the edge of the bed and sitting up. "Is there any way they could help themselves to a little of the winnings before Mr. Hardin came to collect it?"

"No," she snapped. "And let me set you straight about something. Nearly every one of our dealers have been with Belle Chasse from the start. They'd never steal from Papa."

"People change, Ashlee," Rhys pointed out with a lift of his tawny brows.

"Yeah, well, these people haven't," she seethed. "And I'm sorely tempted to tell John what you've said about him." She bolted from the rocker and yanked the sash on her robe a little tighter. "If you accuse John of stealing

253

from Papa, then you're accusing me as well." A dainty finger tapped her chest.

"It's a possibility," he shrugged, reclining on the bed again.

"What?" she exploded. "Me? You're insane! Why would I steal from my own father? I love him. I want him to succeed." Enraged that he would even think such a thing, much less suggest it, she stormed across the room to confront him. "Why? Why would I steal out of my own pocket?"

With his hands clasped behind his head, Rhys raised his chin a notch to look at her. The fury crackling in her eyes turned them an icy shade of blue, and it was all he could do to keep himself from pulling her down on top of him and kissing that sensuous mouth. "A person would have to be deaf and blind not to know about your feelings toward your stepmother, Ashlee. Or realize that Dominique is a fortune hunter." He smiled at the change in her expression. "You may think I'm nothing more than a stupid Yankee, but I'm smarter than you give me credit. And if I could spot it, then I'm sure you were aware of it long ago."

Ashlee's eyes narrowed, suspicious. "And what has that to do with your accusing me of stealing from my father?"

"If there's no money to be had, an opportunist will soon look in other directions for his—or her—wealth." He looked away from her and crossed his ankles, settling his long frame comfortably on the bed. "If Belle Chasse failed and your father lost everything, the chances of Dominique being counted as one would greatly increase. It would be a very simple method of getting rid of her." He glanced up at her and grinned. He could see her mind working on the idea and knew then that Ashlee had already told him the truth. She and John weren't

254

responsible for the losses at the casino. "However," he continued, studying the ceiling above him, "it might not work."

"Why?" she quickly asked, pulling up the rocker next to the bed and sitting down close to him.

"Arthur might sell out before you and Mr. Hardin had saved enough to purchase Belle Chasse."

"Purchase—" Ashlee frowned, not having completely understood Rhys's theory. "Where would we ever—" She straightened suddenly in the chair, her tiny chin dropping. "Oh, I get it. You thought John and I were keeping the money we stole from the gamblers on the riverboats as well as taking however much we could from the casino in order to buy Belle Chasse and expose Dominique to Papa." She smiled broadly. "What a marvelous idea."

Rhys pressed his lips tightly together to keep from smiling. "You mean I was wrong?" he mocked, noticing the shrewd gleam in her eyes.

"You were," she absently replied, then bounced to her feet with a wide grin. "But I'll fix that."

"Whoa there, Ashlee," he warned, quickly jumping off the bed to catch her wrist when she started toward the armoire for something to wear. "That was only conjecture on my part . . . the only explanation I could come up with that would warrant your need to steal."

Ashlee stared at the fingers grasped around her arm for a moment, then jerked free of his hold. "And I thank you for it. Now you've given me a way to solve two problems." She darted past him, crossed to the armoire, and pulled the door open.

"What do you mean?" he frowned, following her.

"It means, Mr. Sinclair," she threw back over her shoulder as she searched through the garments in the wardrobe, "that you, in your bumbling Yankee way, have struck upon a method to free Belle Chasse of a nuisance."

"By continuing with your little masquerade?" he finished.

"That's right," she admitted flippantly.

"Well, I've got news for you, young woman," he growled, grabbing her arm and spinning her around. "Your days of parading around the waterfront dressed like a prostitute are long gone."

"Oh, really?" she jeered. "Well, I've got news for you, Yankee, they're not and there isn't a thing you can do about it!"

Rhys met her angry glare with his own. "Would you care to wager a diamond stickpin?"

Ashlee's cheeks pinkened instantly, but she was not about to relent. "Bet anything you like. You're not going to stop me." Twisting free of him, she turned slightly, took the first dress she grabbed from the armoire, and walked to the bed with it clutched in one hand. Tossing it down, she headed for the dresser. "Be sure and shut the door on your way out, Mr. Sinclair." She opened a drawer and took out a clean chemise and pair of stockings, frowning once she turned back to find that he hadn't moved or gave any indication that he intended to. "What's the matter? Didn't I make myself clear? Get out!"

Ashlee noticed something about Rhys as he stood glaring back at her that she had never seen before, and it frightened her. As angry as he was with her, his eyes had darkened to nearly an ebony hue, but it was the small scar on his cheek that caught and held her attention, for it gleamed almost white against his tanned complexion. For a moment, she feared what he would do. Some of her courage faded.

"I'm only going to tell you this one time, Ashlee," he snarled, and she thought how much he looked like the sketch of a fierce Viking warrior Priscilla had shown her

256

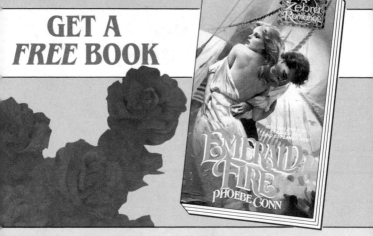

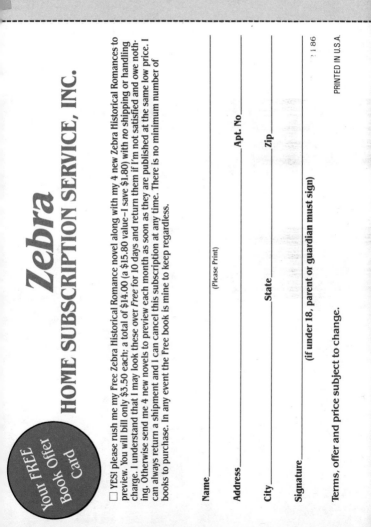

when Ashlee was a little girl. Even on paper, the pencil drawing of the man scared her, and now, it seemed, he stood in her very own room not five feet away. "You're to forget about this silly notion of robbing people or stealing from the casino in order to buy out Belle Chasse just to get rid of your stepmother. If I ever hear that you're planning such a thing, I'll go straight to your father. Am I making myself clear?"

Ashlee's mouth fell open. "Oh—oh, I understand. I think it's called blackmail." Her chest heaving with suppressed rage, she knotted her fists and jammed them on her hips. "And I suppose now that you know about me, you'll just waltz right into my room any time you feel the impulse, expecting me to welcome you with open arms just to insure your silence."

The thoughts of such an alluring sight softened his mood and brought a twinkle to his dark brown eyes. "Well, maybe not with open arms . . ."

Ashlee's entire body stiffened. "How dare you," she hissed through clenched teeth, wanting desperately to hit him with something.

Jerking around, she espied an assortment of perfume bottles sitting on top of the dresser. Giving little thought to which fragrance she could do without, Ashlee scooped up one in each hand, ready to fling them at him. But as she twirled back prepared to do battle, she gave a startled gasp when Rhys lunged for her, pinning her arms at her sides with his own clamped tightly around her.

"Let go of me," she wailed, struggling uselessly.

Imprisoned in his steely hold, Ashlee was powerless to stop him from taking her weapons or to ignore the beguiling sensation his rock-hard body pressed against her own aroused. And when he trapped the thick locks of her hair at the base of her skull in his hand, she fought only briefly before giving in to the passion his mere presence ignited. His lips descended upon hers, and as she surrendered to his kiss, she silently cursed her weakness, hating him for being the cause. Even her body went against her convictions as her hands moved to unloop the ascot at his neck, then unfasten the buttons on his shirt and slip it off his shoulders. The sash of her robe quickly followed, and in the next instant she stood captive in his strong embrace, her naked breasts pressed against the warm, sleek flesh of his wide, muscular chest as his hand roamed possessively down her spine, sparking a liquid fire through her entire being. The fierceness of their passionate kiss never waned even while Rhys lifted her in his arms and carried her to the bed. Bending a knee upon the mattress, he laid her gently down upon it, shed the rest of his clothes, then joined her there. His fingers glided over the silky smoothness of her bare flesh while his lips and tongue tasted the sweetness of her mouth then nibbled on her earlobe. Eager to unite and blend their souls as one, Ashlee drew him down on top of her, willingly parting her thighs as his knee pressed against them. Their desires, forged like tempered steel, spiraled them to dizzying heights, their bodies molded together and moving in perfect harmony until their passion reached its limit. Caught up in the rapture of their desire, they floated breathless and contented in the warmth of their embrace until all that remained were the glowing embers of their romantic interlude, a time destined to play upon their hearts and minds for all eternity.

The pinks and pastel yellows of early morning found Ashlee sitting on the sill of the opened window in her room looking out to view the coming of the dawn. Tears glistened in her pale blue eyes and spilled down her cheeks as she listened to the excited chirping of the sparrows and smelled the sweet fragrance of jasmine in the air. She hugged her arms about her trembling form to still her sobs, while in her thoughts she pleaded for someone to take away the pain she felt.

Rhys had left her shortly before the first faint evidence of sunlight streaked the sky. She had watched him don his clothes from the warm haven of their bed, unashamed of both her boldness and her behavior. He had been the first, and Ashlee knew there would always be a special feeling for him in her heart—even if she married another. He must have sensed her thoughts, for he, too, remained silent. But once he had gone, doubt began to grow—doubt that he would ever feel the same for her. Nothing would erase the fact that Rhys Sinclair was a northerner . . . a carpetbagger. And everyone in New Orleans knew that that breed only used people to better their position. Tears had gathered in her eyes. It was probably why Rhys had made love to her. He wanted something, and it didn't include her. But what could it be? She had no money, no property. Belle Chasse belonged to her father. A sudden revelation tore at her insides, and Ashlee had quickly left her bed, picked up her robe from the floor where it had fallen, and put it on.

"You're very cunning, Rhys Sinclair," she whispered through her tears, absently watching the last of the bright, glowing stars fade into the soft shades of twilight. "You never once truly thought John and I were conspiring to take over Belle Chasse. It was your idea all along. You just wanted me to carry it out so that when Papa decided to sell, you could outbid us." Angrily swiping away the moisture from her face with the back of her hand, she stood, closed the window, and pulled the draperies shut. "You bastard," she hissed, picking up her stockings and chemise. "Well, your little plan didn't work. I know what you're up to and I'll do whatever is necessary to see that you never own Belle Chasse." And the first thing she would do was talk to John. Together they would figure out a way to stop the damn Yankee.

*   *   *

"Good morning, Ashlee," John smiled warmly, rising from his chair and holding out his hand at the one next to him. "Sleep well?"

Ashlee could feel her cheeks pinken, realizing she hadn't slept at all, and quickly glanced around the restaurant to make sure no one was close enough to hear their conversation. "We need to talk," she said quietly, slipping into the chair. She slid it nearer to his, then rested her arms along the edge of the table.

A frown deepened the lines in John's brow. "Why is it I get the feeling that trouble's brewing?" he asked, sitting down again and reaching for the pot of coffee in front of him.

"Because there is," Ashlee admitted, moving her cup closer when he offered to fill it.

"And it involves Mr. Sinclair, no doubt," he added. "Do you think maybe I could finish my breakfast first before you tell me? I hate getting bad news on an empty stomach."

"Empty or full isn't going to change the fact that Mr. Sinclair knows all about us," she confessed, her brows knotted together.

"Ashlee," he moaned, mixing a teaspoon of sugar in his coffee, "I told you before that all we had to do was be careful what we said. There's no way he can connect us with the robberies." He took a sip and wrinkled his nose when the hot liquid burned his tongue. "Except, of course, for the stickpin you stole from him. And you got rid of that." When she didn't say a word, an awful dread formed a knot in his belly, and John slumped in his chair. He didn't even have to look at her to know what expression was on her face. Putting his cup back in its saucer, he folded his arms over his chest, leaned his head back, and closed his eyes. "So start at the beginning," he sighed.

Ashlee looked sheepishly at her hands folded in her

lap. "He tricked me into playing a game of poker with him."

"Poker?" John echoed, sitting erect with one arm on the table's edge, the other on the back of her chair. "Ashlee, you know how your father feels about your playing poker."

"Only because he thinks I can't win," she blurted out in defense.

"Well, did you?"

"Yes," she exclaimed. But remembering the outcome of the match, her shoulders drooped and she fell back in her chair. "And no," she reluctantly added.

John shook his head and leaned both elbows on the table. "Would you care to explain that one?"

Next to her father, John meant more to her than anyone else in the world—except maybe for Priscilla—and she truly hated telling him how stupid she had been even after he had warned her about the Yankee several times. But she knew she must. Otherwise, there was a strong possibility her father would lose Belle Chasse.

"It doesn't matter how, but Mr. Sinclair lured me into playing against him. Now that it's over, I suspect he lost on purpose to enable himself to bet a piece of jewelry on the final hand."

"Jewelry?" John repeated. "What jewelry?"

Ashlee sucked in a deep breath and exhaled slowly. "A diamond stickpin—just like the one I stole from him earlier."

John twisted in the chair to look her straight in the eye. "And he knew just from seeing your reaction."

Ashlee shrugged. She didn't want to tell John the whole story. She was afraid of what he might do if he learned Rhys had followed her to her room and what had happened then.

"So what does he want besides his money back?" he asked, waving off the waitress who had started toward the table.

"He never really said," Ashlee told him. "It's more what he didn't say." She raised a hand to silence him when he started to voice a question. "Let me explain what I think he's after. Once he was convinced that you and I were responsible for the thefts, he proceeded to tell me why he thought you and I needed to steal. John, he accused us not only of stealing from the men on the riverboats, but from the casino as well."

John's mouth dropped open, but before he could say anything, Ashlee hurriedly continued.

"He said he thought we were trying to accumulate enough money to buy out Belle Chasse and expose Dominique as a fortune hunter. Well, you can imagine how much I liked the idea, and I didn't try to hide it. And that's when he did a complete turn around." She leaned forward with her arms braced against the table. "He told me that if I even so much as thought about it, he'd go to Papa and tell him everything!" She glanced over her shoulder at the guests coming into the restaurant. "You know what I think?" she asked in a whisper. "I think that's exactly what he's hoping we'll do."

"Whatever for?" John exclaimed.

"Because by the time we had saved up enough money to buy Belle Chasse from Papa, he would have already sold it—to none other than Mr. Sinclair. I think that's why he's here, why he took a job in the casino, and why he planted such an idea in my head. He wants us to force Papa into selling so *he* can be the one to buy it!"

Frowning, John shook his head and leaned back in his chair. "I don't know, Ashlee," he said after a while. "Mr. Sinclair doesn't strike me as the type to do something so underhanded. He—"

"Of course, he is!" Ashlee snapped. "He's a Yankee, isn't he?"

"And a very wealthy one from what I hear," he barked.

262

"If he wanted to buy this place, he could do it without our help." Leaning forward, he wrapped his hands around his coffee cup and absently studied its contents. "What puzzles me is that he didn't insist on having his money returned or that he hasn't gone to the sheriff with what he knows about us. There has to be a reason for that, and I don't think it's because of what you claim he's planning." He stood up suddenly.

"Where are you going?" Ashlee demanded.

"To ask a few questions," he told her. "And in the meantime, I want you to stay away from Mr. Sinclair."

"That will be a little difficult since Dominique ordered him to escort me to the depot this afternoon to meet her cousin's train," Ashlee jeered.

"Today? Fabron is expected here today?"

"Yes. Hadn't you heard?" she scoffed. "And by this time next week, I'll probably be marching down the aisle with him if Dominique has anything to say about it."

A sadness tugged at the corners of John's mouth, knowing that Ashlee was right. Dominique wanted the girl married and out of the way. But the vows hadn't been exchanged yet, and if God permitted, John would do something to alter the Frenchwoman's plans. "Have faith, Child," he said softly, touching her cheek with a huge hand. "If worse comes to worse, I'll take you away from here before that can happen."

Tears filled Ashlee's eyes at the man's kindness, and she quickly covered his thick fingers with her own delicate ones, grateful for his patience, but most of all his friendship.

Chapter Nine

Since Arthur's marriage to Dominique, the couple seldom went to church, leaving Ashlee to attend services alone or with John whenever she could persuade him to go. She didn't try this morning. She preferred going by herself, hoping that the long walk to the chapel would bring the kind of peace she needed right now.

The streets along the way were crowded with churchgoers all dressed in their Sunday best, and Ashlee smiled sweetly back at those who voiced their greeting to her. It was indeed a cheery day, with bright, warm sunlight falling all around and a crisp, invigorating breeze pulling at the locks of hair peeking out from beneath her bonnet. Ordinarily, Ashlee would have enjoyed the brisk stroll and the companionship of others, but she couldn't get her mind off Rhys and why she hadn't slept at all last night.

Nearing the front steps of the church, she paused and looked up at the tall, spiraling bell tower, listening to the sharp, clear tones pouring out from it. It was usually here that she felt most reverent, but today the only feeling she could arouse was guilt—guilt about stealing and about her shameless behavior with Rhys. She frowned and started into the church, vowing never to allow herself to be alone with Rhys again. A relenting smile touched her mouth. She wasn't too sure about stealing.

The pews were almost full by the time Ashlee got there, and she had to sit near the front. Normally, she wouldn't mind, but in her emotional state it made her feel as though everyone were staring at her. Quickly taking her seat, she bowed her head and refused to look up until the pipe organ bellowed out the prelude of the first hymn to be sung. Rising with the rest of the congregation, she took the hymnal from its holder and hurriedly leafed through it to the appropriate page.

Ashlee had been told by many of the church members that she had a very pleasant soprano voice and that it was always refreshing to hear it raised in song. The compliment never failed to make her blush but neither did it embarrass her enough to discourage her from singing altogether. Thus, when the first chord was struck, Ashlee joined the rest in singing "Onward Christian Soldiers" in a most joyous manner. However, before the first refrain was finished, she heard the rich tones of a deep baritone voice that was unfamiliar to her. Turning her head slightly to peek out from around the brim of her bonnet and the others in her pew, the notes caught in her throat the instant she saw Rhys standing at the other end. Feeling her eyes upon him, he glanced over at her and nodded, and Ashlee straightened immediately. Was there no escape from the man? How did he know she would be here? Had he followed her?

By the time she had decided to quietly slip down the aisle and out through the entrance of the church, the song had ended and everyone was sitting down again. Ashlee was forced to do the same or draw the entire congregation's attention her way. This would be the longest service she had ever sat through.

She tried to focus her concentration on the minister and the words he spoke, but Rhys's presence, although divided by several people, still had an overpowering affect on her. Even with the cool air inside the church, her nerves made her perspire. She tried, as inconspicuously as possible, to dab at her throat with the handkerchief she had taken from her purse. The congregation rose to sing another hymn, but this time Ashlee remained quiet, oddly preferring to listen to Rhys's smooth, mellow voice carrying the tune quite effortlessly, as though singing in a church was a common Sunday happening for him. She noticed, too, that others around her had chosen to listen rather than sing, and she was struck with a strange feeling of pride, as if their silent approval had something to do with her. When they sat down again, she stole a quick glance his way. But all that she could see of him were his hands resting on the hymnal in his lap and the blue pin-striped trousers he wore. She studied her own book, smiling softly and thinking how that shade was his best color.

When the service finally came to an end, Ashlee politely but hurriedly moved to the aisle, intending to leave the church as quickly as possible. She was sure Rhys would want to walk with her, and right now she didn't have the energy to mix words with him since it seemed they seldom held a conversation that didn't end in an argument. Brushing past the line of church members waiting to compliment the minister on his fine sermon—the subject of which was completely lost to Ashlee—she moved out onto the front steps and quickly descended them. The sidewalk was crowded as well, but she managed only a short delay before heading back toward Belle Chasse, almost sensing the hand that would at any moment catch her arm and spin her around. She had traveled nearly ten yards during which she braced herself for his touch, and without thinking glanced back over her shoulder cursing herself the instant she had and coming to an abrupt halt. Rhys wasn't anywhere near her. In fact, he was just coming out of the church. Ashlee's blue eyes narrowed at what she saw, for he wasn't alone. A string of giggling females followed him, all vying for his attention, and Ashlee was suddenly struck with jealousy.

"The brainless fools," she muttered, yanking on the cords of her purse in a most irate manner. "Don't they know he's a Yankee?" She stiffened then, squared her shoulders, raised her pert nose in the air, and twirled around. Thank God, she wasn't that fickle. Stomping off down the sidewalk, she glanced back only once before she turned the corner at the end of the block and marched toward the hotel . . . alone.

The church bells pealed the hour of noon as Ashlee raced up the front steps of Belle Chasse, and she stopped dead center and turned around. Shading her eyes with one hand, she frowned up at the sun high above her. If only there were some way to slow its descent, maybe even halt it altogether, then she wouldn't have to go to the train depot in two hours. Gritting her teeth, she pounded a tiny fist against her thigh and whirled back to bound up the stairs.

The lobby was crowded with people when Ashlee opened the door and went inside. Some were new arrivals waiting at the desk to sign the register and receive the key to their room, others were checking out, and a steady stream of patrons were entering the restaurant. Ashlee followed the group headed into the dining room. She might be upset, but it never made her lose her appetite. Choosing a table in the far corner away from the center of things, Ashlee sat down facing the wall and took off her bonnet. She might not be alone in the busy dining hall, but at least it would seem that way. She ordered a bowl of soup and cup of tea with a little cream and sugar, then lost herself in thought while she waited to be served.

Her life, it seemed, was falling apart. It had started the

268

day Dominique came to Belle Chasse looking for a job. Arthur was quite taken by the petite Frenchwoman from the first moment he saw her, and Ashlee knew then that it would only be a matter of time before he asked the woman to marry him. What surprised her about the whole situation was Priscilla's reaction when Ashlee came to her with the news. Although Priscilla didn't say a word one way or the other, Ashlee swore she had seen a glimmer of sadness in the woman's eyes. When pressed, Priscilla explained it by stating that she had secretly hoped someday Veronica would be welcomed back into Arthur's home and Ashlee's family could be complete as it should have always been. Ashlee had adored Priscilla for a long time, but after her confession, their friendship grew even stronger.

At first, Ashlee had tried very hard to get along with her stepmother. After all, if her father had found something about Dominique to love, then it meant Ashlee could too. But it seemed whatever Ashlee did was wrong in Dominique's eyes, and the two women wound up at each other's throats constantly. Dominique set very strict rules, ones she said that she had had to follow growing up the daughter of a French duke. Ashlee had never met any dukes or duchesses from any country to know if that were true or not, but somehow she didn't think nobility should work as the hostess in a gambling house. Her idea of royalty was sitting around all day sewing tapestries, attending balls or political functions, and supervising the household staff on such menial things as the laundry, what silver should be used at dinner, and what the menu should be. Dominique hardly fit any of those categories. All she cared about was managing the books. Ashlee's cheek crimped in a disgusted snarl. And marrying her stepdaughter off so that she wouldn't be underfoot anymore.

The waitress brought Ashlee her tea on a small silver

tray along with a matching creamer and sugar bowl. After mixing her drink the way she liked it, Ashlee took a sip and tried to conjure up an image of Perrin Fabron. Being Dominique's cousin presented a strong possibility that the man would be handsome, since Dominique's features were pleasant to the eye. However, since Ashlee hoped Perrin wasn't as delicately boned as his cousin, and a lot taller. She took another sip of her tea and found it difficult to swallow when a knot suddenly formed in her throat. She didn't want to marry a stranger. In fact, she didn't want to marry anyone. Until Dominique had announced her plans for her stepdaughter, Ashlee hadn't even considered marriage. She had been quite content living with her father and helping him manage his business. Now Dominique wanted to change all that. She wanted to push Ashlee aside and stand between her and her father. She swallowed hard. She wanted to put her on a ship and send her across the endless miles of sea to live out her life in exile with a man she didn't even know.

Setting down her cup, she sighed heavily and leaned her head back with her eyes closed. And then, of course, there was Rhys. Whatever was she going to do about him? If she was right and he was trying to take over Belle Chasse, she should warn her father. But in order to show the man any kind of proof at all meant telling her father the truth about what she and John had been doing for the past year. And if she did that, Rhys would merely retaliate by going to the authorities about her and John, and they both would probably wind up in prison. Sitting up straight, she propped her elbows on the arms of her chair, interlaced her fingers, and rested her chin on them. Rhys may have pretended he didn't want her stealing anymore, but she was positive it was only an act—a way to get her to do just the opposite. And she would. But instead of filtering the money back into the casino, she would deposit it into a bank account under her own name and keep adding to it until she had enough to buy Belle Chasse ahead of Rhys Sinclair. That way she'd get rid of both Rhys and her stepmother, and free herself to live the kind of life she wanted. And that didn't include Perrin Fabron! A frown wrinkled her brow and she leaned in to pick up her teacup. There was one problem, however. She didn't have a great deal of time to accomplish such a plan, which meant she and John would have to double the robberies, maybe even branch out into hitting private homes. But how would she explain her need to be away from Belle Chasse so often? A silly smile lifted her mouth. Maybe she'd just appear to have run away. Then once she had enough money, she'd return, visit the bank, and use a proxy to buy Belle Chasse. And she'd only have to run as far as Priscilla. She'd help her!

The waitress returned with her bowl of soup, and Ashlee discovered that she was more hungry than when she had sat down. The excitement of adventure always stimulated her appetite—for both food and danger. Unfolding her napkin across her lap, she paused a moment wondering what John would think about her idea—more so if he would be willing to go along with it. She sighed, picked up her spoon, and started to dip it in the broth when she sensed someone was watching her, a feeling that made her horribly uncomfortable. As casually as she could manage it, she glanced back over her shoulder and spotted Rhys walking toward her table.

"Damn," she muttered irritably, glaring into her bowl of soup. What she didn't need right now was to argue with him.

"Good morning, Miss Redington," he said, then chuckled. "Or should I say afternoon?"

"I'd like it much better if you said farewell, Mr. Sinclair," she crisply replied without looking at him.

Rhys forced himself not to laugh, pulling out a chair next to her and sitting down. "Hmmm," he murmured.

271

"Didn't you sleep well last night? You sound a little on edge."

Icy blue eyes peered up at him, flashing sparks of pure rage, and Rhys noticed the slight coloring in her cheeks. He raised a brow questioningly. But before she could comment—a statement he was sure would be a slur against his parentage by the hateful gleam in her eyes—the waitress returned to take his order. He glanced at the bowl sitting in front of Ashlee.

"The soup looks good," he said. "I'll have that and some coffee."

Ashlee held her breath until the waitress had gone, afraid that if she didn't she would blurt out every foul name she could think of to describe the man sitting next to her. "You have a lot of nerve, Rhys Sinclair," she hissed, gritting her teeth. Wadding up her napkin, she threw it on the table beside her teacup, the desire for food suddenly gone.

Relaxing back in his chair, he smiled softly while enjoying the vision of her lush curves partially hidden beneath her blue and white striped dress, the way her thick ebony curls tumbled over her shoulder and fell against her bosom, and the flawlessness of her creamy complexion and that most tempting mouth. "*I* have a lot of nerve?" he challenged. "You're the only woman I know who ever had the courage to dress like a boy and jump over the side of a steamboat while it's churning upriver." He grinned and leaned closer. "Or take the risk of suffering the consequences disguised as a prostitute."

"You're truly enjoying this, aren't you?" she sneered.

Rhys didn't answer until after the waitress had set down his cup of coffee and walked away. "It was meant as a compliment."

"Oh really?" she scoffed.

Rhys took a sip of his drink then looked at her. "Yes, really. There aren't many young women who would do what you've done to help their father. They'd cry and complain about it, but that's as far as they'd go. It's just a shame you went about it in the wrong way."

"Oh?" she mocked. "And what should I have done differently? Murdered my victims?" She smiled sarcastically. "I wouldn't be troubled with you if I had."

He considered her a moment, wanting very much to pull her into his arms and kiss those sensuous lips as though no one else was in the room with them. He checked the desire and smiled. "You said that you and Mr. Hardin have been engaged in your little venture for over a year now." He waited for her nod then continued. "And yet nothing has improved. The casino is still losing money. It's never occurred to you that someone is responsible for it being that way?"

"Of course it has," she snapped. "But as I already told you, the only person who would have the opportunity besides John is Dominique. And if you accuse him again, I'll dump my tea right in your lap."

Rhys laughed good-naturedly. "Of that, madam, I am sure." Shifting in his chair, he leaned forward with one arm on the table, his other hand propped on his knee. "Then that leaves your stepmother."

"And a very unlikely choice," she replied without the slightest hesitation.

"Why?" he asked simply.

Ashlee fell back in her chair, laughing with a shake of her head. "Because—as you so astutely put it—she's a fortune hunter. Practically everyone at Belle Chasse agrees that she married Papa for his money. Why would she steal from him when it's already her money to spend any way she wants?"

"What do you know about her?"

Ashlee shrugged. "She came to New Orleans from Paris shortly before she met Papa. She's the daughter of some duke, and she's used to having wealth."

273

"What brought her here, and what's the duke's name?" he pressed.

Ashlee shook her head, frowning. "I—I don't know—to either question. She and I don't spend a whole lot of time chit-chatting, if you know what I mean." Her curiosity was aroused when she noticed the vague smile that came over Rhys's face. "What difference does that make?"

He picked up his coffee cup and took a drink as he shrugged one shoulder. "None. I was just wondering."

"There's more to it than that, Rhys Sinclair," she argued, "and I want you to tell me what it is."

Of course there was, but Rhys wasn't about to tell Ashlee what he thought. Knowing her dislike for the woman and given the slightest hint of misdoing on Dominique's part, Ashlee would confront her with the knowledge and ruin any chance Rhys had in solving this bizarre puzzle.

"Eat your soup," he said instead. "You haven't much time to finish lunch and freshen up before the train arrives." He smiled over at her. "I would imagine you'd like to change into something more suited to greeting your future husband."

Ashlee recoiled at the sound of the word, but at the same time took offense to his meaning. "And what's wrong with the way I'm dressed?" she demanded, forgetting all about their prior discussion.

His gaze roamed freely over her from head to toe, sending a tremor of titillating excitement through her while she silently cursed the way he could undress her with his eyes.

"It's a little flashy for a woman who's about to be married," he remarked, then leisurely took another drink of his coffee.

"Flash—" she choked. "How would you know what a woman should or shouldn't wear? Engaged or not!"

A devilish smile gleamed in his eyes but never touched his mouth. "Well, I know if you were engaged to me, I wouldn't want other men looking at you. And that dress certainly attracts the eye." His gaze purposely lowered to her heaving bosom.

Her flesh burned beneath his bold appraisal as though his fingers had caressed her, and Ashlee instantly bolted to her feet. She lowered her chin and her voice as she glared down at him. "And I thank God we're not, Mr. Sinclair." Seizing a fistful of her skirts in both hands, Ashlee yanked them out of the way and stormed off, unaware of the surprised and curious looks she received from the others who had witnessed her outburst.

A smile stretched across Rhys's face as he watched her stomp away, thinking how easy it was to make her angry. His look grew distant and the smile faded from his lips. Just as easy as it was to spark a flame of passion in her. Major Sheffield, the man Rhys had served under during the war, had oftentimes told him that one day he would meet a woman who wouldn't fall for his flattery and charming way, that she would know just by listening to him how much of a flirt he was, and that she would be the woman who would touch upon his heart to linger in his thoughts. He sighed and turned back to the table, spotting Ashlee's bonnet lying there.

"Damien, old friend," he murmured with a lopsided grin, "truer words were never spoken."

"Ohhh, damn," Ashlee moaned, looking at her grandfather's pocket watch for the hundredth time. Half past one. She snapped the lid shut and laid the watch back on the dresser. She had never known her grandfather—he had died long before Ashlee was born—but she had always treasured the timepiece her father had given her. It made her feel as though she had known the older

Redington, and in an odd way, holding the beautifully handcrafted watch gave her peace. It didn't help today, however.

Stepping back, Ashlee studied her appearance in the mirror. She honestly couldn't see anything wrong with the blue and white striped dress she wore. The neckline came high above her bosom, while the entire bodice was gathered from the top of the dress to her waist. Actually, the extra material concealed the fact that she wasn't as well endowed as most ladies. Granted, the off-the-shoulder style of the dress was a little provocative, but Ashlee always thought she needed all the extra help she could get.

"If I didn't know better, I'd say he's just jealous," she muttered, brushing her long dark hair into thick curls.

After one final appraisal of her appearance in the mirror, she turned away from the dresser to look for her bonnet, groaning when she remembered that she had left it at the table in the restaurant. She picked up her purse and started for the door. She had plenty of time to go after it and still meet the train, but as she reached for the doorknob, her lip curled disgustedly as she thought how she'd prefer spending the day in bed—away from Perrin Fabron *and* Rhys Sinclair. She twisted the ivory handle and pulled the door open wide, coming to an abrupt halt the instant she saw Rhys standing just outside. It appeared as if he weren't even aware of her presence as he concentrated on the fountain located in the middle of the foyer and the bubbling water pouring out of the cherub's pitcher to splash noisily at the statue's feet.

"Interesting concept," he finally said. "Artesian, isn't it?"

He turned then to look at her, and Ashlee felt that same electrifying charge sear through her as his gaze swept her entire length before coming to rest on her face. She quickly cast her eyes away from him.

"I think that's what Papa called it," she replied evenly. "You left this at the table."

Ashlee turned back to find him holding up her bonnet. "Thank you," she said, frowning.

"I thought you might need it," he went on, a vague smile parting his lips when Ashlee wouldn't look at him. "The sun's terribly bright today, and with no protection at the depot, I figured you'd want to wear it to shade your face." He grinned openly at the disdainful look she gave him, then hurried to open the door to the courtyard for her.

"I've taken the liberty of asking Mr. Hardin to drive us to the depot," he told her, falling into step with her short, agitated stride, "so there's no need to rush." He fought back his laughter when he heard her irritated sigh. "Perhaps you'd like to take the time to change."

Ashlee stopped dead center on the sidewalk. "I like what I'm wearing, Mr. Sinclair," she spat, arms akimbo, "but if you disapprove, you don't have to be seen with me. As a matter of fact, I'd prefer it. People might get the wrong idea and think I dressed for you."

Rhys chuckled. "I'd like to oblige, Miss Redington, but I'm afraid I can't. You see, your stepmother ordered me to escort you to the depot, and since I work for her—"

"Who's going to tell her that you didn't?" Ashlee cut in. "I certainly won't."

Rhys shrugged. "It's a chance I'd rather not take. I wouldn't want to get fired."

Ashlee stared at him a long while before answering. "Mr. Sinclair, everyone at Belle Chasse knows you're a wealthy man. You don't need this job. From what I've heard, you could probably buy the place with pocket money."

"Pocket money?" he laughed. "Not quite."

"Then why are you hanging around?"

"I thought you knew," he replied, trying very hard to

look serious. "It's the only way I can be close to you and not be obvious." He took her arm and started them down the sidewalk again. "And besides, I promised some friends of mine that I'd see their money returned."

Ashlee pulled her arm free of him. "Then I'm afraid you're wasting your time. The only thing you'll win being close to me is my undying dislike for you, and I've already told you several times that your friends' money and yours is gone." She lowered her voice and added, "Just as I wish you were."

Her comment did not go unheard by Rhys, nor would he let it pass. "Ahh, my dear Ashlee," he murmured. "Had you stated such last night, I would have thought you delirious with passion."

"How dare you!" Ashlee exploded, turning on him in a rage, one hand raised to strike him.

Rhys quickly raised his own and cautioned. "Careful. Someone might see and question what it was that made you angry."

His warning brought an immediate reaction from her. She dropped her hand and fearfully looked about the courtyard, afraid that it was already too late. To her relief there was only one other couple strolling the grounds, and they were obviously too caught up in each other's presence to give notice to anyone else. However, her fury still shone clearly in her pale blue eyes as she gave Rhys one last damning glare then turned for the lobby door.

Rhys gave her wide berth as she stormed through the hotel's entrance hall, knowing that if he pressed her again, she would more than likely change her mind about striking him. He winked devilishly at Michael's questioning look.

"She's anxious to meet her fiancé," he quipped as he passed by the desk. "But then, aren't we all?"

A knowing smile spread across the other's face. "That we are," Michael called after him, chuckling to himself and thinking how much things had changed around Belle Chasse since the Yankee had arrived.

By the time Rhys caught up to Ashlee, she had already boarded the carriage. She sat in the center of the seat with her skirts spread out on either side of her as a silent warning to him that he was not welcome to sit next to her. Her nose was raised in the air, and she was studying something across the way from her as if she didn't expect anyone to be riding with her. But Rhys wasn't going to be the least bit discouraged. Signaling to John, who sat quietly in the driver's seat observing it all, Rhys climbed into the carriage, took his place opposite the brooding young woman, and leaned back comfortably to enjoy the ride to the train depot.

The station, located on the north side of town, was only a fifteen-minute trip, but to Ashlee it seemed forever. She could feel Rhys's warm gaze on her the entire time, and she didn't have to look at him to know where it rested. She tried to concentrate on the scenery they passed by and pretend as though he weren't even there with her. Finally, out of desperation, she picked up her bonnet lying next to her and put it on, hoping the distraction would be enough to draw his eyes away from the feast he so eagerly devoured. To her dismay, however, her fingers were clumsy as she repeatedly tried to tie the satin ribbons in a satisfactory bow beneath her chin. Even though she couldn't see it, she was sure her attempts had failed miserably. Without thinking, she glanced at Rhys and gave an inward moan to see him smiling crookedly at her, his amusement shining in his deep brown eyes. Her irritation, nevertheless, fell short of a much deeper emotion when the distant whistle of the train screamed its high-pitched, earsplitting announcement that Perrin Fabron was about to arrive.

The carriage rolled to a smooth stop alongside several others whose occupants had come to the depot for much the same reason as Ashlee. Yet, she doubted any of them regretted being there more than she.

"Train's a little early," John said, setting the brake and climbing down to help Ashlee from the carriage. "Good thing we came when we did."

"Yes," Rhys agreed with a wry smile. "We certainly wouldn't have wanted Miss Ashlee's fiancé to think she wasn't anxious to see him." Stepping lightly to the ground, he straightened and looked at her as though confused by the heated glare she gave him.

"I would appreciate it if you kept your comments to yourself, Mr. Sinclair," she snapped, readjusting her bonnet when it seemed one side dipped lower than the other. "You're here only because Dominique thought I needed an escort. As you can see, John is quite capable of fulfilling that task, so you, sir, may stay with the carriage."

She turned then and looped her arm into John's, ready to leave Rhys behind. But he wasn't about to give in so easily.

"I would love to oblige, Miss Ashlee," he hurriedly replied, stopping the pair before they had taken a step, "but I'm afraid I'm a man of my word, and I did promise your stepmother—"

Ashlee's spine stiffened. "That you'd what, Mr. Sinclair? Annoy me?" She smiled sarcastically. "She'll be pleased to hear you've succeeded." Without further comment, she tugged on her companion's arm to start them off again, knowing that Rhys would be following close behind.

The depot's platform was crowded with people, and it appeared nearly everyone in New Orleans had someone to meet at the train. Ashlee was forced to let go of John and walk ahead of the two men. They moved to the far end where it wasn't as congested, thus offering a better view of the huge locomotive chugging down the track toward them. With her back to John and Rhys, she closed her eyes and prayed Dominique's cousin wouldn't be on it.

Standing shoulder to shoulder with Rhys, John crossed his arms over his huge chest and kept an eye on Ashlee in case she should turn around to look at him. He didn't want her seeing him talking to Rhys.

"I think it's time you and I talked, Mr. Sinclair," he said quietly so that Ashlee wouldn't hear.

Until this moment, Rhys wasn't absolutely sure Ashlee had told John Hardin that he was on to them, though he couldn't imagine why she would keep it a secret from the man. John had as much to lose as Ashlee. "I'm listening," he answered as he, too, eyed the trim figure standing a few feet ahead of them.

John shook his head. "Not here. I'll buy you a drink at the casino after we get Mr. Fabron settled in."

"All right." Rhys agreed, casting the man a sidelong glance. He certainly was a big man, and Rhys could only hope their meeting would be nothing more than conversation. He didn't relish the thought of having to physically defend himself, since the only advantage Rhys might have over the man was being lighter on his feet. Even then he was sure he wouldn't escape unharmed.

The train's shrill whistle rent the air a second time. Everyone turned to watch the huge engine spewing steam, like some fierce dragon snorting from his nostrils, as the locomotive slid along the track and came to a stop. Ashlee said her prayer again, only this time she added the thought that maybe Rhys would buy a ticket and be on the train when it pulled away. She sighed, disheartened, then braced herself and concentrated on the passengers getting off the train.

A steady stream of people disembarked from the three cars, making it quite difficult for Ashlee to see everyone. She stood on tiptoes and craned her neck, though she wasn't sure why. She was in no hurry to find Perrin. Several minutes passed and when the crowd finally began to disperse, the way opened up and presented two men standing about five feet apart from each other, both looking all around them as if expecting someone to meet them. Ashlee's heart thumped in her chest the instant the taller of the two turned and looked her way. He was young, broad-shouldered, dressed superbly in snug-fitting clothes that left little doubt to his masculinity, and not at all unpleasant to look at with his coal-black hair and dark eyes. And when he smiled, warm and sincere, Ashlee could feel the blush rise in her cheeks. She still had no intentions of marrying the man, but at least he wasn't some doting old man on the verge of senility with only one thought in mind—bedding his fiancée before the vows were spoken. And from his appearance and gentle manner, Ashlee concluded he was a gentleman, one who knew how to treat a lady. She thought of Rhys, and a smile crept over her mouth. It would be a delight playing one against the other. And she'd start right now.

"If you'll excuse me," she cooed, deliberately resting her eyes on Rhys's tall frame and realizing her mistake almost immediately. The gentleman who awaited her was handsome, but the comparison with this Yankee was like choosing a hay wagon over a landau. Her cheeks pinkened again, and she quickly turned away, not wanting Rhys to notice. What difference did it make? He could never guess what she was thinking, and she'd play this one to the hilt. With a dainty lift of her skirts, she started toward the man, ready to introduce herself and welcome him to New Orleans simply for the benefit of the one closely watching her. But before she had traveled two steps, the stranger turned his head away when a definitely female, highly enthusiastic voice called out to him from somewhere in the crowd at the other end of the platform.

Ashlee's color heightened even more once she realized

the dreadful mistake she had made, for in the next moment the gentleman had dropped the bag he carried, spread his arms wide, and eagerly enveloped the young lady who had come to the depot to meet him. Wishing there were some place she could hide, Ashlee stood transfixed to the wooden boards beneath her feet and mutely watched the couple walk away. She didn't have to look at Rhys to know how much he was enjoying her faux pas. She could almost hear him laughing. But it seemed her mortification had only begun when the second man, a much shorter, much thinner, horribly plain little creature, started her way. Ashlee held her breath as she watched him advance, positive—without anyone telling her—that this was Perrin Fabron.

"Excusez-moi, s'il vous plait," he said weakly, taking a kerchief from his sleeve to dab nervously at his chin and neck. "I was to meet my cousin, Dominique Redington. But I fear she has forgotten me." He shrugged narrow shoulders and muttered, "As always."

Ashlee didn't have to rise up on her toes to see over the man's head, for Perrin was a good five inches shorter than she. She doubted his spindly frame could hold him upright if he was ever caught in a gust of wind stronger than the gentlest of breezes. Glancing toward the heavens, she wondered what she had done that was so wrong to warrant such punishment. She sighed resignedly and looked back at him, noticing for the first time the vague resemblance he bore to her stepmother. In fact, the longer she studied him the more clear the likenesses became. He had the same dark eyes and thin, chiseled features as Dominique, and if it weren't for the masculine clothes he wore, Perrin could easily pass for Dominique's sister, even a twin. She cringed inwardly at the thought of being married to such a milksop and considered telling him that his cousin had moved to Barbados.

"Mademoiselle?"

Ashlee blinked, realizing that she had been so caught up in thought that she hadn't paid any attention to his queries. "I'm sorry, what did you ask?"

Perrin opened his mouth to repeat his question, spotted John and Rhys over Ashlee's shoulder, and visibly paled. *"Mon Dieu,* are they with you, *mademoiselle?"*

It took her a moment to understand whom he meant, but once she did, Ashlee suppressed the urge to laugh. It was even worse than she first thought. He not only looked like a weak-kneed fool, he was one. And once her father met Perrin Fabron and discovered for himself what a poor choice of a husband he'd make, Ashlee was sure he'd call off the marriage. Turning her head to see what John thought of the dolt Dominique had chosen for her and allow herself a moment to gather her wits before answering the little man, Ashlee saw Rhys instead, and her humor vanished. If it had been anyone else standing there with that same smirk on his face, Ashlee wouldn't have minded. Especially since she didn't think any more of Perrin than Rhys obviously did. But Rhys wasn't laughing at the Frenchman as much as he was laughing at the awkward position Ashlee was in, and she knew it. Well, she'd show him that it didn't bother her at all!"

"Pay no attention to them," she whispered, smiling sweetly. "They're just hired help. And please accept my apology for not speaking up right away. I'm Ashlee Redington, and your cousin sends her regrets for not being able to meet your train. She and Papa were invited to spend the weekend at the home of a friend in Jackson—political, of course. They should be back this evening sometime."

Perrin appeared to relax a bit with Ashlee's announcement that the two men who accompanied her were not there to do him physical harm, even though his eyes continued to shift between the pair as if expecting them to disobey their mistress and attack him anyway.

"Oh—oh, there ees no need to apologize, *Mademoiselle* Ashlee," he said, his high-pitched voice cracking several times. "I will not flatter myself by thinking you were *transporte de joie*—overjoyed—to meet with me. Prearranged marriages are, shall we say, seldom happy occasions?" He finally managed to bring himself to look at her and ignore the other two. "And I have known my cousin longer than anyone. She can make life miserable if you go against her wishes." He stuffed the kerchief back beneath the lacy cuff of his shirt sleeve and smiled. "But do not tell her I said thees," he confided. "I do not wish to hear her rantings when I have only just arrived."

Perrin Fabron wasn't at all what Ashlee had secretively hoped for. He was too short, too thin. His features were too sharp. He looked as though he might never have the need to use a razor. His manner was almost feminine, and even his well-manicured nails were longer than most men wore them. Yet, despite all that, there was something about him that she liked. She sensed a special kindred would grow between them, and the source of that relationship would be his cousin. She still had no desire to marry him and doubted that she ever would. But his openness to someone he didn't even know about his feelings toward Dominique hinted that he disapproved of the woman's methods and demands, and that was something on which Ashlee and he could easily agree.

"You have my word on it," she smiled warmly, tucking her arm in his and turning them toward the place where John had tied off the carriage. "I decided the day Papa married her that the less she knew, the better off I'd be."

Her answer surprised Perrin, and for a moment he stared blankly at her. "You do not like my cousin?" he hesitantly asked.

"It's no secret, Perrin," she laughed. "You'll only have to spend the day at Belle Chasse to realize that for yourself."

His soft brown eyes took on a twinkle before the smile

285

reached his lips. *"Mon chere*, you and I have a lot in common," he grinned. "I can't tell you how afraid I was that I might learn that you and my cousin were, shall we say, good friends?"

"Far from that, Perrin," she smiled. "Far from that."

As they neared the luggage wagon and the single piece left sitting on it, Perrin stopped to pick it up.

"Oh, don't bother with that, Perrin," she said, looking back toward the other two who followed. "Rhys, bring Mr. Fabron's bag for him, please." The command was spoken as if given to Harold Brown, the doorman at Belle Chasse, rather than to the one man who could so easily set her heart thundering in her chest. Ashlee wisely gave him no time to deny her instructions when she turned back to Perrin, took his arm again, and started them off toward the carriage. To any who might have observed the exchange, it would have appeared just as Ashlee had intended it to look—an employer giving a servant an order. To Ashlee, however, it was her silent way of telling Rhys to keep his distance from now on.

"I was surprised when Dominique told me you were arriving by train, Perrin," she said sweetly, sounding as though they were lifelong friends. "I would have thought you would have taken a ship that sailed directly into port." A puzzled frown flitted across her brow when she noticed how pale the young man became.

"I traveled with a friend," he replied quietly, unable to look her in the eye. "The trip made him terribly ill and when our ship docked for supplies, he got off and refused to sail any further. I did not want to leave him alone in thees strange country, so we took the train the rest of the way here."

"Oh, Perrin, why didn't you say so before?" She stopped and glanced back at the empty depot. "He's more than welcome to stay at Belle Chasse."

"Oh, he did not come here, *ma chere*," Perrin quickly

amended, his face turning a bright red. "He had business in Baton Rouge and took the train there."

"But, Perrin," she laughed, "there isn't a—" Ashlee caught herself before she finished telling the little man that there was no train from New Orleans to Baton Rouge. The only way one could travel from this city to that one was by steamer. He was hiding something, and she decided not to press the issue just now. Maybe later, after she had assured him that he could trust her . . . "I mean there wasn't a need for him to continue on. He could have visited here for a while." She took his arm again and started them on their way. "Will he be staying in America long?"

"*Non.* Philippe only wishes to stay a short while." He glanced over at her and smiled weakly. "As I, *ma cherie.* I miss Paris already."

"Well, perhaps when your friend is through with his business in Baton Rouge, he'll come to Belle Chasse for a few days. Dominique would probably enjoy—"

"*Mon Dieu, non!*" Perrin exploded loudly, then remembering the men who walked behind, he quickly lowered his voice. "Pardon, *mademoiselle.* I do not mean to sound rude, but Dominique knows Philippe and does not approve of our friendship. She must not learn that I have brought him with me. I beg you, *ma chere,* do not tell her."

Ashlee could see the fear in his eyes. From what he had revealed, she could only conclude that Perrin had gone against his cousin's demands and that he was afraid of the consequences should the woman find out. Ashlee liked Perrin more and more with every minute that passed. She took his hand and gave it a gentle squeeze. "The only way she'll find out is if you tell her, Perrin," she whispered with a smile, stopping alongside their carriage. "However, I will ask one thing of you if I'm to help keep your secret. You must tell me everything you know about

287

my stepmother."

Perrin's eyes widened considerably. *"Chantage?* Blackmail, *ma petite?"*

Ashlee started to correct his misinterpretation, spotted John and Rhys within earshot, and decided to wait. "Just put Mr. Fabron's bag on the seat, Rhys. You may ride up front with John," she ordered, quickly accepting Perrin's help into the carriage. Once everyone was settled and John had directed the rig toward the street that would take them to Belle Chasse, Ashlee turned to her companion with an apologetic look on her pretty face. "You misunderstood me, Perrin. I would never tell Dominique anything. Not even the time of day. What I meant was that I must know how you two feel about each other so that I'm careful with my words. And I'm only asking about her past as a favor. She never talks about her childhood or what she did before she came to New Orleans, as if it's a big secret. I'm curious, that's all."

Perrin's narrow face contorted with his frown, and Ashlee raised a quizzical brow.

"Is it a secret?" she asked.

"Non," he quickly replied, beads of perspiration dotting his upper lip. He withdrew his handkerchief and patted his face. "I will tell you anything you wish to know, *chere,* but first I would like to rest a while. It was a long trip."

"Of course," she relented, leaning back in the seat where she could watch him from the corner of her eye without his knowledge. Dominique made this little man very nervous. That was obvious. The woman's past suddenly made Ashlee very curious.

Chapter Ten

Men, afflicted with the kind of fever bed rest wouldn't cure, filled the casino at Belle Chasse the moment the place opened for business, regardless of the fact that it was the Sabbath and many of their wives threatened to leave them if they did. The huge hall buzzed with excited voices, the clicking of the roulette wheels, and tinkling of glasses being filled and refilled with any favorite drink the patrons hoped would soothe the pain over their losses or boost their courage to play on.

As Rhys stepped into the gaming room he could feel the tension in the air, clearly remembering the days when he, too, allowed the fervor over a game of chance to rule his better judgment. He had had to lose nearly everything he owned before he learned how to control the gambling fever that afflicted every man who picked up a pair of dice or held cards in his hand. He had been one of the lucky few who could earn a comfortable living by sitting down at a poker table. Taking a cheroot from his pocket, he scanned the crowd for the one who asked to meet him here, thoughts of joining a game the last thing on his mind.

John Hardin's huge frame and shaved head weren't hard to spot as he stood at the bar, waiting. Striking a match, Rhys lit his cheroot, tossed the charred wooden stick in a nearby ashtray, and started across the room. Knowing this time would come and in order to be prepared, he had done a little research before coming to the casino on the man Arthur Redington trusted so completely. Michael, always the talkative sort, had told him everything he needed to know about the gentle giant who watched over Arthur's daughter as though she were his child, and how there was no mistaking the love John Hardin had for his employer. That, along with Ashlee's confession, convinced Rhys that he could trust John with the knowledge that he and Arthur were partners. It would also give him the insurance that Ashlee would stay home. Without John's help, it would be impossible for her to continue her little excursions up and down the Mississippi. Once he reached the bar Rhys ordered a mug of ale, neither man speaking until after he had been served.

"I think what we have to say isn't meant to be overheard," John quietly announced as he leaned back against the edge of the bar, his attention focused on a nearby game of blackjack and the men who played it. Then, without further comment or a glance Rhys's way, John turned, picked up his own mug, and started off toward the back of the casino and the private rooms reserved for special games of poker.

Rhys's mouth twisted in a wry smile, wondering if that were the only reason John Hardin preferred privacy. There was still the chance he meant to land a few well-placed blows to Rhys's chin before allowing him the opportunity to explain. He took a puff on the cigar, watched the huge man through the gray haze for a moment, then lifted his drink from the bar and followed.

The room John chose was at the end of the long hallway, far from the noise of the casino and the possibility some drunk might come banging on the door before Hank Newell spotted him. Stepping inside, John waited for Rhys to enter, then shut and locked the portal behind them. The space had only one window with bars across it, much like those in Ashlee's room. Crossing to it, John pulled aside the draperies to let in more light, then turned back to pull out a chair and sit down at the table in the center of the room. When he looked up and saw that Rhys hadn't moved, he nodded at a chair opposite him and waited until Rhys had done as he indicated.

"I did some snooping around, Mr. Sinclair," he began, his green eyes staring out at Rhys from beneath thick brows, "and I've learned quite a bit about you. Would you care to hear it?"

Leaning back in the chair, one elbow propped on its arm, he nodded, then clamped the cheroot between his teeth.

"Be sure and correct me if I've gotten anything wrong," John half smiled, bracing his upper torso against the table with his forearms, his hands wrapped around the mug of ale sitting in front of him. "You come from some place in Maine, a big family who owns a lumber mill and plenty of timberland. You served under Grant during the war and spent the last two years in Vicksburg under a Major Sheffield. When the war ended, you liked the south so much you bought a plantation called Twin Oaks up near Vicksburg, but didn't tell anybody. Some time back you won a riverboat in a game of poker, and again kept it a secret. You earn your living by playing cards, and all in all you're probably one of the wealthiest men to walk into Belle Chasse. So tell me, Mr. Sinclair, what's the real reason you took a job here? You want more than just the money Miss Redington and I stole from you."

Grinning, Rhys studied the cheroot he rolled between his fingers. "Very good, Mr. Hardin. Mind if I ask how you came by all your information?"

"It took a little doing, but I managed it. Let's say I tricked a poker friend of yours . . . Judge Lott? I told him that I was in the market for a business associate with a lot of money, one that knew a great deal about managing a gambling house. He thought of you right away. But he made me promise not to tell anyone about your financial holdings. Said you didn't want it known. As for the rest of it—about your being here for some other reason than wanting your money returned—it was purely speculation. Am I wrong?"

"No," Rhys replied with a shake of his head. "And since we're laying all our cards on the table, I'll tell you what I've learned about you." He grinned. "Stop me if I get something wrong."

John raised a quizzical brow.

"About twenty years ago you left England when you got into a little trouble, and came here. The night you arrived you witnessed some men trying to rob another man and stepped in. That man was Arthur Redington. He offered you a job and you took it. A few months later, some Englishmen paid you a visit, demanding the money they thought you owed them. Without question, Arthur gave it to them, and you've felt indebted to him ever since. There probably isn't a thing in the world you wouldn't do for him, including some ridiculous scheme of stealing as a way of helping him keep Belle Chasse. Am I wrong?" he mimicked.

Twisting in the chair, John laid one arm on its back rail while he tapped the fingers of his other hand against the table top. "Arthur never would have told you that. Who did?"

Rhys shrugged. "Doesn't really matter. What does is that because I know about your past, I feel I can trust you."

"Trust me?" John exclaimed. "To do what?"

Rhys leaned forward. "I need your help, but I also

need your word that no one will find out what I'm really doing here."

"Which is?"

"Your word first," Rhys instructed in a very serious tone.

Because John had little else to offer, he held the pledging of his oath very dear and something he didn't freely give. What made it even more difficult was that until he spoke it, he had no way of knowing what secret he would be honor-bound to keep for this Yankee. "Your condition is quite high, Mr. Sinclair. What you ask could put me in a very compromising position—should such knowledge go against my conscience."

"Then put it at ease, Mr. Hardin, for I assure you that you and I have the same goal in mind as far as Belle Chasse is concerned." When John didn't respond or even blink an eye, but simply stared back at him, Rhys added, "To see that its ownership remains with Arthur Redington. And on that, you have *my* word."

Several moments ticked away while John considered what his companion had said. Then, finally, he nodded. "My word," he answered.

Noticing that the tip of his cheroot no longer burned, Rhys tapped the cold ash in the dish sitting on the table and fumbled for a match in his vest pocket. "When I first came to Belle Chasse, I had only one thought in mind . . . finding you."

"Me?" John asked, watching Rhys relight his cigar.

"Yes," he replied. He was quiet for a second or two then said, "Thomas thought he recognized the driver of the carriage that so hastily helped a young boy escape us. A young boy who later turned out to be Miss Redington."

The stern expression on John's face slowly melted into a smile. "So that's how you figured it out."

"Actually, there were several clues," Rhys admitted. "But coming here searching for you put us on the right track. And it was the only reason we came. We had no intention of talking with Arthur. I mean our business at Belle Chasse wasn't to discuss politics, even though that's the way it worked out."

"So you're here for political reasons?"

"No," Rhys quickly denied. "That's not what I meant. Once Arthur found out that Thomas Bryan was running for a seat in the Senate, he asked us to join him for dinner. It was during that conversation that I found out his casino was in trouble—financially. At my friend's suggestion, Arthur asked for my help in finding out why."

"And you agreed . . . just like that . . . with no strings attached," John finished with one brow raised skeptically. The gesture brought a chortle from his companion.

"Is that what you really think?" Rhys smiled.

John's green eyes never wavered from the man as he lifted his mug and took a long drink. "Suppose you tell me."

The smile lingered for a while as Rhys thought how foolish he had been for ever misjudging John Hardin. He was too smart for the kind of game Rhys had mentally accused him of playing. He took a puff on his cigar, then laid it in the ashtray. "I made him a deal, seeing as how I'm always a businessman first. I told him I wanted to buy in, that he was to use that money to further his political career, and that, in turn, I'd do some investigating. But the condition was that no one, including you and his wife and daughter, know anything about the transaction. Thus, the reason why I'm now one of his dealers."

"And he agreed?" John's usually expressionless face registered his surprise. "I can't believe it. I thought that next to Ashlee, Belle Chasse meant everything to him." Frowning, he pushed himself up from the table and went to the window to stare outside.

"I'm sure it does," Rhys tried to reassure him. "But so

294

does rebuilding the south. And the only way he can help is to become a senator. That's his main goal right now. Selling me a portion of his business isn't the same as giving it up all together. It means he's simply put his trust in me to find where his losses are, put an end to them, and get the place turning a profit again."

"But to take on a partner—" John shook his head as he braced his hands on either side of the window frame and leaned his weight against them.

"Not equal partners, John. I didn't want it that way. I'm not interested in owning Belle Chasse."

"Then why did you buy in?" he asked almost angrily, turning around.

Rhys thought of Ashlee right away and smiled. "For several reasons, I guess."

"Such as? And why do you need my help? To do what?" Each question raised in volume.

"For one," Rhys began, "it's the way I do business. I prefer the kind of holdings that don't require any managing on my part, just a steady income I can count on. Secondly, it was a way of guaranteeing Arthur that I would find out what was going on with his casino and put a stop to it. After all, what part owner would allow such a thing to continue? It would be the same thing as taking money out of his own pocket. And it was a way to give Arthur the funds he needs to run for office. You might not believe it, but I'm as anxious to see the south recover as you or any other southerner."

"And what about Ashlee and me? It wasn't just your money we stole."

"No," he sighed, "it wasn't. But I'm not going to turn you in if that's what you're asking. Nor am I going to tell Arthur. I see no need, since what the two of you did was meant as a way to help him. As for my friends . . . I guess they'll have to wait for their money."

"Mr. Sinclair," John frowned, "they'll be waiting a

long time. We don't have their money anymore and we never will."

"Then I guess maybe you'll have to work it off," he casually replied.

"Doing what?" The question nearly rattled the roof.

"Something that will probably take a great deal of effort on your part, Mr. Hardin." A lazy smile kinked his mouth. "But a simple enough task. I want you to make sure Miss Ashlee never steals another penny."

The anger and frustration slowly ebbed from John's face. "That's all?"

Picking up his cheroot, Rhys leaned back in the chair, took a long drag, then watched the many curls of smoke drifting upward before lightly blowing them away. "Knowing Miss Redington, I'd say that's a lot," he grinned. "And she isn't to know that we've had this conversation. The less people who know about me the better. If I'm right about someone helping themselves to a little of Arthur's money, nothing must change if I'm to catch them."

John studied his companion for a long while. What the man said made sense. He knew how much Arthur wanted into politics and had no way of funding it since his business seemed destined to fail. It surprised him, though, to hear Arthur would sell part of Belle Chasse in exchange for the money he needed for his cause, and more so that he'd sell to a Yankee. But this wasn't just any Yankee. Rhys Sinclair had a fair and honest reputation as a businessman, and it had been confirmed by the highly respected Judge William Lott. Arthur must have known it, too, or he wouldn't have agreed to Sinclair's proposal. And if Arthur trusted Rhys Sinclair, then so would John.

"But isn't there something else I can do?" John offered, sitting down again. "Let's face it. The only reason I was helping Ashlee was to keep my best friend from losing his business. That hasn't changed. I still want to help him."

Rhys stared at him a moment, thinking how much better he liked having John Hardin on his side. "You probably can't do any more than I'm doing. Just keep your eyes and ears open. And remember one thing. Everyone is suspect. Greed has a funny way of turning good people bad."

"And that's what you thought happened to me," John added, no emotion of any kind showing on his lined face.

Rhys had reached for his mug of ale at the same moment John put Rhys's earlier thoughts into words, and he froze, his hand extended but not touching the glass. If someone had ever accused Rhys of stealing from his best friend, he would have done what any honorable man would do and level his gun at him. Unwittingly, Rhys's gaze dropped to John's hands, half expecting to find the black bore of his pistol already pointed at him.

"If that look on your face is any indication of what's going through your head right now, you can relax." The vaguest of smiles lifted one corner of John's mouth. "I've never been one to go looking for a fight, especially since I nearly killed a man with my fists back in London when I wasn't much more than a boy." His green eyes crackled with a glow of humor. "Besides, I would have thought the same thing if I was in your place." He smiled openly now as he picked up his mug of ale and took a drink. "I don't imagine your source told you about that, did he?"

"No. He didn't," Rhys answered, wondering if he sounded as relieved as he felt.

"I didn't really think he could have. Nobody knows about it. Not even Arthur." Cupping the mug in his hands, John leaned against the table and carefully studied the other's face. "But I'd say Ashlee took offense to your accusations." He laughed at the puzzling look his companion gave him, then nodded at the four red marks on Rhys's cheek.

Rhys's hand flew to his face. He had forgotten about the incident until John mentioned it. She had taken offense, all right. But not in regard to any insult Rhys had made toward her friend. The thought raced through his head again as to what John would do if he knew what really happened between the pair, and he cleared his throat, smiling lamely.

"She's very loyal to you," he said, hoping to point their conversation in a different direction. "As you are to her and her father."

"They're the only family I have. I think I can honestly say that I'd kill any man who tried to hurt them," he sighed, staring into the mug he cradled in his huge hands.

Rhys wondered how John would define hurt and quickly took a sip of ale.

"You know what puzzles me, Mr. Sinclair?" John suddenly asked.

"Please . . . call me Rhys," he hurriedly instructed. Maybe if he got John on friendly terms . . . "What puzzles you?"

John nodded his approval that they do away with formalities. "I imagine you've heard that Ashlee's against this arranged marriage of her stepmother's. Actually, if the truth be known, she plans to run away before she'd ever walk down the aisle with him. Yet, she behaved as if she truly liked the—the Frenchman." He fell back in his chair, the delicate piece of furniture squeaking beneath the strain. "At least I won't have to worry about him raising a hand to her as I've heard the French are so quick to do with their women. If he ever tried to hit Ashlee, she'd knock him right on his well-creased trousers." He smiled over at Rhys. "But I'm sure you realize that."

Rhys laughed before he could catch himself. "Yes. She does have a temper and she's not afraid to turn it loose."

He smiled to himself as he took a puff on his cheroot, thinking how angry she would be with John when he refused to help her steal anymore. He had seen the look in her eye and realized his threat to tell her father about her had had very little affect. She had every intention of continuing on with her masquerade. After all, it was only his word against hers as far as she was concerned. But without John's aid, her days of robbing wealthy northerners had come to an end.

"So tell me, Rhys," John said, intruding upon his companion's thoughts. "You've been here now for nearly a week. Surely you have someone in mind who might be behind all this."

Rhys finished off his ale and set the mug down. "Well, I really hate to accuse anyone without any proof, but unless I'm missing something, the only person who has the opportunity is Mrs. Redington. But after going over the books, I've almost eliminated her."

"The books?" John exclaimed. "When did you have the chance to look at them? And how did you get into the safe?"

"Arthur gave me the key and I simply waited until the night desk clerk was asleep. Quite easy if you use a little imagination." Snuffing out his cheroot, he folded his arms along the edge of the table. "And since you brought it up, what can you tell me about Dominique Redington?"

"Besides being a bitch—nothing. She showed up here one day about three years ago, put on a seductive air for Arthur, and had him marrying her within six months. I figured she'd have spent every penny he had by now. That's the kind of woman I took her for. But it's quite the opposite. In fact, trying to get a bloody red cent out of her is impossible. Why do you ask?"

Rhys shrugged. "Well, everyone else who works here is more than willing to talk to me about their past, where they've come from, what they hope to do in the future. But I can't find out a single thing about Arthur's wife. I've heard she claims to be the daughter of a French duke. Is that true?"

"Don't know," John admitted with a shake of his head. "It's what she's told Arthur. Why? Do you think it's a lie?"

Rhys chuckled. "The possibility has crossed my mind."

"You sound like you know something. Care to share it?" John smiled.

"Before she married Arthur, her name was Fabron, wasn't it?" He waited for John's nod then continued. "Well, I sent a telegram this morning to a friend of mine in Washington." He straightened and reached into his inside coat pocket, pulling out a piece of paper and handing it to John. "That's no real proof either. My friend could be wrong, but he's done a lot of traveling in France and he's never heard of a French duke by the name of Fabron. I'm not saying there isn't such a duke, but it certainly raises my curisoity about Arthur's wife."

John refolded the telegram and handed it back to Rhys. "I'll tell you someone else who might know if you asked her. She's done her share of traveling in France, too. And in the kind of places you'd expect to find a duke."

"Who?"

"Priscilla Krayer."

Rhys's brows came together in a frown. "I thought she was a part of the fixtures at the theater."

"She is now. The poor woman has a painful affliction in her knees and hips that makes it too difficult for her to travel. But before that happened, she used to act in nearly all the theaters abroad . . . especially France. She told me once that she even performed for Napoleon. Now where else would you expect to find a duke if not rubbing elbows with the emperor?"

A broad smile stretched across Rhys's mouth. "John, I think you've struck upon something." Pushing back from the table, he hurriedly stood up and turned for the door.

"Wait a minute, Rhys," John cautioned, standing up as well. "I'm going to have to go with you. Priscilla isn't going to tell you anything, my Yankee friend . . . at least not until I've assured her that you mean no harm to the Redingtons." He grinned almost evilly as he rounded the table and went to the door to unlock it. "And once she learns why we're asking, she'll be more than delighted to tell us." Pausing once he opened the door, he looked Rhys straight in the eye, all sign of humor gone. "If everyone around Belle Chasse knew why you were here, they'd all ask what took you so long. And I guarantee, Rhys, you'd have a lot of friends if they did. I can't think of a single person who wouldn't like to see Dominique Redington sent back to France." Extending his hand, he indicated that Rhys should take the lead, then quickly followed him from the room.

John Hardin had a reputation for being a loner. Seeing him as he was now, engrossed in conversation with the Yankee as they left the casino and crossed the lobby toward the back door, raised more than just a few surprised eyebrows. Of those who watched, however, Ashlee wasn't only surprised, she was fearful. Snatching up the hem of her skirts to clear her step, she hurriedly descended the staircase and lost herself in the crowd below in order that she might secretively observe the two men and the direction in which they were headed. She had no way of knowing what they talked about nor did it really matter. What she didn't like was the almost friendly manner in which they behaved. Rhys was the enemy, and John should treat him as such.

Standing on tiptoes, Ashlee peeked out around the people dividing her from the two men in time to see the back door open and shut again. Was it possible that they were on their way to see her? Curiosity getting the better of her, she gently edged through the crowd and fell into step behind the couple that had obviously decided to take a stroll in the courtyard. Once she had moved out onto the stone walkway, she stopped, surprised to find that John and Rhys hadn't taken the path leading to her quarters, but instead were cutting across the lawn toward the iron gate that opened up to the alley. Now, more determined than ever to learn what they were up to, she waited until they had disappeared behind the tall shrubs and trees lining the perimeter of the grounds, then darted across the grass after them, her long, black hair flying out behind her and a blur of white petticoats flashing with each step she ran.

She waited only a moment or two once she reached the gate before peering out past the shrubs to catch a glimpse of John and Rhys. Her mouth gaped open the instant she saw them walking toward the back entrance into the theater. Why was John taking him to see Priscilla? What could she possibly tell the Yankee that he didn't already know? Ashlee's beautiful face twisted with rage. Was he planning to threaten her? Pulling herself upright, she seized the latch on the gate and angrily swung it open. Well, she'd put a stop to it and right now!

She was nearly upon the figure standing at the theater door with his back to her before she realized that Rhys had decided to wait outside for John. She stopped dead in her tracks, afraid to move or even draw a breath lest he hear her and turn around. She had no excuse for being there except that she had followed him, and she certainly didn't want him to think that. He'd merely twist it around to make it sound as if she couldn't stand being away from him for a minute. Biting her lower lip, her eyes trained on his tall, masculine build, she lifted her skirts and quietly started to back away.

Thoughts of Ashlee filled Rhys's head as he stood there in the shade of the huge brick building, wondering where she was at the moment and what she was doing. John hadn't asked him if he had noticed the change that came over her once she had met Fabron. But he had, and he was reasonably sure it was done to spite him. Ashlee was too much of a woman to fall for someone like that little doddering fool of a Frenchman. His fingertips idly traced the bright furrows on his cheek. Yes, she was definitely all woman. Earlier, when they had ridden together in the carriage and were on their way to meet the train, he had found himself worrying about the man to whom Ashlee was engaged. Since none of the staff at Belle Chasse had ever met Perrin Fabron, rumors had run wild on what he would look like. It was the general consensus that because of his French heritage he would undoubtedly be handsome, a flirt, a great lover, and more than likely very rich—everything a woman wanted and needed in a man. The thought that they might be right bothered Rhys, and the only explanation he could come up with was that he was envious.

Leaning back against the cool brick wall, he leisurely glanced up at the bright blue sky with its spattering of clouds, asking himself why it mattered. It shouldn't. But the idea that she would be off bounds should she speak the vows with Fabron was something he didn't care to face. He enjoyed Ashlee. More than any other woman he had known . . . including Melody.

He chuckled suddenly, recalling Ashlee's blunder at thinking the stranger at the depot was her betrothed. Of course, he had thought so too at first and had been instantly struck with a sharp twinge of jealousy. Then the real Perrin Fabron stepped forward, and it was all Rhys could do to keep from laughing out loud. Ashlee had assumed he was laughing at her predicament. But he wasn't. He was snickering over his fears that Ashlee would find her betrothed interesting enough to marry him. After one look at the nervous little Frenchman, Rhys was sure John had struck upon the truth when he said Ashlee would run away before giving in to her stepmother's demands. What woman in her right mind would want to be saddled with someone like him for the rest of her life?

A movement to his right caught his eye, and Rhys quickly looked in that direction, suddenly filled with the sense that he was being watched. Straightening, he stepped away from the building where he stood and surveyed the length of the alley, seeing only one other who shared the place; a merchant near the other end stacking boxes at the back door of his establishment. Rhys shook his head, mentally scolding himself for allowing his thoughts to wander. Being in control of his mind and of his actions, he felt, had been what brought him through the war alive and uninjured. Just because the United States was at peace again didn't mean he could let down his guard . . . especially in a place like New Orleans. There was still fighting going on in the streets from time to time between the newly freed slaves and hostile whites, and the general attitude toward northerners wasn't what he'd call friendly. But more importantly, he'd hired on to do a job, and he mustn't let his personal feelings interfere with getting it done. He shrugged one shoulder a bit rebelliously. Maybe he'd limit his thoughts about Ashlee to the moments he was alone in his room.

The theater door creaked open behind him, and Rhys quickly turned around, half expecting what John's report would be.

"Priscilla never heard of a Duke Fabron," he said simply, "in France or England or anywhere. But then you didn't really think I'd find out anything different, did you?"

Rhys reached up and tugged on one earlobe with a half smile. "No I didn't."

"So what does that mean?"

"It means she lied about her past . . . or I should say her heritage. The question is why?"

"Well, if your suspicions about her are right, I'd guess it has something to do with her reason for stealing from her own husband, wouldn't you?"

"It's the only logical explanation." He fell quiet for a moment, deep in thought, then asked, "Did Priscilla get curious about all your questions?"

"Not at all. I just pretended I thought she'd like to hear about Ashlee's fiancé. The rest came as a matter of conversation. Priscilla loves that young woman like she was her own daughter, Rhys, and I think you should know that. If you need some help other than mine, she's the one to ask. Miss Krayer can be trusted more than anyone else I know."

"Thanks," Rhys smiled, heading back toward the hotel. "I'll remember that. But right now, I think it's better if we keep this just between you and me. I hate to think what Arthur would do if he learned I've done everything but openly accused his wife of being a thief."

"Then you really think she's responsible?" John asked, falling into step with his companion's long stride.

"Well, let's put it this way, from this point on, I'll be trying to prove she isn't . . . for Arthur's sake."

"Any ideas how you'll go about doing it?"

Rhys stopped at the iron gate, lifted the latch, and swung it open, letting John pass through it ahead of him. "How early in the morning does she usually make a bank deposit?"

"First thing. Around eight o'clock when the bank opens."

"Does anyone accompany her?"

"Hank, usually." John stopped suddenly and turned to

face Rhys. "You don't think she has a partner in this, do you? 'Cause if you do, I can guarantee you it isn't Hank Newell."

"No, that's not what I was implying," Rhys smiled reassuringly, laying his hand on John's thick shoulder. "I was just hoping that maybe I could be the one to take her to the bank. I'd like to stick with her for a few days, learn her routine, the people she talks to, that sort of thing. If I'm right about her, sooner or later I should be able to set up a pattern in her behavior. Then when she does something out of the ordinary, I'll check into it. It's about all I can do for now." His hand dropped to his side and he stared off into the distance for a moment before he looked back at John and smiled. "Unless, of course, I can win her over."

"Win her over?" John repeated with a slight frown. "What do you mean?"

"Make her think she can trust me, get on her good side, convince her that a woman needs a man's help. However, that means I'd have to find out what she's up to first—"

"Well, good luck, Rhys," John snorted, starting off again. "Dominique Redington doesn't trust anyone. Even her stepdaughter. That's the reason she's in charge of the books."

"It's what she wanted everyone to think," Rhys corrected. "If no one was allowed to look at them, she could fill in any figure . . . she . . . wanted. . . . That's it!" he exclaimed with a snap of his fingers.

"That's what?" John frowned, stumbling to a stop and turning back around.

"Two sets of books," Rhys confided in a whisper. "One to show her husband should he ever ask to see them as well as Ashlee on the nights she takes care of the records. A second set to keep track of the money she's embezzling."

"You really think so?" The lines in John's face

deepened even more.

"I've come up against a dead end everywhere else I've tried. Let's say it's worth looking into."

"But she wouldn't keep them in the office. It'd be too risky, don't you think?"

"Why?" Rhys challenged, draping his arm over John's wide shoulders and leading them both back toward the hotel. "No one's allowed in there except her husband and stepdaughter."

A slow dawning came over John's weathered face. "You know, Rhys, I think you've got something there."

"Uh-huh," Rhys grinned. "Now the problem is finding it."

"Well, let me know if there's anything I can do," John offered.

"You'll be the first," Rhys nodded, opening the door to the lobby.

Ashlee's blue eyes had narrowed to fine slits while observing the two talking together as if they were long lost brothers, laughing, sharing secrets, patting each other on the back! She had hidden herself in the bushes and had waited for John to come out of the theater again, hoping she would be able to eavesdrop on their discussion. But she had realized her mistake in standing where she had when all she could hear was a single word now and then, none of which made any sense. She could only assume they were talking about her, and from the way things appeared, Rhys had convinced John that he was on their side. The fool! Didn't John know that it was only a ploy, a friendish method of tricking John into letting down his guard so that the Yankee could walk right in and take over her father's business? Well, he hadn't duped her. Yanking the sleeve of her dress free of the branch it was snagged on, Ashlee let out a throaty growl at the rending tear of cloth she heard and stumbled out into the open to examine the damage. It was only a small hole, one that could be easily mended. But how it had happened never would. It was Rhys's fault and she ought to make him pay for it.

"Everything is his fault," she muttered. "Things were just fine until he came along." Well, not exactly fine, she silently amended, but at least not as nerve-racking. Ashlee spun around and headed toward the gate. She'd go and talk to Priscilla. Maybe John had deserted her, but Priscilla never would. After all, women always stuck together.

"Ashlee, what happened to you?" Priscilla cried once she looked up from the script she was reading and saw the young woman standing in the doorway of her apartment.

Ashlee gave herself a quick once-over. "Nothing," she frowned. "Why?"

"Because your dress is torn and you have leaves in your hair. Did you fall?" She laid aside the manuscript and awkwardly stood up. Her affliction was bothering her more than usual today.

Ashlee could feel the blush rise in her cheeks, and for a second she considered lying. But the woman was never fooled, and since Ashlee had honestly come here to ask her about John, she changed her mind. "It's a long story," she mumbled, turning to close the door behind her. "I was hiding in the bushes out back."

"Hiding? Whatever for?" Priscilla exclaimed.

"I didn't want John and that . . . Yankee to see me."

"John? Yank—" Priscilla shook her head. "Ashlee, you're confusing me." Pointing to the chaise lounge, she waited until Ashlee had sat down in it, then pulled her rocker closer and did the same. "Suppose you start at the beginning. You've come for a reason, and if I'm to help, I must know what provoked your visit."

Ashlee studied her hands folded in her lap for a minute, trying to decide just how much to tell the woman and where, exactly, to begin. But too many thoughts were running through her head, and the longer she contemplated their order, the more mixed up she became. Totally frustrated, she bolted from the chair and began pacing the floor.

Priscilla watched her companion's nervous trek from one side of the room to the other and back again until she couldn't stand it a second longer. "Ashlee," she snapped, "sit down. You're making *me* nervous."

Like a scolded child, Ashlee did as she was told and plopped herself on the chaise lounge again.

"It can't be as bad as you're putting on," Priscilla frowned. "Now tell me what's wrong."

Ashlee took a deep breath and exhaled it in a rush. "He knows. That damn Yankee knows everything."

"I assumed that much," Priscilla calmly replied. "Otherwise you wouldn't be here. So what's the problem? Is he threatening to turn you in to the authorities?" When her companion vigorously shook her head, Priscilla's brow furrowed. "Then he's planning on telling your father."

"No, no, nothing like that," Ashlee said, sliding to the edge of her seat. Reaching out, she took one of Priscilla's hands. "I don't know how he's done it, but Mr. Sinclair has turned John against me."

"Oh, Ashlee," Priscilla moaned. "Now you're being silly. No one in the world could do that and you know it. And why would he even try? What's to gain by it?"

"That's just it," she argued. "Rhys Sinclair wants Belle Chasse for himself and the only way he can do it is to stop John and me from stealing and giving the money to the casino. If the place goes under, he'll be the first in line to buy it." She rushed on when she saw the doubtful look on the other's face. "John was here a few minutes ago, wasn't he?" She didn't wait for an answer. "And I'll bet he didn't tell you that the Yankee was waiting outside the back door for him, did he? Of course not!" she exploded, not giving Priscilla a chance to say anything. "Whatever Sinclair's up to has something to do with me. That's why he talked John into coming here. To try and convince you not to help me if I asked. He's already tricked John." She curled her upper lip disgustedly. "I could tell that by the way they were acting." Irritated, she collapsed back in the lounge chair and folded her arms over her chest. "I never should have been fooled into playing poker with him."

All during the young woman's recital, Priscilla had tried to grasp the point of Ashlee's accusations but couldn't. She was talking in circles. John's visit had been nothing more than friendly, and he never once mentioned Ashlee. And what was this about playing poker?"

"Ashlee," she sighed, "I haven't the faintest idea what you're talking about. John came here because he thought I'd be interested in hearing about your fiancé. That's all we talked about other than his wanting to know how I was feeling. So for whatever misguided reasons you have, you are wrong about John."

Ashlee's blue eyes widened in surprise. "That's all? Are you sure?" she asked, sitting up.

"Yes," Priscilla nodded. "In fact, it was a very pleasant visit. We even talked about the days I used to perform with the theater in Paris."

"Paris?" Ashlee blurted out. "What brought that up?"

Priscilla shrugged. "I don't really remember. . . . Oh, wait, yes I do. He wanted to know if I had ever met Perrin's uncle."

"His uncle?"

"Yes. Dominique's father, the duke."

"Why would he want to know that?" Ashlee mumbled to herself.

"You know something, Ashlee," Priscilla murmured, leaning forward to pluck a leaf from the girl's long dark hair, "until John mentioned it, I hadn't realized that I'd never heard of a Duke Fabron all the while I was in Europe." She laughed and rested back in the rocker, absently twirling the leaf between her finger and thumb. "And when I said so to John, he told me that maybe the duke wasn't the theatergoing type. But I don't agree. And I don't know why I never thought about it until now."

Suddenly interested, Ashlee touched Priscilla's knee, drawing the woman's eyes to hers. "What are you saying?"

"Nobility always attends the theater. Duke Fabron never has." A strange smile came over Priscilla's face. "I don't think there is such a man."

"But Dominique claims—"

"Yes," Priscilla interrupted. "Yes, she does, doesn't she?" Placing her hands on the arms of her rocker, Priscilla arduously pushed herself to her feet and stiffly walked across the room to the window. "Certainly does raise one's curiosity about the woman. Or should I say, her past?"

Ashlee quickly stood up and hurried over to stand by her friend. "But why would she lie? Titles mean nothing to Papa if she thought it was a way to trap him."

"I don't know why," she said, staring out at the late afternoon sun. "But I think John does." An odd smile touched the corners of her mouth and she turned to look at Ashlee. "Why don't you ask him?"

Ashlee's smooth brow wrinkled into a puzzled frown. Not so much as to the matter of her stepmother's stories and why John suddenly found the knowledge of interest, but because of the unexplainable, almost foreign look in Priscilla's eyes. It was as if Ashlee had never seen this woman before, and a cold chill raced across her shoulders. She stumbled back a few steps.

"Yes. Yes, I think I will ask him," she said in nearly a whisper. "Priscilla, are you all right?"

The question was enough to bring the woman out of her peculiar trance. She blinked several times, saw the worried look on Ashlee's face, and chuckled as a slight blush rose in her cheeks. "I didn't mean to frighten you, love," she apologized. "I guess I just got carried away. I know how terrible things have been for you since that woman came into your life, and my creative mind simply took over looking for a way to get rid of her. There's probably some logical explanation for her mysterious father that will make us all look like fools."

"Do you really think so?" Ashlee hesitantly asked.

"Uh-huh," Priscilla nodded, reaching out to wrap her arm around Ashlee's shoulders and draw her companion back to the chaise lounge. "Now, suppose you tell me about Perrin. Is he handsome?"

"Handsome?" Ashlee laughed, sitting down again. "Didn't John tell you? He's shorter than I, very plain-looking, and somewhat of a dandy. Hardly the kind of choice I'd make for a husband."

"Oh, dear," Priscilla moaned. "That makes things rather difficult, doesn't it? I did so hope he would be the answer to your unhappiness."

"Oh, he's very nice, Priscilla, don't misunderstand me. But he isn't the sort I'd want to spend the rest of my life with." Her nose wrinkled disdainfully. "Much less have his children." She shivered at the thought of the two of them in bed together.

"But you don't have much of a choice," Priscilla pointed out with a frown.

"Not as far as Dominique is concerned, no. But that doesn't mean I'll marry him."

"Ashlee, you can't go against your father's wishes. It's what he wants, too," Priscilla warned.

Ashlee grinned impishly. "Papa hasn't seen Perrin yet. I think he'll change his mind once he has."

"And what if he doesn't?"

Ashlee shrugged and bounced to her feet. "Then I'll worry about that when the time comes." Bending down, she kissed her friend on the brow, then turned for the door. When she had reached it, she stopped and glanced back over her shoulder at Priscilla. "At least one good thing has come of all this," she smiled tenderly. "You and I don't have to keep our distance anymore."

Priscilla chuckled. "Except where your father is concerned."

A devilish twinkle gleamed in Ashlee's blue eyes. "That's never stopped me before, has it?" Swinging open the door, she grabbed a handful of her skirts and exited without another word.

Priscilla stared at the closed door long after Ashlee had gone, her tired blue eyes taking on a hint of sadness. She wouldn't tell the young woman that she had thought John Hardin's visit was out of the ordinary, that she had suspected he had come to see her for a different reason than he had let on. They didn't have the kind of relationship that would warrant his whimsical need to talk to her about Ashlee's fiancé, and he wasn't the type who enjoyed gossiping. He had wanted something from her. He had wanted to know about Dominique Redington's past, and he had gotten it—as much as Priscilla knew about it. Priscilla hadn't liked Dominique Fabron from the first moment they met. She was sure the feeling was mutual, for the simple fact that Priscilla had pegged the woman as an opportunist incapable of loving anything other than money and power, and the Frenchwoman knew it. What tore at Priscilla's heart then as well as now was that there wasn't anything she could do to stop Dominique. Arthur would never have listened to her, and if she had said anything to Ashlee, it would have only made things worse by widening the gap between her and the man she had loved all these years. Choking back her tears, she picked up the script she had laid aside when Ashlee came in and forced herself to concentrate on the words written there, silently reaffirming her pledge that she would never tell anyone how she truly felt. It was her own form of punishment for what she had done.

Chapter Eleven

A dark frown settled over Ashlee's brow as she walked through the courtyard ribboned with the shadows of late afternoon sunlight, the knot in her stomach reminding her that she had skipped lunch. She had already decided to talk with John just as soon as she could, but she'd have a bite to eat first. He wasn't going anywhere, and at the moment, food seemed of more importance. Her mouth twisted into a disapproving snarl. Food was always important to her, and maybe this time she could dine alone instead of having her appetite spoiled by unwelcomed company. The thought of Rhys turned her head in the direction of the staff's quarters located on the other side of the courtyard from her own, as if she expected to find him standing there watching her. The instant she realized what she had done and how he would misinterpret the gesture should he happen to have seen her, she snapped her attention back to the path she took, frowning all the more. Although her life at Belle Chasse wasn't exactly the way she wanted it to be, at least she had been in control of it for the most part. The Yankee's presence had changed all that. Hardly a moment went by that she wasn't running into him or finding herself forced to listen to the silly chatter of the female employees about how handsome and charming he was, and the ways in which they plotted to draw him into conversation. And now that everyone had gotten a look at Ashlee's fiancé, the cordial greetings she had usually received had turned to sympathetic nods, almost as if they knew about her and Rhys and were trying to discreetly convey their regrets over her loss of the better choice.

"If they only knew . . ." she fumed, reaching the lobby door and yanking it open.

The entry hall was nearly empty, a usual occurrence for this time of day since it was too early for the dinner crowd and the casino didn't really get busy until later in the evening. Thus, it was easy for Michael to spot the beautiful brunette right away as Ashlee headed toward the restaurant.

"Oh, Miss Redington," he called, stopping her just inside the doorway. "A wire just arrived for you."

"Who's it from?" she asked as she neared the desk and took the envelope he held out to her.

Michael straightened as though insulted. "I'm sure I wouldn't know, Miss Redington. I'm not in the habit of reading other people's mail." The sparkle returned to his green eyes. "Besides . . . it was sealed."

Ashlee smiled in return. "Since when has that stopped you?" she teased, tearing open the flap and pulling out the message to read. "Hmmm," she murmured after a while, "good news and bad news."

"Oh really?" Michael questioned, bracing himself against the desk top on his folded arms. "Would you care to share?"

"Of course," she grinned. "How else will everyone at Belle Chasse learn what was in this?" She shook the paper in front of him. "It's from Papa. He and Dominique have decided to stay in Jackson one more night."

"That's it?" Michael frowned.

Refolding the telegram, she put it back in the envelope and nodded. "Uh-huh."

"Well, how do you get good and bad news out of that?"

"The bad news is that I won't see Papa until tomorrow. The good news is that we don't have to put up with Dominique again tonight!" She smiled devilishly. "Don't you agree?"

"Yes, ma'am," Michael laughed.

"I thought you would," she bantered, tossing the note down on the desk next to him. "Well, I guess I better go and tell her cousin. I wonder if he'll be as relieved as we are." She winked at Michael and started for the staircase.

"He isn't in his room, Miss Redington."

The announcement turned Ashlee back around. "He isn't?"

Michael shook his head.

"Do you know where he is?"

"Well, not exactly. I just took over the desk for Charles as Mr. Fabron was leaving, but Charles said your fiancé received a message. Don't know from whom, but he asked Harold to get him a carriage. So wherever he's going, it's too far to walk. He left just before you came in. You might be able to catch him if you hurry."

"Thank you, Michael," she replied, lifting her skirts a mite to dash off toward the hotel's front entrance. Perrin Fabron didn't know anyone in New Orleans—or so she was led to believe—and the message he received as well as his sudden need of a rig raised more than just her curiosity. Something very mysterious was going on, and she couldn't help but suspect Perrin's unexpected departure was in some way connected to his cousin's secretive past. She opened the door and went outside.

The street in front of the hotel was bustling with carriages, horses and people traveling along its sidewalk, and Ashlee's shoulders drooped. She knew that unless

Harold had some idea where Perrin had gone, it was useless for her to even consider trying to follow the Frenchman, for he had already lost himself among the crowd. And if she hadn't had the burning desire to unravel this enigma concerning her fiancé and his cousin, she would have turned around and gone back inside. John had even sensed something wasn't quite right, and since he had made friends with the Yankee, she doubted he would share his discoveries with her. She was on her own, and the only way she'd learn anything was through her own determination.

"Harold," she called down to him as she hurriedly descended the stairs.

"Yes'm?" he smiled back at her as he finished unloading the luggage from the landau of their latest arrival.

"Michael told me that Mr. Fabron ordered a carriage."

"Yes, ma'am, he did. Just a couple of minutes ago."

"Do you know where he went?" she hopefully asked, then nodded politely at the couple who stepped down from their rig, assuring them that Harold would bring their baggage in straight away.

"Yes'm," he replied, glancing up to wave the driver on. He waited until the carriage had pulled away before turning back to her. "I heard him tell the coachman to take him to the hotel La Rouge."

"La Rouge?" she repeated, completely surprised. Frowning, she looked away and muttered, "This is getting stranger by the minute."

"Ma'am?"

Ignoring Harold's puzzled expression, Ashlee instructed him to have a rig brought around for her while she returned to her room for a bonnet and her purse, and she hurried off before he could answer. A few minutes later he helped her board the coach and stood back to watch the conveyance rattle off down the street, shaking his head and wondering if he would ever be able to figure out a woman's moods.

There were many hotels in New Orleans, several of which were of the same caliber as Belle Chasse. La Rouge wasn't one of them. Located in the run-down section of town patronized by those whose luck had turned bad since the end of the war, it was the kind of place a lady didn't visit unescorted. If Ashlee's head hadn't been so full of thoughts about Perrin and his reason for coming to such a shabby establishment, she might have reconsidered venturing there alone.

"Wait here," she told the driver as she climbed down from the carriage. "I shan't be long." Turning for the front door, she readjusted her bonnet, glanced both directions down the sidewalk that passed before the hotel, then started for the entrance, praying Harold hadn't been wrong about Perrin's destination.

The first thing Ashlee noticed about the interior of the hotel was how dimly lit it was and the musty, rank smell that rose up to assail her nostrils. Holding her breath, she quickly searched through her purse, withdrew her handkerchief, and pressed it beneath her nose, wondering if she could make it through the whole experience without retching. She set her sights on the mousy little man sitting behind the desk and started toward him.

"Excuse me, sir," she said, moving the handkerchief only long enough to speak.

He looked up from the paper he'd been reading and stared at her over the rim of his spectacles. "You lost?" he asked, not bothering to rise. "Or just come to poke fun at those less fortunate than you?" His dull brown eyes looked her up and down.

Ashlee gritted her teeth to keep from replying. She would have liked telling him that anyone with any kind of moral fiber could change their destiny if they wanted it badly enough, but she decided such advice would be wasted on this sort of creature. He obviously enjoyed wallowing in his self-made misery. She straightened her spine and stuffed the handkerchief back in her purse.

"I'm looking for someone," she said intrepidly.

"Here?" the man snorted sarcastically, studying his newspaper again. "Who? Your mother?"

Ashlee's temper flared. "Sir, I have not come here to be insulted by some poor excuse of a human being, and I take offense at the mere sight of you. So I think I should warn you by saying that my father is not without influence in this town and therefore advise that you keep a civil tongue in your head if you do not wish to pay the consequences." When he lifted his eyes to look at her again, Ashlee expected to see a glimmer of worry in his expression, possibly even a little fear because of her threat. But his reaction wasn't what she thought it would be, and she groaned inwardly for thinking she could intimidate such a person.

"Ain't nothin' your old man could do to me what ain't already been done, lady," he sneered. "So why don't you just wander back to the rich side of town where you came from and leave us honest people alone?"

Ashlee instantly regretted every word she had said. This wasn't the kind of individual that words would scare. At one point in his life he was probably a wealthy man, but because of the war he was living like a pauper in a decrepit hotel that only slightly resembled the way things used to be. It was very possible that this was the way her father could wind up. She bowed her head and sighed. She never liked being put in her place . . . even when she deserved it.

"Sir, I apologize," she murmured. "I had no right to say what I did."

This time his expression did change, but not the way Ashlee would have preferred as he raised one brow suspiciously at her. This wasn't going at all the way she

320

hoped. She sucked in a breath and tried again.

"Since neither of us wants me here, perhaps we can bring this meeting to a quick and hasty end. If you'll just tell me what it is I wish to learn—"

"Tell you?" he cut in, laying down the newspaper and coming to his feet. He leaned forward to brace himself against the desk. "Nothin' comes cheap these days."

Clamping her teeth together to calm her rising ire, she gritted out, "How much?"

He shrugged. "Don't know 'til ya tell me who it is you're looking for. Lot of your kind comes here when they don't want their friends to know what they're doing. Your father, maybe?"

Ashlee's emotions came full circle, and for the first time in her life she wished she were a man. She'd make him regret his insinuation. "He's a Frenchman, dark hair, dark eyes, short, very thin. I was told he was coming here," she recited, digging through her purse for what money she had with her. Laying three coins on the counter, she said, "And this is all I have."

The desk clerk eyed the silver as though it weren't enough, then scooped up the money and stuffed it in his pocket before he sat down again and picked up his paper to read. "Top of the stairs. Second door on the right."

"Thank you," she sneered, turning and heading for the staircase.

The steps creaked beneath her slight weight as she climbed them. Ashlee wondered how the rickety treads would manage to hold a man twice her size if someone as tiny as she could make them moan. When she reached the top, she paused and looked back down them. Better still, would they allow her to descend them? With a heavy sigh, she lifted her gaze to appraise the long, narrow hallway ahead of her, shuddering at the dirt and grime she saw. The walls and woodwork obviously hadn't been painted in years. The window at the end of the corridor had two cracked panes and was covered with a thick yellow film that made it impossible to see out of. The curtain that hung from its bent rod was torn and frayed and a dingy color of what once might have been a bright shade of blue. The threadbare rug was caked with dry mud and stained in several places where Ashlee assumed it had rained in through the cracks in the ceiling, and cobwebs hung in every corner. She shook her head in disgust and moved toward the room where the desk clerk had said she would find Perrin. How could anyone live in such a place? And what had brought Dominique's cousin here?

Standing in front of the door, Ashlee stared at its unsmooth finish of blistered varnish and the black marks around the knob and down one edge, trying to decide if she should just mind her own business and go home. She truly had no right in following him. They weren't married, and if everything went the way she wanted it to, they never would be. Yet, she felt compelled to satisfy her curiosity. During their ride to Belle Chasse, Perrin had shown a nervous reluctance to talk about his cousin, even though he had guaranteed Ashlee that he would answer all her questions after he had rested. Then, all of a sudden, he received a message from someone in a town where he was supposedly a stranger and dashed off without telling anyone anything, contradicting his claim that he wanted to lie down for a while. A frown wrinkled her brow. Who could he have possibly met here? She leaned in to listen through the cracks in the door and straightened instantly when she heard the laughter of two men, her cheeks heightening with color. Dear Lord, what was the matter with her? What Perrin did was his concern, not hers. And if she knocked on the door, what would she say? Pardon me, Perrin, but I was passing by on my way to the dressmaker's and . . .

She stifled a gasp when she heard footsteps from inside

the room coming toward the door. Dominique seldom spoke French around Ashlee except in anger. But Ashlee had learned enough of the language to know the men were saying good-bye to each other and that at any moment one of them would open the door and find her standing there. She glanced back toward the stairway and shook her head. Perrin would see her leaving the hotel. She quickly looked the opposite direction. The corridor at the end of the hall divided and went both ways. If she hurried, she could round the corner and hide there until after Perrin had left. Lifting her skirts, she raced on tiptoes as fast as she could, her heart thundering in her chest when the clicking of the latch echoed loudly all around her.

Reaching the end of the hall, she dashed to her left out of sight, stopped, and fell back against the wall to catch her breath as she listened to the men speaking in French. She couldn't understand most of what they said but enough to know that they planned to meet again as soon as they could. Tempted beyond caution to sneak a glance at Perrin's friend, Ashlee leaned to her right and slowly peeked out at the pair in time to see Perrin briefly kiss the man full on the mouth in a way that suggested they were more than just friends.

For a moment, Ashlee thought she had only imagined the embrace until a sick feeling washed over her and her head began to spin. Dizzy, she braced herself back against the wall and closed her eyes, a flood of turbulent emotions coursing through her to grip at her heart unrelentingly. She felt betrayed, used, degraded, even ashamed. But the strongest, most overwhelming of them all was pure, unbridled outrage. Surely Dominique knew of Perrin's preference for men, and yet she was still willing to force them into marriage. What kind of a life would that have been for either of them? Was getting rid of her stepdaughter so important to Dominique that she would marry her off to someone who would never love her as a man should love his wife? Had this woman no compassion? Even for her own kin? Ashlee fought back the wave of nausea that turned her stomach upside down. Had Dominique planned to tell her? Or did she intend to let Ashlee find out on her wedding night? Tears sprang to her eyes. God, this was a nightmare!

She gave no thought to the chance the men were still in the hall as she left her hiding place and raced for the stairs. But once she reached them and saw Perrin starting back up, she couldn't force herself to take another step. She hardly knew the man, yet something about him—perhaps the pathetic look on his face when he glanced up and saw her—struck a compassionate nerve. A long while passed as they stared at each other, neither knowing what to say. Yet both sensed the need to comfort the other. Finally, it was Perrin who drew up the courage to speak first.

"Zee desk clerk told me you were here, *mon chere.*" He looked down at his feet. "I should have left a message with Michael."

Ashlee wanted to cry and to scream at the same time. She wanted to hit something with her fist and exchange the pain in her heart for that in her hand. She wanted to wake up and find it had all been a hideous dream. She bit her lower lip and swallowed the lump in her throat, realizing that Perrin must be suffering a lot more than she. This wasn't the kind of thing a man wanted anyone to know about, especially his fiancée. Suddenly filled with sympathy, she smiled weakly and started down the stairs.

"I have a carriage waiting outside, Perrin," she spoke softly, taking his arm. "I suggest we go somewhere and talk this out."

"*Oui, mademoiselle,*" he murmured, unable to look at her.

The sun was beginning to set when they left La Rouge. Ashlee knew John would be worried about her once he learned that she had left the hotel alone and hadn't returned now that it was getting dark. But she also realized what she and Perrin had to say to each other should be discussed in privacy. The only place Ashlee could think of that would guarantee this was a secluded little spot along the riverbank at the edge of town. Before the war started and before Dominique had entered her life, she and her father used to go there on warm Sunday afternoons to watch the huge ships sailing into port. It was peaceful there, and it just might serve to bring the same kind of peace to two very troubled souls.

Neither of them spoke as they traveled the distance. Ashlee was sure Perrin was sorting out the answers he would give her, even though she wasn't positive what to ask. He helped her from the carriage, then held out his arm for her as Ashlee instructed the driver to wait. Arm in arm, they walked the narrow path that wound through a sparse stand of trees to the river's edge. Ashlee withdrew from him and went to view the dark brown waters of the Mississippi tipped golden by the dying sun.

"I did not wish for you to find out this way," Perrin half whispered, his voice tight with anguish.

Ashlee swallowed hard. "Does Dominique know?" she asked without turning around to look at him.

"*Oui*," he said softly.

"And it didn't matter." It was stated more as fact than as a question.

"It mattered, *mon chere*," he corrected. "My cousin thought of me as a disgrace to our family and said I would marry so that no one knew."

"Except your wife," Ashlee snapped and instantly regretted having lost her temper. She wasn't truly angry with Perrin. He was an innocent victim of Dominique's malicious plan. If the woman honestly thought Perrin

325

brought shame to their family, she would have had him married off long before now. What Ashlee couldn't understand was why Perrin had agreed. She turned to look at him. "Who is the man I saw you with?"

"His name is Philippe Dorset."

"The one you said came here with you from Paris?" The one who supposedly went on to Baton Rouge?"

"*Oui*," Perrin nodded weakly.

"Is he your—your—" She couldn't bring herself to say it.

"I care a great deal for Philippe," he replied with a sigh, moving to stand closer to the muddy shoreline.

"How long have you know each other?"

Perrin bent and pick up a stick lying at his feet, tossing it out into the water. "For many years, *mon chere*."

"And your cousin knew about . . . you two?" Ashlee hoped her words conveyed her sympathy and understanding for the man.

"*Oui*," he answered, turning back to look at her, his thin face twisted in a puzzled frown. "But why all these questions, *Mademoiselle* Ashlee?"

She smiled softly back at him, then took his trembling hand and drew him down on the fallen log next to her. "Because I have no say in the matter of choosing a husband, Perrin. And if you'd like to know the truth, neither did my father. It was Dominique's idea. But you, being a man, should have been able to decide whether or not you wanted to marry me, and since your . . . preference is not marry anyone, well, I don't understand why you agreed. I don't mean to hurt you, Perrin, and this isn't meant as a slur against you, but I don't want to get married either . . . to anyone! I'm quite content living as I am." She twisted to look him straight in the eye. "So tell me, Perrin, what did she threaten you with?"

A look of near panic flashed across his face. He stood

and walked away from her. "I—I already told you, *ma cherie.*"

Positive now that she had struck upon something, Ashlee quickly came to her feet and went to stand beside him. "Perrin, there's only two people in this entire world that can stop the marriage between us, and that's you and me. And the only way we can do it is to be honest with each other. I can't believe that you would willingly travel all the way here to marry someone you've never met, someone you don't want to marry just to please your cousin. Why should she care what you do back home in France? She's never going back there to live. I know why she chose me. She wants me out of the way. But why you?"

Perrin's delicate chin quivered as he chewed on his lower lip, and Ashlee was sure she saw tears in his eyes.

"Is this the way you want it?" she said more softly than before, yet pleadingly.

Perrin gulped and shook his head, and Ashlee gently touched his arm.

"Then tell me what it is, Perrin. You can trust me. I have as much at stake as you." She watched him for a moment, and when he still wouldn't answer but seemed to shake even more at her insistence to face the truth, she moved to stand in front of him. "She frightens you, doesn't she, Perrin?"

He raised a boney hand to his mouth and chewed on one knuckle, his eyes darting from the ground to Ashlee and back again. Then in a burst of emotion he whirled away from her and went to stand near a tree, propping his elbow against the trunk and burying his face in the crook of his arm. Ashlee half expected him to start weeping loudly at any second, and if it hadn't been for the pain she knew he was suffering, she would have lost her temper with him. Perrin was nothing but a tormented soul in a

327

man's body, and losing her patience with him wouldn't do either of them any good.

"Perrin," she began again, coming to stand next to him, "whatever it is that your cousin is holding over you can't be so great that the two of us—working together—can't overcome. You haven't been able to do it alone, and neither can I. But if we work as a team, we just might show Dominique that there are two people in this world she can't bully. And think of what we'll gain by proving it!"

"It isn't as simple as that, *mon amie*," he groaned, dropping his arms at his sides and turning away. "I am in debt to Dominique."

"You can't be serious," she exclaimed, catching his elbow and spinning him back around. "You actually think you should be grateful that she's forcing you into marriage? That's blackmail, Perrin, pure and simple."

"*Non, non, mon petite,*" he wailed. "It ees not that kind of debt. I owe her money."

Ashlee straightened, quite taken aback with his announcement. To force someone to marry against their will meant the amount Perrin owed had to be staggering. It also meant Ashlee wouldn't be able to help. "Oh," she murmured with a frown, moving to sit back down on the log.

"I 'ave a weakness for cards, *chere*, as well as a good bottle of wine. When I indulge in both at zee same time, it ees disastrous." He sighed, disheartened, and settled down next to Ashlee on the tree trunk, his clasped hands dangling between his knees. "Because I owed so much to so many and they were zee kind who wanted payment, my cousin had to give them all the money she had so that they would not take our house and land and leave us to wander zee streets."

Ashlee's head shot up. "What?" she gasped.

"*Oui,*" he nodded. "They would not be content with

merely sending us to prison, and killing me would not give them zee money I owed." Absently staring off into the distance, he sighed and shook his head. "Dominique was very angry with me and said one day I would pay her back. I didn't know then how much it would cost me."

"But what about her father? Your uncle? Wouldn't he help?"

A strange look came over Perrin's thin face as he turned his head to look at her.

"The duke, Dominique's father," she advised when it seemed by his expression that he didn't understand. "Where was he that he didn't offer to pay your debt instead of Dominique?"

"Ashlee, I thought you had already figured it out," he replied, frowning. "Dominique's father ees not a duke. *Mon Dieu*, we don't even know who her father ees."

"But she said—" Suddenly everything fell into place. The reason Priscilla had never heard of a Duke Fabron was because there was no such person. And Dominique's fetish over keeping track of every penny Belle Chasse earned came from the fact that she had never had any wealth of her own. But why had she lied about her father being a duke? Once more she set her gaze on the man at her side. "Will you tell me why it was so important to her that we think she was the daughter of royalty?"

Perrin shrugged one narrow shoulder. "It ees not so much that you or *Monsieur* Redington believe as it ees that she believes, *mon petite*. Dominique was a very young child when her mother died, and she was forced to live with her aunt and me. I think she began to make up zee story out of loneliness because she always said someday her father, zee duke, would come for her, that she would have all zee money and fine clothes she wanted." He sighed as he flicked a piece of lint off the knee of his trousers. "It was no surprise to any of us when she announced one day that she was going to New

Orleans, and I thought I would never have to pay back zee money I owed her." He gave a short, sarcastic laugh. "I was wrong."

"Perrin, is there a chance she could be the daughter of a duke?" Ashlee posed speculatively.

"Of course," he quickly agreed. "And since we do not know who her father ees, she could be zee daughter of zee king of England! But no matter whose blood runs in her veins, she ees still illegitimate and therefore has no claim to anything."

"Didn't your mother know who the man was? I mean, she'd surely know something like that about her own sister, wouldn't she?"

Perrin fell quiet for a moment, his gaze dropping to the ground at his feet. When he spoke again, his voice held a sympathetic note. "To put it quite bluntly, *mon amie*, there were so many men in my aunt's life that it was impossible to tell who fathered her child."

"Did Dominique know this?"

"*Oui*," he nodded. "And she hated me and my mother for knowing as well." He twisted on the log and took Ashlee's hand. "And she will kill me if she learns I have told you. So you must not say a word, Ashlee. Promise me that you won't." The lines around his eyes deepened with the pleading look he gave her.

"I won't," she quickly assured him, patting his hand. "I wouldn't gain anything by it except, maybe, to make her hate me even more. And you know, that's something that really puzzles me. Her dislike for me is so intense, and I can't honestly figure out what I've done to her to make it that way."

"*Chere*," he laughed, "you are not alone. I know of no one Dominique likes."

"So what do we do, Perrin?"

"Do?" he questioned. "About what?"

"About our situation."

"I do not see where either of us has a choice. You must marry because your father wishes it, and I must marry because I owe Dominique money. If I refuse, she will have me thrown in prison." He grimaced and looked out at the river. "Or murdered. And if that happened, Dominique would choose another man for you to marry. At least as my wife, you will have no demands made upon you. You would be free to do whatever you liked."

"In Paris," Ashlee finished, a bit sardonically.

Perrin turned and looked at her. "*Oui*, in Paris. I do not wish to live here."

"And I do not wish to live in Paris, Perrin," she countered. "What kind of a life would that be for me? Do you honestly think I'd be happy in a strange country where people don't even speak the same language as me? I'd be lost and lonely . . . and poor."

"But I would take care of you, Ashlee," he argued in nearly a whine.

"I'm sure you would. You'd see that I'm never hungry or cold and that I was properly clothed. But it would end there. What of love, Perrin? What would happen if I met someone and fell in love? I couldn't marry him or have his children because I would belong to you." In a sudden flurry of emotions, she hurriedly stood up and walked toward the edge of the river where the thick grass thinned out and turned to muddy sand. "You'd be happy, Perrin," she added, her throat tight. "You'd go on living as you had before, only better. You wouldn't be in debt to your cousin anymore. In all actuality, I'd be the one who paid. My freedom and happiness for yours." She faced him again. "I won't do it, Perrin, I'll run away first."

Distressed by her announcement, he sprang to his feet, his mouth gaping open. He started to speak, to beg her to change her mind, and suddenly knew that he had no right to ask anything of her. She was right. She would be the one to suffer. Clamping his mouth shut, he dropped his head and stared down at his feet. It wouldn't be fair, but he didn't see how they could do anything to change it.

"I cannot blame you, *mademoiselle,*" he murmured. "I would do the same if I could. But there ees more."

"More?" Ashlee's dark brows knotted worriedly, fearing the worst was yet to be told.

"*Oui,*" he admitted, looking sheepishly up at her. "Running away would not solve my problem. It would only make my mother's life more miserable."

"Your mother?" Ashlee repeated, coming to stand near him. "Why?"

Perrin's dull brown eyes saddened with the thought of the sick and aging woman he had left behind in Paris, and a lump formed in his throat. Blinking several times to hold back the tears that threatened to fall, he clutched his hands tightly to his chest and took a deep breath. "Zee only way Dominique would pay my gambling debt was if my mother would turn over zee deed to our property. About six months ago, I received a letter from her telling me that since I could not repay zee money, I was to marry you instead, and only then would she give back zee deed. If I refused, she would sell zee house and property and put my mother out into zee streets to beg. Then she would have me shot." He smiled weakly. "So you see, *mon amie,* I have no say in zee matter either. I do thees for my mother."

Ashlee stared at the little Frenchman for a long while, wanting very much not to believe a word he had said. The only thing that convinced her he was telling the truth was the simple fact that she knew Dominique was capable of just about anything, including putting an old woman out of her home, penniless. It seemed they were both caught in a well-thought-out scheme from which neither of them could escape. But Ashlee had never been a quitter, and she knew that if she thought about this long enough, she'd come up with a plan. After all, hadn't it been her idea to rob the gamblers on the riverboats? She inwardly cringed at the thought of how that had turned out. She sighed heavily and raised her chin in the air, absently looking at the pale blue sky streaked with the burning reds and oranges of the sunset.

"I know how you feel, Perrin," she admitted, visions of Rhys stealing into her thoughts. "I owe a great deal of money to a man who won't rest until I've paid it all back. And like you, I have no way to do it."

"You have a weakness for cards, *mon amie?*"

Laughing, Ashlee shook her head and turned around. "No. It isn't anything like that. You see, my father's business is failing, and it has been since the war broke out. Some weeks we lose, some we make a little profit, but the majority of the time we break even. It doesn't leave anything left over for the things my father really wants to do."

"And what ees that?" Perrin questioned.

"He wants to be elected to the Senate, to represent Louisiana in Washington. But it takes money to campaign for such an office, and every penny he makes goes right back into Belle Chasse just to keep it open."

"So you borrowed money to help out?" Perrin guessed.

"No," she chuckled, glancing back over her shoulder at him. "Not exactly. I stole it."

Perrin's thin face paled as his hand flew to his mouth. *"Mon Dieu,"* he gasped, sinking back down on the log. "You have more courage than I, *ma cherie.*"

"I don't think courage had much to do with it," she confessed, sitting down next to him. She clasped her hands and rested them on one knee. "It was done out of desperation . . . and love."

"And then you got caught?"

"Well, sort of. You remember the two men who came with me to the train depot this afternoon?"

333

Perrin nodded his head and twisted around on his perch to give Ashlee his full attention.

"John, the bigger of the two, has been a friend of my father's for as long as I can remember. He was my partner." She smiled over at him when she heard Perrin mutter something in his native tongue, a phrase she didn't understand but felt certain expressed his feelings about John's intimidating size. "About a year ago, we came up with a scheme that would allow me access to the staterooms on various riverboats sailing north out of New Orleans, where a big poker game was being played. I'd slip laudanum into the gamblers' drinks, wait for them to pass out, then take their money and leave the boat."

"Did your father approve of thees?" Perrin asked. It astounded him to think that any man would allow his daughter to do such a thing. "It ees so dangerous."

"He didn't know. And still doesn't. And that's why I'm in trouble," she added, crimping one side of her mouth. "One of the players on board the last steamer we robbed somehow figured out who I was—even though I was wearing a disguise—and suddenly appeared on my doorstep. He wants his money back, and I have no way to give it to him because I already filtered it into my father's casino."

"Who ees thees man?"

"The one who came with John and me to the train depot. His name is Rhys Sinclair."

Perrin straightened in surprise. "But I thought he worked for you."

Ashlee realized how confusing the whole thing must seem to Perrin. If she hadn't experienced each detail as they happened, she probably wouldn't understand either. "He does," she said, pushing herself up to her feet. Unaware of what she was doing, she began to pace back and forth in front of him. "I don't know why he took

334

a job working for my father. Mr. Sinclair is wealthy enough to own a place like Belle Chasse, not work in one. But I can tell you what I suspect." She stopped her aimless walking and quickly sat down beside Perrin again. "He came to Belle Chasse looking for the woman who had robbed him. Then he learned about Father's difficulties and decided to take advantage of the situation."

"What do you mean?" Perrin asked, his curiosity aroused.

"I think he's hanging around like some vulture waiting for the right time when he can buy out my father for half of what Belle Chasse is worth."

"Why do you think that?"

"Because after he learned why I was stealing, he told me that if I continued, he'd tell my father. But he never once asked me how I intended to pay back the money I had taken from him. I don't think it matters to him anymore. Purchasing Belle Chasse is much more profitable. And now that you're here, he can just sit back and wait."

"Me?" Perrin exclaimed. "What have I to do with it?"

"He knows that after we're married, I'll be returning to Paris with you. I'll be out of the way, don't you see?" She stood up suddenly with a devilish smile brightening her blue eyes. "Won't he be surprised when he learns that you and I have changed our plans to wed?"

"What?" Perrin gasped, jumping to his feet and grabbing her arm. "Ashlee, we must get married. My mother will—"

"Oh, don't worry, Perrin," she assured him. "I have a plan that will solve your problem and delay mine a bit."

"A—a plan?" His doubt shone clearly in his eyes.

"Uh-huh," she grinned. "Dominique gave you two choices, didn't she? Either pay back what you owe her in exchange for the deed to your mother's property or marry me to have it. Since we both agree that we don't want to get married, that leaves us the first alternative. We'll pay her the money."

"Oh, *ma cherie*," he moaned. "I 'ave already told you. I cannot pay her. I 'ave no money."

"Well, neither do I," she smirked playfully. "But I know how to get some."

Perrin's chin sagged and beads of nervous perspiration popped out on his brow. *"Mon Dieu,"* he groaned. "You do not mean—"

A reckless smile flashed across her face. "That's right, Perrin. I'm going to steal it."

Chapter Twelve

It was dark by the time Ashlee and Perrin returned to the hotel. As she watched Perrin ascend the stairs to his room Ashlee mentally braced herself for the lecture she was sure John would give her. There was no sense in making him a part of it, and what she had to say to John must be said in private. Turning for the front desk and Michael, she asked the clerk if he knew of John's whereabouts, setting her steps in the opposite direction toward the entrance into the restaurant when advised John had been seen heading that way a short time earlier. But once she moved inside the dining hall and spotted John's broad shape at a far table, her body stiffened in anger and her feet wouldn't move another inch.

"Mary," she hissed through clenched teeth at the waitress who passed by, "please tell Mr. Hardin that I'd like to speak with him in Mr. Redington's office. That is, of course, if he can tear himself away from Mr. Sinclair's company."

"Yes'm," the girl replied with a nod of her head. The puzzled frown on the young maid's face disappeared the instant her mistress's eyes fell upon her. She turned to do as bade without further comment, unaware that Ashlee's attention had already moved back to the two men sitting at the table.

"How cozy," she sneered when John laughed at something his companion said. "I wonder what lies the Yankee told him to win him over so easily. Well, it isn't going to work, Rhys Sinclair. John's loyalty is with my father, and all I'll have to do is remind him of it." She raised her nose in the air as if Rhys had eyes in the back of his head and could see the gesture, lifted her skirts in a very prim manner, and exited the restaurant.

As she passed by the front desk she informed Michael that once Mr. Hardin joined her in the office she did not want them to be disturbed and that it was his responsibility to see that they weren't. Michael quickly guaranteed Ashlee that he'd make doubly sure no one bothered them, smiling politely at her until she had turned away and gone into the other room. Only then did he raise a quizzical brow at the empty doorway. Miss Redington, for as long as he could remember, never ordered anyone to do anything. She always asked. But then he couldn't say it surprised him any. Miss Redington's nature had changed over the past week and he guessed it had something to do with the Yankee.

Ten long minutes passed before John made an appearance. Ashlee had listened to every single tick of the clock that sat on one of the bookshelves, swearing she could see the hand on its face move as she watched. And the longer she waited, the shorter her temper became. She cursed the day she met Rhys Sinclair, for that chance meeting had played havoc with her life, the worst of it being the apparent friendship he had made with the man who stood before her now. If John trusted the Yankee, he would have second thoughts about helping her. She motioned him farther into the room and closed the door behind him.

"What's so important, Ashlee, that I couldn't finish my dinner?"

His tone lacked the concern he usually showed for her, and Ashlee gritted her teeth as she watched him lower his beefy frame into one of the wing chairs before the desk. Not only wasn't he going to scold her for leaving Belle Chasse unescorted, but he obviously hadn't even missed her! She let out a long, exasperated sigh and came to sit down next to him.

"What's so important?" she repeated with a mocking smile that quickly turned into a sneer. "Have you forgotten already? Or has Mr. Sinclair changed your mind?" She bounced to her feet and began pacing the floor. "I've noticed you've been spending a lot of time with him. Has he convinced you that he's not out to buy Belle Chasse for himself? And before you say a word, let me point out that even if it's true, there are others who would love owning a place like this for half of what it's worth." She stopped and whirled around to glare at him. "What's important, John, is that we continue with what we were doing. We may not be able to bring Belle Chasse out of the trouble it's in, but at least we're helping Papa hang on to it."

"By running the risk of being caught?" John's light brown eyebrows slanted upward with the question. "Again?" He nodded at the empty chair. "Sit down, Ashlee."

Unlike most men, John never tried to disguise his feelings whenever he and Ashlee talked, and she knew by the look on his face that their jaunts up the Mississippi had come to an end. Disheartened, she sank down in the chair. It would be interesting to hear his reasons.

He quietly studied the beautiful face staring at him for a moment, afraid that what he would tell her would tarnish their relationship, that she wouldn't understand why he had to deny her his help. But he had made a promise to the Yankee, and for that reason, as well as the fact that he agreed with Rhys about protecting Ashlee, he

339

would tell her no.

"Ashlee," he began softly, leaning forward to brace his elbows on his knees, his hands clasped between them, "I think you know how much you and your father mean to me. You're the only family I've ever had, and Arthur is more than just a good friend. That's why I so willingly agreed to help you steal. That and because I knew you'd try it without me if I had said no. I had regrets about it the very first time I watched you board the steamer, knowing that you were entirely on your own from that point on. Or at least until we met upriver a ways." He gave her a half smile then stood and went to stare out the window. "I was afraid we'd get caught sooner or later, but I just kept on helping because I knew how much it meant to you . . . and it meant a lot to me. I didn't want to see Arthur fail. After a while, I started to believe that we'd never get caught, and I think you did too. That's when we started getting careless. And that's when it was our misfortune to rob Mr. Sinclair."

Ashlee's dark brows came together when she heard him chuckle. So far, he hadn't said anything that she found terribly amusing.

"Or I should say our good luck." He glanced back over his shoulder at her. "Anyone else wouldn't have wasted a second going to the authorities about us. All he wants from us in return is not to steal anymore."

Ashlee's delicate chin had dropped as she listened to his calm admission that he believed Rhys Sinclair would not cause them any trouble. It also surprised her to hear that he trusted a total stranger. That was something John Hardin had never done in all the years she had known him. But more than anything, it hurt her to think that John was going to simply sit by and watch her father's business fall into the hands of a northerner, because she was sure that that was exactly what Rhys Sinclair was planning. Tears suddenly burned her eyes, and she

340

quickly looked down at her hands.

"Ashlee, I'm not abandoning your father." John had already seen the pained expression on her lovely face. He hurried to sit down in the chair again and take her tiny hands in his much larger ones. "It's because of your father that I won't let this go on any longer. He'd never forgive me if something happened to you. Sinclair made me realize that. I'll simply find some other way to help Arthur, but not at your expense. Do you understand?"

Ashlee's chin quivered as she bravely lifted her eyes to look at him. "I understand that you've allowed a Yankee to come between us."

"Ashlee, no," John groaned, coming to his feet when she stood up and moved away from him. "I thought you knew me better than that. No one will every destroy the feelings I have for you and your father, and nothing anyone can say or do will ever change that."

"Then prove it by helping me this one last time."

The plea was spoken softly, but there was an unmistakable challenge in the pale blue eyes that watched him, and for an instant John nearly broke his word to Rhys. He didn't want Ashlee to think he had deserted her. There was no one in the world except her father that meant anything to him, and it pained him to let her assume there was. He wanted to tell her that. He wanted to let her know that even though Sinclair was a Yankee, he was a man who could be trusted, and that the reason he wouldn't help her steal was because she didn't have to anymore. But he had promised not to say anything and that he would keep Ashlee home where she belonged. So rather than explaining, he was forced to remain silent, taking comfort in the fact that if everything went as planned, it wouldn't be long before he could recite the truth. Venting a long, tired sigh, he said, "I didn't think friends had to prove anything to each other, Ashlee." He lowered his gaze and started for the door. Reaching it, he paused and looked back at her. "But maybe I was wrong."

The tears that had only moistened Ashlee's eyes now fell freely as she watched the door swing silently shut behind John Hardin. He was right. Friends shouldn't have to prove anything. If her life weren't in such a turmoil, she never would have put such demands on him. But it seemed that everything she cared about was drifting away from her, and all she had really wanted was to be assured that he wasn't part of it. Haphazardly, she wiped her face with the back of her hand, a brave smile lifting the corners of her mouth. Well, maybe she had lost one friend, but she had found another, and Perrin needed her more than she needed John right now. Squaring her shoulders, she took a deep breath to strengthen her sagging spirits, vowing that she'd find another way to acquire the amount of money it would take to buy Perrin's freedom. But first she had to get rid of the Yankee.

As expected, the casino was crowded with finely garbed men and women hoping to beat the odds and take home more money than any of them could spend in a lifetime. A thin haze of cigar smoke hung above them like an early morning fog, merging with the pungent odor of whiskey and ale to waft up and attack Ashlee's nostrils as she paused just inside the entrance. It was not something new to her, but this time it turned her stomach. She frowned, wondering why she had shaken it off before, as she searched the mass of people for Elaine's blond head. If anyone knew where to find Rhys Sinclair, she would, for it seemed she kept a very close watch on the man. Spotting the woman near the bar, Ashlee moved farther into the room, one finely arched brow slanted upward. She couldn't understand why Elaine was attracted to the pompous northerner.

"Elaine," she said, once she reached her, "have you seen Mr. Sinclair this evening? I know he has the night off, but I thought maybe he'd spend it here."

"I think he went to his room to change his shirt, Miss Redington," the pretty blonde informed her. "He was playing poker and there was an accident with a tray of drinks. Would you like me to go and tell him that you're looking for him?"

Oh, I'm sure you'd love to hear me say yes, Ashlee mused, her pale blue eyes darkening a bit. *What a perfect excuse to be alone with him in his room . . . where no one could see what went on.* She sucked in a breath and cast her gaze away from the woman. "No," she answered, "I'll do it myself." Turning, she hurriedly walked away, deciding that she'd go without talking to him rather than give Elaine the opportunity to do what she'd been longing to do since the Yankee first appeared at Belle Chasse. Ashlee missed the puzzled look on the blonde's face.

"You know, Kelly," she said to the man behind the bar, "Miss Redington sure has been acting strangely since Rhys started working here. Do you think there's a connection?"

"Depends on what you call strange," Kelly replied, watching Ashlee's slender figure move across the room away from them as he finished wiping dry the glass he held.

Elaine shrugged. "Oh, I don't know. Possessive, I guess you'd call it—like she don't want nobody to talk to him except her."

"You're not jealous, are you, Elaine?" he grinned.

"Jealous?" she laughed. "Are you joking? Rhys don't give none of us women here a second look. He's nice enough if you can manage to get him to talk to you, but that's as far as it goes. How can I be jealous of something that ain't there?" She shook her head and watched

Ashlee make her way in the direction of the private gaming rooms and the hallway that led to the staff's quarters further on. "No, I'd say Miss Redington is the one who's jealous." She laughed again. "Though I don't see nothing for her to be jealous of. If she'd just open her eyes, she'd realize Rhys ain't interested in anybody but her." A bright smile flashed across her face as she turned back to Kelly. "And just wait until Mrs. Redington comes home tomorrow. She'll put a stop to that!"

The portly bartender couldn't refrain his laugher. "Yeah, well, I'm sure Miss Ashlee's fiancé won't do anything about it. That little milksop is afraid of his own shadow."

Elaine's amusement faded with the mention of the Frenchman. "I know. And it's a shame. Miss Redington deserves better than that." Her gaze drifted back to the hallway where Ashlee had gone. "I sure hope something good happens to prevent their marriage," she murmured sadly, silently wishing there were some way she could help.

Ashlee hadn't realized exactly how it would look to Rhys to find her standing outside the door of his room until after she had rapped loudly and announced her presence. The instant she had, she longed to race back down the hallway and disappear from sight before he could open the door and see her. She had allowed her disapproval of the way Elaine behaved around the man to cloud her thoughts or she wouldn't have put herself in such a compromising position. When she heard the knob rattle and the latch click free, she steeled herself for the pleased look he would give her once he opened the door and saw her there. But it hadn't been enough once the portal swung wide, for she hadn't imagined he would answer the summons half dressed.

Wide, muscular shoulders gleamed in the soft light of the lamp's glow coming from behind her in the hall, caressing every ripple, every inch of iron-thewed flesh. Ashlee couldn't pull her eyes away from the sleek expanse of his chest, the thick-muscled ribs, or the lean, flat belly that seemed to fill her entire vision. A scorching heat rose in her cheeks, and her head began to spin.

"I—I—" she stammered, touching cool fingertips to one temple in an effort to still her reeling world. But the gesture only seemed to rock her wavering balance, and before she knew what was happening, her knees buckled and she fell into the outstretched arms that had quickly moved to catch her.

Rhys's tawny brows came together in a harsh frown as he scooped Ashlee's tiny frame up against his chest and carried her into his room, kicking the door shut behind him with the heel of his shoe. She had been the last person he expected to see on the other side of the door or he would have taken the time to don his shirt before answering her knock. He had no idea why she fainted, but it worried him. She must have known whose room this was, and even if she hadn't, she surely wouldn't have swooned at the mere sight of him. He laid her gently down on the bed, readjusted the pillow beneath her head, then touched her cheek with the back of his hand. She wasn't hot, but there was an unusual paleness to her otherwise rosy complexion. He smiled softly, wondering how loudly she'd scream once she woke up and found herself lying in his bed.

A coolness touched Ashlee's brow, stirring her from the peaceful haven she had sought, and her eyelids fluttered open. Confused, she tried to focus on the tall, broad figure hovering over her, and she gasped when the shape took on a recognizable form. She slapped away his hand and the damp cloth he held, awkwardly trying to push herself up. But Rhys's unrelenting grip on her shoulder held her down.

"Lie still," he ordered sharply. "I'm not going to do

anything to you. I just want to make sure you're all right. You fainted, and it worries me."

"And what lady wouldn't," she snapped, "if she was met at the door by a half-naked savage?"

The sparkle returned to his dark brown eyes. "Savage?" he questioned. When a dark coloring stained her cheeks, he inwardly relaxed knowing there was nothing seriously wrong with her. "When was the last time you had something to eat?" He turned away and plucked a fresh shirt from the opened drawer in the dresser. Slipping his arms into the sleeves, he glanced back at her with a raised brow when she didn't respond.

"Noon . . . I guess," she mumbled, looking away. The silk shirt he chose to wear did little to hide his well-proportioned physique.

"More like this morning," he corrected, remembering how she had stormed away from their table without touching her bowl of soup. "And I suppose you're all cinched up under that dress."

"I beg your pardon," she exploded, sitting up and swinging her legs off the bed. "What I have under this dress is none of your concern." She started to rise, felt a little dizzy, and decided to stay put . . . for the moment, anyway.

The humor glowed in the amber depths of his eyes, but he managed not to smile. "It is, when you appear at my door and faint dead away. I'd like to think that it was the sight of me that had something to do with it. But knowing how you feel about me, I rather doubt that was the case."

Ashlee dared not look at him. She could feel the color rising in her cheeks again. He had hit upon the truth—or at least part of it—and the expression on her face would tell him so. She didn't want to give him that kind of advantage.

"What has brought you here, Ashlee?" he asked curiously, pulling up a chair and turning it around.

Straddling the seat, he laid his arms across the back and waited, unaware that the shirt he had neglected to button gleamed white against his darkly tanned, bare chest and was enough to make any maid swoon.

Although Ashlee forced herself to stare straight ahead, she could still see him out of the corner of her eye. Even with that restricted view, his handsomeness unnerved her. She should stand up this very instant, remind him how improper this situation was, and request that he meet her in the dining hall once he had fully clothed himself. But the queasiness in her stomach, as well as the fact that she was still a little light-headed, warned her not to move lest she find herself in his arms again.

"I came to tell you that your services at Belle Chasse are no longer required. Business has been slow and we really don't need an extra dealer right now. As for the money I owe you, if you will give me an address where I might send it, I will forward it to you as soon as possible." She could almost feel the lopsided grin on his face, and when she took the chance to steal a look his way, her cheeks flamed anew as his warm perusal swept her from head to toe. Her flesh burned at every point where his gaze rested.

"Did your father send you here?"

Ashlee's eyes flared in outrage. Her father would be appalled if he knew his daughter had gone to a man's room . . . escorted or otherwise. And besides, if Arthur wanted to fire an employee, he would do it himself, not send someone else to do it for him. She ground her teeth and sucked in a breath. "Papa is still in Jackson with Dominique."

"Then letting me go isn't his idea."

Now she was insulted. "I have the authority in such matters, Mr. Sinclair. If I feel Belle Chasse doesn't need someone, I have the right to fire him."

"I'm sure you do." The twinkle appeared in his eyes again. "But since it isn't by your father's orders, then I'm afraid I must decline. He hired me. He'll fire me." He cocked a handsome brow at her, daring her to respond. "Besides, the job isn't the only reason I'm sticking around."

"I said I'd pay you back," she shouted.

"Or the money you owe me."

It wasn't so much what he said, but the suggestive gleam in his eyes and the flash of white teeth when he smiled that sent a nervous tremor down her spine. Realizing that the Yankee would leave Belle Chasse only if he wanted to, no matter how much she offered or how long she argued, she knew it was time she did the walking. She had been foolish in coming here as well as thinking she could get him to do something she wanted. No amount of threats would budge him, and now that he had obviously won John over to his side, the promise of a sound beating from the man was ludicrous. Praying her legs would hold her, she stood up, wobbling a little until she caught her balance.

"I think this discussion has come to an end, Mr. Sinclair," she said, taking a step.

"Without knowing what it is that attracts me to Belle Chasse?"

"I'm not interested," she retorted crisply, hurrying toward the door. But in the next instant, he was blocking the way. She stumbled back a step.

"You should be," he murmured softly, his eyes sparkling, his mouth curved in a vague smile. "You're the reason."

Ashlee's heart pounded so loudly in her chest she wondered if he could hear it. Would she have any voice with which to speak if she opened her mouth?"

"I'm . . . engaged, Mr. Sinclair."

Rhys shrugged his wide shoulders carelessly. "Engaged, yes. Married, no. There's a difference. And from what I've seen and heard, you'd rather not be either." His grin broadened. "At least not to Mr. Fabron."

Ashlee tried to display a look of complete surprise and total shock at his insinuation. "You're not suggesting I'd prefer you?" She gave him a disapproving once-over. "At least Perrin is a gentleman. You, sir, are a cad!" She took another hurried step backward when he advanced.

"Why? Because I don't try to hide my feelings for you?"

"Feelings?" she scoffed. "All that finds you panting at my heels is lust, Mr. Sinclair."

He laughed openly at her description. "A little crude, but adequate, I suppose." The corners of his mouth twitched with amusement and his eyes glowed warmly as he stared into hers. "I won't deny that that has something to do with it. But I am capable of other emotions as well. If you weren't so hardheaded and could lay aside your prejudices for a while, you might see it for yourself."

Pale blue eyes narrowed into glaring slits. "Hasn't it ever occurred to you that I simply don't find you as appealing as you think you are?"

He raised a dubious brow, continuing toward her until the backs of Ashlee's legs bumped the nightstand and she could go no farther. "Then you're quite the actress, little one," he whispered, toying with a silky lock of her hair.

Ashlee forced herself not to look at his handsome face or the dark brown eyes that could so easily melt away the image of bravado she fought to create whenever he got near her. Instead, she lowered her gaze to the long, deeply tanned fingers caressing the strand of hair he had lifted off her shoulder. But before she knew it, she had followed the length of muscular arm covered with white silk and ruffled cuffs to the hardened, well-formed curve of his half-naked chest where the shirt fell away. Her

349

pulse quickened and throbbed at the base of her throat, seeming to strangle the breath from her. She had to break away before she was consumed by the overwhelming power he had over her, before he recognized it and took advantage of the situation . . . before she let him.

"This is not something we should be discussing." Did the nervousness she felt register clearly in her words? She gulped and moved to step past him, but he caught her arm just above the elbow, drawing her eyes to his.

"I think it is. Before it's too late," he spoke softly.

Ashlee's brows crinkled inquiringly. "Too late for what?"

"Too late for you to change your mind about marrying Mr. Fabron."

He started to pull her closer, but Ashlee quickly raised a hand to stop him, instantly regretting her decision when her opened palm touched warm, bare flesh and rock-hard muscles across a flat, lean belly, setting her fingertips aflame. The same heat scorched her cheeks and took her breath away. Gasping for air, she made a feeble attempt to free herself of the unyielding grip around her arm.

"Let go." The command sounded weak and insincere.

"Why, Ashlee?" he asked. "Are you afraid of the truth?"

Desperate, she said the first thing that came to mind. "Let me guess. The truth as you see it would be that I'd prefer to remain single so that you and I can—can—so that I wouldn't have to be unfaithful. Maybe things are done differently up north, Mr. Sinclair, but being married has never stopped lovers from meeting."

"Is that what you want us to be? Lovers?" He smiled lazily.

"No!"

All signs of humor faded from his eyes, and when he answered, Ashlee knew she should take heed to every

350

word he spoke. "Neither do I. Nor should we have to be. What has happened between us was something I failed to control, and I can only blame it on a moment of weakness. I was quite taken by your beauty, your courage, and what I thought was your willingness. I should have known better. For that I apologize. You're a lady, Ashlee, and I should have treated you as one." His eyes took on a faraway look as he gently lifted a tendril of hair from her brow. "But since there's nothing I can do to change everything back the way it was before we met in my stateroom, I'm left with one alternative. To win your love and your hand in marriage."

Ashlee felt as if the breath had been knocked from her. Surely, he was joking! Maybe Perrin wasn't the kind of man she wanted for a husband, but what made this Yankee think he was any better? There was no denying that he could set her blood on fire by a simple caress or a few spoken endearments, but that wasn't enough on which to base a lasting relationship. It was absurd, and she'd tell him so. She jerked her arm free.

"Spare me the chivalry," she spat. "I knew what I was doing there in your cabin. And again last night. But what I *wasn't* doing was looking for a way to get you to offer marriage. The only thing that might interest me about you is your money. And if that's all I wanted, all I'd have to do is get Perrin to the altar tomorrow. He has enough wealth to solve all my problems. And I wouldn't be stuck with you!"

Amused by her sudden flare in temper as she brushed past him to present him with a lovely view of her slender back and rounded hips, Rhys studied her a moment, then moved to the chair he had vacated earlier. Resting his foot on the seat, he leaned forward with his weight braced on one elbow against his knee and clasped his wrist with the other hand.

"All of your problems, Ashlee?" he challenged.

"Marrying him won't solve any of them."

"Oh?" she scoffed, turning around. "And what makes you think that?" It was difficult for her not to lower her eyes to the muscular length of thigh he displayed beneath snug-fitting trousers, where the garment was stretched to accommodate his casual stance. Her pulse quickened again.

One corner of his mouth lifted in a crooked smile. "Because I've done a little research on your fiancé and found out that he hasn't a penny to his name."

Ashlee's tiny chin dropped in outrage. "How dare you!"

"And," he calmly continued, "from the company he keeps, I doubt he'll ever be interested in pleasing you as a husband would want to please his wife. I, on the other hand, can serve you in both respects." His brown eyes sparkled with humor. "And of course, with my help, your father would be able to keep Belle Chasse and pursue his political career as well. I hardly see where you have much of a choice, Ashlee. It would make more sense to marry me."

Incensed, Ashlee blurted out, "Oh, but I do have a choice. One I've already made." She lowered her chin and her voice, glaring back at him. "And it doesn't include you."

He eyed the lovely visage trembling with anger, thinking she looked the most beautiful when her pale blue eyes crackled with unleashed fury. Rhys was tempted to sweep her up in his arms and kiss away her ire, but he decided on another approach. Dropping his foot to the floor, he went to the bed and stretched out on the mattress, his arms folded behind his head, his ankles crossed as he gazed up at the ceiling above him. "Then perhaps it is too late."

There was something about his casual manner and the tone of his words that made Ashlee suspect there was more he wished to say. Although she had no idea what it was, she knew she wouldn't like it and elected to let it pass without question. She turned for the door. "Good. Then we understand each other." She touched a hand to the doorknob.

"Have you considered the reason why you fainted, Ashlee?"

An unexplainable chill shot through her. She didn't move.

"Of course, I could be wrong," he went on, his rugged brow marred by a frown. "It could be because you haven't had anything to eat all day. Or maybe I surprised you by answering the door dressed as I was. Then again—"

Ashlee knew she should ignore him, open the door, and get as far away from him as possible. She knew it, yet she stayed right where she was. "Then again what?" she asked.

"Oh, I'm probably wrong," he confessed, swinging his long legs to the floor and sitting up. "Just forget it." He concentrated on buttoning his shirt.

Straining to keep her temper under control, she clamped her teeth together and faced him. "You brought it up, Mr. Sinclair. You obviously thought it was worth mentioning. So why not just say it and get it over with?" Each word was spoken slowly and with great clarity, as if she thought him too stupid to comprehend otherwise.

Dark brown eyes glanced up at her, the picture of innocence. "Only because I thought you should consider the possibility. It could cause you a great deal of trouble later if I'm right."

"About what?" she hissed impatiently.

He stood up and tucked his shirttail into his trousers. "Have you noticed that certain smells upset you lately? Ones that never did before?"

Just being reminded of the odor of cigar smoke and ale

353

and the way it had turned her stomach when she entered the casino a little while ago revived the unpleasant affect it had had on her. She closed her eyes and gulped down the bile that threatened to rise. How could he have possibly known that?

"Why do you ask?" she questioned, after the spasm had passed.

"Well," he frowned, as though giving the matter great consideration, "I remember my mother acting that way."

A tingling sensation raced up the backs of her arms and across her shoulders. "Your mother?"

Rhys purposely made her wait for an explanation while he nonchalantly strolled up beside her. He raised a sympathetic brow and leaned a shoulder against the door, his arms crossed over his wide chest and one knee bent. "Uh-huh. Every time she was expecting a child."

Ashlee could feel the blood drain from her face. The pain in her chest made it difficult to breathe. It couldn't be! No! A babe would complicate things. If her father learned of it, he would never allow Perrin to return to Paris without her . . . even if he had paid his debt to Dominique and freed himself of any obligation he had to the Redington family. He wasn't interested in being a husband, much less a father! The title rang in her ears, and she closed her eyes. By sheer dint of pride alone, she managed not to burst into tears.

"But like I said, I could be wrong," Rhys pointed out, a devilish twinkle appearing in his eyes as he watched her. "We'll just have to pray that I am."

There was something threatening in his tone. Ashlee's eyes flew open and she glared at him, her head cocked to one side questioningly.

"Well, you certainly don't think I'd let the mother of my child marry someone else, do you? I'm a man who accepts his responsibility. I'd go straight to your father and tell him the truth. In fact," he sighed, pushing himself away from the door, "I think that's what I'll do anyway."

"What?" Ashlee shrieked, clutching his shirt sleeve when he started to walk away. "What do you mean that's what you'll do?"

Rhys lowered his chin and shook his head at her as if he were scolding a young girl. "Well, it wouldn't be very fair to your fiancé, Ashlee. The man is expecting to meet his bride at the altar, not a woman who's"—he paused and glanced over his shoulder as though someone might be outside the door listening, then whispered—"shall we say, taken a lover?"

Rhys's head snapped sharply to the right with the force behind the stinging slap Ashlee presented him. "I have *not* taken a lover, Rhys Sinclair," she growled, blue eyes shooting icy sparks of pure, untethered rage. "Taking a lover means it's a willing relationship. Ours is hardly that!" She doubled up a tiny fist and waved it threateningly beneath his nose. "And if you tell my father anything, I'll deny it. You have no proof, remember?"

Despite his smarting cheek, Rhys still smiled. "My apologies, madam, for thinking we were lovers." His tawny brows gathered in a curious frown. "And if not, then what would you call us?"

"Enemies," she sneered.

"Hmmm," he replied thoughtfully, returning to the bed. "If all enemies fought as we, there would be no wars as we know them." His dark eyes sparkled as he lay down and stretched his long legs out in front of him. Leaning back against the headboard, he clasped his hands behind his head. "As for the proof you mention, aye, 'tis true. You have my grandfather's stickpin." He grinned wickedly. "And I have Thomas."

Some of Ashlee's confidence fled. "T—Thomas?"

Rhys nodded. "You remember him, don't you? He was

one of the men you robbed. He sat right next to me at the table. In fact, he was the one who invited Sally White to watch the game." Rhys struggled not to laugh when Ashlee's face paled considerably. "He's also a highly respected politician and your father's host for the past two days. I don't think I'd have too much trouble convincing your father of the truth." He kicked his shoes to the floor. "This is one game, Ashlee, that you can't win. Even if you cheat." He wiggled his index finger at her, motioning her to come closer.

With slow dawning, Ashlee realized his intent. It was his plan to blackmail her, to have her at his beck and call whether it be in the broad light of day or dark shadows of the night. When he felt the urge, he would summon her and expect her to respond without hesitation and with her arms opened wide. Well, he had another thing coming. With her nostrils flared and her chin lowered, she advanced. She cursed the day she stepped on board the *Mississippi Queen*.

Rhys knew by the look in her eyes that his life was about to be threatened. With quick agility, he sprang from the bed, wondering exactly how she planned to bring a bloody end to his well-being and moving to his left where he wouldn't be trapped by the wall at his back.

"If I had a pistol, I'd shoot you, you—you guttersnipe, you viper, you *Yankee!*"

"Now, Ashlee—" he warned, a smile stretching wide across his face.

"Don't you 'now, Ashlee' me, Rhys Sinclair. Maybe your northern women would be intimidated by you, but I won't be!"

With the prowess of a great African lioness protecting her cub from certain danger, she stalked him, ready to attack at the second it presented itself. She shadowed his moves without fear or worry of the consequences. He stepped to the right. She followed. He circled in back of the chair. She slid it out of her path. They made a complete trek of the room. When Rhys found the bed blocking his way, he jumped up on the mattress, then landed on the floor on the other side, hoping the huge piece of furniture might slow her down a bit and all the while grinning broadly at the fiery temptress who had murder on her mind. But the amused smile quickly vanished when he saw her reach for the water pitcher sitting on the nightstand, and he raised a hand to stop her. The weapon was hurled in his direction, and he nimbly ducked to one side, cringing when it made a thunderous crash against the wall behind him and showered water everywhere. Shocked that the little chit had actually tried to bash in his head with it, he twisted around to look at the shattered pieces lying on the floor. He turned back with the intent of telling her it had gone far enough and was hit in the face with a pillow. It surprised him rather than doing any harm other than snapping his patience and ending his desire to continue with their game. But before he could voice his objection, Ashlee, who now stood in the middle of the bed with the pillow gripped in both hands, brought her weapon around and struck him a second time. It burst into a snowfall of feathers when the seam gave way, seeming to nearly fill the room with an avalanche of fluffy white down.

"Enough!" he bellowed, swiping at the flurry of tiny goose feathers flittering about his head.

"Not yet it isn't," she howled. "You're still alive!"

Through the blizzard of floating plumage, Rhys saw her twist and drop to her knees as she reached out for something else from the nightstand, obviously thinking it would finish the job. Catapulting himself through the air, he caught her around the waist and tumbled them both facedown on the bed just as an urgent knock pounded against the door. He clamped his hand over her mouth to stifle her screams.

"Mr. Sinclair, are you all right?" the voice from the hallway called out. "I heard something break."

Rhys grunted when an elbow found his ribs. He shifted and laid his weight on top of her, not enough to hurt, but enough to make it impossible for her to move. "Yes, I'm fine. I just had a little accident with the water pitcher."

"You want me to send someone to clean it up?"

Rhys chuckled, thinking that what Ashlee deserved was to have one of the employees walk into his room and find her there in bed with him . . . even fully clothed. "No, I'll take care of it. But thank you anyway." A long moment passed, and Rhys sensed the man was still there. "Was there something else?"

"Well—ah—yes," came the muffled, hesitant response. "Mr. Fabron is looking for Miss Ashlee, and Elaine said she—well—Have you seen Miss Ashlee, sir?"

Seen her? he thought devilishly. *I can feel every inch of her.* "Sorry," he said instead. "I can't help you."

"That's all right, sir." His voice rang with relief at learning his employer's daughter was not in the man's room. "But if you should, would you tell her that her fiancé would like to have dinner with her and that he'll be in the restaurant?"

"I'll tell her," he grinned, surprised by Ashlee's sudden burst of strength as she wiggled beneath him. He waited until the sound of the intruder's footsteps faded down the hall before lifting himself from her.

But rather than gaining her freedom as Ashlee expected, she was roughly tossed on her back and pinned down again with his body covering hers. Her growl of outrage over such abuse was muffled beneath the hand held tightly against her mouth.

"Your fiancé is looking for you," he chaffed, his brown eyes aglow with mischief. He wrinkled his brows at her when he couldn't understand what she said. "What was that? You don't care if your fiancé is waiting? You'd rather be here with me?" A silly grin parted his lips. "Why, Ashlee, you don't really mean that, do you? Here just a minute ago, I thought you were trying to kill me. You mean that fire in your eyes was lust, not vengeance?" He caught her waist when she worked her hand free and tried to scratch his face, tucking her arm beneath him as he slid to one side of her, his long, muscular leg draped over her. "You know, we could have saved a lot of time if you had just said so when I opened the door."

Drawing on every ounce of strength she had left, Ashlee strained to push him from her. He didn't budge, but she did manage to free her other arm that had been trapped beneath her by her own weight. With lightning speed, she grabbed the hand that covered her mouth, yanked down, and brutally bit his little finger.

Rhys would have bellowed in pain if it hadn't been imperative for him to concentrate on protecting his head from the rain of blows Ashlee began pouring on him. And if he hadn't asked for everything he was getting, it would have made him angry. Chuckling, he caught her fist in mid-swing, came up on his knees to straddle her hips, and balanced the weight of his upper torso by leaning forward on his hands, her wrists trapped beneath them. The eyes that glared back angrily at him were exquisite. There wasn't a flaw in her smooth ivory complexion, and even though her mouth was set in a hard line, Rhys was still tempted to kiss the full red lips. For a fleeting moment, he hoped she was carrying his child. Arthur Redington might be furious at first, but once Rhys explained the advantages of having him rather than Perrin as a son-in-law, as well as the probability that Rhys would love her in a way the Frenchman never could, he was sure Arthur would forgive them both and agree to their union. Of course, getting Ashlee to agree was another thing entirely. A roguish grin brightened his dark eyes when

Ashlee arched her hips against him, striving to catch him off balance and push him from her. The effort failed, and she groaned as she collapsed beneath him again.

"If you don't let me up this instant, Rhys Sinclair, you'll live to regret it," she snarled. "You may have everyone else wrapped around your little finger, but Dominique won't take kindly to what you've done after I tell her. And I'll be sure to add a few details that aren't true." She strained against him one more time, then reluctantly surrendered to his greater strength. "You'll be out of a job and out on your ear!"

White teeth flashed beneath his smile. "Somehow I don't think you could ever be angry enough with me to ask for your stepmother's help. And besides, if you told her what has gone on between the two of us, she'd have you married to Perrin within the hour. That isn't what you want."

"And what makes you so sure of that?" She pushed against him again and to her surprise he released her. Scrambling from the bed, she made a futile attempt at straightening her attire. As she combed her fingers through her hair a sprinkle of goose down floated free, bringing with it an enraged growl as Ashlee batted the feathers away.

Amused by the sight of her, Rhys stretched out comfortably on the bed, his head propped up on a fist. "You're too much of a woman to want to be strapped with someone like Fabron for the rest of your life."

At breakfast that morning, Ashlee would have agreed. But that was before she had met Perrin. Now that she had, she had to admit that she liked him. And she took offense to the Yankee's remark about being married to someone like Perrin. She faced him in a whirl of cotton, crinoline, and tiny feathers. "I'll have you know, you river rat, that Perrin Fabron is a very sensitive, gentle man. He's kind, considerate, soft-spoken, and wouldn't dream of laying a hand on me." She gritted her teeth and glared at him, daring Rhys to argue.

"And somewhat of a dolt," he finished with a lopsided grin.

"What if he is?" she exploded. "At least I won't have to worry about being pawed every time I turn around."

"Pawed?" he laughed. "Is that what you'd call it?"

"It is when I'd rather be left alone."

"So what you're saying is that if you had a choice, you'd prefer to be left alone instead of allowing yourself to enjoy a man's advances"—he quickly corrected himself—"your husband's advances."

"I most certainly would," she hurriedly replied, failing to recognize the direction in which he led their conversation. "What lady wouldn't?"

Rhys shrugged one shoulder. "None that I know of."

Suddenly, it was all very clear to her. "I think it's time I left." She stumbled backward toward the door.

"Why, Ashlee? Are you afraid you might be wrong?" He sat up and swung his feet to the floor. Rising, he added, "I think it's something you should find out about before you've committed yourself to a life of loneliness."

"Don't you touch me," she commanded, backing into the thick oaken panels behind her.

Rhys paused only a hairbreadth away and nodded his head slightly. "All right," he concurred. "I won't touch you. I won't have to." He leaned in with both hands pressed against the door on either side of her head, trapping her between his muscular arms. "I'll just stand here, admiring." His gaze dropped to her mouth and chin. "We won't even have to talk." Warm brown eyes lowered to her heaving bosom, and Ashlee felt as if her entire body was on fire. "But tell me, Ashlee. Could your sensitive, gentle little man stir the desires in you that you know are there? The yearnings of a woman longing to be fulfilled? And if not, will you be content to let them wither and die, just as you will surely do of loneliness?" He stepped within an inch of her, the warmth of his body searing her from head to toe as he plucked a tiny feather from her hair, studying it a moment before he set his eyes on her once more. "I think not," he whispered.

Ashlee tried to watch the giddy descent of the feather when Rhys set it free, wanting very much to convince herself that his closeness, the masculine scent of him, even his warm breath falling softly on her cheek, had no affect on her, that she might as well be the only one in the room. She tried. But suddenly his knuckle was beneath her chin, lifting her mouth to his. She closed her eyes. Let him kiss her. It wouldn't change how she felt about him. It wouldn't prove anything except that what she had said was true. She would gladly live out her life in her own way, not having to answer to a man or play the wifely role in bed. Who needed them, anyway? Her mother hadn't. But then, if that *were* true, why were her lips trembling? Why was her body anticipating his touch?

A soft chuckle shattered Ashlee's trance, and her eyes flew open when he stepped away from her. A bright scarlet hue stained her cheeks when she realized how it had appeared to him and that no amount of guarantees on her part would sway him into thinking otherwise. Feeling weak and dizzy, she fell back against the door as she watched him slowly lower himself onto the bed again, a smug look on his face.

Tears boiled up inside her, and rather than give him that victory as well, she spun around, yanked the door open, and ran out into the hall, mindless of the prospect that someone might see her. She had to get away, as far from him as possible. She dashed out into the courtyard, cut across the lawn, and raced through the foyer and into her room, slamming the door shut behind her.

"Damn him!" she sobbed, falling to her knees. "Damn him for being right."

Chapter Thirteen

Ashlee successfully avoided seeing Rhys for the next week. There were times when it hadn't been very easy, but she had managed with Perrin's help, using the excuse that they needed to be alone so that they could get to know each other better. Dominique had been quite agreeable, especially when neither Ashlee nor Perrin argued with her decision that the wedding take place in one month. She had originally thought two weeks was long enough to wait, until Ashlee pointed out that there were a lot of her father's friends who would like to attend, which meant sending out invitations and waiting for the replies. Thus, the couple was free to come and go as they wished, since everyone thought their many absences from Belle Chasse had something to do with wedding plans. It didn't. Perrin would spend the days with Philippe and his evenings in the casino playing cards; Ashlee would go for long carriage rides in the country or occasionally visit Priscilla.

During that week's time, Ashlee came to the conclusion that she was, indeed, going to have Rhys's baby. Every morning she woke up sick to her stomach, and by noon she was feeling fine again. She learned to avoid places where the smells were offensive and, therefore, wound up having to lie to her father about her job in the casino. She told him that she didn't have the time for it with all the wedding plans she needed to make. Arthur hadn't argued, telling her that he would have had to hire someone sooner or later, anyway, once she and Perrin were married and leaving for Paris. It saddened Ashlee to have to give it up, but at the same time made her not have to work alongside of Rhys.

She hadn't told anyone about her condition. It would be months before it would start to show, and she had decided to deal with it then. Hopefully, by that time, everything would have worked out for the best. Perrin and Philippe would be back in Paris, her father would be campaigning for the Senate, and she . . . Tears gathered in her eyes every time she thought about the baby. Once her father learned of it, he would demand that Perrin return from Paris and marry her, no matter how awful their quarrel had been. That was what she planned to tell him when Perrin suddenly packed his bags and booked passage on a ship sailing for France, the truth being that he had actually paid off his debt to Dominique from the money Ashlee and he were scheming to steal. As for Rhys, she didn't know what she would do about him. Ashlee was sure once he found out about the baby he would go to her father, unless she somehow figured out a way to make him leave Belle Chasse before then.

Perrin had proved himself to be an excellent card-player, and along with his subtle charm, he quickly made a great many friends of the regular patrons of the casino. As long as he didn't imbibe too much of his favorite wine, he could walk away from the table a winner. Ashlee had watched him play, soon observing that his problem with poker was that whenever the stakes were high he became very excited. To calm his nerves, he'd order a drink or two. But he couldn't stop there. One glass led to another, and by the end of the night he left the gaming tables with less money than when he started. After one week, he was nearly penniless.

"It's a shame you don't know how to cheat, Perrin," Ashlee teased one afternoon as they traveled back to the hotel.

Frowning, he snapped the reins a little harder than the last time. "I tried once, remember, *ma chere?* And we both know what happened." Pulling back sharply on the left rein, he guided the rig onto the avenue that would take them directly to Belle Chasse's front steps. "Even sober, I am no good. Zee only way I could win ees by 'aving a partner who would deal me a good hand." He nodded recognition at the driver of the carriage they passed on the street, missing the bright smile that came over his companion's beautiful face.

"A partner," she repeated cheerfully. "You know something, Perrin? I think you've given me an idea."

His head jerked around to stare openmouthed at her. He didn't like the sound of it. "An idea, *cherie?*"

"Uh-huh," she beamed. "And it's a lot less dangerous than my old way of stealing money."

"Mon Dieu," he groaned, falling back in the carriage seat.

Since John's refusal to help Ashlee relieve a few unsuspecting gamblers of their extra cash, she hadn't been able to come up with an alternative plan until now. She had doubted Perrin was strong enough to row a boat out to meet the steamer as John had always done, so she had given up the thought of robbing steamboats. Priscilla had offered no help whatsoever when she asked her about it, and by the end of their conversation the actress had told Ashlee that if she didn't promise to forget about stealing altogether, she'd tell John. Ashlee had given her word, but only in regard to the riverboats. Thus, she and Perrin were on their own. And now he had been the one to figure out a way of getting them the money they needed.

"So tell me, *mon petite,*" he sighed. "'Ow we will do thees?"

Ashlee smiled sympathetically at the little man, knowing that he was willing to help only out of necessity. She reached over and patted his hand. "It will be very simple, I promise."

"Simple," he grumbled, hauling back on the reins when the carriage approached the steps in front of the hotel. "Since I 'ave come to America, nothing has been simple."

Ashlee laughed. "This will be," she guaranteed him, sliding to the edge of the seat where he could help her down. "And all you have to do is play cards." She laughed again at the suspicious frown he gave her. "I'm going to be your partner."

Perrin's milky complexion paled even more as he watched her ascend the stairs on her way to the lobby's doors. His cousin hadn't warned him about his intended bride's strong-willed disposition, and he was glad she hadn't. It would have been very intimidating. But now it was Ashlee's spunk and determination that made him relax. With her, he would be free of the hold Dominique had on him. He smiled broadly and quickly bounded up the stairs after her.

"Please, Ashlee," he whispered as they went through the lobby toward the restaurant. "Tell me what you 'ave planned."

Grinning, she pulled him aside where no one would hear. "Like I said before, you're going to play cards and I'm going to be your partner. Only to those sitting at the table with you, I'll simply appear to be the dealer."

Perrin's brown eyes widened instantly. "You mean, cheat?"

"Shhh!" Ashlee warned when a couple stepped out of the restaurant and started in their direction. She watched them until they were far enough away. "Yes, that's exactly what I mean. I'll deal you the best hands of poker you've ever seen in your life. By the time the game's over, you'll have more than enough money to pay off your cousin and buy two tickets back to Paris."

Perrin dropped his gaze, and when he spoke his words came out in a choked whisper. "You'd do that for me?"

"For us, Perrin. I don't want to get married any more than you do."

When he looked up at her, his eyes glistened with unshed tears. He blinked them away. "It will save me, *cherie*, but Dominique will find someone else for you to marry."

"I know," she nodded. "But that will take time. If I'm lucky, I'll have worked something out by then." She smiled encouragingly and slipped her hand into the crook of his arm. "Now, however, we must concentrate on the game. For this to be successful, it must appear that it all came about very innocently. *And*," she added, stressing the word, "you can't have a single drink the entire time you're playing cards." She smiled at his distressed look. "It's your downfall, Perrin. I've watched you play enough times to know. Whenever you get a good hand and the stakes are high you start drinking, and the only thing you wind up with to show for it is a headache the next morning. Am I wrong?"

He shook his head sheepishly.

"You have to keep your wits about you. This game will be the most important one you've ever played in your life because it won't be just for you. It's for your mother and me as well. Do you understand?"

"Oui, ma chere."

"Good," she smiled, giving his arm a squeeze. "Now, I'll tell you what my idea is. Besides noticing what you do wrong when you play poker, I've also seen who it is you're playing with. You've made a lot of friends since you came to New Orleans and we're going to use that to our advantage."

"How?"

"Those men who sat across the table from you are very wealthy businessmen, Perrin. You're going to suggest playing a private game of poker somewhere away from Belle Chasse. You can tell them that Dominique doesn't approve or something, but you must get an invitation to play in a private home. We can't let her, Papa, John, or Mr. Sinclair know about this. When you've gotten it, then you tell them how much your fiancée loves to watch and if it's all right with them, I can be the dealer. Do you think you can do that?"

"If it means paying off my debt to Dominique, *oui*, I can do it," he said with a firm nod of his head.

She smiled brightly. "I knew that's what you'd say." Glancing away, her dark brows came together with a perplexing thought. "Now our only problem is what to use for money. It will take more than you and I have." She shrugged, dismissing it for the moment. "I'll think of something later. Right now I'd like to have something to eat, wouldn't you?"

"*Oui*," Perrin quickly agreed. "All of thees has made me very hungry."

Their spirits high, they both giggled about the secret they shared and turned for the restaurant's entrance, certain everything would work out the way they wanted it. But their gaiety was short-lived when they nearly collided with Dominique and Rhys as the couple left the dining hall. For Perrin, facing his cousin struck terror in his heart, positive she knew what was going on just by looking at him. Ashlee didn't have the same reaction, however. She was angered to see Rhys with her stepmother when her father was nowhere around. But the emotion was quickly forgotten once she saw the possessive way Dominique had hooked her arm into her companion's, as if they were the lovers making wedding plans. Dominique had always been a flirt, Ashlee knew that. But for some strange reason, Ashlee didn't approve of the woman's choice this time, and she couldn't explain why. It bothered her not knowing.

"Here's our little lovebirds," the Frenchwoman purred, hugging Rhys's arm a little tighter as she gave the couple a sickeningly sweet smile.

"Yes, so we are," Ashlee commented dryly, looking past them into the restaurant as if she hadn't the time for social chatter.

"If we had known you were dining here this evening, we would have asked you to join us. Wouldn't we have, Rhys?" She gave him a demure smile, then settled her gaze on her stepdaughter again.

"Where's Papa?" The question was clipped and icy, but full of unspoken disapproval over the woman's behavior as Ashlee continued to survey the customers in the dining hall.

Dominique's eyes darkened and the smile faded from her lips. She understood what her stepdaughter was implying. Her gaze shifted from Ashlee to the man who stood trembling at her side. Why couldn't her cousin have been a man, one with a backbone? She laughed inwardly. But then if he had, she wouldn't have been able to force him into marrying Arthur's spoiled bitch of a daughter.

"Your father's at another one of his meetings, Ashlee, just as he has been every night this week."

Cold blue eyes found her. "And rather than dine alone, you asked Mr. Sinclair to join you."

The expression on Dominique's face hardened, and sparks of hatred flashed between the women. A moment passed before a sardonic smile twisted the elder's mouth. "Ashlee," Dominique murmured acidly, "I wouldn't think you, of all people, would be jealous. After all, you

369

have Perrin."

Instead of the rage Dominique expected to see erupt, Ashlee grinned almost pleasantly. "Yes, Dominique, *I* have Perrin." She nodded politely, sent Rhys a murderous glare, and moved into the restaurant.

"Ma chere," Perrin gasped when they had walked far enough away that neither Rhys or Dominique would hear him. "You 'ave such courage. I would never speak to her like that." Guiding his silent companion to a table, he held out a chair for her, then sat down opposite her. A puzzled look came over his face when he noticed Ashlee's sad expression, and he glanced back up at the empty doorway where his cousin and Mr. Sinclair had once been. While the two women had words, he had watched the tall, handsome man with Dominique and briefly questioned the attention Sinclair gave Ashlee, deciding that he had mistaken what he thought was more than casual interest. Now he wasn't so sure. "Ashlee," he said somewhat sympathetically, reaching for her hand as she toyed with the stem of her water goblet.

Snapped out of her reverie by the touch of another's hand on hers, she blinked and looked up, a bit surprised and embarrassed. "Forgive me," she laughed nervously. "Did you say something?"

"We are friends, are we not?" he questioned softly.

Ashlee nodded.

"And friends can say what they feel?"

Her brow wrinkled. "Yes," she replied, curious.

Perrin studied her a moment, praying he hadn't misjudged her and that what he was about to say wouldn't send her rushing off in a fit of temper. He needed her, and if he was right, she needed him just as much. The waitress came to pour them both a cup of coffee, and he waited until the woman had left before speaking his mind.

"You know my secret, Ashlee. You 'aven't told

370

anyone. I trust you, and I want you to trust me with your secret."

Ashlee pulled her hand away. "I don't have any secrets, Perrin," she said with all the conviction she could muster. "What makes you think I do?"

"Zee eyes never lie." The statement was said with tenderness. "Zee Yankee, *Monsieur* Sinclair, he means something to you, does he not?"

"Means something?" she repeated, pretending as if she found the subject amusing. "Whatever are you talking about?"

Perrin touched one hand to his chest. "In here, *mon amie.*"

Ashlee shook her head and looked away. "I don't think so, Perrin. The only thing he means to me is trouble."

"*Oui,*" Perrin agreed. "But zee trouble ees in your heart." He raised a hand to silence her when she jerked her head back to glare at him, her mouth opened to hurl an angry retort. "It ees difficult to hide zee truth, *cherie,* from a friend. You love him, no?"

"Love?" Ashlee exploded in a fit of laughter. "Oh no, Perrin. Never that."

"But he loves you."

"Oh?" she chuckled. The laughter died away, and she folded her arms across the edge of the table and leaned in. "Then tell me why he spends every free moment he has with my stepmother? Or hadn't you noticed?"

Perrin shrugged. "*Oui,* I 'ave noticed."

"Well, wouldn't you agree that that's a funny way to behave if you're in love with someone else?" Her mouth curled in a sarcastic smirk. "Or maybe he's just doing it to make me jealous."

Perrin shook his head and picked up his water glass. "There ees no arguing with a closed mind."

"A closed— Perrin, there's nothing to argue about. I

371

won't deny that I find the man attractive. My mind isn't that closed. But he's a Yankee, and he's here at Belle Chasse for one reason. And it isn't me! He's waiting for the right moment when Papa's ready to sell." Angrily, she picked up her napkin and flipped it open across her lap. "Now, if you really want to be my friend, you won't bring it up again. We have more important things to think about. Like, for instance, who we want to have at the poker game."

Perrin shrugged one shoulder. He wouldn't say another word about it. He didn't have to. They both knew Ashlee cared more for the Yankee than she wanted to admit. "'Ave you thought of a way to get the money to stake me?"

Stirring a teaspoon of sugar into her coffee, she said, "There's always enough in Papa's safe. We'll just borrow it."

Perrin's chin sagged and he rolled his eyes as he fell back in his chair. If they pulled this off, it would be a miracle.

"Tell me, Rhys," Dominique said as they strolled about the courtyard, "what is it that fascinates you about Belle Chasse?"

Rhys smiled secretively as he watched the petite woman at his side. It had taken a great deal of patience on his part to get Dominique where he had her now. He had spent the last six days—and nights—saying just the right thing at the right moment to imply that he was more interested in making money and owning property than anything else in his life, and that he didn't care how he managed it. He still hadn't figured out what it was that she was doing with her husband's money, but instinct told him that it had nothing to do with the rebuilding of the south. She had made it quite clear on several

372

occasions that she was still loyal to France and someday planned to own the property that was rightfully hers. She even went so far as to tell Rhys that in her opinion Arthur should be using his energies and his money to better himself, not aid rebellious southerners who were too proud to admit they were wrong. She had confessed to Rhys that that was one topic on which she and her husband constantly argued.

"Fascinates me, Mrs. Redington?" he asked guardedly. "Why do you think I'm fascinated with Belle Chasse?"

"Because there has to be something here to keep you interested enough to stay. A man like yourself wouldn't waste his time if there wasn't." She sat down in the wrought iron settee, spread out her skirts, and eyed him carefully. "What I don't understand is why you lowered yourself to work for my husband. He has told me that you're a very rich man."

Rhys prayed his answer wouldn't be the wrong one. If he had misjudged her, he'd come too far to scare her off. "I find work amusing."

"Amusing?" Her dark eyes glowed in the yellow light of the torches dotting the walkway. "What a strange answer."

Walking a few steps past her, he pulled a cheroot from his pocket, tilted his head for her approval to light it, then struck a match. "I am a man who grows easily bored, Mrs. Redington. When that happens, I try to find something that will amuse me. Working for someone when I have enough money to buy the place three times over becomes a game to me. Especially when my employer isn't aware of it. Of course, in your husband's case that isn't true. He knew that when he hired me."

Dominique cocked a suspicious brow. "So what was your reason if not to poke fun at those less fortunate than you?"

373

Rhys savored the taste of his cheroot, then blew the smoke away. "I don't own a place like Belle Chasse and find the prospect intriguing. Like all of my business ventures, I study it inside out before I make any plans."

"Plans? What do you have planned for Belle Chasse?" Her smile was insincere.

"It seems to be a profitable little business. I'm thinking of making Arthur an offer."

"To buy him out?" Dominique was genuinely surprised. "Arthur has never mentioned that he wanted to sell, Rhys. What makes you think he'd be interested?"

Rhys grinned confidently. "Every man has a price, Mrs. Redington."

"Hmmm," she agreed. "And I'm sure Arthur isn't an exception." Her gaze drifted toward the hotel. "And he'd use that money on his foolhardy campaign instead of investing it in something more practical."

"Sounds to me as if you're the one with business sense, Mrs. Redington. Arthur's very fortunate to have a wife who can handle his affairs. I hope he appreciates you."

A vague smile deepened the faint lines around her mouth. She reclined back in the settee and lifted her gaze to him again. "Not nearly as much as he will someday."

Maybe it was the look in the woman's eye as she sat there watching him that made Rhys think there was more to her statement than just the words she spoke. Or, perhaps, his suspicious nature was reading something into it that wasn't really there. Dominique Redington was a hard woman to figure and one who wouldn't let anyone get close to her unless she could use them to her advantage. And that's exactly what he was sure the Frenchwoman was doing with Arthur Redington—using him to her advantage. What confused him, however, was that Arthur couldn't see it. Granted, Rhys had only known the man for a short time, but since everyone else

374

at Belle Chasse had come to the same conclusion as he, it seemed only logical that Arthur would too—sooner or later. Or was he that blinded by love? Rhys took a long drag on the cheroot and looked away. If he was, then finding out that his wife only married him for his money would surely kill him. A sadness gripped Rhys, and he suddenly hoped he was wrong about her.

"I'm sure you've heard the rumors about Belle Chasse, Rhys," Dominique said, breaking into his thoughts. He turned his head to look at her. "Why would you want to buy something that is failing? It's not a very wise investment."

Rhys chuckled softly. "True. But the potential is there. And when a business is failing and the owner's aware of it, he's more than likely willing to let it go for considerably less than it's worth. Don't you agree?"

"Is that how you handle your business dealings?"

He grinned. "Most of them."

Leaning to one side, Dominique rested her elbow on the arm of the settee and idly tapped her chin with a fingertip, studying him for several minutes. Rhys had the vague feeling he was being measured up for something and could only hope he was suitable for whatever she had in mind. He had spent the past several days covertly following her each time she left Belle Chasse, not knowing any more about her private life now than when he had begun. It seemed her outings consisted of nothing more than a visit to the bank, a French bakery, and a boutique.

"Arthur tells me you were an officer in the Union Army during the war," she said after some considerable thought. "Does that mean your loyalties lie with the north?"

An innocent enough question, Rhys thought, for someone other than Dominique Redington. Could this be what he waited for? He smiled crookedly and studied his

375

cheroot. "My loyalties lie wherever it's most profitable, Mrs. Redington. North, south, east, west, here, or abroad. I learned long ago that the only person who will look out for my welfare is me. A rather narrow way of looking at things, I suppose. But it's what's kept me alive and wealthy all these years." Only his eyes moved to capture hers. "I think you and I have much the same feelings. Am I wrong?"

Dominique's dark brown eyes glowed with her smile. "Perhaps." She shrugged. "Perhaps not. I do think there's a difference, though, in that I can only dream, where you have the assets to fulfill them."

The door to the lobby opened up and with it came the blend of laughter and excitement from the casino, distracting Dominique for a moment as she watched two strangers step out into the courtyard. Then, with a sigh, she came to her feet.

"Thank you for having dinner with me, Rhys. I never have liked eating alone, and lately it seems like that's always the case." She held out her hand to him and watched as he placed a gentle kiss upon her knuckles. "But now I think we both should get back to work. You are working tonight, aren't you?"

"Yes, ma'am," he nodded. "May I walk you to the office?"

"Thank you, no," she declined. "I thought I'd go to my room and lie down for a while, first." She touched long, well-manicured fingers to her temple. "I seem to be coming down with a headache."

"Would you like me to tell your stepdaughter? Perhaps you'd prefer that she did the books tonight," he offered, wondering if the headache were a lie. From what he'd heard about the woman, she hadn't been sick a day since she came to New Orleans.

"I'll be fine in an hour or so, I'm sure. But thank you for your concern." She turned toward her quarters, calling back over her shoulder, "Good night, Rhys."

"Good night, Mrs. Redington," he replied, lingering until after she had gone into the foyer and closed the door.

Dominique hurried into her room, extinguished the light, and rushed to the window where, in the darkness, she could watch his tall figure turn and head into the hotel lobby through the back entrance. She'd give him plenty of time to enter the casino, find his table, and deal out a round of poker before she left Belle Chasse. Dominique was about to break her own rule, but this was something important. She was sure Jourdain would understand and agree once she explained why she had come to see him twice in one day.

There were a lot of French bakeries in New Orleans, but none of them were as busy as Jourdain LaFoe's. Located on one of the main streets, it attracted customers from the time it opened in the morning until every last piece of pastry and loaf of bread were sold. Thus, it was no surprise to Dominique to find the place bustling with people when she drew her carriage to a stop outside its front door. Nor did it bother her to be seen by so many. They would merely think she had a craving for something sweet just as they had had.

LaFoe frowned the moment he saw Dominique, thinking there was trouble until he saw her smile and nod her head slightly. He greeted her as he did anyone else entering his shop and continued on with what he was doing, waiting on each customer in turn so as not to draw undue attention to the one who had set his nerves on edge. By the time he got to her, he was shaking visibly.

"*Bonsoir*, Madame Redington," he smiled, his dark eyes flitting past her to the door and the last customer making an exit. He lowered his voice and asked nervously, "Ees something wrong?"

"*Au contraire, mon ami,*" Dominique laughed. "Everything is fine."

"But we agreed—"

"I know what we agreed, *Monsieur* LaFoe," she interrupted, walking back to the door and closing it. She faced him again. "Shall we talk where it's private?"

LaFoe bobbed his head and extended a hand toward the curtained archway leading to the back room. Once his visitor had gone there, he cast a nervous look about the place as if half expecting an armed group of men to burst into the shop, then hurried to catch up.

"So tell me what is so important that you come here now?" he demanded in French, feeling safer talking in a language the Americans couldn't understand should they be overheard somehow.

Removing the bonnet she had worn, Dominique tossed it carelessly down on a table with her purse and crossed to the buffet and the wine decanter sitting there. Pouring two glasses full of the rich red drink, she handed one to Jourdain. "I'd like to propose a toast," she smiled, also speaking in their native tongue. "To our success." She held the glass high.

"Dear God, Dominique," he moaned, his shoulders dropping. "You took the chance coming here to toast our success? Are you insane? Our success depends on secrecy."

"And money," she added, her enthusiasm heightened even more with the discovery she had made.

"Yes, money," he agreed almost angrily. "But what has that to do with your being here?"

"It has everything to do with my being here, Jourdain. I have found someone who I'm sure will want to help. A man whose interest lies only in adding to his wealth, whether it be in money or property. And we can offer him more land than he ever dreamed of owning."

LaFoe stared dubiously at her. "What man, Dominique? I know of no one in New Orleans."

Smiling confidently, she began to stroll about the room. "His name is Rhys Sinclair. He's a Yankee, but he told me only a few minutes ago that his loyalties are to himself, not his country or any of his friends." She stopped her pacing and whirled on him. "He's the kind of man we need, Jourdain. He's perfect."

LaFoe's dark brows came together. "How much do you know of him? Only what he tells you?"

"At the moment, yes. That's why I'm here. I want you to contact our people and find out everything you can about him. I'll wait until you have before I approach him with an offer. But do hurry. I've been getting pressure." She frowned angrily and took a drink of her wine. "And my stepdaughter is still causing trouble."

"I thought your cousin was supposed to take care of her."

Dark flashing eyes glared up at him. "Perrin? The spineless ninny is worse than I remember. He follows her around like a lost puppy." She finished off her drink and set the glass down. "I wish the ceremony were tomorrow."

"And when is the wedding?"

"Not for three weeks yet." Grabbing her bonnet, she quickly put it on and picked up her purse.

"Why so far away? I thought—"

"I know. I know," she cut in irritably. "But I couldn't raise suspicion by insisting they wed two days after he arrived. And Arthur still isn't convinced he's doing the right thing by marrying off his daughter and sending her away." Her brown eyes darkened as she stared off into space. "I should have considered Ashlee more carefully before I became involved with her father."

"It wouldn't have made any difference, Dominique," LaFoe argued. "We all agreed that Redington was the

379

man we needed."

"Yes, but his daughter makes me nervous. She's been suspicious of me since the day we met."

"And it will all be over very soon," he encouraged, taking her elbow and guiding her from the room. "As for Mr. Sinclair, I will send a telegram about him in the morning. Until we hear from our people, I suggest you watch what you say and do around him. We can't be too careful, you know."

They paused near the front door.

"Have you heard when the next shipment will take place?"

"They're making arrangements now," LaFoe advised. "Why do you ask?"

Looking out at the street through the storefront windows, Dominique casually readjusted her bonnet and tucked in a stray curl. "Because I want my share to be the biggest this time. And I can't do that unless I have Mr. Sinclair's money."

"Patience, Dominique, patience. Carelessness could send us all to prison," he warned, opening the door for her.

"And mine grows short," she hissed. "Being married to someone like Arthur takes every ounce of strength I have. I long for the day when a real man holds me in his arms and shares the wealth I have obtained. And that day shall come, Jourdain. You will see." A demoniac light glowed in her eyes for just an instant then vanished. She smiled. *"Bonsoir, Monsieur* LaFoe," she nodded politely and stepped out onto the wooden walkway toward her carriage, thinking that Rhys Sinclair would be that man.

Ashlee lay awake well into the early hours of morning, after the casino had closed and the hotel had grown quiet for the short time before everything would begin again.

Her plan to have Perrin invited to a private poker game with her as the dealer had worked out better than she imagined it would. After dinner, she and Perrin had gone to the casino with the intention of proving to him that he could play the game without needing to drink to boost his courage. Through a stroke of luck, he sat down with Lloyd Winchell, a local merchant with a passion for gambling and a great deal of money to support his hobby. Lloyd was a likable sort, with sandy-brown hair and narrow green eyes. He wasn't married and loved to entertain as often as possible, claiming that a big house like his was meant to have guests. He took an instant liking to Perrin—almost to the point of ignoring Ashlee—and after the first round of poker was played, Lloyd invited him to his house the next night. It caught Perrin so completely off guard—he figured he'd have to be the one to suggest it—that the poor fellow just sat there with his mouth open and it was only Ashlee's quick thinking that saved the moment. She had been standing behind Perrin. When she sensed Winchell had taken Perrin's silent hesitation to mean no, she quickly touched her fiancé's shoulder in what appeared a loving fashion and told the merchant that she and Perrin had made a promise to spend every moment they had together. Seeing no difficulty with that, Winchell happily invited her as well, since those he had already asked to come would be bringing companions anyway. Ashlee had smiled her acceptance, even though the presence of other women meant she might have to spend the time in another room talking about needlepoint or how cool the spring was this year or something else as insignificant while she frantically searched her mind for a way to suggest she be the dealer at their game. Perrin had saved her, and Ashlee thought it was a touch of genius.

"*Monsieur* Winchell," he had said, "if you will not

think it too bold of me, I would like to ask your help."

"My help?" Lloyd had laughed. "How can I help? To do what?"

"To settle an argument between my fiancée and me."

Ashlee had known the man's curiosity was aroused by the way his close-set eyes darted from Perrin to her and back. "An argument? Over what, Perrin?"

"Ashlee says she ees zee best dealer in all of New Orleans. I 'ave told her I do not think that ees possible. Allow her to deal, and you be zee judge."

Ashlee could have kissed Perrin right there and then. Now, if he could only bluff his way through the rest, they'd be leaving Lloyd Winchell's house with enough money to pay off Dominique and Rhys Sinclair. But before they could do that, she'd have to visit her father's safe. Sitting up, she swung her legs off the bed, deciding there was no time like the present. She had heard her father go to his room about a half hour earlier and figured that by now he'd be asleep along with his wife. As for the others at Belle Chasse, she'd have to take the chance. Slipping back into her dress, she hurriedly buttoned up the front, slid into her shoes, and left her room.

As always, the night clerk was asleep in his chair, propped back against the wall. Ashlee simply walked right by him, unlocked the office door, and went inside without disturbing him. She didn't bother lighting the lamp, since the moonlight trickling in through the window was enough to light the way to her father's safe. Upon reaching it, she took down the portrait, set it aside, and withdrew the key from her pocket. There were always two metal boxes kept there: one with the bank deposit and another with a good sum of money used to give the dealers each afternoon when the casino opened. It was from the latter that Ashlee took what she needed. If she could manage it, she would offer to distribute the cash tomorrow afternoon instead of Dominique, thus avoiding the possibility of the woman discovering some was missing before Ashlee had the chance to return what she had borrowed. Stuffing the wad of money down the neckline of her dress, she placed the box back in the safe, closed the door, and hurriedly hung the portrait back where it belonged.

In her haste to leave the office before someone found her there and because of the dim light, Ashlee accidentally bumped the edge of the desk with her hip, knocking a book lying there to the floor. Her heart lurched in her throat and she remained perfectly still, listening for the desk clerk to stumble to his feet and come barging in at any second. Several long, agonizing moments passed before she decided that the noise hadn't awakened him, and she quickly bent to retrieve the book. She couldn't read the title in the muted light but knew that it belonged on the shelf with the others when she looked up and saw an empty spot. As she passed by, she tucked it back in place and left the office in a rush, failing to notice the dark figure of someone outside the window who had observed her every move.

Cool night air touched Ashlee's hot cheeks as she stepped out into the courtyard from the lobby, and she paused to enjoy it. Taking the money she needed had been relatively easy now that it was over, but it was something she was glad she didn't have to do every day. She frowned disgustedly. Stealing had never really bothered her before. It had always been a sort of game for her, one she always won. Being caught had ruined that, proving how dangerous and foolish the idea had been. Although she didn't like admitting it, she knew John was right when he said they had been lucky that it was Rhys Sinclair who figured it out. Anyone else would have seen them thrown in prison whether they had returned the money or not. She moved out into the courtyard, strolling aimlessly. Of course, Rhys wasn't through with them. That was what was so distressing. She didn't know what he wanted for sure. Nearing one of the many wrought iron settees scattered about the gardens, Ashlee slowly sat down, her attention drawn to the dark shape of the building where at this moment her father slept. She loved the man so dearly that at times it hurt. She'd always love him, no matter what happened, even if her actions in the next few days destroyed his feelings for her. It was a chance she had to take, and she prayed that sometime in the future, not too distant a future, he would come to understand why she had exposed the woman he loved— or thought he did. Dominique was evil, and she had to be disposed of.

Suddenly Ashlee sensed she wasn't alone in the courtyard, and the hairs at the nape of her neck tingled. She wanted to stand up and race for the safety of her room, certain that was all that would save her. But for some unexplainable reason she discovered that she couldn't move, that instead of doing what she knew she should do, she just sat there, listening, straining in the deafening silence for any sound that would tell her where the intruder was. Then it came, the snapping of a twig behind her, and Ashlee's hand flew to her mouth as she jerked around to see who it was. Rage instantly replaced her fear when she espied Rhys standing a few feet away, a bright smile on his handsome face.

"How dare you," she growled, coming to her feet.

"How dare I what, Ashlee?" he mocked. "Go for a walk in the courtyard? I think I have as much right as you."

"I mean sneaking up on me like that!"

He paused once he reached her. "I wasn't sneaking. I could see that you were deep in thought, and I simply didn't want to disturb you."

Her disbelief showed clearly in her eyes. She collapsed back in the settee. "A little late to be out strolling, isn't it?"

One corner of Rhys's mouth twitched upward. "I was about to say the same for you."

"I couldn't sleep. What's your excuse?" She sat up straight and glanced all around them. "Or were you supposed to be meeting someone?" She raised a brow in sarcastic humor. "My stepmother, perhaps? The two of you seem to be very close these days."

Rhys shrugged his wide shoulders. "I've never been one to avoid a beautiful woman's company." Without asking her permission, he sat down next to her on the narrow bench, folded his arms over his chest, and stretched his long legs out in front of him. "How have you been feeling lately? It's been a while since we talked."

Ashlee's cheeks flamed instantly, and she was thankful that he wouldn't be able to notice it in the darkness. Sitting so close to him didn't help either. Hoping that it didn't appear he bothered her, Ashlee slowly came to her feet. "Your concern is touching, Mr. Sinclair, but not necessary. I've been taking care of myself long before I met you, and I think I can continue without your help."

"And we both know how that turned out," he reminded her with a smile.

"Is that why you're still here?" she countered. "To badger me? Do you find some evil satisfaction in constantly reminding me that you were the one who solved the big mystery concerning the robberies on the Mississippi?"

Drawing his feet in, Rhys placed his hands on his knees and casually pushed himself up. "I already told you why I'm sticking around, Ashlee. I'm here because of you."

She stumbled back a step when he moved closer. "Well, you're wasting your time, Yankee. I'm engaged, and even if I weren't, I wouldn't give you an ounce of consideration."

"Engagements can be broken," he spoke softly, his

dark eyes reflecting the moonlight that surrounded them. "And love doesn't just happen. It has to be nurtured, like a seed planted in the earth. It must be given time to grow. I'm in no hurry, Ashlee. I'll wait for as long as it takes." He moved to within an inch of her. "It will be a small sacrifice for such a promising reward."

Suddenly, his arm was around her waist, pulling her against his hardened frame, his other hand trapping the back of her head while his lips descended on hers. He kissed her tenderly and passionately enough to make her head spin, and Ashlee had to fight with herself to remember how much she hated and despised him. His fiery kiss branded her to the very core of her inner self, shattering the lies and awakening the truth in her. She cared about him . . . to what extent, she wasn't sure, but enough to realize that there would be a terrible emptiness without him. His mouth moved hungrily over hers, and much against her will, she returned his kiss with equal passion and the desire to have him hold her in his arms for all eternity. Then it was over. . . . Just as abruptly as it had begun, Rhys let go of her, and Ashlee felt an odd sense of aloneness even though he stood so very close.

"My only hope," he whispered, "is that you come to realize it before you hurt the others in your life."

Tears welled in her eyes as she watched him turn about and quietly walk away.

Chapter Fourteen

Night had slowly embraced the city into its silkened arms, enshrouding it with a sprinkling of bright silver stars on a cushion of black velvet. In the west, faint streaks of gold stained the sky as the last evidence of day slipped behind the horizon, silhouetting the dark shape of a carriage winding its way up the twisting, narrow road toward the stately manor perched majestically atop a knoll. Ashlee viewed the beauty that surrounded her with some trepidation. She couldn't name the cause, only that the nervous qualm that had knotted her stomach forewarned of impending doom. Covertly, she stole a glance at her silent companion. Even in the faint light of the carriage lanterns, she could see the beads of perspiration dotting his brow, and Ashlee knew Perrin was experiencing much the same doubts as she. Perhaps, not about her talents, but of his own. Their success—or failure—this night would shape their future. For the first time since Perrin told her of Dominique's hold over him, she realized that if their plan succumbed to a fate not of their making, she would be obliged to marry him. Her conscience would never let her rest knowing that her selfish act in refusing him had driven an innocent woman from her home. She thought about praying, asking for

God's help in this matter, and quickly banished the idea from her head. What they were about to do was morally wrong, and God would have no part of it. This was up to her and Perrin. They'd have to achieve it on their own. She reached over and patted his hand.

"We'll do just fine, Perrin," she smiled encouragingly, though the words sounded shallow in her ears. "You'll see. We'll walk out of Winchell's home with enough money to solve all our worries."

A vague smile parted his lips, and he nodded.

"Did you bring the money?" she asked, hoping to ease the tension. From the look on his face, she quickly realized she had only made it worse.

"*Oui*, but don't tell me where you got it, *ma chere*. I do not think I could go through with thees if I knew you had stolen it so that we could cheat someone else out of more."

"Borrowed, Perrin," Ashlee corrected, squeezing his hand. "I borrowed it. There's a big difference."

Perrin sent her a dubious look then snapped the reins, urging the horses up the slight incline toward Winchell's house. "Borrowing, *mon amie*, means zee donor gave his permission."

"Borrowing means you intend to pay it back. Which I do," she argued, grinning. "Come on, Perrin. Let's have fun tonight. Think of this as a contest. You and me against four wealthy intelligent businessmen. We're about to show them that they aren't as cunning as they think they are when it comes to dealing with money." Her smile broadened. "Or with Ashlee Redington and Perrin Fabron."

Perrin's shoulders dropped. "I wish I was as confident as you, Ashlee."

"Nothing will go wrong," she assured him. "And think of the reward you'll get. Tomorrow morning you will walk into the office, hand Dominique the money you owe her, then book passage on the first ship sailing for Paris with the deed to your mother's property in your pocket."

Perrin's mouth twitched as he tried to suppress a smile. "It will be gratifying to see zee look on her face."

"Gratifying?" Ashlee laughed. "It will be exhilarating. I'd love to be there to see her reaction."

Feeling considerably better, Perrin smiled openly. "I promise to tell you everything."

"You better," she teased, then lowered her voice to a whisper as the carriage neared the front steps of Winchell's house. "You remember what I told you about the game, don't you?"

"*Oui*," he nodded, the worried look gone from his dark eyes. "You will deal me a good hand, then a bad one, so that no one will suspect. When zee ante ees high, I will win." He hauled back on the reins, set the brake, and quickly jumped to the ground to help his companion from the carriage.

"I'd wish you luck," she whispered playfully, "but you won't need any." When she started past him, he caught her elbow.

"*Non, ma chere*, I 'ave all zee luck in zee world," he murmured. "And it began zee day I met you at zee train station." His eyes softened and a half smile lifted one side of his mouth. "I want you to know, Ashlee, that even if thees does not go zee way we planned, I will always be grateful to you for trying." He glanced down at his shoes. "And if I had been given zee opportunity to choose my own bride, I would have chosen you."

"Perrin," she cooed. "That's the most beautiful thing anyone's ever said to me."

"It comes from my heart, *mon amie*," he admitted.

"Then we must promise to always remain friends and to keep in contact after you've returned to France."

"That ees one promise I will never break," he grinned, holding out his arm for her. "Shall we get on with business?"

Laughing gaily, she curled her hand into the crook of his arm and started up the steps.

Lloyd Winchell's home was probably one of the most elegant in all of New Orleans, and to be invited there was an honor only the wealthy enjoyed. Against the backdrop of a velvety black sky, each window in the place glowed with a warm light, emitting a friendly atmosphere to the guests ascending its stairs. The double front doors stood open to welcome Ashlee and Perrin inside, and once they crossed the wide porch adorned with a long column of white pillars that supported the roofline of the two-story high veranda, they were met by the butler who expressed his employer's pleasure at their arrival. Upon taking Ashlee's shawl, he held out a directive hand toward the parlor, stating that Mr. Winchell and his other guests could be found there. Perrin thanked the man and led his companion across the white marble floor toward the room the butler had indicated.

"Miss Redington and Mr. Fabron," Lloyd Winchell smiled warmly once the couple had stepped into view through the parlor door. "I'm so glad you've come." He set aside his glass of wine and crossed the room, welcoming them with a friendly handshake for Perrin and a light kiss to the back of Ashlee's fingers. Then, encircling Ashlee's slender waist in a manner much like a man would do with his daughter, he turned her toward the others who awaited introductions. "You remember Daniel Ryan, don't you, Miss Redington?"

"Of course," she smiled politely as the gray-haired man came forward to greet her in the same style as Lloyd had done. "I've seen him at Belle Chasse many times."

"Ah, yes," he laughed, his brown eyes twinkling. "One of my weaknesses and the reason I find myself here this evening. And I must say I was delighted when Lloyd told me you would be the dealer tonight. It will make losing a little more tolerable."

"Be careful, Perrin," Lloyd cut in. "Daniel always says that before a game, then winds up cleaning the rest of us out."

"That may have been true in the past, Lloyd," Daniel objected. "But I've never played against Mr. Fabron, and you're the one who told me how good he is."

"Well, why do you think I invited him?" Lloyd chuckled. "I've been waiting a long time to see you lose." Ignoring his friend's mocking glare, Lloyd turned to the one about whom they spoke. "Perrin, allow me to introduce Daniel Ryan, one of the few remaining planters in the area who somehow managed to hang onto his money. We're still questioning his methods."

Ryan reached out and shook Perrin's hand. "Listen to who's talking," he countered, though his eyes remained on Perrin. "None of us have figured out how Lloyd's business can bring in enough to maintain a house like this, but we never outright imply anything." He cast his friend a sarcastic grin, then added, "Congratulations on your upcoming wedding, Perrin. Without a doubt, you'll have the most beautiful bride in all of Louisiana."

"*Merci*," Perrin nodded with a smile Ashlee's way. "I must agree."

"And this other grinning jackanapes," Lloyd continued, holding out his hand toward the remaining guest, "is Richard Bonnett. Richard, Ashlee Redington and her fiancé, Perrin Fabron."

Stepping forward, Bonnett presented Ashlee with a deep nod of his head, then shook Perrin's hand. "And you're Dominique Redington's cousin, I hear."

"*Oui*," Perrin replied.

"Well, it's an honor to meet you, sir."

"May I get the two of you a glass of wine?" Lloyd

offered, guiding Ashlee to a chair.

Perrin would have enjoyed an entire bottle but graciously declined. Ashlee accepted.

"I was under the impression your wives would be joining us this evening," Ashlee said as she took the glass Lloyd held out to her.

"Ordinarily, my wife would have," Daniel said, "but her brother is paying us a visit and she decided to take him to the theater tonight instead. And rather than leave Richard's wife alone, she invited her to go with them. I hope that doesn't make you uncomfortable, Miss Redington."

"Not at all, Mr. Ryan," she smiled. "Until my father married Dominique, there were countless occasions when I had to be hostess to a group of men." She took a sip of her wine, then looked at Lloyd. "But shouldn't there be five players, Mr. Winchell?"

"There will be," he assured her, starting to say more when his attention was suddenly drawn to someone standing in the parlor's doorway. "Ah, there he is now."

The goblet shook in Ashlee's hand and she nearly spilled some of the wine over the rim when she turned her head to look at the newcomer. There, haloed in the framework as he smiled back at her, stood Rhys Sinclair. He was dressed in a subtle, yet always elegant manner, and Ashlee couldn't help but stare. The simple beige trousers, though well-fitted, failed to disguise his muscular thighs. His white silk shirt with a peach-colored ascot and his dark brown coat with velvet lapels boldly hinted at the powerful shoulders and chest that lay hidden beneath the rich cloth. His presence never fell short of stirring Ashlee's blood, but this time it was born out of a different cause. She was certain she could fool the other players when she dealt off the bottom of the deck, but Rhys Sinclair was another matter altogether. He made his living playing poker and could probably spot cheaters by the look in their eyes. She glanced down at her glass of wine . . . or the way their hands trembled.

"And of course, you know Miss Redington."

Winchell's voice penetrated Ashlee's thoughts. She blinked and lifted her gaze to the men who stood before her now.

"Miss Redington," Rhys nodded with a cordial smile.

She could feel the tremor work its way up her spine. "Mr. Sinclair," she answered weakly.

"Well, now that everyone's here," Lloyd said, rubbing his hands together in anticipation of what was to come, "shall we begin?" When the others eagerly agreed, he stepped away from Ashlee to direct his guests from the parlor and didn't see the troubled look that came over the beautiful brunette's lovely face. For if he had, he might have expressed his concern over what he would have misread as ill health. As it was, Rhys was the only one who noticed.

"May I escort you to the table, Miss Redington?" he grinned, holding out a hand.

Panic rising high, Ashlee could only stare at the long, tanned fingers and the gold band of his diamond ring, silently cursing her neglect in asking Lloyd Winchell who his other guests might be. But she had been so sure that she and Perrin would be in total control of the game that she hadn't even given a thought to the possibility that one of the players might know more about the less than honest methods of winning. Yet, on the other hand, what made her think that Rhys was any better than Winchell, Ryan, or Bonnett? After all, hadn't she beaten this arrogant Yankee at his own game? Her confidence sparked anew, she set aside her wine goblet and stood, ignoring his offer.

"Thank you, Mr. Sinclair, I'd be honored," she smiled sweetly, "but I don't think that would be proper, since I'm here with my fiancé." She moved past him and took

Perrin's arm. "Shall we go, my darling?" She cast Rhys a demure look over her shoulder, then intrepidly strolled from the room.

"*Mon Dieu*, Ashlee," Perrin whispered nervously in her ear as they neared Lloyd's study, "what will we do now?"

Her blue eyes sparkling with devilment, she replied, "Do Perrin? Why, we'll play poker."

Ashlee couldn't remember the last time she had had so much enjoyment out of a simple game of cards. The men were delightful and didn't seem to mind losing some of their money to the charming little Frenchman at their table. And Perrin displayed a masterful technique of hiding his glee over the cards Ashlee purposely dealt him. To any who might have observed, they would have merely applauded his expertise and envied his luck. Even Rhys seemed surprised by the man's agility with the cards, and with each round that was played, Ashlee's fears all but disappeared while Perrin's winnings grew.

Two hours passed, and although Perrin would lose three or four hands in a row, those that he won awarded him with twice the amount of money he had forfeited previously. Through it all, Perrin kept his word, declining Lloyd's offer of wine or sherry and settling for a cool glass of water or occasional cup of tea.

When the hour neared midnight, Ashlee knew that the next hand would have to be the one that would send her and Perrin home with enough money to pay off Domonique and free them from a marriage neither of them wanted. But in order to raise the ante high enough to do them any good, Ashlee realized she would have to execute some stunning artistry with the cards she dealt each player. By giving each man just enough to make him take the chance of betting a little higher to stay in the game, the mound of silver in the center of the table would grow. Then, when it came their turn to draw against the cards they elected to keep, she would have to give them enough to make them think they could win the game, thus tempting them to raise the ante even higher. Everything depended on her now, and although the evening had gone smoothly so far, Ashlee could feel herself break out in a fine veil of perspiration. One slip on her part, and it would all be over.

When Lloyd Winchell first asked Rhys to join the poker game he was having in his home, Rhys had thought to decline. Ashlee's strange behavior toward her fiancé had warranted his close attention, for he suspected it was only a front and that sometime in the near future the two of them would reveal what it was they were truly planning to do. Then Winchell had announced the names of the others who had already accepted and that they were in for a treat since their dealer would be Miss Redington. Rhys could only surmise that the little vixen had something in mind when she finagled an invitation to a game usually played only by men, and after the first round was dealt, he knew what it was. He had played against the best, and although Ashlee was good, he had spotted her dishonesty right off. She might not be able to play the game well when someone else was the dealer, but she certainly could handle the cards. It was a unique plan, and if he hadn't been expecting something, he would have been distracted by Ashlee's charm and beauty during the game just as the other men obviously were. Of course, sitting directly across the table from her helped. It gave him clear view of her hands and the way she held the deck of cards. What he couldn't quite figure out, though, was what she hoped to gain by cheating. Stacking the deck so that Fabron could win would work this time. But if they thought to continue, it wouldn't take very long for someone to make a connection between his good luck and the fact that his fiancée just happened to be the dealer at the time. Knowing that he didn't stand much of a chance at winning tonight, Rhys settled back in his chair, content to play the cards Ashlee gave him while he patiently waited for the evening to come to an end. As soon as the three of them returned to the hotel, he'd confront the pair with what he knew.

There were several times during the course of the evening that Perrin wished he could compliment Ashlee on her skill. If he hadn't known about her intentions, he would have just assumed Lady Luck stood at his side. He smiled secretively as he watched the slender hand pass out five cards to each player.

The opening bet was placed, and Perrin matched it before looking at his hand, the briefest of frowns wrinkling his brow once he had. Would this be the round that would send them home the big winners? It didn't seem likely, since the only high card he held was the queen of diamonds. Another bet was placed, and Perrin discarded all except the queen and the ten of diamonds, hoping to draw a flush. He nearly laughed out loud when he realized luck and prayers had nothing to do with the cards he'd receive.

A strange excitement seemed to electrify the room once each player had added the new cards to his hand, even though none of the men let on that they thought to be the winner this time. But Ashlee knew. To Lloyd, she had dealt two queens and two deuces. Ryan received three kings. Richard Bonnett was given a flush, while Rhys was honored with the second highest hand in the game of poker—namely, a straight flush. As for Perrin, he collected an ace, king, and jack—all diamonds to match the queen and ten he already had. Ashlee relaxed back in her chair to watch each man calmly add a substantial amount to the pot.

Rhys leisurely studied the cards he held, then folded them up and laid them face down on the table in front of him. If this had been an ordinary game of poker, he would have known what to do without hesitation. The chances of someone else having a higher hand than his were quite slim, since it wasn't very often that a straight flush was dealt, whether done so honestly or with a little help. But knowing the way Ashlee's mind worked and what it was that she hoped to accomplish, he was able to find a flaw in an otherwise sure thing. More than likely she planned to lure him into betting every penny he had on him, knowing that the cards Perrin held would beat him. He had a fifty-fifty chance of winning, but as he lit a cheroot and looked out over its tip at her, he was sure the odds had changed. And from the look in her eye, they weren't in his favor. He nodded back at her, checked Ryan's bet and raised it, then took a puff on his cigar and settled his attention on Ashlee again.

The teal-blue gown she wore added heightened color to the pale depths of her sparkling eyes, and its square neckline revealed only a small portion of white creamy skin for him to appraise. But that simple sight easily stirred memories of what lay hidden beneath, and Rhys frowned as he picked up his glass of wine and took a drink. She had managed to avoid him for nearly a week, but there hadn't been a moment that passed that he didn't think of her or recall the intimate times they had shared. He had tolerated another man's claim on her only because he was sure nothing would come of it. Yet his patience was dwindling. He wanted Ashlee more than anything he had ever wanted in his life, vowing that as soon as this mess with the casino was straightened out he would go to Arthur and make him a proposition. His gaze drifted to the little man sitting beside Ashlee. And if he were right about Perrin Fabron, it wouldn't take much to buy him off.

"Well, Rhys," Lloyd grinned, "it's up to you. It'll take one hundred dollars to see my cards."

Doubting very much that he had any chance of

winning, let alone Lloyd's chances, Rhys shoved the required amount into the heaping pile in the center of the table. "Then let's see them," he smiled.

Hopefully, Lloyd uncovered the two pair he held, groaning when Daniel Ryan topped them with three kings. Next came Bonnett's flush, and three pairs of eyes expectantly turned on Rhys. He didn't disappoint them as he laid down what should have been a winning hand nor did he reach out to scoop in the mound of silver. Taking a long drag on his cheroot, he squinted over at Perrin when some of the smoke got in his eyes and waited.

"My God," Daniel Ryan exclaimed, "it would take a royal flush to beat that. Perrin, can you do it?"

Perrin could feel the sweat dot his upper lip, and he thought how badly he needed a drink right then. Maybe the others would believe that it was merely his good fortune to have been dealt such a rare and magnificent hand, but the Yankee who sat there staring at him with a vague, almost surrendering smile on his face knew better. Unable to swallow the lump in his throat, Perrin tugged nervously at his shirt collar. He was tempted just to throw in his cards, but the stack of money laying there on the table was his for the taking, and he knew there was more than enough to settle his account with Dominique. Yet, if he played the cards, would the Yankee call him out for the cheater he was? Torn by indecision, he sat there as mutely as a granite statue.

When Perrin didn't immediately lay down his cards, declare his victory, and gather in his winnings, Ashlee feared her skill at handling the deck had failed her, that perhaps she hadn't given him the cards she had planned for him to receive. Yet so far everyone else revealed the hands she had selected for them, which meant the odds were high that he would as well. So why was he just sitting there? Leaning forward a mite to see his face more clearly, she quietly called his name.

Perrin's head snapped around to look at her. "W—what?"

"Mr. Ryan asked if you can beat a straight flush. Can you?" she asked hopefully.

Perrin rubbed trembling fingers across his mouth and gulped, but made no further gesture to indicate his willingness to disclose the cards he held. Finally, out of desperation, Ashlee slowly took his wrist and lowered his hand to the table where everyone could see the product of her hours of scheming.

"My God," Lloyd moaned. "I don't believe it. Rhys's hand is one that I've seldom seen, but for it to be beaten by that is absolutely awesome."

"And absolutely the end of me," Ryan laughed, pushing back from the table. "I bet every last penny I had, thinking my three kings was a sure winner."

"Well, what about me?" Bonnett argued. "How often do you get a flush and still lose? Perrin," he chuckled, standing up, "next time *I* get the honor of having Miss Redington sit by me."

Certain he had been found out, Perrin's eyes widened into huge circles. *"Monsieur?"*

"Wait a minute, Richard," Lloyd broke in before the man could explain. "If you're implying that Perrin's good luck was because he was sitting next to Miss Redington, I think I should remind you that I, too, sat beside her. You saw my cards."

All but ignoring the nervous couple who stared at him, Richard laughed. "Maybe love has something to do with it. Should I insist my wife come with me next time?"

"I don't think your wife will let you come next time," Daniel added, chuckling. "Or aren't you going to tell her how much you lost tonight? I know I'm not telling Sarah."

"See the advantages of staying single?" Lloyd grinned,

coming to his feet. "Well, gentlemen, I think we better call it an evening."

"I should have called it an evening about two hours ago," Daniel replied, standing. "How about you, Rhys? I would think losing with the kind of hand you just had would make you swear off gambling for a while."

Rising as he snuffed out his cheroot in the ashtray, he grinned. "Believe it or not, it isn't the first time it's happened, and I doubt it will be the last. You can see how much it bothered me."

"Yes, well, you have a little more gambler's blood in you than I do, I'm afraid," Daniel admitted. "I'm going to have to sell four or five acres of my plantation to make up for what I've lost here tonight."

"Will you listen to him, Lloyd," Richard mocked. "That man is trying to make us feel sorry for him when we all know he probably spent more on that silk top hat he wears than he did on this game." He cast Daniel a playful smirk, then turned to the couple who had quietly observed the good-natured bantering. "It was a pleasure meeting you both, and I hope we can do this again sometime. Only I plan to walk away the winner." Reaching out, he shook Perrin's hand, smiled broadly, nodded at Ashlee, then turned and strode from the room, all the others following close behind.

At the front door everyone said their good-byes and thanked Lloyd for inviting them. Bonnett and Ryan quickly got in their carriages and drove off, leaving Perrin, Ashlee, and Rhys to walk alone together down the stone pathway toward the single rig awaiting them. Perrin still hadn't quite gotten over the shock of his success or he wouldn't have done the unforgivable and offered the Yankee a ride back to the hotel, since it appeared the man would have to walk otherwise. But then Perrin didn't have the same feelings toward Rhys Sinclair that Ashlee had. Besides, there just might be enough money in his wallet now to pay off his cousin *and* Mr. Sinclair. Yes, Perrin's future was looking brighter by the minute. Early tomorrow morning he would find Dominique and reclaim the deed to his mother's property, then book passage for him and Philippe on a ship bound for France, hopefully sailing by the afternoon. Handing Ashlee into the front seat of their rented surrey, he took his place beside her and waited while Rhys climbed in behind them. In his gleeful state, he failed to notice the displeased look on his lovely companion's face.

Ashlee sat stiffly in the seat all the way back to Belle Chasse, almost feeling the intense brown eyes watching her. The prickling of doom that had assailed her earlier was stronger now, and she could only blame it on Rhys's reaction when Perrin's winning hand was revealed. Lloyd, Ryan, and Bonnett had clearly expressed their amazement and their disappointment at losing. Rhys hadn't said a word. In fact, the expression on his face hadn't changed in the slightest—almost as if he knew what cards had been dealt to Perrin. Yet, if that were true, then why hadn't he challenged her fiancé? He, as well as all the others, had lost a substantial amount of money on that one game. An ordinary man wouldn't sit back calmly and let that happen if he thought he had been cheated. Ashlee closed her eyes, moaning silently. Rhys wasn't ordinary. She had realized that from the first moment she saw him standing on the gangplank of the *Mississippi Queen*. No other man in her life affected her the way he had. She would miss him once he had grown bored with Belle Chasse and moved on. Unknowingly, she laid her hand against the hard flatness of her belly, thinking that she would miss Rhys but would never be able to forget him. His child would see to that. And if she were lucky, it would be a boy, a son with the same dark blond hair and brown eyes of his father. Suddenly, the

401

need to cry formed a knot in her throat and she swallowed hard. Could it mean that Perrin had been right when he guessed Ashlee loved this arrogant, cocky Yankee? Was that the reason she could never seem to get him out of her thoughts? Or the cause that flared her jealousy every time she saw him with another woman? Her eyes flew open and she defiantly blinked back the tears. God forbid! Rhys Sinclair was everything she was supposed to hate.

Their surrey rolled to a stop outside Belle Chasse along with the many others already there awaiting owners who were still patronizing the casino at this late hour. Rhys was quick to jump down and offer his assistance to Ashlee in descending the rig, which she reluctantly accepted, then volunteered to walk her to her room while Perrin disposed of the carriage. Ashlee started to decline, but Perrin, who hadn't sensed his fiancés's disapproval, eagerly thanked Rhys for his kind suggestion and drove off, leaving Ashlee there in openmouthed astonishment.

"It wouldn't have done much good to argue, Ashlee," Rhys told her as he took her elbow and firmly started her up the stairs. "You and I have to talk, and if your fiancé had objected, I would have simply insisted a bit more strongly."

Irritated, she tried to yank her arm free, but Rhys's grip tightened. "We have nothing to say to each other."

"Well, I disagree. I think you have a lot of explaining to do, and at the moment, I'm offering you the chance to do so in private. But if you push me, we'll stand right here and discuss it where anyone and everyone can listen in." He never broke stride as he half dragged, half shoved her up the stairs, nor did he give her a choice. Jerking open the door, he all but thrust her through it, then continued his angered trek across the lobby and out the back into the courtyard, his hand still clamped securely around Ashlee's arm. He stopped suddenly, obviously disturbed by the amount of people wandering about the gardens, glanced in the direction of Ashlee's chambers, and changed his mind, turning them both toward the staff's quarters.

"Where are you taking me, Rhys Sinclair?" Ashlee demanded, nearly having to run to keep up with his agitated gait.

He didn't answer her, instead storming into the hallway that led to the private rooms belonging to the employees and dragging Ashlee with him. The only comfort she was granted was the absence of someone in the corridor who would see them, but her fear of his intentions once he got her alone almost made her wish that the hall had been crowded with people. She stifled a gasp when he viciously caught the ivory knob in his hand, swung the door to his room open, and shoved her inside. Ashlee stumbled, practically fell, then whirled back to face him.

"You can't treat me like this," she hissed.

Rhys slammed the portal shut behind him and glared at her in return, his chin lowered, his brows drawn in an angry frown, and his hands placed low on his hips. "I'll treat you any way I see fit, Miss Redington."

"By what right?" she demanded testily. "Who do you think you are?"

"I'm a man who allowed you to make a fool of him, not once but twice, and then had to sit through an evening watching you stack the deck against him. You're damn lucky, Ashlee, that I was the only one who saw it."

"What?" she shrieked. "Are you saying I cheated?"

"Are you denying it?"

"Yes!"

"Then you're a liar."

Ashlee didn't like the way the muscle in his cheek flexed. It was time she left. Lifting her chin, she said, "I don't have to stand here and take this."

"You'll do whatever I tell you," he countered, biting

off each word. "And you'll start by telling me what the two of you hoped to achieve tonight."

"I haven't the vaguest idea what you're talking about, Mr. Sinclair. Now stand aside and let me pass." She jumped backward when he took two steps toward her.

"Well, I doubt your doltish fiancé could have pulled it off alone, or for that matter come up with the idea in the first place. It had to have been yours."

"Stop calling Perrin names," she shouted.

"Would you rather I went and talked to him about it?"

Ashlee knew what a mistake that would be. "Talk about what?" she repeated, refusing to give in.

Rhys's frown deepened. "Or would you prefer that I went back to Lloyd Winchell's and talked to him? Or maybe I should talk to your father. I warned you before, Ashlee, that I wanted your thievery to stop, and I meant it."

"Oh, I'm well aware of that," she sneered. "And I know why. But what you want and what I plan to do are two very different things, Mr. Sinclair. So warn all you like. I'm not going to listen. As for talking to Mr. Winchell or my father, go right ahead. I think they'd listen to me before they would some"—her disapproving gaze ran the length of him—"some Yankee."

His dark eyes held hers for a long moment before he nodded his head slightly. "It's possible."

Ashlee smiled victoriously.

"So I guess I'm left with no alternative but to talk to Mr. Fabron. I'm sure all I'll have to do is tell him to hand over the money he won tonight and he will." He turned for the door.

"Wait," Ashlee exploded, bolting after him. "You can't do that!"

He looked at her over one shoulder. "And why not?"

"Because—because—" Her mind raced for an answer. "He needs it to pay off a loan."

"Then why didn't he simply borrow the money instead of stealing it?" he asked suspiciously.

"For the same reason he couldn't pay it off in the first place. He doesn't have any money," she snapped. "You know that. Or at least you said you did."

Rhys considered her for a moment. "Then what you're saying is that tonight will be the one and only time. You're not planning to make a habit of it?"

"There's no need to," she assured him. "What Perrin won is enough."

A strange smile parted his lips, and he looked away with a shake of his head. "Why is it I have a hard time believing that?" His brown eyes captured hers again. "Who does he owe?"

Ashlee straightened indignantly. "That's none of your business!"

"It is when a good portion of his winnings is my money—won, I might add, by cheating me out of it. Who does he owe?"

"Go to hell," she blurted out, reaching past him for the doorknob. She gasped when he cruelly took her wrist and yanked her away from the door. "Let go of me!"

"Not until you tell me who he could possibly owe so much money to."

His demand struck an insolent nerve. Glaring into his eyes, Ashlee quickly stomped the heel of her shoe into the tip of his toe. He winced, even though the thickness of his leather boot cushioned most of the blow, but did not release her. His temper soared.

"There are times, Ashlee Redington," he ground out threateningly, "when I wish you weren't a woman."

"Why? So you could hit me?" Pale blue eyes flashed. "I'll bet it wouldn't make a difference if we were up north right now. I'm sure that's how your kind treats their women."

"Our women don't behave the way you do!" he

405

shouted. "In fact, I can't think of a single other *southern* lady who would consider dressing up in boy's clothing just so she could steal!"

"Maybe that's because there isn't another woman around who is willing to do *anything* to help her father the way I am."

"And what good will you do your father if you wind up in prison?" he challenged, giving her a rough shake that sent her long strands of silky hair shimmering all around her.

Enraged by his treatment of her, Ashlee dug her fingernails into the hand clamped firmly around her arm and struggled to get free. "If I do, it'll be because you turned me in," she howled, then cried out in pain when Rhys grabbed her wrist.

"I'm not your enemy, Ashlee," he growled.

Tears glistened in her eyes, but the determined, stubborn look she gave him clearly told him that it would take more than physical abuse to break her spirit. "Yes, you are!"

Rhys sucked in an angry breath, intending to list the flaws in her character that made him appear that way to her. But while he mentally went over the order in which they should be recited, the soft fragrance of her skin and hair assailed his senses and dulled his desire to verbally attack her. In truth, there wasn't a thing he could name about her nature or her beauty that displeased him. The fury that had darkened his eyes vanished. "You're blind, Ashlee," he whispered, slowly enveloping her tiny frame with its soft curves within the strong circle of his arms, her own drawn behind her back as he lowered his head.

The feel of his rock-hard body pressed against her instantly shattered Ashlee's desire to fight him. His touch, his smile, the scent of him, even the thoughts she had about him, stirred the passion she longed to bury deep inside herself, an emotion she hoped never to be aroused by him again. But as his lips gently kissed the corner of her mouth, the tip of her nose, then brushed against her temple before softly tracing the outline of her jaw to her chin, she knew how foolish it was to even consider such a possibility. And if she didn't bring this moment to an end and quickly, the hardened shell she had spun around her feelings toward him would crumble.

"Rhys . . . don't," she breathed, tears burning the backs of her lids as she fought not to cry.

"Why?" he whispered tenderly, kissing her temple. "Are you afraid?"

She pulled her wrist free of his hold and placed her opened palm against his chest to push him away. But the warmth of those steely muscles beneath her fingertips sent an electrical charge through her entire body, and she stifled a sob. "Yes," she answered, her voice quivering.

"Of what?" he asked, his tanned brow furrowed in a confused frown. "Of me?"

Ashlee dropped her gaze and shook her head. "Of me," she admitted after a long moment. "Of falling in love with you."

Surprised to hear her mention the word love in connection with him, a smile flashed across his face until her meaning registered. "Would that be so terrible?" he proposed, feeling a little injured by the implication.

Willing herself to be angry again, she jerked free of him and whirled away. "Yes!"

"Why?" he pressed, mentally searching for some logical reason.

"Because—because you're everything I've learned to hate. Loving you—even liking you—wouldn't make any sense." She shrugged out of his reach.

"For God's sake, Ashlee, you talk as if I'm a bowl of spinach and your father just sat you down at the table and told you to eat it whether you liked it or not." He tried to take her arm again and lost his patience when she quickly evaded him, jerking forward to firmly latch onto her wrist. She struggled briefly before he subdued her by crushing her against his chest. "Listen to me," he ordered almost angrily, catching her chin in one hand and forcing her to look at him. "First and foremost, I'm a man, a living, breathing human being who's capable to feeling every emotion you can name. I'll admit that until this very moment, I wasn't really sure. But now, in all honesty, I must tell you that what I feel for you isn't just infatuation. It isn't even admiration for your courage or that stubborn pride of yours. It goes much deeper than that. Ashlee, to put it simply . . . I love you." He wrapped both arms around her and hugged her to him, gently kissing the top of her head. "Maybe you don't feel the same toward me right now, but given time, I think I can change your mind. I can show you that not all men born north of the Mason-Dixon line should be thought of as the enemy. But more than that, I can make you happy."

Tears streamed down her face, and for a moment Ashlee wasn't sure if they were tears of joy or of sorrow. She felt trapped in a web of deceit and could see no way out of it. Her father would never understand. She and Perrin had played such a convincing game that even if Perrin went back to Paris and left her free to marry whomever she chose, to suddenly show an interest in a man she had claimed to hate would make her father think she was fickle. And when the truth about the baby that she carried became obvious . . . At first her father would, of course, think the child was Perrin's. It would only be logical. But what would he think of her once she and Rhys admitted the baby belonged to them? But would any of that really matter as long as Rhys loved her? She swallowed hard and bit her lower lip. No, it wouldn't, for in her heart she knew that she loved him as well, and through that love they would conquer any obstacle.

"Forever?" she whispered, lifting her eyes to his. "Will you love me forever?"

"Yes, little one," he answered softly without a trace of a smile. "I'll love you forever."

"No matter what might happen to pull us apart?" Her lower lip quivered and a tear raced down her cheek when she blinked.

"No matter what," he quietly assured her, wiping away the moisture from her face with his thumb.

A brief smile lifted the corners of her mouth before Ashlee threw her arms around his neck and pulled him down to meet her urgent kiss. The instant their lips touched, a burning fire exploded within them. Since their first chance meeting, the shortest of glimpses they had caught of each other—she on board the steamboat, he on the gangplank ready to embark—had made them sense something special about the other, subconsciously knowing this time would come. Whether it was of their own making or destiny's plan, they eagerly welcomed this moment.

Discarded shoes were kicked aside and quickly followed by a sampling of cotton, silk, and crinoline. The couple clung to each other almost frantically as they shared the rapture of their embrace, their naked bodies touching full length, fingertips exploring luscious curves and sinewy ripples. Rhys's world pivoted on its own axis, a glorious awakening to the pleasure a willing woman's caress had aroused, knowing that in this moment she was not caught up in the heat of passion but had come to him freely and of a desire to be wholly his. Dark hair fell loose from its pins and shimmered full about her shoulders. He brushed his face against the soft curls, stirring from them the sweet smell of jasmine, and his mind reeled from its heady scent. He kissed her throat and felt the rapid beat of her pulse at the base. His lips trailed the delicate line of her shoulder then lowered to the firmness of her breast, its rose-hued peak taut and anxiously awaiting the moistness of his tongue as he tasted of its sweetness. His hands glided along the smooth curve of her waist and hip, descending the back of her shapely thighs and up again to touch well-rounded buttocks and draw her close against him. Ashlee moaned, and he quickly pressed his mouth on hers again, lost in the savagery of their desires. In an effortless sweep, he lifted her in his arms and carried her to the bed. With hungry impatience, he gently laid her down upon the feathery cushion, then pressed a knee between her thighs and slowly lowered his body against hers.

Ashlee responded eagerly, cradling his face in her hands and drawing his opened mouth to hers. Their lips touched, their tongues met, and the fierceness of their kiss sent a scorching heat through every fiber of their being. Unconscious of any world other than their own, Ashlee arched her hips to welcome his first thrust, moving in blissful harmony with the sleek, hard body possessing hers until an ecstasy exploded within her. The celestial orb that had been her haven shattered in a million tiny stars, draining her strength, sating her passion, and leaving her breathless in the sweet contentment of their desires.

A long while passed as they lay entwined, their eyes closed, Rhys's face nuzzled against her throat as he breathed in the intoxicating scent of her. Giddy with the mystical power she seemed to have over him, Ashlee lovingly traced the welts her nails had made across his wide, muscular back with her fingertips, laughing softly. He raised his head to look at her questioningly.

"It would appear, my knowledgeable Yankee, that I have, indeed, taken a lover."

Grinning wickedly, Rhys propped his head up on his fist and smoothed her ruffled hair away from her cheek. "So it does," he agreed, studying the delicate line of her

410

jaw and the tempting fullness of her tiny mouth. "But that can be corrected with a little work."

"Corrected?" Worry creased the fairness of her brow as she turned her head to look at him, and he laughed.

"Not the way you're thinking, love," he assured her. "I will make it right with your fiancé and your father, and then we can be married." His eyes lowered to the flawless length of her creamy white throat, then feasted openly on the full swell of breasts she immodestly displayed, chuckling when she playfully rolled over onto her stomach and spoiled his view. He settled for the shapely curve of her back and buttocks.

"My father might pose a difficulty, but Perrin and I have already taken care of the problem of our engagement," she cheerfully announced, kissing the tip of his nose when he frowned back at her. "Dominique was blackmailing him into marrying me. It seems he owed her a great deal of money, but after our little adventure tonight, he has enough to pay her back." Resting up on her elbows, she cradled her chin on her fists and smiled brightly. "I would imagine Perrin will be on a ship heading back to Paris by tomorrow afternoon."

"You mean she was blackmailing her own cousin?" He knew the woman was evil, but he hadn't guessed just how much.

"Yes. And to think my father actually loves her. I wonder what he'd say if he knew."

"You don't plan to tell him?" he asked.

"I wouldn't dream of it," she exclaimed, sitting up and scooting off the bed to retrieve her clothes.

"Why not?"

"Well, for one thing, I don't think he'd believe it, and that would only cause ill feelings between the two of us. I love him too much to let that happen." She shimmied into her camisole. "Besides, Dominique was really only trying to get rid of me, not hurt my father."

"And why is that?"

Ashlee smiled impishly and reached for her petticoats. "I'm what you'd call a thorn in her side."

"A beautiful thorn," he quipped, making her giggle. Rising, he yanked the coverlet from the bed, wrapped it around his lean hips, and tucked in the corner. "That's an awfully vicious thing to do to someone . . . making them marry someone they don't want to marry."

"Oh, Perrin's not so bad, Rhys. I like him. Very much." A spark of devilment danced in her eyes once she had slid into her dress and began to fasten the buttons. "In fact, I'm not really sure I'd prefer marrying you instead of him. I've always longed to go to Paris."

"There are easier ways to get to Paris, Ashlee," he admonished, catching her tiny frame in his arms.

Laughing gaily, she added, "But Perrin's uncle is a duke. I'd be a member of royalty. Could I say the same married to you?"

"Is that really so important?" he asked, giving her a squeeze.

Ashlee shrugged. "It could be. And besides, you take a lot for granted thinking that just because you want to marry me, I'll accept." Pretending to be offended, she wiggled out of his hold and held him at arms length with the point of her finger against his chest. "In fact, Mr. Sinclair, you'll have to win my approval or I'll be obliged to carry through with my former wedding plans."

Rhys knew she was teasing, and decided to play a game of his own. "I only offered because I thought that was what you wanted. But," he continued, turning away from her so that she couldn't see his face and the smile that lit up his eyes, "if that's not the case, then I'll have to give it more thought."

"You do that," she bantered, heading for the door. "But don't take too long. You might be sorry." Pressing her fingertips to her lips to keep from laughing out loud

412

and spoiling everything, she twisted the knob and pulled the door open as she threw back over her shoulder, "Good night, Mr. Sinclair."

"Good night, Miss Redington," he countered, turning his head in time to catch a glimpse of teal-blue skirts as the door closed slowly behind her.

Chapter Fifteen

"More tea, Mr. Fabron?"

Startled half out of his wits, Perrin nearly dropped the empty cup he'd been holding for the past fifteen minutes as he stared blankly out the restaurant window, laughing nervously up at the young waitress holding the teapot. *"Oui, mademoiselle,"* he replied, returning the delicate piece of china to its saucer.

"May I get you anything else? Eunice just baked caramel nut rolls. They're very delicious."

Perrin shook his head. *"Merci, non,"* he frowned, reaching for the sugar bowl.

"All right then," the waitress smiled. "I'll check back in a few minutes in case you change your mind."

Perrin's thoughts had wandered off again, but when the young woman turned to leave, the movement of her dark skirts caught his eye and brought him around again. *"Mademoiselle?"* he called out, stopping her before she had gotten very far.

"Yes?"

"'Ave you seen my cousin thees morning?"

"Not yet, Mr. Fabron. Mrs. Redington doesn't usually come to the restaurant much before noon. But I told Michael to send someone for you just as soon as he sees her. Just as you requested I do."

He glanced up at the clock on the wall opposite him. That was still another two hours from now. He frowned. "I must speak with her."

"Well, Michael said that sometimes she goes to the office first before coming here and works for an hour or so. Maybe that's what she'll do today," she smiled encouragingly.

"*Oui*," Perrin nodded weakly and watched the waitress walk away. He hadn't slept much last night. He had been too excited about being able to pay off his debt to Dominique, and if it hadn't been so late, he would have gone to see Philippe and told him the good news. Instead, he paced the floor much of the night, sleeping a few hours and getting up before anyone else at Belle Chasse. Michael was already at the front desk, and Perrin stopped long enough to tell him that he'd be going out for a couple of hours should his fiancée or his cousin be looking for him. Then he rented a carriage and drove to the docks, where he booked passage for two on board the next ship sailing to France. He was pleased to learn it would be tomorrow afternoon. He had gone to Philippe's then, and they spent the next two hours talking excitedly about their plans once they returned home again, and about the surprised look on Dominique's face when Perrin handed her the money he owed and told her he would not marry Ashlee. The longer they discussed it, the more anxious Perrin became. He wanted to get it over with, to finally be free of his domineering cousin, and he hurriedly left Philippe's to return to Belle Chasse. By the time he stood in the hotel lobby, he could have taken on the world and won. He was no longer afraid of Dominique. Then he was told she hadn't risen yet, and he was forced to spend the time waiting for her in the restaurant. Seconds stretched into minutes, minutes into hours. With each tick of the clock his courage faded and worry that something would go wrong returned him to his old self—a nervous, cowardly little man.

"Mr. Fabron, are you all right?"

Perrin jumped at the sound of his name and accidentally bumped his cup of tea, knocking it over and spilling the contents onto the white tablecloth. A string of muffled oaths, uttered in French, followed as he quickly blotted up the mess with his napkin, more annoyed with himself rather than the young waitress who had summoned him. *"Excusez-moi,"* he moaned. "I am such a *maladroit.*"

"That's all right, Mr. Fabron," she assured him as she, too, helped clean up the spot. "It was really my fault. I shouldn't have surprised you so."

"I was—how do you say—daydreaming," he murmured apologetically.

"Well, don't let it bother you," she smiled. "It happens all the time. You're not the first and you won't be the last. Now let me take care of this while you go and speak with Mrs. Redington."

"Dominique?" he exclaimed. "Has she—"

"Yes. Michael just sent word that she's in her office."

"Merci," he sighed, sounding as if the weight of the universe had been lifted from his shoulders. But he was slow to rise. What should have been a glorious moment for him turned into one he feared. Something was going to go wrong. He was sure of it. Even though Ashlee guaranteed him it couldn't. He sucked in a deep breath and headed out of the restaurant.

It wasn't until he reached the door of the office that he stopped and checked his coat pocket for the wallet he had placed there. Filled with the money he and Ashlee had stolen, its thickness gave him the confidence he needed. He rapped loudly on the door.

"Come in, Perrin," Dominique called out. "I've been expecting you."

His brow instantly dotted with perspiration and the hairs on the back of his neck stood out. Had Michael told her? Or did she possess the power to see through doors? He gulped and turned the knob, and his apprehension mounted once he saw her sitting behind Arthur's huge desk. She reminded him of the Mother Superior back in Paris where he had gone to school, and of the time he had been summoned to her office for disciplinary action. He had been just as frightened then as he was now.

"*Bonjour,* cousin." His voice shook and he forced a smile, hoping she wouldn't notice it as he closed the door behind him.

Dominique's dark eyes seemed to devour him. "It was until a few minutes ago," she answered, her tone threatening. She smiled suddenly, something that made Perrin tremble, and held out her hand toward one of the chairs near her. "Please sit down, Perrin, and tell me what it is that's brought you here."

He hurried to do as she ordered, certain his wobbly knees would buckle if he didn't, plastering a courageous smile on his thin face as he reminded himself that he was about to be free of her. "I—I—" He gulped down the knot in his throat. "I've come to pay zee money I owe."

One dark brow slanted upward. "Have you?"

"*Oui,*" he quickly replied, fumbling in his coat pocket for his wallet, too excited to realize his announcement hadn't surprised Dominique. Standing up again, he withdrew the bills from his purse and held them out to her over the desk. "It ees all here, Dominique, every *centime.*"

She stared at the thick wad of currency her cousin offered, not moving to take it from him. Puzzled by what appeared to be her disinterest in it, Perrin's gaze shifted back and forth between her and the money in his hand before he slowly lowered it to the desk top, deciding that maybe she preferred not having to touch him. He couldn't remember a single time when she had, even as children.

"And I suppose you think I should give you the deed to your mother's property in return," she said with a vague smile, although her expression was anything but friendly.

Perrin nodded hesitantly.

"That's rather presumptuous on your part, wouldn't you say," she challenged, leaning in to sweep up the stack of bills and place them in the metal box sitting on the desk next to her, "seeing as how you stole this from me to begin with." Closing the lid on the container, she stood and put it back in the safe. "Are you that stupid, Perrin, that you thought I wouldn't notice some was missing? You, more than anyone, should know how cautious I am about money." She closed the safe, locked it, and faced him again. "I suppose Ashlee was the one who got it for you. She's the only one besides Arthur and myself who can open the safe. Well, you can tell her that I said even though what you gave me was more than what she took, I consider the extra to be payment to keep me from telling her father what she's done." Her dark features hardened as she glared at him. "Now get out, Perrin, before I change my mind and have you thrown in prison like I should have done years ago."

Perrin's entire body shook uncontrollably. His whole world had just tumbled down around him, and he could see no way out. Tears of frustration and helplessness filled his eyes, and rather than have his cousin see this, he quickly turned away and staggered to the door. Even Ashlee would be angry with him now. She had given him a simple duty to perform and he had failed. If only his mother weren't depending on him, he would put a pistol to his head and end it all. Groping for the doorknob, he awkwardly pulled the portal open and stumbled out into the lobby. But he knew he would never have the courage

419

to do such a thing. He was a spineless fop and everyone knew it. What he regretted was losing Ashlee's friendship, for he was sure that once he told her what had happened, she would turn against him as it seemed the world had done.

Ashlee was awakened from a blissful sleep by the frantic pounding on her bedroom door. She sat straight up in bed, disoriented for a moment while the blurred images around her slowly took shape and settled into the familiar furnishings in her room. Combing her hair back from her face with her fingers, she tilted an ear toward the door, wondering if she might have dreamed the rude method someone employed to force her out of bed. The urgent rapping sounded again.

"Who is it?" she called sharply. If it was anyone other than her father, that person was about to receive a stern lecture on manners.

"It's me," the faint voice replied. "Perrin."

"Perrin?" She glanced at the clock, then hurriedly donned her robe and scrambled from the bed. Something was wrong or Perrin wouldn't have behaved in such a way and risked coming to her door in the full light of day where everyone would see him. If nothing else, Perrin was a gentleman. She twisted the key in the lock and yanked the door open. "What happened?"

His complexion darkened a bit once he took in her attire. He looked down at his feet, then back at the door that stood open in the foyer the way he had left it when he rushed in. "I—I— Perhaps, I should wait for you in zee courtyard."

"Oh, for heaven's sake," she remarked impatiently, grabbing his coat sleeve and pulling him into the room. "It's too late to worry about someone seeing you." She closed the door and guided him away from it, just in case

420

he was followed and the person thought to eavesdrop through it. "I assume you went to see Dominique?"

Perrin bobbed his head but wouldn't look at her.

"And?" she pressed.

He wouldn't answer as he stood there twisting a button on his coat.

"Did she take the money?"

Perrin gave her a brief look, then nodded.

"And she gave you the deed to your mother's property."

His lower lip quivered.

"Perrin," she warned, slapping his hands when he nearly tore the button from his coat. "Look at me and tell me she gave you the deed."

Tears welled in his dark eyes, and in a burst of sobs he spun away from her. "*Non*, she did not. She took ze money and put it in ze safe. She said she knew you had stolen it, and ze extra was payment to keep her quiet. She will not give me ze deed, Ashlee, and I am not free to go home. I 'ave failed, and because of it, I 'ave lost ze only true friend I 'ave ever had." He collapsed into the rocker and buried his face in his hands, crying miserably.

Ashlee felt as if she had been dealt a stunning blow by his recital. For several moments she was unable to speak or think clearly or even breathe. Last night, in Rhys's arms, she had been convinced that for once in her life she would be in command of her destiny and that by morning light her problems would be solved. Perrin would be going home to live out his days any way he chose, and she would be free to marry the father of her child. Now, because of one woman, all of that had changed. She closed her eyes and fought back the tears of anger and frustration, flirting with the idea of whether or not she had the courage to point a gun at Dominique and pull the trigger.

The sobs of another penetrated Ashlee's thoughts, and

421

she opened her eyes and glanced down at the broken man before her. Here was a lost soul who probably hadn't hurt another person in his entire life, who didn't have the nerve or the desire to cause someone pain, and his own flesh and blood had deliberately set out to destroy him. She had truly meant it when she told Rhys that she liked Perrin very much, and to hear him cry like an abandoned child twisted her insides. Falling to her knees, she slowly drew him into her arms, comforting him until the heart-wrenching sobs had ceased.

"Oh, *ma cherie*," he whispered, hugging her to him, "what shall we do?"

"Do?" she questioned softly as she stroked his hair. "There is nothing left for us to do, Perrin. She's trapped us." Her own tears threatened to spill down her cheeks as she thought of the happiness that would have been hers had she married Rhys. She blinked them away. "Dominique has left us no choice."

Only Rhys knew the real reason why he elected to walk to the telegraph office and back rather than renting a carriage. It had nothing to do with the bright, sunny afternoon, the warm breezes, or the sweet fragrances of flowers filling the air. His lighthearted mood had evolved the moment he had opened his eyes this morning and remembered the pleasant way the evening before had come to an end. The only thing that bothered him about the night past was that he hadn't actually heard Ashlee say she loved him, but her response to his caress had been enough to make him think she did. And when he mentioned getting married, she hadn't objected. The problem now, of course, would be convincing Arthur.

A frown settled on his brow when he thought of something else that had to be resolved: the matter of his suspicions concerning Dominique Redington. And all of it would have to wait a few days, including the speech he had prepared for Arthur. The telegram he received an hour ago said Major Sheffield wanted him to come to Vicksburg on business as soon as he could get away. Rhys hadn't seen Damien but once since resigning his commission more than a year ago. He admired the man very much and had attended Damien's wedding to Rachel Montgomery, a beautiful blonde Rhys had made friends with while serving in Vicksburg with Major Sheffield. They had tried to keep in touch after Rhys was reassigned to General Grant's division, but that had proved rather difficult. Grant's army never stayed in one place very long.

Rhys returned to Vicksburg after the war ended, with the purpose in mind of visiting the couple and the young daughter Rachel had given birth to nearly a year and a half before. As Rhys thought about it now, it had been the happiness he had seen in Damien's eyes that made him decide it was time he settled down as well. All he had had to do was find the right woman. He smiled to himself as he climbed the stairs to the hotel's entrance. If he had been told then that the woman he would choose to spend the rest of his life with would be a southern lady, he probably would have laughed at the possibility.

"Did you get your telegram off all right?" Michael asked as Rhys strode to the front desk.

"All taken care of," Rhys smiled.

"So when will you be leaving?"

"Just as soon as I talk to a couple of people." He glanced over his shoulder toward the restaurant as a cheer went up that sounded as though the patrons were celebrating something joyous. A curious frown flitted across his brow before he turned away dismissingly and asked, "Have you seen Arthur this afternoon?" He'd talk with him first, then find Ashlee and explain why he had to go to Vicksburg for a while.

"He's in the dining room," Michael advised hesitantly, wondering if he should warn Rhys of what was going on in there before the young man walked into the middle of it. There wasn't a person at Belle Chasse who wasn't aware of the feelings Rhys had for Arthur's daughter. He decided against telling him. It really wasn't any of his business, and there was nothing Rhys could do to change it, anyway. Leaning his weight on his elbows against the desk top, Michael sadly shook his head as he watched the handsome northerner walk into the restaurant.

Rhys's curiosity was piqued anew once he had clear view of the group crowded together in the center of the room, in the middle of which stood Ashlee, Perrin, Dominique, and Arthur. It appeared from the wine glasses everyone held and the smiles on their faces that there was cause for celebration, and Rhys's first thought was that Arthur had furthered his bid for the Senate seat. But when Ashlee lifted her glass to her lips and spotted him over the rim of it, he changed his mind. The jubilation that crackled in the air had nothing to do with her father, for the smile that was on her face did not reflect in her eyes. When Rhys's gaze shifted to the little man at her side, he sensed the festivity concerned them.

"Rhys," Arthur called out excitedly once he noticed the way his daughter's attention had been drawn away and the reason why. "Come share a glass of wine with us and help toast the happy couple."

Something stirred in the pit of Rhys's stomach, a mixture of anger, betrayal, and pain. He couldn't take his eyes off of Ashlee. A toast to the happy couple could only mean one thing, and had it not been for the many faces watching him at that moment, he would have turned around and marched from the room. Numbly, he took the glass Arthur shoved in his hand and allowed himself to be drawn into the circle of friends surrounding the woman he loved, a woman who now belonged to someone else.

424

"I'll tell you, Rhys, I could hardly believe it when Dominique told me what they'd done," Arthur rattled on, unmindful of the cold, hard look on his companion's face. "They just up and eloped this afternoon, ran off to Bertrandville. But I guess it doesn't really matter as long as they love each other. Don't you agree?"

One of the reasons Rhys had never asked Melody to marry him was because he knew he simply didn't love her . . . not in the way a man should love a woman and hope to be happy the remainder of their years together. He'd wanted the kind of marriage his father and mother had, a relationship that had lasted because of their deep feelings for one another. He had found that kind of love with Ashlee and had honestly thought she felt it too. He was wrong. But what truly hurt him more than her sudden decision to wed someone else was how easily she had deceived him. She had played him for a fool and won.

"Yes," he replied solemnly, his eyes locked on hers. "What really matters is that they love each other. Do you love him, Ashlee?"

But before she could answer him, Dominique stepped between them and hooked her arm in Rhys's, pulling him away. "Well, of course she does, Rhys. Everyone at Belle Chasse knows that. And tonight we're throwing a party in honor of the newlyweds. You will come, won't you?"

"Actually, no, Mrs. Redington," he said, setting down his glass of wine untouched. The merry chatter of those around them was grating on his nerves and he wanted to leave just as quickly as he could. "I'm afraid I won't be able to. I have to leave New Orleans for a few days, and I'll be catching the train in about an hour. In fact, that's why I came into the restaurant in the first place. I was looking for Arthur to tell him about it."

"Nothing's wrong, I hope," she said almost convincingly.

Rhys shook his head. "Just business. I should be back

day after tomorrow."

Setting her own glass on the table next to his, Dominique glanced discreetly back toward her husband to find him totally absorbed in conversation with those around him, then pulled Rhys further away from the group. "And speaking of business, Rhys," she continued, keeping her voice low, "when you return, I'd like to discuss something with you."

If he hadn't felt so drained, Rhys might have pressed her to talk about it now. As it was, all he wanted was to escape this madness. "I'll look for you as soon as I return."

"All right," she concurred with a smile.

"Now, if you'll excuse me, I have some packing to do." Graciously freeing his arm from her possessive hold, he started to walk away.

"But surely you have a moment to congratulate the bride and groom," she objected, one dark brow raised in a challenging way. "It would be the polite thing to do."

Rhys stood perfectly still for several seconds, fighting desperately to hold back the words he truly wanted to say—that being polite was the last thing he cared about doing. But over the past few weeks he had learned to recognize Dominique's sly tactics in goading someone into being careless enough to reveal something that they wished to keep secret. She was doing it now. And he was sure she had sensed his surprise and maybe even his pain over Ashlee's elopement. Not only didn't he want Dominique to know it for certain, but he didn't want her telling Ashlee of her suspicions either. Above all else, he didn't want Ashlee to think he cared.

"You're right, of course," he said dryly, then offered his arm to the woman again. "If you'll be kind enough to accompany me, I can express my good wishes to the entire family at one time."

The day Rhys Sinclair walked into Belle Chasse,

Dominique realized that he was someone special, different from the men she was used to dealing with, different from Arthur Redington, and she had mentally cursed her misfortune in not having met him sooner. If she had, she would be his wife now. He was different but he was still a man who could be manipulated, just as she had been able to do with Arthur. What she hadn't understood was Rhys's apparent attraction for her stepdaughter. He didn't strike her as the type who would get involved with a woman for any other reason than personal gain. Ashlee had nothing to offer. Before the month was out, Belle Chasse would be stripped of its last penny. Slipping her arm into his, she smiled up at him, thinking what an elegant couple they would make on her ranch in Mexico.

Rhys hated the weakness that allowed his gaze to instantly fall on Ashlee. He hated it, but he knew why. It would take a long time, if ever, for him to forget her. She had wounded him deeply with her hypocrisy, and he would carry the scars forever, never fully trusting a woman again. He thought of Melody, and his heart ached. He might not have loved the pretty little blonde, but at least she had never lied to him. She had been faithful to him even though there was no hope that he would ever ask her to be his bride. She had married someone else, he was sure, only because he had destroyed that love, and he was glad. He didn't deserve someone like her.

He was struck with a sharp twinge of jealousy when Ashlee's new husband extended his hand to shake another's in a gesture of appreciation for their kind words. He was the one who should be standing at Ashlee's side, not Perrin Fabron. He cringed inwardly, realizing that once everyone had given the couple their blessing, toasted their happiness, and then left the newlyweds alone, Perrin would take her to their room for the night. He couldn't bear the thought of another man holding her in his arms the way he had done only a short twelve hours ago. Anger flared up inside him, and he gritted his teeth to keep from bellowing his rage.

"Ashlee, Perrin," he heard Dominique say, and he quickly checked his emotions. "Mr. Sinclair would like to congratulate you."

A strange hush fell over the crowd standing around the couple, but Rhys wasn't aware of it. All he could see was the beautiful face with its pale blue eyes looking back at him, the silky glow of raven-black hair sprinkled with baby's breath and piled high in luscious curls, the delicate line of her cheek, and the full, tempting mouth with its corners turned downward. It was an image that would live in his mind for all eternity, a picture that would haunt his dreams and spill over into his waking hours to plague him. He knew then that he would never be free of her. He sucked in a deep breath and let it out slowly, silently.

"Mr. and Mrs. Fabron." He nodded to Arthur. "Mr. Redington, my congratulations." He felt his throat tighten and paused a moment to regain control before looking back at Perrin. "Sir, you are, no doubt, the luckiest man among us this day. Treasure what you have, and take special care of her." His eyes drifted to Ashlee. "She is rare, indeed." Had his pain not been so great, Rhys might have noticed the tears that glistened in Ashlee's eyes. He didn't. "And may you both find happiness," he added, bowing slightly before he turned and strode from the room.

Rhys tried to concentrate on the soothing beat of huge iron wheels roaring down the tracks as they marked off each section laid end to end, hoping somehow that the steady rhythm would have some effect on his shattered emotions. After he had left the restaurant, he went directly to his room and packed his bags. His original thought had been to take only a few of his things since he hadn't planned to be gone very long. But as he stuffed his shirts and trousers, his razor and brush into the satchel, he realized there was no longer anything for him to come back to and angrily gathered all of his belongings together, mindless of how wrinkled they'd become as he jammed them into his bags. The train wasn't scheduled to pull out for nearly an hour, but Rhys had left Belle Chasse and gone to the depot anyway. He much preferred waiting there among strangers than in a hotel where everyone was celebrating the marriage of the woman he loved.

The trip from New Orleans to Jackson, where he was to change trains and head to Vicksburg, took more than six hours. There was an hour delay while he waited for the next train, and he spent the time sitting alone in a restaurant rather than going to visit Thomas. He wasn't in the mood for explaining his depression, something his good friend would spot in a second. It was nearly midnight before he boarded the passenger car and took a seat in the back away from everyone else. The hard, narrow boards on which he sat didn't bother him until exhaustion took its toll, then he had to shift around for several minutes just to find a comfortable spot. The next thing he knew, the train whistle announced their forthcoming arrival in Vicksburg, and he woke up more tired than when he had fallen asleep.

The first pale lights of dawn had already started to streak the sky. Rhys sat thoughtfully staring out the window at the horizon, painfully reminded that somewhere in the distance Ashlee and her husband lay nestled in each other's arms. He blinked, angrily forcing his attention to focus on the rooftops of Vicksburg and the reason he had come here. Major Damien Sheffield's telegram had been brief but urgent. He hadn't said much, actually, but the simple fact that he had asked Rhys to visit him as soon as possible spoke a thousand words. Damien was still enlisted in the army, detailed for special duty concerning the war in Mexico, and Rhys could think of no reason for the major's asking him to come other than needing his help in some way.

A vague smile touched the corners of his mouth as he thought of seeing Rachel again. Although Rhys honestly doubted it was true, she had many times told him that he was the reason she had managed to survive the madness of the war and, in part, had been responsible for getting Damien and her together. Rachel and her black mammy had been forced to leave their plantation and move to Vicksburg shortly after the Union Army had invaded the city. They met at the hospital where Rhys had been assigned to help with the incoming wounded, both Yankee and Confederate. He remembered thinking that in all his years he had never seen such a beautiful woman with more courage and compassion than Rachel Montgomery. Being the pampered daughter of a huge plantation owner, she hadn't closed herself off somewhere and hidden from the atrocities of war, as everyone had expected. Instead, Rachel had volunteered to help the young men who suffered far greater than she.

Rhys had taken on the challenge of making her smile, something he was reasonably certain she didn't do very often. It hadn't been easy but he had managed, and because of it they became good friends. As the train chugged to a stop and he stood to retrieve his bags, he wondered if maybe this time she could return the favor. He certainly didn't think there was anything left in the world to smile about.

The Sheffields' plantation was about three miles out of town, which meant Rhys would have to hire the use of a horse to get there. Since he doubted the livery would be open at this hour and because he was hungry, he decided first to get a room at the hotel, then find a restaurant that would be serving breakfast. Two hours later, he was riding east out of Vicksburg.

The major had purchased Cypress Grove just before the war started and never had the opportunity to live there until peace had been restored. Abandoned all that time left it prey to looters and the destruction that always accompanied such battles. The house and all the other buildings had been destroyed, and although Damien had thought it a waste, it left him free to design the place the way his architectural blood required it be done. Rhys hadn't had the chance to visit during its reconstruction and now, as he reined his horse down the long drive lined with huge cypress trees on either side and espied the mansion at the opposite end, he felt certain the previous owners would be pleased with what Damien Sheffield had done.

The lane circled around in front of the two-story structure. Rhys was so caught up in the beauty of the mammoth colonnade across the front of the open veranda that he didn't see the young groom rushing toward him until his horse had nearly run over the poor soul. Full of apologies for his carelessness, Rhys dismounted in a somewhat embarrassed state and relaxed only after the stableboy assured him that no harm had been done. Even then, Rhys remained where he was, watching the well-dressed boy walk away with his horse.

"Good help is hard to find these days, Rhys," a voice on the porch told him. "I'd appreciate it if you wouldn't try to eliminate what little I have."

Feeling much like the fool when he recognized Damien's voice, Rhys couldn't bring himself to look at the man. "I didn't sleep well last night," he explained with a smile.

"So you thought to nap while you rode over here," Damien teased.

431

Rhys glanced up sheepishly. "Something like that."

Grinning broadly, Damien motioned his friend to the porch. "Then why don't you come inside and have some coffee. That ought to wake you up." He waited until Rhys stood beside him before adding, "I'll make sure everyone stays out of your way until you do."

The two men stared solemnly at each other for several seconds before the humor that sparkled in their eyes lifted the corners of their mouths and they burst into laughter.

"I've missed you, my friend," Damien chuckled, draping his arm around Rhys's shoulder and drawing him into the foyer.

"And I've missed you," Rhys answered. "It's been a long time."

"Too long," Damien agreed. "Have you had breakfast?"

"Yes. I ate in the hotel's restaurant."

"You didn't take a room there, did you?" Damien frowned. "Rachel will be very upset if you have. She was looking forward to having you stay with us a while."

Rhys shrugged, following Damien into the study. "Only because my train arrived so early." He sat down in the chair Damien pointed to and took the cheroot he offered. "How is Rachel, by the way?"

"Fine," Damien smiled, his dark eyes glowing with love.

"And the rest of your family?"

Striking a match, Damien lit his cheroot, then held the flame out for Rhys. "Derrick's in Baton Rouge on business and Lyndsy's with her mother having a bath. They'll be down soon."

"I can't wait to see her."

Damien raised a dark brow, his smile hidden beneath the thick mustache. "My daughter or my wife?"

"Both, actually," Rhys laughed, knowing Damien

only teased. "But I was referring to your daughter. How old is she now?"

"She was two last February."

Rhys shook his head, unable to believe he had been gone that long. "She was only a baby the last time I saw her."

"Not anymore."

"How does your brother take to living here? I imagine it was quite a change from Illinois."

"Derrick's doing all right. In fact, he's the one who really runs Cypress Grove." Damien took a puff on his cheroot and smiled. "I don't know what I would have done without him. My work for the army keeps me pretty busy. Too busy to pay much attention to the problems of a planter."

"And that's the reason for your telegram," Rhys speculated. "You need my help too."

Rising from the corner of the desk where he leaned, Damien sighed heavily and ran his fingers through his dark hair as he rounded the huge piece of furniture to sit down in the chair behind it. "Yes. I needed someone who wasn't an enlisted man and thought of you right off, someone who wouldn't raise suspicion." He was distracted for a moment when a young black girl appeared at the door. "Yes, Harmony?"

"Ya'll want your coffee here, Mr. Sheffield?"

"Yes, please," he smiled. "And tell Rachel that Rhys is here, will you?"

"Yes, sir," the maid nodded and quickly disappeared.

"I cannot get that young woman to call me by my first name," Damien admitted with a chuckle as he stared at the empty doorway. "She was one of the slaves Rachel's father owned, and even though she's free now and I pay her a salary, old customs are hard to break for her. There are times when I have to force her to take the money she's earned." He shook his head. "She's very loyal to Rachel.

In fact, most of the people who work for us were slaves for Rachel's father and came here asking to live after the war was over." He laughed good-naturedly. "After three years, I still feel like the outsider in my own home."

"Well, you are, in a way," Rhys pointed out. "You're a Yankee and always will be. Believe me, I know how you feel. It'll just take a little time, that's all."

"Mmm," Damien agreed with a nod.

"So," Rhys urged, "what's so important that a major has to stoop to asking a civilian's help?"

Harmony returned then with their coffee, poured both men a cup, and left again, closing the door behind her as Damien asked her to do. He took a sip, then settled back in his chair.

"Are you aware of what's been happening in Mexico lately?"

"Just rumors," Rhys replied. "I heard the United States is pressuring France into withdrawing their troops and that Maximilian has fled north out of Mexico City somewhere."

"Querétaro," Damien advised. "And yes, France is withdrawing her troops—reluctantly. For the past two years we've suspected that some French-Americans are aiding Napoleon's army in Mexico, but we weren't sure until just recently."

"Aiding? In what way?"

"Gold and rifles. They're being smuggled into the country by wagon train."

"Wagon train? From where? Who's behind it?"

"That's where you come in," Damien smiled. "The *where* is New Orleans. The *who*, we don't know. I saw Thomas Bryan last week when he came to Vicksburg for a political rally, and he told me you were living down there for a while. That's what gave me the idea. If the people in that city are used to your being around, they wouldn't

434

question your moves. What I was hoping was that you could do a little investigating for me . . . you know, poke around a little, see who's sympathetic toward France . . . that sort of thing. If we're lucky, you might stumble on to something."

Rhys quickly lowered his eyes. He didn't want his friend to see the anguish he was sure had twisted his face. Not just yet, anyway. He wanted to think about this first before he said anything or accused someone. He took a sip of coffee and glared into the cup. But what was there to think about? Dominique had already admitted her loyalties were with France, and it would certainly explain the shortages at Belle Chasse. But how? How was she doing it? For what gain? He knew her well enough by now to know there had to be something in it for her or she wouldn't be taking such a chance. Did Arthur know? He mentally shook off the idea. That was impossible. What man would be foolish enough to hire someone to find out why his business was failing if he already knew the reason? It would be the same as sentencing his wife to prison. Besides, Arthur loved Dominique. If he suspected what she was doing, the last thing he'd want would be to have someone else find out about it. No, Dominique was in this alone as far as anyone else in the family was concerned. Now all Rhys had to do was learn who her accomplice was.

And then what? he mused, frowning. *Tell Arthur his wife is committing treasonous acts?* Setting aside his cup, he took a puff on his cheroot, his gaze absently drifting back to the man who had silently watched him the entire time.

"Funny thing about the human expression," Damien said quietly. "It speaks louder than words."

Rhys chuckled, yielding to the truth. "It wouldn't if I knew how to control it."

"Very few men can when they're caught off guard," Damien smiled encouragingly. He fell quiet for a moment, watching his friend, then asked, "Will you tell me what you know?"

Rhys shrugged. "That's just it. I don't really know anything right now. I have my suspicions, but no proof."

"Then tell me what you suspect. Maybe we can figure something out working together."

"I'm afraid it's rather involved." Rhys's mouth twisted into a sarcastic half smile. "Or should I say, I'm rather involved."

Although Rhys and Damien hadn't known each other but a few years, Damien had come to consider the man a true friend, one he trusted and cared about a great deal. He sensed not only from what Rhys had admitted but also from the look in his eyes that the discovery Rhys had just made affected him on a personal level, one that might engage betrayal of a friend. "Would you care to elaborate?"

Snuffing out his cheroot in an ashtray, Rhys stood and crossed to a window where he idly stared outside. "It's a long story," he said after a while.

"And one that concerns someone very close to you," Damien guessed.

Rhys nodded and continued to gaze out the window. "About a month ago, I met a woman—an exceptional woman—and I think I fell in love with her right then. Her father's casino was in financial trouble, and she resorted to stealing as a way to keep the place from going bankrupt. I was one of her victims. It took me a while to find her, but once I had and she told me her reasons for stealing, I decided not to turn her in. The money she had stolen was gone anyway, so nothing would have been gained by it."

"Dear God, Rhys," Damien broke in, "you're not

trying to tell me that you think she's the one we're after, are you?"

With a smile, Rhys glanced back over his shoulder at Damien and shook his head. "No, not at all. Her loyalties are with the United States—the south—so much so that the only people she'd steal from were northerners." He looked out the window again. "It's her stepmother that I suspect."

"Why?" Damien asked quietly, knowing now the cause of his friend's distress.

"Her name is Dominique Redington—Fabron before she married Arthur a little over two years ago. She came to New Orleans from Paris and admitted to me that she still considers France her homeland."

"There must be more. That's hardly enough to accuse her of something like this."

"Oh, there is," Rhys admitted, sighing heavily as he returned to his chair and sat down. "Arthur Redington owns a hotel, restaurant, and casino called Belle Chasse. Perhaps you've heard of it." He waited for Damien's nod, then continued. "The casino has been losing money for some time now, something everyone blamed on the war. After talking with Arthur and playing a little poker, I didn't agree and I told him so. There were just too many paying customers for it not to turn a profit. So I took a job as a dealer—at Arthur's suggestion—to enable myself to do some snooping around without anyone getting suspicious."

"And what did you find?"

Rhys shook his head. "Nothing much, really. I just have a gut instinct, that's all."

"About Arthur's wife."

"Uh-huh. I got the chance to look over their books and everything checked out—too perfectly, if you ask me. So I decided to try a different approach. I began dropping subtle hints Dominique's way about how I'm the kind of man who cares nothing about ethics, only making money. Before I left yesterday afternoon she told me that she'd like to discuss some business with me when I return. I could be wrong about her, Damien. But after hearing what you had to say, there's just too many coincidences."

Damien was thoughtfully quiet for several minutes as he took the last puff on his cheroot before snuffing it out. Rising, he began to stroll aimlessly about the room, his handsome features twisted in consideration. Finally, he turned to face his friend. "Is there any chance Arthur Redington is involved? You never mentioned it."

"No, I don't think so. For one, he's very tied up in politics. But more than that, it was really his idea about my finding the cause for his casino's shortages. If he knew what his wife was doing or was helping her achieve it, he certainly wouldn't point someone in that direction. He loves her very much, and that's what makes my part in this difficult. For his sake, I hope I'm wrong."

"And for your sake, I hope so too," Damien comforted.

Rhys nodded his appreciation and took a breath to say more when the sound of tiny feet running outside in the foyer drew both men's attention. Knowing that they had to belong to Lyndsy, Damien smiled brightly and hurried to open the door.

"Da-da!" the little child exclaimed as she raced into her father's opened arms.

"Good morning, sweetheart," he beamed, giving her a kiss on the forehead. "Did you have your bath?"

Round dark brown eyes grew larger when Lyndsy spotted the stranger standing in her father's study, and the smile vanished from her face as she stared fearfully at Rhys.

"You don't have to be afraid of him, Lyndsy," Damien

laughed. "He's a friend of mine. Can you say hello to Rhys?"

Lyndsy stubbornly shook her head and buried her face in her father's neck, bringing laughter from both Damien and Rhys.

"I think I'm losing my touch," Rhys chuckled.

"Oh, don't let it bother you. She's this way to everyone she sees for the first time. When you're ready to leave, she'll be begging to go along." He patted the young girl's head, then asked, "Where's your mother?"

A tiny finger pointed back out to the foyer just as Rachel called out their daughter's name.

"She's with us, Rachel," Damien answered, motioning for Rhys to follow as he stepped into the hall, the little girl perched on one hip.

"Lyndsy," Rachel scolded with a soft smile, "I told you that you had to wait for Daddy. He's busy."

"I think we were just about through," he objected, holding out his other arm toward his wife. Pulling her close, he kissed the corner of her mouth, then turned them all toward Rhys. "Well, what do you think? Do I have the two most beautiful women in the world right here beside me?"

There had been many times during those months before Rachel admitted she loved her Yankee major that Rhys had wished they were more than just friends. Seeing her now, dressed in soft pink satin, her lush blond hair pulled back from her oval face with a ribbon and falling in thick curls over her shoulders, reminded him why. She would make any man proud as she obviously did her husband, and Rhys was struck with a twinge of envy for the happiness they had found together. Little Lyndsy was the proof of their love.

"Yes," he smiled. "I think you do."

Suddenly embarrassed by their flattery, Rachel laughed and pushed away from her husband. "I've been cursed with the two biggest liars in the state," she rallied, eyeing them both before she admitted, "but it's nice to hear." Holding out her arms, she waited for Rhys to step forward, then drew him into her embrace. "We've missed you, Rhys. Perhaps I more than my husband."

Laughing, Rhys teased, "Are you saying there's still hope for me after all?"

"About as much hope as there is that it will snow next week," Damien commented dryly, although his green eyes sparkled with humor.

"An attitude like that can get you in trouble, friend," Rhys bantered. "Take this little lady for granted, and someone like me will start to move in."

"Well, I'm not too worried about you," he returned grinning. "You already told me you were in love."

"Really?" Rachel asked excitedly. Tucking her arm in his, she guided her companion through the hall toward the back of the house and the gardens outside, her husband and daughter following closely behind. "Let's sit in the gazebo and you can tell me all about her."

For the next hour the three friends sat in the summerhouse watching Lyndsy play while they sipped lemonade, talking of the days gone by, what each had been doing since the war ended, and of Rhys's love for a woman who had married someone else. It helped for Rhys to talk of it with people who cared, and although neither of them could do anything to change it, their comforting words relaxed him and made him feel that perhaps the world hadn't come to an end because he had lost the woman he loved. He admitted that it would be painful for him to return to Belle Chasse knowing that Ashlee would be there with her husband. Maybe it sounded strange to hear him say it, but after talking it over with them, he decided that going back would be his wedding present to Ashlee. If her stepmother were, indeed, aiding France in its bid for Mexico, Rhys would expose her, freeing Ashlee of the deceitful woman who had made her life miserable for the past two years. Then, in one final gesture of love, he would finance her father's quest for the Senate, hopefully winning the man's forgiveness for his part in unmasking Dominique for what she truly was. This would be his gift to Ashlee before he left Belle Chasse, intending never to return.

Chapter Sixteen

The newlyweds had been given the biggest suite of rooms Belle Chasse had to offer—and the guarantee they wouldn't be disturbed the entire night. Ashlee and Perrin had excused themselves from the celebration, which seemed would continue until dawn, and the huge crowd of well-wishers that kept pouring into the place sometime around midnight. Neither of them felt much like rejoicing. What they had done was a mockery to the sanctity of marriage, and once the truth was known, Arthur Redington would carry the shame of it—no matter how noble their cause.

Being alone with a woman in his room had been something Perrin had never experienced before, and it unnerved him. Especially since everyone who had watched them ascend the stairs on their way to their chambers had cheered him on as they would some victorious gladiator bowing before his emperor. The only thing that helped soothe his troubled spirits was the fact that Ashlee hardly seemed aware of his presence. If he was capable of loving a woman, then Perrin loved Ashlee. And he envied her courage. But none of that made it any easier for him, and within minutes he had grown restless. He couldn't face the aspect of spending the entire night alone with a woman, even though everyone considered her as his bride.

Whether Ashlee sensed Perrin's uneasiness or not, it had been her suggestion that, once the hotel quieted for the night and the possibility of their being seen was minimal, the two of them would appear to be going for a stroll in the courtyard. Then, when they were sure no one watched, Perrin would slip through the iron gate that led out into the alley, and from there he would be free to go to Philippe for the night. Perrin had wanted to believe that she was doing it for him, but he knew that wasn't true. He had seen the change come over her the minute Rhys Sinclair walked into the restaurant that afternoon and could only assume she preferred to be alone. He had wanted to say something that would comfort her. He couldn't. The Yankee's absence would contradict any hopeful statement he might have. Although he honestly knew his cousin would have found someone else for Ashlee to marry, Perrin couldn't help blaming himself for the seemingly impossible situation in which he had placed his one and only true friend. Thus, he chose to keep silent and allow Ashlee her time to grieve.

An early morning shower had begun by the time Perrin started back to the hotel, and while it dampened him to the bone, it also gave him the security that few if any people would be walking the streets—especially at this hour. The dismal gray sky did little to lighten his mood, and the closer he got to Belle Chasse, the more depressed he became. He was such a weak-willed person that he hated himself for it, even though he knew he lacked the spirit to change. He paused beside the gate at the edge of the courtyard, let out a nervous sigh when he saw no one there, then dashed across the grounds toward the rose trellis anchored to the floor of the balcony outside his room. It seemed dangerously high, but it was the only alternative to his taking the inside stairs and running the

444

risk of being seen by the desk clerk. Mumbling a prayer, he grabbed hold of the delicate latticework and pulled himself up. The feat took only a minute or two, but to Perrin it seemed the world had stopped moving while everyone in it held their breaths. Finally, when he had climbed over the railing and stood on the solid wood flooring of the balcony, he was able to calm his pounding heart and ease the pain in his chest. Now, all he hoped for was that Ashlee had had the foresight to leave the French doors of their sitting room unlocked. Hurriedly tiptoeing to his destination, he grabbed the knob and twisted, smiling happily when it turned in his hand.

"Good morning, Perrin," a voice in the darkness said once he had stepped inside.

Not having expected to find Ashlee awake, hearing her speak startled him to such a degree that he jumped sideways, hit his shoulder against the door, and slammed it shut with a loud bang.

"*Mon Dieu,* Ashlee," he groaned. "Don't do that to me. You nearly scared ze wits out of me."

"I'm sorry," she apologized, moving into the gray light filtering into the room. "Was Philippe glad to see you?"

"Surprised is ze better word," he said, slipping out of his wet jacket. "He had already heard about ze wedding."

"Hasn't everyone?" she said sarcastically, plopping down in a chair.

Perrin noticed for the first time that she was still wearing the dress she had on when he had left her, rather than a nightgown and robe. Moving to the lamp, he lit it, then faced her again. "Have you not been to bed, *mon amie?*"

"Couldn't sleep," she muttered, resting her chin on her fist while she absently stared out at the rain dripping off the rooftop.

A sudden chill shook his body, but Perrin ignored it. "Oh, Ashlee," he moaned sympathetically, kneeling down beside her chair. "I never should have left you alone."

"Why?" she laughed, looking at him. "Do you think your being here would have made a difference?" Tears sprang to her eyes and she quickly turned her head away. "I could be in a crowded room right now, Perrin, and I'd still be alone." She bit her lower lip. "I'll always be alone. Without Rhys—" A sob choked off her words. "Oh, Perrin, he didn't give me a chance to explain. He left before I could."

"Then you must go to him," Perrin firmly told her.

She bolted from her chair. "I don't know where he went! No one knows. He packed all his things and left. He's never coming back. Never! He hates me and I'll never see him again."

"You're wrong," he argued. "He will come back."

"Why should he?" Tears streaming down her face, she began to pace the floor like a wild animal trapped in a cage. "He said he wanted to marry me, and the very next morning he learns I married someone else. What is he supposed to think? That I—that we only forged the marriage papers to give us some time to look for the deed to your mother's property?"

"But we did, Ashlee," he said, coming to his feet.

"He doesn't know that," she sobbed. "He left before I could tell him."

"Because he hurts, *ma cherie*," Perrin assured her. "He will come."

"And how long do I wait?" she snapped, losing all control. "A month? Two? Or shall I wait until the baby's—" Her hand flew to her mouth when she realized she had let her secret slip out. And the surprised look on his face that turned to pity told her that he had understood. Whirling, she raced for the door.

"Ashlee, wait!" he called after her, but she had already fled out into the corridor and down the hall by the time

Perrin had fully recovered enough to try and stop her. He stumbled to a halt just outside the door, muttering an oath. Because of his stupidity and lack of character, a good friend suffered. Well, not anymore. He glanced down at his wet clothes. He'd change first, then find John Hardin. Together they would figure out what could be done.

Ashlee didn't stop running until she suddenly found herself at the back door of the theater. Odd how she always came to Priscilla whenever she needed comforting. She touched the knob and pulled the door open. But she doubted the woman could help this time. Making her way through the darkened area backstage, she had just about decided to turn around and forget about telling Priscilla anything, when the pretty blonde surprisingly appeared before her as if she had known Ashlee was coming to see her. They both came to an abrupt halt, staring at each other for several seconds.

"Ashlee?" Priscilla questioned. "What are you doing here at this hour?"

Dropping her head, she tried to wipe the tears from her face without Priscilla noticing. "I needed to talk with someone. You're the only one who ever listens." She glanced up pleadingly. "Please?"

Smiling, Priscilla held out a hand and said, "Have I ever denied you?"

Ashlee shrugged one shoulder. "No."

"Then come. I've made some tea. We'll drink it while you talk and I listen."

Ashlee hesitated, then took Priscilla's hand. It felt so wonderful to know that no matter what she did, this woman would stand beside her. It seemed to Ashlee that Priscilla loved her with that special kind of attachment a mother feels for her daughter. Maybe Veronica had walked out of Ashlee's life, but God sent Priscilla to take her place, and she thanked Him with all her heart.

"Have you heard the news?" Ashlee asked, watching Priscilla pour tea into two cups.

Setting aside the pot, Priscilla handed one cup and saucer to her friend, then sat down in the chair next to her. "News?" she repeated. "Probably not. I wasn't feeling well last night and went to bed early." She took a sip of tea, watching Ashlee over the rim of her cup. "So why don't you tell me."

Ashlee lowered her eyes. "If you'll promise to hear the entire story before you say a word."

"Why is it," Priscilla sighed, shaking her head, "that I get the feeling I'm not going to like this?"

Ashlee glanced up sheepishly and bobbed one shoulder. "Because, as usual, I've done something stupid."

"I'm used to that," Priscilla responded mockingly. "It's the degree that's always a surprise." She set her cup on the table and folded her hands in her lap. "I'm ready. Tell me what new stupid thing you've done, and I'll try not to say a word. And when you're finished, we'll try to figure out how to undo it."

Ashlee knew that she deserved every unkind word Priscilla might throw at her and that maybe the actress would change her mind about helping once she'd heard it all. But that was a chance Ashlee had to take. Sucking in a deep breath, she began relating every detail leading up to her sudden appearance a few minutes ago. The only change in Priscilla's expression came when Ashlee told her that she was carrying Rhys's child. Her initial look of surprise quickly softened into what Ashlee thought might be pleasure.

"So, you see," she continued on when Priscilla just sat there staring off into space, "even if Perrin and I can find the deed which would free him to go home, that only solves half my problems. I'll still be very much pregnant and very much single."

"How did you manage to get a hold of marriage

documents?" Priscilla asked suddenly.

Ashlee blinked, surprised by the question. "The same way I usually get a hold of anything I need. I stole them. Why?"

Blue eyes twinkled with humor. "Rather ingenious, even though it did have some repercussions. I don't think I would have thought of that. Where's Perrin now?"

"I left him in our room." Ashlee wasn't sure, but it seemed as if Priscilla found the whole situation amusing. "Priscilla, you realize how serious this is, don't you?"

"Oh, yes. Serious, but not hopeless." She pushed herself up from the chair. "And first things first. It's too early for Dominique to be in the office, isn't it?"

"Yes," Ashlee said, slowly coming to her feet.

"All right, then. Number one on our priority is to find that deed. We're going to search that entire office until we have, and once we've got it in our hands, we'll give it to Perrin and send him and his companion back to Paris. This afternoon, if it's possible." Priscilla's tired, crippled body seemed to take on new life with the thought of doing something as adventurous as duping Dominique Redington. She reached out, took Ashlee's hand, and pulled her toward the door. "As for your Mr. Sinclair, I'm afraid I have to agree with Perrin. He'll be back. And my guess is it won't be very long."

"I wish I were as sure as you," Ashlee sadly admitted.

"Well, if I'm wrong, darlin', we'll do the next best thing," she grinned brightly, devilishly.

"What's that?" Ashlee frowned, leery.

"We'll send John Hardin after him."

The woman's smile was infectious, and before Ashlee realized it she had burst into laughter, imagining the sight of Rhys bound and gagged and thrown over John's horse. Then she thought of her father, and the vision faded as did her merriment. "What about Papa?"

"Oh, he'll come around. Especially after you tell him

why you and Perrin faked the marriage."

"You mean I should tell him?" Ashlee gasped.

"You're damn right, honey," Priscilla rallied. "It's about time he learned what kind of sneak that woman is."

"It'll hurt him."

Priscilla shrugged indifferently. "Won't be the first time. And maybe—just maybe—he'll realize he brings on most of it himself." She frowned and pushed Ashlee toward the door. "Now, let's get going. We haven't got all day, you know."

The next twenty minutes found them thoroughly searching every drawer, shelf, and nook they came across in the office, still finding nothing. Disheartened but not about to give up, Priscilla stood in the center of the room trying to decide where she would hide something she didn't want anyone to find. She remembered a play she had been in where the heroine had hidden a letter from her lover inside a book, then placed the book on a shelf with dozens of others. It worked for her, Priscilla decided, staring at the bookcase; maybe it had worked for Dominique as well. Relaying her idea to Ashlee, the two women prepared to thumb through all the volumes before them, positive that this time they'd be successful.

Starting at opposite ends, they methodically removed one book at a time, flipped through its pages, then returned it to its place, thus making sure none were skipped over. It was a nerve-racking job, for it seemed Arthur Redington owned every book that was ever published. But neither Priscilla nor Ashlee even considered giving up. Their mission was too important.

"Anything yet?" Priscilla asked, plucking a leather-bound edition from the shelf.

"No," Ashlee sighed, a sense of panic starting to build as she returned one book and picked out another. "But it's got to be here. It just has to."

"Don't worry, Ashlee. If we don't find it here, we can

always pay Dominique a visit. As vain as she is, she'd much sooner tell us where she's hidden it rather than sport a black eye."

Shocked by such a suggestion, Ashlee gaped at her friend, positive she didn't really mean it until it suddenly dawned on her that Priscilla would beg for the chance. "You'd really do it, wouldn't you?"

An impish smile kinked Priscilla's lips. "Uh-huh," she admitted, "and I'd love doing it." She glanced over at Ashlee. "I'd even let you help . . . if you wanted to."

Fighting back laughter, Ashlee concentrated on the task at hand. "No wonder Papa forbids me to be with you. At times, you are a bad influence," she snickered, failing to see the sad look that came over Priscilla's face. She picked out another book and started leafing through it, a curious frown settling on her brow when it seemed to be some sort of ledger. The back pages were empty, while those in front and halfway through had dated entries. The sick feeling that began to wash over her wasn't because of the staggering amount accumulated over the months, but simply because she had recognized the handwriting. It belonged to Dominique. Stepping back, she stared up at the bookcase and the location of where the ledger had been, remembering the last time she had held this book in her hand. It had been three nights ago while she visited her father's office to borrow the money she and Perrin needed for the poker game. This was the book she had accidentally knocked on the floor, the one that had been laying on the desk, the one Dominique used to record the true income of the casino.

"Ashlee, what's wrong?" Priscilla asked, having seen the young woman's strange reaction. "Did you find the deed?"

"No," Ashlee replied in hardly more than a whisper. "It's something I wish I hadn't found." She held out the book. "Look for yourself and see what you think."

"It's a ledger," Priscilla observed after she had carefully examined several pages. "What was it doing in the bookcase? I would think your father would keep it in the safe or at least lock it up in one of the desk drawers."

"Papa doesn't know about it." There was pain in her voice.

"What do you mean?" Priscilla gasped, for she could make no sense of it.

"What she means, dear Priscilla," a voice in the doorway said as the two women spun around to find Dominique standing in the framework, a derringer clutched in her hand and pointing at them, "is that the book you hold is a second set of records, the true account of the casino's earnings." She stepped further into the room and closed the door behind her, one dark brow raised appreciatively. "It's been in the bookcase now for nearly two years, and no one's ever thought to look for it there. You're smarter than I gave you credit, Ashlee."

"Save your praise, Dominique," Ashlee sneered. "I was looking for the deed you refused to give back to Perrin. Had I suspected what you were doing, I wouldn't have waited this long to get my hands on the proof." She took the ledger from Priscilla and shook it at her stepmother. "What have you been doing with Papa's money?"

"It was just as much my money as it was his," she raged. "I earned it."

"Earned it? Doing what? Lying to him?"

The gun leveled at her victims, Dominique crossed to the desk and took a key out of her pocket to unlock one of the drawers. "Yes, lying to him," she admitted, her dark eyes snapping with hatred. "I lied every time I said I loved him, and the fool was too blind to see it."

From the day this woman walked into their lives Ashlee had prayed for a way to make her father truly see what kind of a person she was. But not this way. She had

452

wanted her father to make the decision, not have it forced on him. He loved her, and finding out that their entire marriage had been based on deceit would surely break his heart. She blinked back the tears that filled her eyes and slid her hand into Priscilla's. Why couldn't her father have fallen in love with someone like this sweet lady? Why couldn't he have fallen in love with Priscilla? Dominique had ruined hers and Perrin's futures, and now she was about to shatter the life of a man who meant everything to Ashlee. Why? What drove her?

"Tell me your reasons," she asked softly, too drained of emotions to even sound bitter or angry.

Lifting a metal box, which Ashlee assumed was filled with money, from one of the desk drawers, Dominique glanced up, sneering. "For power. And wealth. I was tired of living my entire life in poverty, and I came here to New Orleans to change that."

"But why steal? You got all that the day you married Papa. And when he's elected to the Senate—"

"You little fool," Dominique laughed wickedly. "Do you honestly think this is my idea of power and wealth?" Her hand swept out to encompass the room. "I'm talking about *real* power and the kind of wealth being a countess brings." She picked up the box and came to the center of the room.

"A countess? If you wanted to be a countess, then why did you marry my father?" Ashlee demanded.

"Let me guess," Priscilla cut in, a strange smile curling her lips. "The only way Dominique would ever become a countess was if she bought the title." She raised questioning brows at the woman and when Dominique nodded in response, Priscilla continued. "That's where your father came in, Ashlee. He had the money she needed. Everything went along smoothly for a while, until you started causing trouble. So she blackmailed her cousin into marrying you and taking you back to France to live, just to get you out of the way. But what puzzles me," she went on, looking at Dominique again, "is how you tricked him into marrying you. Other than being a little romantic at times, he's basically a good judge of character. He should have spotted you right off."

"The way he did you?" Dominique jeered.

Frowning, Ashlee looked at the woman at her side. "What does she mean?"

Priscilla's face paled, and she quickly lowered her eyes. "I don't know," she answered after a moment's hesitation.

"Oh, yes you do," Dominique smiled acidly. "Arthur told me all about you. And you know what I think? I think that even though he pretends to hate you, deep down inside somewhere he still cares. Perhaps, he even still loves you."

"Shut up," Priscilla warned through clenched teeth when Ashlee stepped away from her, a pained expression on her young face and the look of understanding in her eyes.

"What is she talking about, Priscilla?" Ashlee challenged, unshed tears tightening her throat.

"Go on, Priscilla. Tell her," Dominique dared. "It's time she stopped living in a dreamworld anyway. Tell her who you really are, and then try to get her to understand why you walked out on your husband and little girl. Try and convince her that you're no different than me, that all you ever wanted was something Arthur couldn't give you."

Ashlee blinked and a tear ran down her cheek. Suddenly, everything made sense to her: the strange remarks Priscilla had made in defense of Ashlee's mother, even though the woman had claimed to have only met her once; the way she defended Arthur's feelings toward his first wife; why this woman understood Ashlee so completely. This wasn't Priscilla Krayer

454

standing before her. This was Veronica Darnell, Ashlee's mother.

For years Veronica had guarded her secret, holding back when she really wanted to tell Ashlee the truth, beg her forgiveness, and explain what it was that drove her away from New Orleans. She had tried to come back into her daughter's life, but Arthur wouldn't allow it. His reasons, at the time, were logical. So Veronica had done the next best thing: taken on another identity and vowed to Arthur never to reveal the truth about herself to Ashlee. But it never lessened her love for her daughter. And now, with a few spiteful words from a woman who cared nothing for the Redington family, Veronica feared that even that would be taken from her. Ashlee would never understand, and the love the girl had had for her mother would turn to hatred.

"You bitch," Veronica snarled, slowly advancing on Dominique. "You conniving, heartless bitch."

"Stay where you are!" Dominique ordered, the gun pointed and ready to fire.

"I should have put a stop to you the minute you strutted into Belle Chasse two years ago." She continued to advance. "I should have stood up to Arthur. I should have done something then to spare him the pain your deceit will bring him."

"I'll shoot if you take one more step—"

The warning fell on deaf ears. Veronica Darnell wasn't listening. In a blind rage, she threw herself at the woman just as a shot rang out. Ashlee screamed as she witnessed her mother's body lurch when the bullet struck, then fall to the floor, eyes closed, a bright red, splattering of blood staining the bodice of her dress.

"Oh my God," Ashlee shrieked, rushing to kneel at the unconscious woman's side. "Mama!"

This hadn't been what Dominique planned when she returned to her room to get her gun after seeing Veronica and Ashlee go into the office. She had sensed trouble. Arthur's first wife never stepped foot on Belle Chasse property. Yet she never dreamed they were looking for the evidence that would convict her of treason. She had wanted to bleed the casino of its profits a little longer before she joined LaFoe and sailed for Mexico. But that had all changed now. She had to leave and right away. Tucking the metal box under her arm, she quickly cocked the second hammer of her derringer when the office door swung open and Michael rushed in.

"What—" he began, pulling up short the instant he saw the gun pointed at him. Dominique waved him away from the exit and he obeyed, stunned and totally confused by what he observed. Had Arthur's wife gone mad?

Bending slightly, Dominique grabbed Ashlee by her hair and hauled her to her feet, jamming the muzzle into the girl's neck just below one ear. "I'll kill her," she hissed at Michael, shoving her captive toward the door. "One move out of you and she's dead."

Michael remained perfectly still, afraid to even breathe lest she mistake it for aggression on his part, and watched the pair back through the opening into the lobby. A second later the door slammed shut and the key turned in the lock. Only then did he move, rushing to the woman lying on the floor.

Perrin and John were coming through the courtyard, having gone to the theater looking for Ashlee, when they heard the explosion of gunfire. Both men stopped abruptly, each suddenly dreading what it might mean. Especially when the sound came from the direction of Arthur's office. For John, it seemed like an eternity before he could get his feet to react. He bolted off across the grounds then, not bothering to wait for his companion. By the time he entered the lobby and turned toward the office, others, who had heard the disturbance, were coming from all directions to see what had happened and to offer help if it was needed.

"Over here, John," Hank Newell called once he saw him. "It's Michael. He's locked in Mr. Redington's office. Have you got the key?"

"To hell with keys," John growled, waving Hank aside as he neared the door. Clasping his wrist in one hand, he lowered his shoulder, turned to one side, and threw his weight against the wooden barrier. It creaked and some of the framework started to split, but the door remained sealed.

"Wait, John," Hank urged, moving in alongside of him. "We'll do it together." Taking a similar stance as John, Hank nodded when he was ready, and the two men hurled themselves forward with the force of two raging bulls, cracking the casting trim and jamb, and tearing the door from its hinges to send it crashing to the floor. After one look at Michael sitting in the middle of the room with Veronica held in his arms, Hank quickly volunteered to go for the doctor, spinning around and nearly colliding with Arthur as he stormed into the room.

"What the hell is—" Arthur stumbled to a stop, his gaze quickly taking in the scene before him, the concern and anger that had distorted his face changing instantly to one of horror and pain. "Veronica," he breathed, coming forward to fall on his knees beside her. "My God, what's happened to you?" His eyes drifted worriedly from her sleeping face to the grave wound she had sustained, wanting very much to take her in his arms, yet afraid to touch her. For some odd reason he was blaming himself for this. If he hadn't closed her out of his life and set himself apart from her, he could have protected her from this. His self-pity turned to rage. "Who did this?" he demanded. When no one answered, he looked up at the man who held her. "Michael, who did this?"

Almost pleadingly, Michael glanced up at John as if

wishing he were the one who had to tell this man that his wife had suddenly seemed to lose a grip on reality, that from what Michael could figure out, Dominique had shot the pretty actress, kidnapped Arthur's daughter at gunpoint, and fled Belle Chasse. His thoughts instantly changed direction. He'd nearly forgotten about Ashlee. Ignoring his employer's question and the angry look on Arthur's face, he turned his appeal to John. "Ashlee's been kidnapped."

"What?" both John and Arthur exclaimed at the same time.

"I'll explain later. Right now you've got to stop them."

"Who's got her and which way did they go?" John asked backing toward the door.

Michael gulped, knowing Arthur would never believe him. "Dominique, and I can't tell you where they went because she's the one who locked me in here."

John didn't have to be told the reasons. He knew. Rhys's suspicions about the woman were obviously true. He spun around, spotted Perrin among the crowd that had filed in behind him, and raced from the room once he had told the young man to help Michael with Miss Krayer.

"That's a lie," Arthur growled. "What possible motive would she have? She's my wife, for God's sake, and Ashlee's her stepdaughter!"

"I don't know, Mr. Redington," Michael sadly admitted. "All I can tell you is what I saw. I heard a shot, came running in, and found Mrs. Redington standing over Miss Krayer with a gun in her hand. When she saw me, she grabbed your daughter, held the gun to Miss Redington's head, and left, locking me in here."

"I think I can explain," Perrin told the two, stepping forward. "But first we should take *Mademoiselle* Krayer to a comfortable place where ze doctor can attend her."

He motioned for two of the men standing behind him

to come forward, waiting until after they had gently carried Veronica from the office before he ushered everyone else from the room. What he had to say wasn't meant for anyone other than Arthur to hear. Taking a deep breath and wondering if he would have the courage to tell every detail to the man, he faced Arthur again and froze, a curious frown on his brow as he watched him bend down and retrieve a book from the floor. Several long minutes followed while Arthur examined the pages. From the expression on the man's face, Perrin knew Arthur didn't like what he saw.

"What ees it, *Monsieur* Redington?" he questioned softly, watching Arthur round the desk and sit in the chair behind it.

Tired, pain-filled eyes looked up at Perrin as Arthur tossed the book down on the desk. "A motive, Perrin."

"A motive?" he repeated, stepping close enough to flip open the first page and scan the entires. "What ees thees?"

"It's the true earnings of my casino, a set of records my wife was hiding from me." Arthur watched Perrin's face for some sort of reaction, but when he just stood there silently, he asked, "This doesn't surprise you, does it? Why not?"

Perrin didn't want to tell him. "It ees a long story, *Monsieur*."

"Young man," Arthur growled, leaning forward on the desk, "my life is falling apart right now, and you have all the answers. I want to hear them, and I want to know why you've kept them a secret from me."

"He only learned the whole truth a few minutes ago," John said from the doorway, "like the rest of us did."

Arthur bolted to his feet. "Did you find them? Did you find Ashlee?"

John slowly shook his head. "But I've organized a search party and given them orders to tear this town

459

apart. They'll find her. I promise you that." He stepped further into the room. "How's Miss Krayer?"

Arthur collapsed back in the chair. "She was taken upstairs to a private room. She's still alive, but just barely." His head dropped forward and he cradled his brow in his hands. "Why? Why did she do it?"

"That part of it I can't answer," John said, going to the buffet and pouring Arthur a glass of whiskey. Coming to the desk, he handed the drink to the man.

"But you knew about it?"

"Not until Rhys pointed out the possibility."

Arthur's head shot up. "Rhys?"

Drawing in a chair, John sat down and motioned for Perrin to do the same. "Yes. Rhys suspected Dominique was stealing from you a long time ago. He just couldn't prove it, nor could he explain why."

"How did he get involved?"

A vague, mocking smile lifted the corner of his mouth. "Quite by accident, I'm afraid," he sighed and settled in his chair to recite the entire story from beginning to end, starting with the robberies on the steamboats, all the way to Ashlee and Perrin's phony marriage and the fact that Ashlee now carried Rhys's baby. When he had finished, he rose and refilled Arthur's empty glass, then poured himself and Perrin a drink.

"She's in love with him," John added after a while. "And she told Perrin that Rhys had asked her to marry him."

The glass trembled in Arthur's hand as he stared at it, tears filling his eyes. Finally, after a long silence, he shook his head. "This is all my doing."

"How can you say that?" John argued. "How could you have possibly known about Dominique? None of us here liked her, but we never suspected her of stealing. If anything, she appeared to be almost possessive about money."

460

Arthur snorted derisively, lifted the glass to his lips, and downed the entire shot of whiskey in one gulp, enjoying the way it burned and seemed to set his stomach on fire. "Because I married her out of spite."

"Spite?" John echoed, surprised. "To who?"

"Oh, I didn't know it at the time," he jeered. "I thought I really loved her because I thought she loved me. I married her to prove to Veronica that I was worthy of marrying, to show her that a woman *could* fall in love with me."

Confused, John glanced over at Perrin for help, but he merely shook his head and shrugged. "Arthur, you're not making any sense. How would Veronica know that?"

A strange smile came over his face, his blue eyes sparkling with tears. "Well, since everyone's confessing, I guess it's time I did, too. That lady who's lying upstairs right now struggling for her life, the one who probably threw herself in front of Dominique's gun to protect my daughter, isn't Priscilla Krayer. Her real name is Veronica Darnell, my first wife. And before you get the wrong idea and think that maybe I hadn't recognized her after all this time, I'll tell you that I did. I knew who she was the minute she walked back into my life eight years ago."

"And you never told Ashlee?" John could hardly believe his friend would do such a deplorable thing.

Arthur glanced up sheepishly and shook his head. "We're a fine bunch, aren't we, John? A bunch of misfits held together by the love of one girl." He blinked and a tear trickled down his cheek. "Find her, John. Find her so that I can get down on my knees to her and beg for forgiveness."

In the darkness of her prison, Ashlee sat perfectly still, her knees drawn up to her chest, her bound wrists encircling them. So many thoughts crowded her mind that she was too stunned to give precedence to any of them nor did she have the energy to weep. In a matter of seconds, she had found her mother and lost her, for Priscilla had surely died of the wound inflicted upon her by the evil woman who held Ashlee captive. She was torn between loving and hating her father for the secret he had kept all these years. But more than anything else, she knew she was going to die before she could explain to Rhys. Ashlee had heard Dominique and Jourdain LaFoe discussing the French ship that would be leaving port late tomorrow afternoon and their plans to be on board, positive that when they left the bakery shoppe, they would leave her bound and gagged and hidden in the secret room below the floor, once used by runaway slaves. LaFoe had wanted to kill her right then, the moment Dominique dragged her into the shoppe, but her stepmother had stopped him. They needed a hostage, she had said, in case someone stumbled upon her hiding place before their ship was ready to sail. Ashlee realized then how determined and cruel and unfeeling this woman was. How could her father have possibly fallen in love with someone like her?

The only time Ashlee saw light while imprisoned in the tiny space below the bakery shoppe floor was when LaFoe brought her something to eat: once at noon, she guessed, and then again at suppertime. Her meals consisted of a small loaf of hard-crusted bread and a jar of water to drink, and even then the man seemed reluctant to give her anything at all. He considered her a nuisance while Dominique claimed her stepdaughter was a necessity, and Ashlee thought how unimportant a human life was to either of them.

The last time LaFoe paid her a visit was when he came to retie her arms in back of her, stuff a rag in her mouth, and bind her ankles. Ashlee assumed it was night and that neither of them would be guarding the entrance to her cell for a while. If she were to escape, it would have to be now. But after an hour of twisting and wiggling and awkwardly searching the darkness for a sharp object with which to cut the ropes, she collapsed to the dirt floor in exhaustion, her last thought being of Rhys and the baby she would never hold in her arms.

Chapter Seventeen

The shrill, piercing scream of the train whistle exploded in the quiet air, scattering birds from their lofty treetop perches surrounding the depot to flutter off in a wild frenzy while the porter marched up and down the platform heralding all passengers to board. With luggage in hand, Rhys paused near the steps of the car in which he would ride, turning back to shake Damien's hand, ruffle Lyndsy's hair, and kiss Rachel affectionately on the cheek. His visit with them had made him feel a lot better than when he first arrived the day before, but seeing them stand there as a family brought back to mind the thought that he and Ashlee would never be able to enjoy such happiness together. And even worse than that was knowing that his return to New Orleans would bring an end to someone else's happiness—namely, Arthur Redington's.

Damien and he had spent the past evening talking at length about how Rhys would go about connecting Dominique Redington with the gold and rifle shipments coming out of New Orleans and sent to Mexico. All they had decided was that perhaps he should make the first move by asking her opinion on how he might acquire land in that war-torn country, with no further explanation for his need other than hoping someday to settle down there. If she were indeed, working with the French government, it just might be all it would take to tip her hand. Then, if that happened, all Rhys had to do was contact General Brooks, the man in charge of a special investigating division there in New Orleans. He would take care of the rest. It had sounded simple enough, since that made it possible for Rhys not to be directly involved. But as he boarded the train, took a seat near a window, and smiled out at his friends standing on the platform waving good-bye, he realized that even though he might not be the one to arrest Dominique, it would still happen because of him.

By midmorning and halfway to Jackson, where Rhys would switch trains and head for New Orleans, he remembered the light lunch and small bottle of wine Rachel had packed for him. The thought of something to eat was inviting. Picking up his bag from the floor near his feet, he sat it on the empty seat opposite him and unbuckled the strap to peer inside at the selection of foods, his tan brow furrowing when he spotted a letter lying on top. Only his name was written on the envelope, but it was enough to tell him that the note was from Rachel. He hurriedly opened it.

My dearest Rhys, it began, and he settled back in the seat to read every word. *For years I've hoped for a way to repay your kindness to me during my troubled times before I married Damien, to make you laugh the way you made me laugh even though I felt like crying. Well, maybe I can't bring a smile to your lips by telling you that everything will turn out all right—I know if you had said that to me then, I would have doubted it—but things have a way of working out for the best. And they will for you. My only suggestion is to talk with her. Hear her reasons for doing what she did. Although I've never met your Ashlee, we share a special bonding for the simple fact that she is a woman and you*

466

touched our lives. I cannot believe she did this to deliberately hurt you. Rachel.

Suddenly Rhys remembered the last conversation he and Ashlee had had.

"Oh, Perrin's not so bad, Rhys," she had said, smiling. "I like him very much. In fact, I'm not really sure I'd prefer marrying you instead of him. I've always longed to go to Paris."

"There are easier ways to get to Paris," he had argued.

"But Perrin's uncle is a duke. I'd be a member of royalty. Could I say the same married to you?"

Rachel's letter shook in his hand, and he stared angrily out the train window. "Is that really so important?" he recalled asking her.

"It could be. And besides, you take a lot for granted thinking that just because you want to marry me, I'll accept. In fact, Mr. Sinclair, you'll have to win my approval or I'll be obliged to carry through with my former wedding plans."

Rhys had thought Ashlee was only teasing. But now as he reconsidered everything she had said and what became of it, he wasn't sure at all. He reread a part of Rachel's letter. *Hear her reasons.*

All right, he thought. *That's just what I'll do.* He folded the letter and put it back in the envelope. *But it won't change the fact that she's married.* He stared out the window again. *Nor will it stop me from loving her.*

"How's Priscilla—I mean, Veronica—this morning?" John asked as he took a chair beside Arthur in the dining room.

"Ze doctor thinks she has a broken rib or two where ze bullet hit, but he says she will be all right," Perrin smiled wearily. "Thank God for that."

"Yes," John agreed. "Thank God for that." Lifting the

silver pot sitting on the table, he filled his cup with coffee and turned his attention on the man beside him. "Have you been up to see her yet, Arthur?"

Tired blue eyes glanced up at John, then settled on the cup Arthur held. "No," came his rueful answer.

"And why not? She's been asking for you."

Arthur shrugged. "I haven't worked up the courage to face her."

"She doesn't blame you for this," John quickly assured him. "No one does."

"I don't mean that," Arthur responded, shaking his head and falling back in the chair. "I mean I don't want to be the one to tell her that we haven't found Ashlee yet."

Smiling sympathetically, John reached out and patted Arthur's shoulder. "She already knows. I just told her myself. And I also told her not to worry. We've got practically everyone in New Orleans looking for your daughter—and Dominique."

Arthur's gray brows came together in a painful, doubting expression. "Do you honestly think that they're still here in the city after all this time? I don't. I think they left yesterday morning."

"And I disagree," John argued encouragingly. "They disappeared too quickly without anyone seeing them. Dominique is in hiding and wherever she is, she's got Ashlee with her. We'll find them. I promise you that."

"How can you?" Arthur moaned. "Dominique never liked Ashlee and now that we know about her, she won't hesitate to"—the word stuck in his throat—"she won't hesitate to kill her." He closed his eyes and swallowed hard. "Just the way she tried to kill Veronica."

"And I say you're wrong. As long as Dominique is still in the city, she'll need Ashlee to guarantee free passage from here once she decides to leave. And she can't do that without one of our men spotting her. I've hired nearly every man in New Orleans to guard all the roads leaving

468

the area. The train depot is covered, and there are several men posted at the docks. She'd have to be a bloody magician to get by them."

"I wish I had as much faith as you," Arthur murmured. "And I wish Rhys was here. He'd know where to look for my daughter." He glanced over at Perrin. "Are you sure no one knows where he is?"

Perrin shook his head. *"Non monsieur.* No one knows."

"Not even Thomas Bryan?"

"His telegram thees morning says he has not heard from Rhys. But he suggested I send a wire to Rhys's family, that maybe he went home for a while."

"God, I hope not," Arthur sighed. "We'd never catch up to him until he'd gotten all the way to Maine."

"Who wouldn't you catch up with?" a voice beside the group asked, and they looked up to find Michael standing there, his hair mussed, his clothes wrinkled, appearing very much as though he'd been awake all night—which indeed he had.

"Rhys Sinclair," John volunteered.

"Why would he go to Maine?"

"His family lives there," Perrin advised.

"Well, I know that. I just don't understand what makes you think he'd be going home."

John pulled out the empty chair beside him, grabbed Michael's arm, and yanked him down into it. "Let me explain something to you—from beginning to end—so that your eavesdropping is worthwhile this time."

"Eaves—"

John quickly raised his hand to silence the man. "Michael, you're thought of as Belle Chasse's own private telegraph. You know more about what's going on around here than anyone, but usually you only have half the story. The night before Ashlee and Perrin supposedly ran off and got married, Rhys had asked Ashlee to marry him. Now, without hearing Ashlee's side of that conversation, we have no way of knowing if she accepted or not, but from what she told Perrin, we feel safe in assuming she had. So, how do you suppose Rhys felt the next day when he walked into this restaurant to discover that she had married someone else? If he loved her enough to ask her to be his bride, then learning that she chose someone else must have really hurt him. And when a man is hurting, he usually goes where he can find comfort and understanding. In other words, he goes home. Now do you get it?"

"Yes," Michael replied. "But that isn't where he went."

The three others exchanged surprised but hopeful looks.

"You mean you know where he is?" Arthur urged.

Taken aback by the almost angry faces staring at him, Michael pushed back in his chair. "I know where he went, but I don't know if he's still there. Why?"

"Why?" John exploded. "Michael, Rhys knew about Dominique weeks ago, or at least he was suspicious. He'd been following her, keeping track of the people she'd been with. If anyone knows where to look for Ashlee and Dominique, Rhys does! For God's sake, man, tell us where to contact Rhys!"

"Vicksburg," Michael quickly answered. "He got a telegram from his former commander, a Major Sheffield in Vicksburg, and he went there to see him. But I don't know if he's still there or where he was going afterward. He didn't say." The last was shouted at the three men who had bolted from their chairs and were running out of the restaurant. "Hey," he yelled after them, "doesn't anyone want to know why I came in here in the first place?" When none of them so much as hesitated but darted through the restaurant door and into the lobby, Michael shook his head. "I guess not," he mumbled, then waved down one of the waitresses. His companions would take care of wiring Rhys in Vicksburg. Right now, he wanted something to eat.

"All aboard!"

Standing on the platform at the Jackson railroad station, Rhys checked his timepiece against the town clock clearly visible from the depot. By late afternoon he would be back in New Orleans. Snapping the lid shut, he slid the watch back into his vest pocket, picked up his baggage, and climbed the steps to the passenger car. It was hot inside, and once he took a seat, he opened the window next to him to catch what little breeze there was, vaguely hearing the rapid ticking of the telegraph coming from the office a few feet away before the train spewed forth a huge ball of steam, then jerked forward and started the final lap of his journey. Settling down as comfortably as possible on the hard seat, he crossed his arms over his chest and lowered his chin, thinking to nap part of the distance. He didn't see the telegraph operator rushing out of the office, paper in hand.

"What ya got there, Willie?" the station porter asked.

"An urgent message for one of the passengers on that train," he said disgustedly, waving the telegram in the air as the last car passed them by. "Now what do I do?"

"I don't know," his companion replied. "How urgent is it?"

Willie shrugged. "Says somethin' about there being trouble and for this Mr. Sinclair to return to New Orleans immediately."

"So what's the problem?" the other asked. "Ain't that where the train's goin' anyhow?"

"Well . . . yeah."

"So, the guy's doin' what the telegram wants him to do, only he don't know it. I wouldn't worry about it. Just throw the dumb thing away."

471

Willie opened his mouth to tell the man that that wouldn't be right, that it was his job to see a telegram delivered, but his companion was already walking away. The train whistle sounded in the distance, and when he turned around in its direction, he realized that forwarding the message would be rather foolish after all, since whoever sent it would probably be waiting at the depot for Mr. Sinclair anyway. He wadded up the paper and returned to his office.

The train had come to a complete stop at the depot in New Orleans. Nearly all of the passengers had left the car before Rhys even considered picking up his baggage and getting off. He knew what was waiting for him, and he truly longed to avoid it. But this wasn't just a matter of personal conflict. It was an issue that concerned the United States, and this thought alone made him step down from the train.

The long shadows of the dying sunlight graced the wooden platform on which he stood. Rhys lingered there a while, studying the shoreline and the monstrous silhouettes of the ships anchored in deeper waters, idly wishing he could board one and leave his past behind. He thought of Rachel's letter and the advice she had given him, knowing that in order for him to forget about his past, he would have to first settle the unanswered questions that haunted him. He would have to talk to Ashlee.

Descending the steps to the depot, he started across the hard, dusty ground toward the place where he could rent a carriage that would take him to the hotel. He had to hurry his gait when another rig came thundering in his direction. Quickly standing aside, he considered shouting at the driver in no uncertain terms that the man should learn how to manage a team before ever taking up the reins. But any disparaging words he thought to recite fled the instant he saw the passenger riding inside. Draped completely in black, the woman wore a veil that hid her face and reminded him of the first time he saw Ashlee. When the rig raced on by him, Rhys unknowingly took a step forward, as if intending to follow her, and paused when her carriage rolled to a stop at the end of the long pier. Feeling quite the fool once he realized what he had almost done, he watched the driver climb down, then turn to assist his passenger to the ground. It was then he recognized the man who had nearly run him over. He was Jourdain LaFoe, the bakery shoppe owner, whose establishment Dominique frequented every day Rhys had followed her. Mildly curious, he watched the pair gather their things from the carriage, then hurriedly walk the pier toward one of the ships preparing to set sail.

"Ain't hardly safe to walk the streets no more, is it, mister?" a voice behind Rhys said, and he turned to find that a driver from one of the rigs for hire had pulled his carriage in beside him.

"Doesn't appear that way," Rhys smiled, then glanced back at LaFoe and his companion one more time before facing the driver again, asking, "Can you take me to Belle Chasse?"

"Sure thing. Climb in," he said, reaching down to take Rhys's luggage and set it on the seat beside him.

They traveled several blocks in silence while the driver of the conveyance concentrated on guiding them through the busy avenue toward the hotel. Rhys thought of the last time he had hired a rig to take him to the same destination. He'd only been gone a couple of days, but even so, the city seemed different to him. Maybe it had something to do with his reason for returning a second time.

"You a stranger to New Orleans?" the driver asked over his shoulder as they rounded the last corner toward

Belle Chasse.

"No," Rhys replied, honestly wishing he were.

"Oh, yeah? Well, maybe you'd be interested in hearing about all the excitement that's been going on," the man said, twisting slightly in his seat to look at Rhys.

Oddly enough, Rhys found the fellow's enthusiasm amusing. "I might be. Suppose you tell me what it is, and I'll let you know."

"Well, I figured there was a chance, seein' as how you're going to Belle Chasse and all."

Rhys couldn't explain why, but the man's statement twisted his insides. "You mean about Miss Redington's marriage a few days ago?" Angrily, he turned his head and blankly watched the scenery passing by. "I already know about it."

"Naw," the driver continued, studying the street ahead of him again, "that's old news. What I mean is about Mrs. Redington shooting that actress lady then kidnapping her own stepdaughter. Damnedest thing that's ever happened around here for as long as I can remember." He intended to say more, possibly add his thoughts about why Dominique Redington had done what she did and the odds he gave on the stepdaughter still being alive, when his passenger suddenly bolted from his seat in back of him, grabbed him by the scruff of the neck, and tore the reins from his hands. Before he could shout a protest, he was hurled backward onto the floor of the carriage and lay there dazed, watching the man move up front to take his place. Hurling an oath at the mare, the stranger viciously snapped the reins and sent them flying off toward the hotel at the end of the street.

"What the hell do you think you're doin', mister?" he yelled, trying to push himself up on his knees. But the rocking motion of the carriage as it raced down the street only threw him back to the floor.

When the rig neared the front steps of Belle Chasse,

Rhys jerked back on the reins but didn't wait for the carriage to come to a complete stop before jumping from it. Nor did he pay any attention to the man who had finally managed to haul himself upright and now stood shaking his fist at him. Rhys just bounded up the steps two at a time, raced through the door Harold Brown held open for him, and headed across the lobby to Arthur's office.

"Mr. Sinclair," someone called from the direction of the casino, and Rhys glanced that way to find Hank Newell standing in the doorway. "Thank God you're here."

"Is it true?" he demanded. "What I just heard about Ashlee?"

"Yes, sir," Hank replied solemnly, coming forward with his hand extended toward the dining hall. "Mr. Redington and the others are in the restaurant. He said to bring you there if you showed up." The two men hurried toward the entrance. "We didn't think you were coming when you didn't answer the telegram."

"What telegram?" Rhys frowned, pausing in the archway to scan the group of people inside the dining room.

Pointing out the table where Arthur, Perrin, and John were seated, they headed toward it as Hank supplied the information. "Michael told us that you had gone to Vicksburg, and Mr. Redington sent a telegram this afternoon asking you to come. Apparently, you never received it."

"I was already on the train. I left Vicksburg early this morning."

"Well, I guess it doesn't make any difference now," Hank replied. "You're here, and that's all that matters."

Rhys gritted his teeth. "As long as it's not already too late," he growled, turning his attention on the group of men who instantly came to their feet the moment Hank announced Rhys's arrival. His apprehension grew once he saw the worried, frightened look on Arthur's face. He sucked in a breath to calm his own anxiety, speaking quietly but firmly as he motioned for the others to sit again. "Arthur. Tell me the whole of it, and don't leave out a single detail. I want to know what happened and what you're doing to find Ashlee," he instructed, sitting down next to the man.

"It's all so involved," Arthur replied, shaking his head, his hands trembling as he reached for the coffeepot to refill his cup. "And so bizarre."

"Arthur," John cut in, "maybe I should tell it."

He looked up at his friend, smiled weakly, and nodded. "I'd appreciate it."

John smiled in return, patted Arthur's hand, then turned his full attention on Rhys. "We have men out searching for her right now, Rhys. It's all we can do at this point. We thought maybe you could give us an idea where, once you've heard what happened." Rhys nodded, and John took a breath to recite the events of the past two days. "It all came to a head the day before yesterday," he began, "but it started long before that. Dominique was blackmailing Perrin into marrying Ashlee by holding the deed to his mother's property and threatening to sell it if he didn't follow through. Now, since Perrin didn't want to get married anymore than Ashlee did, they figured that maybe they could pay back what he owed her in return for the deed. But when Perrin went to her with the money he owed, she took it and said that it didn't do any good because he had stolen it from her in the first place."

Rhys's eyes moved from John to Perrin. "Had you?"

"Ashlee did—some of it—to stake me at ze poker game. But I owed Dominique much more than what Ashlee took."

"So that left the two of you no choice but to get

476

married." It pained Rhys to have to say it.

"That's what I thought, but Ashlee had a different idea."

"What do you mean?" he asked suspiciously.

"Ashlee said that ze deed was rightfully mine, since I had paid back ze money I owed Dominique, and that if she wouldn't give it to me, then we'd steal it back."

"Then why did you get married?"

Perrin glanced nervously at John, then Arthur, and finally back at Rhys. "We didn't. Ashlee stole ze documents and we told everyone we had eloped." When Rhys only stared at him without a hint of emotion, Perrin quickly went on to explain. "We needed time, *Monsieur* Sinclair, time to find ze deed, and we were afraid that Dominique would force us to marry for what we tried to do. Ashlee wanted to explain, but you left before she could, and none of us knew where you went or if you were coming back. Forgive us, *Monsieur* Sinclair. I know you love Ashlee and she loves you. We did not do thees to hurt you but to save ourselves."

Rhys felt as if he'd been thrown from a horse and dragged a hundred miles. He closed his eyes and silently cursed his own stupidity, his hardheadedness, and his lack of faith in the woman he loved. "What happened then?" he asked after a while.

"Ashlee went to Priscilla for help," John volunteered, "and the two of them started searching the office. From what Priscilla told us, she and Ashlee didn't find the deed, but they did find the second set of records you suspected were there." When Rhys turned his head to look at Arthur and offer an explanation, John cut in. "He knows, Rhys. He knows everything. We all do. Dominique told Priscilla and Ashlee that she wanted the money so that she could become a countess . . . that she had to buy the title." Frowning, John shook his head. "That's the part we don't understand. Where could she

477

buy the title of countess? There are no countesses in Louisiana."

Suddenly, it all fell together. "But there are in Mexico."

"What? Mexico? Why Mexico?" came the chorus of questions from the other three, and Rhys raised a hand to silence them.

"The reason I went to Vicksburg was to talk with my former commander, Major Sheffield. He's in charge of a special force investigating certain allegations that a group of French-born citizens are smuggling gold and rifles to Mexico out of New Orleans for the French troops fighting there."

"Oh, my God," Arthur moaned, dropping his head in his hands.

"I'm sorry, Arthur," Rhys comforted. "I know how painful this is for you and I wish I could say it wasn't true. But it's the only explanation I have for Dominique's actions, and the evidence you've given to me rather confirms it."

"But why take Ashlee?" Perrin asked.

Rhys shrugged. "My guess would be that Dominique knew she wouldn't be able to leave New Orleans right away and needed a hostage that would guarantee free passage—" The image of a Frenchman racing for the docks flashed in Rhys's mind. He blinked and concentrated on the incident at the train depot. The man had been Jourdain LaFoe . . . a *Frenchman* . . . a shoppe owner . . . a place Dominique visited everyday. There had been a woman with him . . . a widow . . . or at least, Rhys thought so. He closed his eyes, recalling how the sight of a woman dressed in black reminded him of the first time he saw Ashlee. But Ashlee hadn't been a widow. It had been a disguise. . . . "That's it!" he exploded, bolting from his chair.

"What, Rhys? What is it?" John urged, coming to

478

his feet.

"I think I know where to find Ashlee," he said, turning to Hank who had stood by silently during the entire conversation. "Hank, I want you to take a group of men and go to the docks. Board every one of the ships and tell the captain that you're under orders of Major Damien Sheffield to arrest Jourdain LaFoe and the woman who's with him."

"Why do you want him to do that, Rhys?" John questioned.

"Because unless I'm mistaken, that woman is Dominique."

"But we have men already stationed at the docks. One of them would have seen her," John argued.

"They never would have recognized her. She's dressed in widow's clothes." He turned back to Hank, giving the man a shove. "Hurry!"

"Hank," Perrin shouted, jumping from his chair, "I'm going with you. It will be my pleasure to see her put in jail."

"And I'm coming with you, Rhys," Arthur said, throwing his napkin down on the table. Rising, he squared his shoulders, tugged at his vest, raised his chin in the air, and looked the other in the eye. "It's about time I apologized to my daughter."

"For what, Arthur?" Rhys soothed. "For falling in love? I guarantee she understood that."

Wanting very much to believe it, Arthur smiled. "Then let's find out for sure. Let's go and get Ashlee."

Somewhere around noon, Ashlee lost track of time. She had been given her last meal the night before, and as each minute dragged by, she feared that this was how her life would end, that Dominique and LaFoe had already left her behind and boarded their ship sailing for Mexico,

479

that maybe in a month or a year or possibly a decade from now someone would find her remains in this tiny dark cavity of a room.

There had been only one time several hours earlier when she had thought she heard a noise from someplace above her, and then it had been so faint that she hadn't been able to distinguish it. It might have been Dominique or LaFoe moving around, or it could have been a mouse scurrying through a wall somewhere. Whatever caused it lasted only an instant or two, then quieted again, and now the silence that was her only companion seemed to hammer in her ears and drive her sanity further away.

Her arms and legs ached, and her hands were numb from the ropes tied too tightly around her wrists. The effort it took to try and free herself became increasingly difficult, and the desire to even motivate herself began to fade. After all, what did she have to live for? Her mother was dead, her father's life had been destroyed, and Rhys had deserted her, probably even hated her for what she'd done. She closed her eyes when they filled with tears, willing herself not to cry, for she knew she would never stop if she gave way to her distress. If only she had the means to end her life quickly. . . .

Ashlee's eyes flew open and she struggled to sit up. She wasn't sure, but she thought she heard a noise, and this time it sounded like a bell tinkling, the one that hung over LaFoe's front door. Could it be? Was it possible that someone had come to rescue her? She sat very still, listening, and several moments ticked by before she heard another noise. Footsteps! She was sure of it! She came up on her knees, straining to listen and determine if there were more than two people. If so, it had to mean that it wasn't just Dominique and LaFoe returning, but someone else, someone who could save her life. She screamed at the sound of muffled voices just above her, but with the rag stuffed in her mouth and held tightly in place by another wrapped around her head, it came out as nothing more than a soft moan, too soft for anyone to hear. In a panic, she collapsed in a ball, falling forward so that she could rub her face against her knees and hopefully pull the gag from her mouth. She worked frantically, desperately, wondering why she hadn't thought of this earlier and praying that whoever it was didn't leave before she had the chance to call out to them. She didn't really want to die, not yet. After what seemed a hundred years, she had worked the gag loose. She spit out the wad of fabric in her mouth and screamed as loud as she could.

"Down here! I'm down here!"

Tears of joy filled her eyes as she sat there, waiting, listening. First the furniture would have to be moved, then the rug that covered the opening to her prison—the trapdoor in the wooden planking. Her stomach knotted when her unearthly companion of late seeped in through every crack and ran its icy fingers over every inch of her flesh, mocking her, testing the limits of her sanity. Had she truly heard the bell? The footsteps overhead? A single tear trickled down her cheek as she knelt there staring up into the darkness, vaguely aware of the silence pounding in her ears again.

Having slept fitfully for only a few hours, Rhys rose before the first light of dawn was clearly visible. He dressed, didn't bother to shave, and haphazardly ran a brush through his dark blond hair. His room seemed to close in on him, haunting him with visions of Ashlee lying lifeless somewhere where he'd never find her, and he cursed the stubborn pride that had driven him away from her. Stepping out onto the balcony outside his room, he heard a door shut from somewhere below him and saw the darkly clothed, full-figured shape of a woman leaving the staff's quarters on her way toward the kitchen, thinking that it must be the cook, Eunice, preparing to start her day as though nothing out of the ordinary was going on. It pained him to think that the world continued on as though the life of one person, one helpless woman, wasn't important, and he frowned almost angrily at the unsuspecting servant.

He had been so sure of finding Ashlee in LaFoe's bakery that even now, hours afterward, he still couldn't accept the fact that she wasn't there. If it hadn't been for John, who had to practically drag him away after they found the place empty, he would still be searching for her.

He had been dealt a second devastating blow when Hank brought him the news that the ship Dominique and LaFoe had boarded had already left port by the time the young man and his group arrived at the docks. That meant more waiting—and a lot of praying. The navy had dispatched a frigate to pursue the vessel almost immediately, but crucial time would be lost while the navy ship chased down their foe, brought it to bay, and boarded and seized its prisoners. Even then, Rhys had no guarantee that Dominique would tell him where to find Ashlee, and if she did, that he would do so quickly enough.

The faint, rich smell of brewing coffee drifted up to him as he stood at the balcony's railing, bringing him around and stirring up his need for conversation . . . with anyone. It would help get his mind off Ashlee. Passing through his room and out into the hallway, he pulled the door shut behind him and headed for the stairs. The lobby was empty except for the night desk clerk, who slept soundly in his chair. Rhys only paid the man a fleeting glance before entering the restaurant on his way to the kitchen out back. As he neared its swinging door, he called out to Eunice so as not to frighten her

482

with his early, unexpected visit.

"Mornin', Mr. Sinclair," she sang once he had stepped into view. "What y'all doin' up at this hour?"

"Couldn't sleep," he sighed. "And I thought I smelled coffee."

"Sho' nuff did," she smiled, pointing toward the stove. "Help yo'self." She watched him out of the corner of her eye as he found a cup and filled it. Then, when he sat down on one of the tall stools at the end of the table and glanced up at her, she busied herself with her work, taking down a huge metal bowl and setting it beside the containers of lard and milk as she prepared to make the morning ration of bread and rolls. "Ah doan think nobody been sleepin' good since Miz Ashlee disappeared."

Rhys had only talked with the black woman a few times since coming to Belle Chasse, yet by her tone and the soft look in her eyes whenever she spoke of Ashlee, he knew she cared a great deal for the young woman. He took a sip of his coffee and thought how it seemed there wasn't a person in the entire place that didn't like Ashlee. He leaned forward and braced himself against the table top.

"Ya know," Eunice went on, measuring out flour from the huge bag sitting on the floor beside her, "Miz Ashlee, she done knowed what kind of woman that Dominique was the first she met her. We all did, ah think, 'ceptin' for Mr. Redington." She shook her head and reached for the lard. "And for dat woman to be tied up with that LaFoe—"

Her thought trailed off, but Rhys could see the disapproval on her dark face. "You sound as if you knew him personally."

"Only what I heerd," she admitted. "And ain't none of it good."

Although Rhys wasn't really interested in LaFoe, since he didn't think the Frenchman was anything more than a

483

henchman for Dominique, listening to Eunice vent her own anger and frustration over the situation eased some of his tension. He took another drink of his coffee, then asked, "Like what?"

"LaFoe, he didn't own dat shoppe for very long. He done bought it a couple of years 'fore the war started, and it was a sorry day for a lot of slaves in dis area."

"Slaves?" Rhys repeated. "Why would his purchase of a bakery have any affect on slaves?"

"'Cause the man what owned it 'fore him, he worked with the underground railroad, hidin' slaves what wanted ta be free. LaFoe, he didn't care 'bout that." She doubled up her fist and punched the ball of dough she had made, almost as if she believed it was the Frenchman she held in her hands. "Lotta folks never got north 'cause of him. And now he and that awful woman are gone, and nobody knows where they took Miz Ashlee."

Rhys wished he could say something to soothe her distress, but he knew that anything he said would sound shallow. The only hope they had was that the navy would catch up to Dominique before it was too late. He stared angrily into his cup. If it wasn't already too late. He took a deep breath and forced himself not to think about it.

"Have you always lived in New Orleans, Eunice?" he asked, looking at her again. But Eunice hadn't heard him, and he raised a curious brow. She was thinking of something else, and whatever it was made her smile, a smile that was almost evil. "Eunice?"

"Y'know what ah think, Mr. Sinclair?" she grinned, her dark skin glowing with perspiration. "Ah think we oughta tie up dem two and throws 'em in the little room under the floor in LaFoe's place to rot. Kinda fittin', seein' as how he wouldn't use it to help people, don't ya think?"

A cold chill embraced Rhys, drawing him to his feet. "What little room?" he asked, praying he would hear the answer he wanted.

Confused by her companion's sudden change, for it seemed to Eunice that he didn't approve of her method of punishment, she frowned and took a step backward. "Why, the one where the slaves hid. Weren't you listenin'? Ah said the man what owned the place—"

"Where, Eunice?" he exploded. "Where is it?"

"W—why, ah doan rightly know, sir. Ah ain't never seen it. Most of 'em is hid under a rug or somethin'."

Rhys knocked over the stool as he bounded past it to descend upon the poor, frightened woman. Eunice retreated in a hurry, thinking him mad. But when he reached her and she felt certain he was about to lay his fist to her jaw, he did the unexpected. Taking her by the arms, he yanked her forward and kissed her on the cheek.

"Eunice," he grinned, "you're an angel sent from heaven."

"A—ah is?" she questioned, frowning as she watched him race from the room.

Never breaking stride as he dashed through the empty restaurant and into the lobby, Rhys hardly slowed down at all when he came to the front door, swinging it open with the thrust of his palms against it, then bounding down the steps two at a time. The street was vacant, and he stopped at the edge of the sidewalk, trying to decide if he should take the time to saddle a horse or run all the way to LaFoe's bakery. But his dilemma was answered for him when he heard the clatter of a carriage at the end of the block and looked in that direction to see Perrin heading his way.

"Perrin!" he shouted, darting off toward him. "Turn that damn thing around. I know where Ashlee is!"

He didn't have to be told a second time. What Rhys called out to him had been something he wanted to hear ever since Dominique had taken Ashlee away. Jerking sharply to the right, he spun the rig around, waiting only

485

long enough for Rhys to jump in beside him before he cracked the reins against the horse's rump and bolted them off down the street at a breakneck speed.

"Where, *monsieur?*"

"At LaFoe's, Perrin," he smiled excitedly. "Eunice told me."

"Eunice? Ze cook? How would she know thees things?"

"She didn't, really. She talked about the man who owned the building before LaFoe and how he hid slaves in a secret room below the floor. I'm not positive Ashlee's there, but it's a damn good chance."

The carriage slid around a corner, throwing both men to one side, but neither of them gave it a thought. Ashlee's life might depend on them getting to her as soon as possible. They raced down several more blocks, rounded another corner, then thundered the final stretch in record time. The rig had hardly come to a full stop before both Perrin and Rhys jumped from it, not caring if the horse wandered off as they dashed across the sidewalk and through the front door of the little shoppe.

"Where? Where do we look?" Perrin asked, his eyes scanning the floor of the front room once Rhys had lit a lamp.

"Not here," Rhys advised, taking the lantern in one hand, Perrin in the other, and pulling him through the curtained archway. "Eunice said the entrances are usually hidden by a rug or something— There!" The word exploded from him as Rhys pointed to the table and four wooden chairs sitting on top of a braided rug, and he hurriedly set down the lamp.

Frantic, the men hurled the furniture away, sending the pieces crashing against the wall. Next came the rug that literally flew through the air as they yanked it from its place to reveal the trapdoor hidden beneath.

"Bring the light," Rhys ordered as he knelt down,

seized the handle, and lifted upward. "Ashlee!" he called into the dark pit. "Ashlee!"

A rustling came from below, then a voice, tiny and weak. "Rhys?"

It was the sweetest sound he had ever heard, and Rhys closed his eyes, thanking God for allowing him to find her, while at the same time cursing the woman who was responsible for putting Ashlee here and vowing revenge. If it were the last thing he ever did, he would see that Dominique paid for this injustice.

"Hurry, Perrin," Rhys shouted. "Bring the light. We must get her out of there."

Half running, half stumbling back across the room, Perrin collapsed to his knees, his thin features twisting into shocked disapproval once the soft light of the lamp fell upon the pale blue eyes staring back up at him. "*Mon Dieu*, what have they done to you?"

"Help me get her out of there," Rhys instructed, taking the lantern from him and setting it down on the floor.

Stretching out on their stomachs, Rhys and Perrin caught Ashlee under each arm and easily lifted her from the black cavity. A moment later they had freed her bonds, and Ashlee threw her arms around Rhys's neck, sobbing miserably.

"She'll never hurt you again, Ashlee," he whispered, holding her close. "Never." Then in an effortless sweep he lifted her in his arms and said, "It's time I took you home."

Standing before the window of her room staring idly outside, Ashlee thought how wonderful it felt to have the warmth of the bright, golden sunshine touching her face and vowed never to take it for granted again. Her ordeal had been the most frightening thing she had ever

487

experienced, and there had been a time, while she was alone in that small cubicle, that she thought she might go insane. Then Rhys found her.

Rhys she thought, the one person she never expected to see again. Why had he come back? Was it because of her? Had someone sent for him? A thousand questions whirled about in her head, all of them too painful for her to voice. She wasn't sure she wanted to hear the answers. She preferred thinking that he came back because he still loved her.

Once they had returned to the hotel, Rhys had carried her to her room, cloistering her off from everyone at Belle Chasse except for Sarah, a young chambermaid employed by the hotel. Sarah had been given instructions to help Ashlee bathe, wash her hair, put on a fresh nightgown, then see that she had all she wanted to eat before lying down. Ashlee had been too weak to argue, and she probably wouldn't have anyway. She always felt safe in her room.

She had slept until noon, when Sarah reappeared with a lunch tray. The girl's bright, winning smile greatly cheered Ashlee as Sarah sat by her bed, chattering merrily. By the time Ashlee had finished eating, she was ready to receive visitors. She asked to see Rhys first. After all, he deserved an explanation.

"I love you, Ashlee."

She didn't move, afraid the voice she had heard wasn't real, afraid that she had only imagined him saying the words she longed to have him recite. She closed her eyes and listened to his footsteps bringing him closer.

"I want you to be my wife, Ashlee."

Tears stole between her dark lashes and spilled down her cheeks.

"I want you to bear my children. I want you to live the rest of your life with me."

She felt herself being drawn into his arms, and she opened her eyes to convince herself that he was really here, really telling her all these wonderful things . . . that he had forgiven her for what she had done to him.

"I want you to say yes," he whispered, lowering his head.

Their lips met in a warm and gentle kiss as if it were the first time, then he started to release her. Ashlee quickly brought her arms up around his neck, pulling him back and kissing him with all the fervor and love she could give. A long while passed before the embrace ended, but neither would let go. Held tightly in each other's arms, they turned to stare out the window at the glorious day, basking in the warmth of the sunshine and of their love.

"I have to explain," she said simply, quietly.

He brushed his lips against her temple. "There's no need. Perrin told me everything."

"And you don't hate me?"

He chuckled softly. "Never."

"Did he tell you about—"

"The baby?" he finished, smiling down at her. "Yes. He also told me that if you hadn't confessed everything to me—about the phony marriage and that you were carrying my child—he would have told me. He knew a long time ago how much you cared for me but that you were trapped by circumstances and couldn't give in to your feelings. He's a good friend, Ashlee. One to be proud of."

"I know," she replied with a gentle smile. "Can you understand, then, why I couldn't desert him when he needed me?"

"Yes. And there's someone else who needs you just as much, right now."

She frowned up at him. "Who?"

"Your father."

Tears gathered in her eyes with the mention of him, and she broke away from Rhys.

"He has the need to explain, just as you felt you had to explain to me. He's hurting, Ashlee. He's blaming himself for everything that happened."

She faced him again. "That's not true. Dominique is the one responsible."

"But he feels that if he had been honest with you the day your mother came back to New Orleans, he might never have married Dominique."

"Why?" she asked, surprised.

Rhys smiled one-sidedly. "Well, he didn't really say, but I suspect he still cares very much for your mother. And I know she loves him."

She looked away from him and walked to her dresser where she idly examined some of the things lying there. "You talk as if she were still alive."

At first, Rhys didn't understand. Veronica's wound had been serious, but not fatal. The bullet had struck her in the side, breaking a couple of ribs but not causing any further damage. She had lost a lot of blood and was very weak, but the doctor assured everyone that given enough bed rest Veronica would be as good as new again before very long. Ashlee's statement puzzled him until he realized that the last time she had seen her mother, Veronica lay before her on the floor, unconscious and bleeding. He crossed the room and took Ashlee in his arms.

"That's because she is, Ashlee. Your mother didn't die. She's upstairs waiting to see you."

"What?" she breathed, her tears starting anew. But this time, they were tears of joy. "Oh, Rhys." She threw her arms around him, kissed him on the mouth as if he had something to do with Veronica's being alive, then took his elbow and excitedly pulled him toward the door with her. "I must see her. I have to talk to my mother. I have to tell her I love her."

"Then let's go," he laughed, extending his hand.

The laudanum the doctor had given her earlier finally

offered some relief for Veronica, and she felt good enough to sit up in bed and read the new play the theater would be presenting in a few weeks. But it was really just a way for her to get her mind off things, and it wasn't working. It had been two days since she was brought to this room, and Arthur had yet to visit her. Both John and Perrin came to see her at least twice each day, and Rhys had just left a few minutes ago when Sarah came to tell him that Ashlee wanted to talk to him. All three men tried to convince her that the reason Arthur hadn't come, even though she had asked him to, was because of the horrible guilt he was feeling. Veronica didn't agree. She was sure that he blamed her for everything . . . just as he always did. She forced herself to stare at the book she held in front of her, but she couldn't focus on the words. Her tears blurred her vision. Frowning angrily, she tossed the script aside and let her head fall back on the pillow. She had some decisions to make, the first one being her choice of a place to live, for once she was well enough to travel, she would leave New Orleans.

A noise in the hallway outside her room startled Veronica out of her thoughts, and she lifted her head to look at the opened doorway just as Arthur stepped into view. Her heart raced and she couldn't stop the smile that touched her lips.

"Come in, Arthur," she beckoned when it seemed he would walk no farther than the threshold. "I'm glad you finally agreed to see me. I have something to tell you."

He stared at her for several moments without saying a word, then dropped his gaze and slowly walked past her bed to the window. There, he rested a hand on the framework, the other shoved deeply in his pocket while he stood staring outside. "Before you say anything, Veronica, I want to apologize."

His voice was tired and full of sadness, and Veronica wanted to stop him but didn't. His apology was the last thing in the world she expected him to offer.

"From the day you left Ashlee and me, I tried to force myself to hate you. I never really succeeded. I buried myself in my work and constantly prayed you'd come back to us. And when you did, my pride got in the way. You'd hurt me, and I wanted to hurt you back. I used our daughter to do it. For a while, I felt good about what I'd done, thinking that you deserved not being able to tell Ashlee who you really were. But then, as the years went by and I could see that she loved you anyway, I became angry because she loved you when I wanted her to hate you, the way I thought I did. And all that time you kept your promise to me. You never told her that you were her mother, and not once did you ever say one bad thing about me. You're a hell of a woman, Veronica." He paused a moment while he rubbed the back of his hand across his cheek, then cleared his throat and took a deep breath. "Now that I think about it, I married Dominique for two reasons. One, because I thought I loved her and that she loved me. But more than that, I thought that maybe Ashlee would love her, too, and in time Dominique would steal away our daughter's affection for you." He laughed bitterly. "I've been a foolish old man," he said, turning around, "and I don't deserve someone like—"

He never finished admitting that he felt he wasn't good enough for Veronica because the moment he faced her again, his attention was drawn to the couple standing in the doorway. He lowered his eyes, frowning.

"I came to apologize to your mother, Ashlee," he said quietly. "Now I can apologize to you at the same time." He looked up beseechingly. "Say you'll forgive me."

Tears sparkling in her eyes, Ashlee held out her arms and hurried across the room to him. She didn't have to tell him. He knew that she already had.

Propped up on one elbow in the middle of the wide bed,

Rhys's gaze lovingly followed the movements of his wife as Ashlee finished brushing her hair and then stood to take off her robe and climb in beside him. They had been married for over a week now. Perrin had gone back to Paris with his friend, Philippe, and Veronica was well enough to go for short strolls in the courtyard with Arthur. Her mother and father had a lot of catching up to do and a lot of wounds to heal, but Ashlee, along with everyone else at Belle Chasse, felt that in time the couple would get remarried.

"How did your father take the news about Dominique?" Rhys asked, kissing her softly on the cheek.

Ashlee sighed, her blue eyes mirroring her sadness. "Pretty good, I guess. I think he feels like I do. Even after all she'd done, neither of us wished her dead." She turned her head to look at him. "Thank you for letting me be the one to tell him."

He smiled and kissed the tip of her nose.

"Do you think things might have been different if her ship had made it to Mexico before the navy caught up to them?"

Lying down, Rhys took her in his arms and rolled her on top of him. "You mean, would she have gotten away?"

Ashlee nodded.

"Perhaps."

"I wonder why she did it," Ashlee sighed.

"Did what?"

"Shoot herself." Her smooth brow puckered in a thoughtful frown. "Must have taken a lot of courage to do something like that."

"Depends on how you look at it, Ashlee," he said, brushing a strand of hair from her cheek. "She didn't want to go to prison. She probably thought being dead was the better alternative, and she knew Arthur wouldn't help her after what she'd done to you."

"I suppose," she agreed, locking her fingers beneath her chin, her elbows resting on his wide chest. "So when do we sail for Maine? I can hardly wait to meet that family of yours."

"In a couple of days," he grinned.

"A couple of days?" she repeated, feigning disappointment. "What will we do until then?"

A devilish twinkle glowed in his dark eyes. "Oh, I can think of something to occupy our time," he whispered, catching her face in his hands and pulling her down to meet his hungry kiss.